FIXER REDUX

GENE DOUCETTE

PART ONE

Area Cryptid

CHAPTER ONE

Given we have not had a verified sighting of K for—by our count—two years, one of the things we've considered is whether it's time to adjust our approach, and allow sightings of persons who do not match K's description. We consider this, because it is no longer an idle speculation that K has stopped performing as Fixer.

Why? He could be dead; he could have returned to wherever it is from whence he came; it could be he simply stopped. Or, there's another explanation. (See the 'did K die?' thread for a larger list of possibilities.) Our point is that we don't know. In the meantime, perhaps someone else has taken his place, and we would be derelict if we didn't acknowledge that possibility.

— @MDevereaux, FindTheBostonFixer.com

The woman was going to fall over.

She was of an age where calling her *mature* was the polite way of discussing her tenure on Earth, but not quite so aged that an unexpected trip to the carpeted floor would result in a broken hip or anything quite so terrible. Late fifties, maybe; early sixties at worst. She walked the walk of a person in unfamiliar shoes or with a recent lower back injury. One of those explanations would probably be why she was about to fall.

Corrigan watched the whole thing happen—before it happened—from his spot in a chair at the edge of the platform stage, at the back end of the room. It was a decent vantage point, as in front of him all manner of law enforcement professionals in plainclothes, and their friends and family, were busy entering the room: a poorly organized invasion, to claim all of the folding chairs not already declared *Reserved*. At the back of the room was a phalanx of media professionals with cameras and cell phones to record and/or broadcast the upcoming event.

It seemed as if there were more people for the occasion than the room was capable of holding, but Corrigan was pretty sure he was the only one seeing it that way. Every person transiting into the room followed the trail of their future selves, so that each person looked—to Corrigan—like a giant centipede-thing, which fooled his mind into thinking each of them was physically occupying their entire five-second timeline, rather than just one point along the path.

It was nearly overwhelming, which was why Corrigan was on the stage at the back of the room, facing forward, with nobody sitting behind him, rather than out in the crowd with all of the other friend-and-family.

Maggie, the honoree he was there for, negotiated this seating arrangement well in advance of the occasion, as a condition of her attendance. She made it sound like a tremendous undertaking, this negotiation, but he doubted it took much more than her asking. Not only did she now have enough clout within the FBI to get her way more often than not, but it wasn't really that big of an ask. He would be in the back, out of the camera shots. To most of the people there, he probably looked like a security person who just felt like sitting down.

He focused on the woman who was about to fall over, which was just an automatic reaction, since she was already the center of attention in the future. He figured her to be the spouse of an older agent. No such older agent was standing next to her, though, so he assumed it was someone who was going to be on the stage. She did have a younger woman by her side, and they shared enough common features to strongly indicate she was a daughter. When the older woman falls over, the daughter cries out in surprise and drops to the ground so quickly, to try and catch her mother, it looks from a distance as if she too has fallen over.

Corrigan used to spend the few seconds before an accident trying to work out how to prevent it. But he was retired now, and didn't do that sort of thing anymore. Plus, the only way to prevent this was to somehow close the distance between, in two seconds, without causing a larger problem than the one he was trying to prevent. He might do that to intercept someone's imminent demise, but not a sprained ankle.

The present caught up with the future, and the woman fell over. Her daughter went down at almost the same time. Just as it did in the future, it looked as if the two of them had stepped in to a hole, vanishing from the crowd. There was a sound of metal folding chairs getting pushed around. People gasped and jumped away, knocking over more chairs.

But it wasn't so terrible; the woman was standing again a few seconds later, and the chairs that had been knocked askew were being re-sorted, and then it was all over. The blushing mature woman laughed it off and then walked—a little pain on her face every other step—the rest of the way into the aisle and to the seat she'd chosen to occupy.

Maggie, in a chair that was about five feet in front of

Corrigan and a little to the left, watched the scene, and then turned around to check on Corrigan. She knew him too well.

She picked up the chair, placed it next to him, and sat back down.

"Are you okay?" she asked, under her breath.

"I was staring."

"You were staring, yes."

In the future that didn't end up happening, Maggie said that Corrigan had been staring at the woman who fell, and that he needed to try and keep his head in the present, but then Corrigan heard all of that and skipped ahead, so she never said any of that aloud.

Not so long ago, Maggie would have tried to get her point across anyway, because she had not actually uttered the thing. Now she only did that when they were arguing, when it was more important to be granted the opportunity to say something out loud than it was to get the point across.

It was fair to say Corrigan Bain was not an easy person to argue with, or even to get along with for extended periods. His head was always wandering into the near future, and that could be maddening to someone who remained in the present. Maggie stuck it out, though, and he loved her for it.

"So, are you okay?" she asked, squeezing his hand.

"I'm doing all right," he said, squeezing back.

He wasn't all right, but he was about the best he could expect to be.

Corrigan didn't like crowds, and he never would. It wasn't a phobia, so much as the fact that a large gathering of people had an incalculably large number of possible futures, and that can be a nightmarish thing for a man who can see all of those possible futures.

He had tricks that helped. The one that worked the most consistently was focusing on one person's specific future and ignoring all of the others. It kept him sane, but was kind of creepy. He also tended to dwell on people who were about to suffer some sort of misfortune, however minor. If this were a few hundred years earlier he probably would have been burned as a witch, as surely it must have looked as if his attention was causing the accidents.

"No, you aren't okay," Maggie said with a gentle laugh. "You're going nuts. Look at you."

"That bad?"

"You look a little panicky, to me, but I know what to look for. If I had you in an interrogation room, I'd say you were just about ready to confess to something. Do you want to confess to something?"

"No ma'am."

She smiled, and air-kissed his cheek.

"Thank you for coming," she said. "It means a lot. Just don't melt down on the stage. These people are supposed to be a little afraid of me, not you."

"That shouldn't be tough," he said. "I'm afraid of you, and you're not even trying."

"Who says I'm not?"

Maggie Trent had been Corrigan's more-or-less exclusive girlfriend for four years and counting, which was perhaps the most miraculous thing in a life full of apparent miracles. It was the longest relationship for both of them, although it was possible the only reason they stuck it out was because they had exhausted all of the reasons they could think of to separate.

For all of those four years—and for the many before, right up to the day they first met—she was also Agent Margaret Trent of the Boston FBI. In another hour, she would be going from that to *highly decorated* Agent Margaret Trent, and another week after that—although this was not yet official—she would be Assistant Special-Agent-in-Charge Margaret Trent.

Corrigan knew all of this, but he didn't fully appreciate how much of a big deal the whole thing really was until a few minutes earlier, when Jim Duplass, the deputy mayor of the city of Boston stopped by to say hello on the way to his seat on the other side of the stage. Maggie stepped up and shook Duplass's hand while everyone with a camera took their picture.

Corrigan didn't start to relax until everyone stopped moving about the room and took their seats. This made it a little easier to tolerate the crowd.

The problem was movement, which was a great deal more difficult to tolerate when people were walking around. Sitting, the room was still a wreck of activity—people fidgeted in their seats—but it wasn't quite so bad. It was a haze of movement, but everyone was pretty well self-contained within their personal spheres of motion.

Corrigan remembered seeing a collection of old photographs where the person sitting for the camera moved too much while the image was being captured, and that was exactly what this looked like. But he could deal. What was much worse was that now that everyone had gotten to their seats, they were all talking—because the ceremony hadn't begun yet—and he could hear not just what everyone was saying but all the things they were about to say, all at once.

Concentrate, he reminded himself.

He picked one person out of the crowd and focused on him —an unimportant-looking man in a suit who didn't appear to be moving much or talking to anyone in particular. He was a good anchor, this nameless fellow: white shirt, blue jacket, red tie. Probably some minor functionary for one government appara-tus or another. He didn't look like FBI—although Corrigan wasn't certain what FBI *looked* like, precisely—so he figured the man worked for the state.

They were in a wing of the statehouse for this event, a small room in a mostly forgotten part of a very large building. It was the sort of room where minority party whips held press conferences to express their discontent with the majority.

"Hey," Corrigan said. "Do you know that guy?"

"Who?" Maggie asked. She hadn't moved her chair back to where it was supposed to be yet, because the ceremony was still a few minutes off, and Corrigan probably didn't look like he was ready to be left alone yet.

He nodded in the direction of the man.

"Oh yeah," Maggie said. "One of the new kids, I forget his name. Larry something. Why?"

"No reason."

She laughed.

"You're doing it again," she said.

"It helps."

"I know it helps, but you're terrible at it. I have honestly never seen someone worse at profiling than you."

"That's unfair. You work in an office full of people trained to do this."

"What was his backstory?"

"I hadn't worked one out yet, but I had him pegged as a statehouse gofer."

"I'll introduce you later and you can figure out where you went wrong."

"That's really not necessary."

"No, mostly just fun."

"And it's working," he said.

"Sorry, I know. Go ahead, pick someone else. I'll you tell you if I know them."

One of the tricks he'd picked up in the past few years was to concentrate on figuring out the pasts of total strangers as a way to avoid fixating on their immediate futures. It was, as Maggie said, a kind of profiling. By studying their current appearance and speculating on what their lives were like, he was effectively forcing himself to concentrate on the present. It didn't appear to matter that he was truly bad at the exercise.

"How about the guy behind him, to the left," he said.

"Whose left, ours or his?"

"Ours."

"That's Jack. You met him twice. Remember that barbecue last summer?"

Corrigan sighed.

"Of course I don't. I remember the barbecue, but not him. I met a lot of people that day."

"It's all right, dear. Being ordinary takes a lot of work."

If overheard, this probably sounded like an insult, but Corrigan Bain had been trying for his entire life to be an ordinary person. But since for much of that life he was also racing around the city of Boston and saving people, the kind of existence where he hung out at the charcoal grill with someone named Jack and shot the shit about the Sox and the Pats and that new chick in vice, fetching a cold one and laughing stupidly at casual sexism...that kind of life was never possible for him before.

It was only recently an option for reasons he didn't fully understand, which was how a lot of his life went. He used to wake up every morning with information in his head—locations he had to be to prevent people from getting into potentially fatal accidents. And every day he'd drive around to those spots and rescue people. He didn't know why, and he only came to understand how about four years ago, roughly the time he and Maggie decided they should call whatever they had going on between them, "dating".

It got easier to manage. He stopped having to race around the city, beating traffic and the clock, to get to certain places at certain times, because suddenly a phone call was good enough. Sure, not everyone was willing to take a call from a stranger seriously, but most of the time it worked.

And then, one morning, it all stopped. Corrigan could still see into the immediate future—that didn't appear to be going away ever—but he stopped waking up with important information.

It used to be that this was the worst thing that could possibly happen to Corrigan Bain, fixer. When the pipeline of information stopped, the nightmares came, and then the ghosts of all the people he'd failed to save started showing up at inopportune moments, like in the middle of the day when he was doing something that didn't have room in it for hallucinations.

It didn't happen. No nightmares or ghosts or guilt that he wasn't saving people. Whatever it was that was compelling him to *fix* the future had decided he was done.

For another six months, he checked the newspapers for reports of accidental fatalities he probably could have done something about, but then he stopped doing that too. It was okay.

He was retired. And as a retiree, he was in a position to go out on real dates, and keep normal hours, and even have vacations outside of the city, something he had been unable to do since before he turned twenty.

It was *almost* normal, and ordinary, and average, and he loved it. But there were times—at parties, or ceremonies like this one—when it was all he could do to just pretend he was like everyone else.

Social norms were incredibly time-specific. One had to laugh at jokes at the right time, for instance. It couldn't happen too long after the joke was told, and it certainly couldn't happen before the punchline had officially been spoken aloud. The laugh had to sound genuine, which was almost impossible when you heard the whole joke five seconds before everyone else. And even if the timing was exactly right and it was the best fake laugh imaginable, people could still sense something wasn't quite right.

He was always going to be Spooky Corry, as the kids called him when he was growing up. It wasn't something he much noticed or cared about when he was working full time as a fixer —people are generally extremely happy to meet the person who has just saved their lives—but now that he was a retired civilian, he was finding it really hard to act normal.

Fortunately, Maggie didn't much care what people thought of her boyfriend, or of her. It was possible she even enjoyed the idea that Corrigan unsettled the people she worked with, on the rare occasion he accompanied her to a function.

Aside from Maggie, he didn't have a fantastic history with the Boston FBI. They had him arrested once, and he'd been the target of more than one bureau investigation. But the agent behind that historical distrust had taken a job with another area office, and nobody else was around to carry on his vendettas. Corrigan doubted there was anyone left in the office who even remembered those investigations.

People stopped fidgeting so much once the ceremony started. Corrigan lost Maggie's immediate company—she had to push her chair back to the front of the stage and take her seat there—but by then he was okay.

When the speeches began, Corrigan was able to focus on the words and keep himself pretty well rooted in the present. Even off to the side, he hated being on the stage, where nearly everyone in the room could look at him if they so wished. They didn't, because the people taking turns behind the podium drew the attention of the room, but if he did something unfortunate, like laugh aloud at a joke that hadn't landed yet, he'd certainly catch some eyes.

There were all there to honor to work of five FBI agents from the Boston field office, who were part of a joint task force consisting of significantly more than five people. Despite sleeping with the head of that task force, Corrigan knew extremely little about what they were doing until the arrests started happening and the media picked up on it. All he'd known about it in the moment was that Maggie spent very little time in the condo they shared, and the work had her smoking more than she let on.

The task force led to what the media was calling a "significant" domestic terrorism arrest. It was actually a dozen arrests conducted in timed raids in three states, coordinated through the Boston FBI office.

Applause.

He heard it coming before it got there. The guy at the microphone had been talking about Deputy Mayor Duplass for the past ten minutes, as a way to introduce the man himself, which led to everyone in the room clapping, which was an awful cascade of noise.

"Thank you everyone!" Duplass half-shouted. He was about 30% politician, 40% revival tent preacher, and the rest was retired law enforcement, family man, with—probably—at least a whiff of graft and corruption. Corrigan kind of liked him.

"When I think about this great country of ours...I think about freedom."

Corrigan bit his tongue. The preamble was exactly the sort of corny he and Maggie would have been giggling about if they weren't being watched. He heard the line coming before it was said, and still had to fight the urge to at least grin stupidly.

"But protecting that freedom comes with a cost. The men and women on this stage with me today are the kind of people who understand exactly what that cost is, and they pay it, over and over, every day."

Maggie turned around to give Corrigan a little smile—and perhaps to check on him. Then she stuck her tongue out and rolled her eyes. She wasn't fooling him; Maggie agreed with most of what Duplass was saying, she just wasn't as corny about it.

The deputy mayor's speech drifted into a lengthy discussion of terrorism, a subject that might inspire a less nuanced political animal in a jingoistic direction. Corrigan thought Duplass handled it well, though.

After the lengthy introduction came the awards portion of the morning, and Corrigan could imagine a near-future in which the event would conclude and he could get to the part where he hides in the corner of a reception hall. Maybe from there, he and Maggie could return to their nice, quiet, unpopulated condo.

Everybody got a plaque, a handshake, and a photograph with Duplass. The applause was continuous and made Corrigan's head ache, but he tried to keep it under control for Maggie, whose name was going to be announced last.

"And finally, the head of the joint task force: Senior Agent Margaret Trent!"

Maggie got up to loud cheers that had begun—from Corrigan's perspective—five second earlier. She walked across the stage, her hand outstretched to greet Duplass, her smile lighting up the entire room. A camera flashbulb went off, and then a second...

And then the entire world exploded.

In a blink, a propulsive wall of flame erupted from the base of the podium, tore Maggie and Duplass apart, and expanded outward from there. *A bomb* was all Corrigan had time to register before the explosion expanded to consume everyone else on the stage, and then the first row, and then Corrigan himself.

He could feel the heat on his face, and the punch in his chest, when the force of the blast hurtled him backwards and he lost control of his body. He was being crushed, and ripped open. He was being murdered.

He was dead.

It hadn't happened yet. It was five seconds in the future. That wasn't enough time to get away from it, but he could try.

He leapt to his feet and charged Maggie and Duplass, still in the middle of their photo op and entirely unaware that they had only a couple of seconds to live.

"Bomb!" he shouted. Nobody could hear him, and he was moving too slowly, like trying to run in a dream, because his body was still reacting to being shattered against the back wall. Did he even make a noise?

To everyone's surprise, including the men there to guard the deputy mayor, Corrigan slammed into Duplass and Maggie and carried them off the stage and onto the floor. He landed with them beneath him, wondering if the lip of the stage and his body would somehow combine to protect them from the blast that was a second away. He took a deep breath, closed his eyes, and waited.

Nothing happened.

Rather, what he expected to happen, did not. The bomb didn't go off.

Plenty of other things did happen, though, since as far as everyone else there was concerned, the weird dude in the corner had just bum-rushed the two most politically important people in the room.

Whenever Corrigan changed the future, for the briefest of moments that future would disappear and get replaced by the version kick-started by his actions. It was, in a way, the only time he felt normal and achieved a modest bit of peace. But he hadn't done anything to disable the bomb; there was no reason to expect it not to detonate.

Yet it hadn't. The future reset with a blink that sometimes felt like it should come with an audible component, and maybe did. Maybe there was a *system reset* sound that only Corrigan Bain, fixer, could hear.

The room turned into a mad scramble of activity. The audience on the floor near where they landed jumped from their chairs and backed up, scuffling metal chair legs on a wood floor. Duplass started shouting, and punching Corrigan, whose entire weight was on the deputy mayor's chest. Maggie was shouting too, but more out of concern.

"Corrigan, what is it?" she asked, trying to push herself out of his grasp.

And then there were the men with the guns. Four of them, in suits, looking angry, grabbing him by the shoulders and pushing handgun barrels in his face and screaming orders at him.

All at once. It was happening all at once, and he was lost. The bomb hadn't gone off and that was a singular point in his future with nothing on the other side. Now he was in a future that didn't appear to understand what to do with him.

"There's a bomb," he said, still too quietly. Nobody could hear him. His ears were ringing from the explosion that didn't happen and he could hardly breathe from the fire that had scorched the air in his lungs and he was being too quiet.

"ON YOUR FEET!" screamed one of Duplass's bodyguards.

"What's wrong with him?" someone in the crowd asked, or was about to ask.

"Who is he?"

"What's wrong?"

"Is there a fire?"

The questions were all coming at the same time, from all directions, and the words were starting to run together. He was losing his grip. He could still see the fire.

Maggie was on top of things, though. She looked him in the eyes, not angry or confused. Just worried.

"Tell me," she said, calmly, holding his face in her hands. "Tell me what happened."

A gun barrel was pushed up against his head and in another three seconds the man to his right was going to kick him in the kidneys. A second after that, the deputy mayor was going to be pulled out from under Corrigan, and the hairpiece he didn't want anyone to know about was going to come loose.

"There's a bomb. In the podium, there's a bomb. Get everyone out of here."

She jumped to her feet.

"BOMB!" she shouted. "EVERYONE OUT!"

The man to Corrigan's right kicked him in the kidney, another one pulled Duplass from under him, and then all of them were on top of Corrigan, punching and pulling. He heard handcuffs out and felt them going on his wrists, all in the future, but that was okay, because the bomb continued to not explode.

Still, he didn't feel like getting handcuffed, so the second before they went on, he altered his own future, twisting under one of the men and rolling onto his back. In one of his futures, the man who had recently had his gun pressed against Corrigan's temple actually got off a shot, which was a good indication nobody responsible for the deputy mayor's safety was listening to the bomb announcement. That was just poor training.

Anyway, a gunshot would just make the whole situation messier, so Corrigan caught his legs up with one of the other men, who tripped sideways and fell into the guy about to fire.

The impact was exactly right to jostle the gun loose, which made sense only because Corrigan had run through multiple permutations of the future in order to get to the one that did what he wanted.

That left one guy unaccounted for. He still had it in his head that Corrigan was a threat. He leveled his gun just as Corrigan got to his feet. In the future, the man took two shots. Neither would hit Corrigan, and one would wound someone behind them. *More bad training,* he thought, as he twisted the gun loose from the man's hand and elbowed him in the nose.

By then, Maggie's announcement had started to really sink in and people began heading for the exits. The crowd scene Corrigan could barely tolerate when it was an ordered passage into the room turned into the utter madness of a rioting exodus. All was shouting and screaming, spaghetti-string futures splitting off in dozens of directions at once. The only good thing about it was that the rush for the exits put some bystanders directly between Corrigan and the bodyguards who seemed intent on ignoring their primary responsibility, that being to get Duplass out of the room he was sharing with an explosive device.

Corrigan lost track of the present as he got caught up in the crowd, until Maggie found him again.

"Let's go," she said, repeatedly. Her words were echoing forward.

"I can't..."

"Yes, you can. You take my hand and follow me and I'll get you out. Come on."

...a wild scene at the State House today as Deputy Mayor James Duplass was attacked during an awards ceremony by this man, *an apparent guest of one of the men being honored. We do not at this time have the man's name...*

—local cable news, 45 minutes after the incident

The total evacuation of a building as large and important as the Massachusetts State House was quite complicated and involved, not to mention chaotic. The word *stately* did not spring to mind, Maggie thought.

The first thing to happen, after she got Corrigan—who was now useless thanks to the aforementioned chaos—out of the room, was that somebody pulled a fire alarm. This put a few hundred more people—from the rest of the building—in the way of their exodus, and slowed it all down. Had it been an actual fire, Maggie wondered how the building designers expected anybody to survive.

The good news was that nobody appeared to be in an active panic. Once the spectators from the room where a bomb was identified, mingled with the people who thought this was a fire drill, everyone calmed down and milled out of the main doors and down the steps, in an orderly fashion.

The State House sat at the top of a hill, among a collection of tightly-packed buildings and narrow streets—a defining characteristic of most of the city—and directly across from the Commons. This convenient fact meant when the entire state government and all of the attendant staff members, hangers-on, and so forth, were evacuated on a Wednesday morning, they had a place to go. There were very few other places downtown where this was the case. It might even have constituted a design specification by whoever decided to put the State House where it was, except both the building and the Commons were older than bomb scares, and possibly also older than bombs.

It was fortunate for everyone that this was happening on a cool day in April. Two months in either direction and it would have been either too hot or much too cold to spend a lot of time in the middle of a field on a steep hill. But April? April was a good time for an evacuation.

Maggie and Corrigan made it down the stairs and across the street, to a bench at the edge of the Commons.

They sat down. She held Corrigan's hand and waited for an indication that he'd rejoined her in the commonly-recognized present.

Corrigan had a habit of slipping out of the present and into the future. There was a stupidly complicated explanation for it that Maggie didn't understand, but the simplified version she did understand went like this: his consciousness drifted forward. She'd seen it happen often enough that she could tell when he was gone, and also when he fought his way back.

It was about three minutes before he returned.

"How are you doing?"

He paused for a few beats, before answering.

"I'm okay," he said.

"Are you with me?"

"I think so."

"Good. Can you tell me what just happened?"

He nodded. He was nodding before she asked.

"There's a bomb in the podium. It went off, and we all died."

"That sounds terrible," she said.

"It was."

"Except the bomb didn't go off, and we didn't all die."

"Yes," he said. "I noticed that too."

"Did you stop the bomb somehow?"

He looked off into the middle distance for a while. The lawn in front of them—and slightly below, thanks to the incline—was full of bored-looking State House staffers, lighting up cigarettes and making lunch plans. Behind them, the street was already full of emergency vehicles and Boston Police cruisers. Two officers were standing on Park Street, talking to someone Maggie recognized as an audience member from the ceremony. She was pointing out Corrigan to the officers.

"I don't see how," Corrigan said. "It's all blurry. There was a lot going on."

"Sure, but one of the things that didn't go on was the bomb exploding. If you didn't stop it, who did?"

"I don't know."

"Maybe the trigger was attached to Duplass somehow, and when you tackled him, you prevented him from setting it off."

She was avoiding the suggestion that the deputy mayor of the city was also a suicide bomber, as that seemed like a step further than anyone was comfortable going.

"I don't think so," he said. "The timing's off. I shouldn't have been able to reach both of you before the explosion. It doesn't make any sense."

Unspoken, was the real possibility that there was no bomb,

and Corrigan had suffered some kind of episode. They weren't going to talk about that.

The officers on Park radioed in Corrigan's location, and a few seconds later, there were five officers standing in front of their bench. Maggie already had her ID out.

"Hi guys," she said. "You probably want to talk to us, huh?"

Another two hours passed, in which Corrigan Bain remained in somewhat voluntary custody. Nobody knew whether or not to arrest him, but everyone agreed he had a lot of things to answer for, but until the room that ostensibly held a bomb was inspected by people who were specifically equipped to handle bombs, nobody knew what to ask him, either.

He and Maggie remained at the bench, flanked by uneasy-looking police officers, for about half of that two hours, until the tent went up.

BPD had a tent. It was there to provide them with a command center a distance from the building, and the fact that it was set up at all, strongly implied they expected this bomb search to be a long-term project.

Maggie thought that made a lot of sense. Whether or not they found a bomb in the auditorium, they'd probably have to search the whole building before letting everyone back in, and it was a big building.

This was Maggie's first bomb scare.

They didn't happen all that often, or not as often as someone raised to expect them routinely due to televised dramas might expect them to happen.

There were other kinds of scares, sure. Anthrax was a good one. Maggie remembered racing to a certain bank building in the financial district that was being evacuated because someone in the mail room found white powder on a chair. It turned out to be baby powder that had puffed out of the pants of an obese mailroom employee. She was dressing—for reasons surpassing fashion, or taste—in Lycra pants which didn't entirely fit; the powder had been applied to prevent chafing.

Assassination threats were a thing now and then, mostly when a head of state was visiting. The FBI usually had an advance team working with the Secret Service, and sometimes she was on one of those teams. Those never got serious enough to warrant any evacuations, and only a couple of low profile arrests. She did have to detain a person claiming to have an interest in blowing up the president, but on investigation it turned out the bombs he was talking about were rotten produce. They still kept him in custody until the president left the city, and then handed him over to the nearest psychiatric unit.

Once the tent was set up, she and Corrigan were led down to it, for what she assumed would be a joint conversation with some representatives of Boston Police, after which maybe they could go home and let the cops deal with the rest of this mess. It was, either way, not an FBI situation until or unless BPD asked for assistance, so Maggie was off the clock.

They were met at the entrance by David Spence, one of the dozen or so BPD detectives she'd worked with in the past—most recently on the task force—at which point it became clear the police had decided it would be in their best interests to separate her from Corrigan.

"Maggie," he said, "c'mon over here."

She looked at Corrigan.

"You good?" she asked.

"Super," he said. Then they escorted him inside.

Maggie thought this wasn't good news, but it wasn't like they could arrest him for notifying them of a bomb in the building.

Unless there isn't a bomb, she thought. Then maybe he was in a little trouble. It seemed weird to think of it that way, but it was true. Best-case scenario: there was no bomb, and nobody had just attempted to assassinate a roomful of FBI agents and the deputy mayor, and Corrigan gets arrested for...well, for something. It depended on how gung-ho they were. Worst-case, there was a bomb, and he was right, and then they had to explain to everybody how he knew there was a bomb. That could get awkward.

David led her past the tent, extracting a pack of cigarettes from his pocket as he went. He took out two and handed one to her without asking or being asked.

She'd worked with him a lot over the past eighteen months, because he was her primary liaison with BPD while working the local angle on the joint task force. They spent enough hours with one another that the shared act of a cigarette break was automatic. Maggie had 'quit', which mostly meant she only smoked when someone else was, and she stopped buying her own packs.

He extended a flame to her first, and then lit his own.

"Sorry you didn't get your moment there, Mags," he said. "I was watching the live broadcast. That sucked."

"There was a live broadcast?" she asked. She just assumed it wasn't interesting enough for a live cut-in.

"Local cable news, yeah. It dropped out as soon as you started shouting about a bomb. It's weird, right? Shout *bomb* on television, and half the city races towards the scene, while everyone at the scene tried to race away from it. Anyway, I'm glad you're okay."

He rubbed her shoulder when he said this, which was something he tended to do. Dave could get kind of handsy around her, something she noticed he didn't do with most of the women he worked with. He hadn't tried anything really hinky, and was harmless enough to get away with the occasional hug, so she'd never called him on it. It probably didn't hurt that Maggie knew he was married with two kids, and a third on the way, and she'd met his wife more than once.

"You know, I'm not sure if we can smoke here," Maggie said. "Aren't the Commons non-smoking these days?"

"I'm a decorated police officer and you run the FBI in this town; we can get away with it."

"I don't run the FBI."

"Not what I heard," David said. "Anyway. I'm guessing that's the boyfriend you told me about, and not some random guy you felt like inviting."

"That's him."

"Good. Well, no, maybe not good. It looks like he's in some trouble here, to be honest."

"He'll be fine. I think I know why I'm not in there. They want his story without the risk that I coach him, I get that. Why aren't you in there?"

"For a similar reason. Do you know Detective White?'

"I don't think I do, no."

"Joe White?"

"Doesn't ring a bell."

"Well there you go. That's why he's in there and I'm not."

"Because you know me?"

"And he doesn't."

"Jesus, Dave, what do you think Corrigan *did*?"

"Hey, you say he'll be fine; I'm sure he will be. Everyone just wants to keep this clean. I'm not happy about it either, for the record. They've got coffee and doughnuts in there."

She laughed.

"There's a Dunkin's a hundred feet that way," she said.

"Aah. Doesn't taste as good when you have to wait in line for it. But seriously."

He stepped between her and the tent. It put him in her line

of sight and got her attention, because apparently, she'd been staring at the tent.

"Oh, we're being serious now?" she asked.

"Yeah. So, what's up with...what's his name? Corrigan?"

"Corrigan Bain, yes."

"Funny name."

"It's his father's last name and his mother's last name."

"Why did he take his father's last name?"

"He didn't take it, it was given to him. His mother didn't know the man's first name."

"Right. I bet there's a great story behind that."

"I bet there is. David?"

"Yeah?"

"Are you questioning me? Right now, is that what you're doing?"

"Little bit. Sucks, huh?"

"Kinda does, yeah."

"Come on, Mags, think this through. Only two outcomes, right? Either there isn't a bomb and your boyfriend is a *little* unstable, or there is a bomb and he's got something to do with the bomb being there. I don't see any better explanations."

"There is one," she said.

"Cool. Do you know what it is?"

She sighed.

"Why don't we see what the bomb squad comes up with first, and take it from there."

"Okay, sure. Look, I'm just asking. As a friend."

"Oh, good. I'm glad you're not arresting me today."

He laughed.

"Mags, it's not like that. I want to help."

"I know you probably do, David," she said. "But right now, you're pissing me off, so I'm gonna go get a coffee. We can pick this up again later."

She dropped the cigarette on the ground and crushed it with her shoe, and then walked off before David could think of something pithy to say.

***

They didn't know exactly what to do with him.

Corrigan sat in a corner of the tent as police officers of varying rank and significance discussed a number of issues regarding the current situation up the hill. Since it wasn't a terribly large tent, he could mostly hear everything they discussed at their little card table, except when they were talking about him; then an effort was made to turn away and speak in whispers.

Nobody told him he was under arrest, so he had no reason to think he couldn't just get up and leave, except for the two large police officers that flanked him. They looked like the real deal: young, healthy, tall and muscular. Kids, both of them, but probably well-trained ones. They'd probably get in the way of him leaving, and then one of the guys at the card table would pick some charges out of a hat—they clearly didn't know what crime to charge him with, or they would have by now—and there would be cuffs, and that was just going to be unpleasant for everyone. So, he stayed where he was.

Corrigan could only guess about half of what was going on, but what he understood was this: the Boston P.D. was running the scene; the bomb squad had been called; they had confirmed that building was fully evacuated; in a few minutes, someone in a bomb suit—or whatever the heck they called it—was going to be entering the hall.

Aside from the obvious problems he would create for himself if he tried to go home—which he really very much wanted to do—one reason he stuck around was to hear what the bomb squad found in that room.

A bomb was in there. He was sure of it. But that was all he was sure of. Given everything that happened after he acted, there was clearly more to this story, and maybe that began with what kind of device it was. Hopefully, he'd be privy to the answer to that question.

After the conclusion of a hushed conversation, one of the plain-clothed officers picked up a chair, dragged it across the ground, and put it down in front of Corrigan.

"How you doing?" he said. "I'm Detective Joe White. Call me Joe."

He extended his hand, which Corrigan took.

"Corrigan Bain."

"Pleasure."

Joe White sat. The chair was of the cheap plastic-metal hybrid folding variety, and Joe was a large enough man to threaten the tensile strength of said chair.

"Can I call you Corrigan?" Joe asked.

"Sure."

"Not one for a lot of talking, I take it."

"No. Not usually, no."

Corrigan wasn't certain he had a good grip on where the present was, and that was the real reason he was keeping his responses short. There was also—probably, he couldn't tell—an unusual pause between White's questions and Corrigan's responses. He didn't want to step on what the detective had to say before he had a chance to say it.

The bomb going off in his future had pretty much wrecked any chance Corrigan had of appearing fully sane and normal for the rest of the day. He knew it, and he knew the only solution was to go home and sit alone for a while, but that wasn't likely to happen soon. Although the isolation of the tent was helping.

"Right," Joe said, rubbing his chin with his hand. "So, I don't know if you know this, but you've caused a real mess."

"I didn't cause it."

"Sorry, no, of course not. I misspoke. Look, you're not under arrest right now, Corrigan, but we'd like it if you stuck around for at least the next half hour, is that okay?"

"What's happening in the next half an hour?"

"Well, we have a team heading into the auditorium now, but they're gonna be out of radio communication. Once they check in, we'll have more information to work with, and we're figuring on that being about a half an hour."

"Okay," Corrigan said. "I can stick around. Why are they out of radio communication?"

"They have a jammer with them," White said. "It keeps whoever put this hypothetical bomb of yours in the room from setting it off remotely. You know, if it's that kind of device. Works great, except our guys can't call out either. Don't worry, they'll get word out. Or, you know, *kaboom*, which is kind of an answer of its own, huh?"

"That's smart."

"Thank you, yeah, we're all smart around here. What do you do, Corrigan?"

"I'm retired."

"Is that right? That's great. We could be the same age. I must not be making the right kind of investments. What's the secret? Family money?"

"You could say that."

He actually did inherit enough money to live comfortably for the rest of his life, provided that life didn't include purchasing multiple personal jets. But he inherited it from someone to whom he wasn't a blood relative, so far as he knew. It was a long story, one he wasn't about to tell Joe White.

"Nice!" Joe said. "Looks like you're keeping it humble, too, good for you. Most trust fund kids, right? Bunch of dicks. So, you were here today because your girlfriend was getting an award?"

White was starting to annoy Corrigan, which he thought was probably intentional.

"Yes," Corrigan said. "We've known each other for over a decade, to answer your next question. I used to have a job that crossed paths with the FBI, and that's how we met. That's to answer the question you were going to follow up with."

Joe put his hands in the air.

"Hey, hey, we're just talking," he said.

"Sure."

"Maybe tell me about that job you had."

"It's hard to explain."

"I bet. Look, I don't want you to take this the wrong way, Corrigan, but I've done a little digging, and your name turned up in a lot of really weird places. You have a talent for being around when shit happens."

"As I said, it's hard to explain."

"My favorite story? A bank robbery where you and your girlfriend stopped a guy with a bomb. You probably think I'm nuts here, but that sounds kind of relevant to where we are right now."

"That was a long time ago."

"Computers! I had someone downtown run a search on your name, and he sent everything to my phone. Sometimes I hate technology, but not today. Today, I love technology. And we're computerizing all the files from fifteen years back and older, so maybe there's more stories about you I haven't gotten yet."

Corrigan remembered the case well enough. It was the first time he and Maggie worked together.

"That was a different situation," he said.

"Maybe so. I'm also told you put up quite a fight with the

deputy's security detail. You have some combat experience, Corrigan?"

"I know how to handle myself. But I think whoever told you that is probably exaggerating."

"Sure. But…"

He was cut off by someone on the other side of the room. Corrigan was pretty sure that someone was the chief of police.

"Joe," was all he had to say, and then Detective White was back at the table, talking quietly. The chief had a phone in his hand.

When Joe White returned, he had a different demeanor entirely.

"They found the bomb," Corrigan said.

"They did, yeah. How about if you tell me how you knew it was there?"

"What kind of device was it?"

"It isn't on a timer, I can tell you that. They're saying it's hooked up to a cell phone."

Joe sat back down in the chair. The chair protested.

"Look," he said. "Give me *something*. Tell me you saw a wire sticking out of the podium or saw someone suspicious in the crowd. Give me an idea of what we're working with here, because buddy, right now I have one suspect and one hero, and they're the same guy. I don't like that."

"Someone in the crowd?" Corrigan repeated. "Why would you say that?"

"*Did* you see someone?"

Corrigan tried to think back to the moments before the bomb, but his sense memory was stuck on the experience of having his entire body pulverized. He couldn't recall anything about the crowd at all.

"I didn't. I don't think I did. It doesn't matter; that isn't how I knew there was a bomb."

"So, tell me."

"You're not going to believe me."

"Probably not," Joe said, "but give it a try."

Corrigan sighed.

"I saw it before it happened," he said.

"Saw what before it happened?"

"The bomb. No, that isn't right. I felt it go off. I experienced it. Before it happened."

"You *experienced* the bomb go off, before the bomb went off, except the bomb didn't go off. You're, what? A dysfunctional psychic?"

"I don't understand it either."

"Really. Which part."

"The part where it went off but it didn't," Corrigan said. "It was different somehow."

Joe shook his head.

"This entire conversation's making my head hurt."

"I need to get out of here. Am I free to go?"

"You have any place to be?" Joe asked.

"You said a half an hour, or whenever the bomb squad called. They called, and I'm here voluntarily. Are you charging me with something, or can I go?"

Joe eyeballed the chief on the other side of the tent. Something unspoken passed between them.

"You can go," the detective said. "But be easy to get in touch with for a little while. We don't want to have to call the FBI to get a hold of you. You want an escort home? There could be media."

"I'll be okay."

"If you're sure."

"I am."

White waved to the two strapping young police officers, who stepped aside to let him pass.

Corrigan walked out into the sunlight, blinked a few times until his eyes adjusted, and took in the scene.

The day hadn't gotten any less crowded since he disappeared in to the tent. If anything, it had gotten worse, as people who hadn't been in the State House had begun to turn up, to bear witness to the slow resolution of the bomb scare. The number of police officers had doubled or tripled, and it looked like if there was a fire in another part of the city, it was going to be a problem, because every firetruck in Boston was at the scene.

It was so enormously busy, Corrigan felt like he'd stepped out of a sensory deprivation tank into the middle of a rock concert.

He'd hoped that Maggie would be waiting, so she could help him get home. He desperately needed a few hours in a dark room, alone, to get his head back on straight. Then he could work out precisely what was going on with this bomb thing. But she wasn't there.

He took out his cell phone. Surely, she was nearby; he'd just call her. That was, assuming the frequency jammers White was talking about didn't reach as far as the tent.

He was about to hit autodial for her number, when he realized he was staring at someone who didn't belong there at all. It was a bald man in orange coveralls, looking sort of like a painter who was missing his equipment. What made him-or *it*, really—stand out, was that his future wasn't visible to Corrigan because, unlike everyone else in the Commons, this being actually lived in the future.

They called themselves Kilroys. And the last time Corrigan saw one, it was trying to kill him.

The creature locked eyes with Corrigan from a hundred paces away, opened its enormous, shark-like mouth, and began to scream.

Then, the ground shook.

What the hell? Corrigan thought. A Kilroy's shriek was terrifyingly loud, if one happened to be sharing the future with one. It didn't cause the ground to shake, though, in the present or not.

There was a lightning flash next—or what looked like one—from inside the State House. It was followed by a loud *BOOM*, as a dozen windows exploded outward. Corrigan turned to look, and in doing so, lost track of the shrieking Kilroy.

Car alarms began sounding off all over the place. For about three seconds, nobody in the vicinity moved, as everyone tried to come to grips with what had just happened.

Then a woman screamed, a siren shrieked, men in uniform began sprinting for the building. Everyone, suddenly had a place to go and a thing to do, and the pandemonium of activity almost brought Corrigan to his knees.

He hadn't seen the bomb go off in the future. He hadn't seen any of this.

What the hell is going on?

"CORRIGAN BAIN!"

Corrigan turned around. Detective White had his gun out.

"Put the phone down," Joe shouted, "and get on the ground, NOW!"

CHAPTER THREE

*We're getting a report...that the man last seen in this video, attacking
the deputy mayor and an FBI agent, has been taken into custody.
We're trying to confirm this, folks. There's a lot of chaos right now, as
you can imagine...*

...he's been identified as Corrigan...[to off camera] is this right?

*...Corrigan Bain, a resident of Cambridge. We're getting this from an
attendee of this morning's event. We are not sure at this time what Mr.
Bain's connection is to the bombing.*

—Channel 4 News, twenty minutes after the explosion

The Commons erupted with activity in the immediate
aftermath of the explosion, and it was wreaking havoc
with Corrigan's head. There were too many people
moving too quickly, too much screaming, too many smells. He
was having a real sensory overload problem. And for some
reason Detective White was yelling at him.

White, who seemed pretty reasonable a few seconds earlier,

was in a hair-trigger sort of state. In the future, Corrigan spun around too quickly and heard the gun go off. He didn't feel himself take that first bullet, but the second one would strike home, below the left shoulder, not far from his heart and probably ultimately fatal.

Corrigan adjusted his future by twisting himself out of the way and saw that second bullet hit a woman standing behind him, in the thigh.

A third bullet would shatter his hipbone if he let it, so he adjusted for that too, but then there was a fourth and a fifth, and while Corrigan could certainly map out a future where he evaded all of them, he couldn't do the same thing for the other people sharing the lawn. White was going to fire wildly and hurt a lot of bystanders in an effort to bring Corrigan down. If there were no other options—if the only future Corrigan saw was one where White fired his weapon—he and the detective would have to live with the consequences.

There were other futures, however. The one with the fewest casualties had Corrigan freezing at the sound of his own name, dropping his phone on the grass, and going down to his knees without turning.

He did this, and didn't get shot. A second later White had him face down in the dirt. He heard cuffs come out.

"Are you arresting me?" Corrigan asked. He had tried three other questions in his future. This was the one with the most promise.

"Yeah, I'm arresting you. What do you think?"

"I don't think you need to cuff me."

"You have the right to remain silent..."

"Detective, what changed between now and two minutes ago?"

"You just blew up some friends of mine, that's what changed.

Now can I finish with the Miranda or do I have to kick you in the head a few times and *then* finish? Your call."

Corrigan let him finish. Then he let him put the cuffs on.

———

Corrigan was in a squad car a few minutes later, his hands behind his back and in some discomfort due to that fact. He was a large man, with thick arms, an ever-thickening midsection, and broad shoulders, so having his hands cuffed behind his back felt like holding a particularly challenging yoga pose indefinitely.

Other than that, he was sort of glad to be out of the crowd again.

The street was almost impossible to navigate even with the dome lights on. The cruiser had to get past emergency vehicles, media, and hysterical civilians, and since almost every vehicle had flashing lights, none of them stood out.

They drove close enough to the front of the State House for Corrigan to get a decent look at the damage. The bomb must have been pretty big: all the windows on the left side were blown out, and black smoke was pouring from two floors. It looked like the building was actively on fire. Whatever bomb squad members had been inside when that happened probably didn't make it, regardless of what kind of equipment they were wearing. Nothing short of a tank would have been sufficient.

"How'd that happen?" he said to himself.

"Excuse me, sir?"

The cop behind the wheel was one of the large young men White used for intimidation back in the tent. Next to him was the other one. White wasn't in the car.

"Just thinking out loud," he said. "This wasn't supposed to happen."

The second one turned to look at him.

"You were expecting something different?" he asked. "Like what?"

He looked ready to hear Corrigan's confession.

"You misunderstand me, son," Corrigan said. "Detective White made it very clear that something was in place to keep anybody from setting off the bomb remotely. You heard him. So, how'd it go off?"

The cop didn't answer. He turned back around, side-eyed his fellow officer, and left it at that.

Even with the cuffs on, Corrigan was having a problem taking seriously the idea that he might be in real legal jeopardy. He'd had plenty of run-ins with the police in the past, and only about half of those encounters were pleasant, but no charges ever stuck.

When he was fixing full-time, he figured out pretty quickly that cops didn't really have the institutional flexibility to allow for somebody like him. In fairness, most people didn't, but since the police generally showed up *after* he'd been there, their issue with what he'd done, and how he'd done it, was sometimes a problem. In a happy world, they'd all know who he was and that he was on their side. In the real world, he got questioned an awful lot, and had been arrested at least three or four times. That was why he always did his best to exit the scene before the police arrived.

Still, it was impossible to look at this as anything other than a misunderstanding that would get sorted out shortly. He just had to wait for some calmer people to assert themselves, realize he wasn't a threat to anyone, and send him on his way.

After all, he didn't have anything to do with the bombing.

The topography of downtown Boston was such that one was almost always standing either on a hill, or at the bottom of one. The State House, from most perspectives, sat atop a hill, but it was actually only on a wayward peak on the side of a slightly larger hill. It was possible, in other words, to go past the building and continue traveling up.

Boston Common was on the side of a hill, too. There were multiple near-flat areas within the Commons—the frog pond, for instance, which was a skating rink in winter—but it was mostly a series of hills or a *part* of a series.

Further downhill was Tremont Street, and halfway down that—for Tremont was also a road that traveled down a hill—was a popular independent coffee shop.

Maggie had been there on many occasions, as they were only a couple of miles from the FBI offices and she was pretty sure she liked their coffee more than the coffee from the Starbucks that was much closer, or the Dunkin's that was even closer still. She had a suspicion that all fresh brewed hot coffee tasted approximately the same, and the real difference was in how one felt about where one purchased the coffee, but that didn't stop her from preferring the boutique cup over the national chain cup; it just made her question the forces that influenced that preference.

Thanks to everything going on at the State House, the shop was line-out-the-door busy, but Maggie had nothing else to do until Corrigan was released, or the bomb was found and removed. She didn't feel like dealing with an interrogation from people she considered colleagues, and she couldn't spend the day staring at the side of a tent, so she waited in line and got her coffee and thought about whether this cup was *that* much better than the five other places she could have gone, without even leaving Tremont, and that was what she was doing when the bomb went off.

She didn't hear it, because she was inside, at the back of the store, where the counter to fetch one's coffee was. She felt it, though.

"Whoa, what was that?" she asked nobody in particular. She looked around the shop to confirm that other people had felt it, in case she had actually suffered some kind of seizure.

"Subway," the young man beside her suggested. "Maybe."

The barista, who spent every day standing right where they were, said, "that wasn't the train." She looked a little concerned.

The bomb, Maggie thought.

It should have been impossible for Maggie to put the idea of the bomb scare aside as quickly as she clearly had, but the truth was that even when she was fleeing the building she never felt like she was in danger. Being around Corrigan could do that to a person. She was far more concerned about him being held for questioning than she was about the reason for it.

There was another explanation. She'd been working a domestic terrorism case for eighteen months, and on five occasions in that eighteen months, she or someone on her team ended up in a room with a device that they didn't know what to do with. Each time, the bomb squad was called, and each time the device was disabled or destroyed harmlessly.

It was how she learned to think about these things over time: hold on until the bomb squad got there, and then everything was going to be okay. Because bombs didn't go off on the bomb squad.

So, Maggie had put the entire idea of it out of her mind. Corrigan was there to get her away from it, and the squad was on the scene to clean it up. All that was supposed to be left was for someone to tell her what the device looked like so she could start working on who put it there and why.

The bomber was supposed to be the threat now. Not the bomb.

Everything outside was madness. Traffic had already been redirected to a slow death on every side street in the city, leaving the four streets surrounding the Commons to firetrucks, ambulances and seemingly every police car on duty, and all of them had their lights on. Black smoke was billowing from the State House, almost entirely obscuring it. The wind picked up the smell of the smoke, and spread it all over the place. Bostonians who, unlike Maggie, had at no time been two feet from the device that just destroyed half a building, stood next to her on the sidewalk and cried. Loved ones were being called. The Marathon bombing, consigned to a distant memory for so many, was suddenly on everyone's lips. A bomb had blown up the State House, and tore open all of the city's old scars.

I shouldn't have left the tent, she thought.

Corrigan was undoubtedly safe, but he was also now at the center of a chaotic scene, and he didn't do very well in that sort of situation. She needed to find him, say whatever needed to be said to the Boston Police, and get him home before he shut down completely. David could help, maybe.

She took out her phone. Looking around, she was perhaps the last person in the area to do so: people were taking pictures, live-blogging, tweeting, updating their Facebook pages, and one or two were actually using their phones like a phone.

Maggie was about to try that herself when she saw the notification flag on one of the applications. It popped up whenever someone put something into a shared cloud drive. Nobody really used the drive anymore now that the task force was done, so there wasn't a good reason for it to have been hit with something new.

Curious, she opened the app.

The first of three new pictures filled the smartphone screen.

"Oh shit," she said, loudly enough to draw some attention from a few of the nearby live-bloggers.

Then she made the first of two phone calls. It wasn't to Corrigan.

"David, it's me. Check the cloud and meet me at the tent."

"A little busy right now, Maggie."

"Then don't meet me at the tent. I'm taking over the case either way."

She hung up. He would look at the drive and understand. She didn't have time to walk him through it.

The second call *was* to Corrigan, who needed to get uninvolved with this thing right now, provided he was still at the scene at all.

He didn't answer. But after several rings, someone else did.

"Agent Trent?" a man asked.

"Yes. Who is this?"

"This is Detective Joe White. I've placed the owner of this phone under arrest. You should head to the station if you want to talk to him. Maybe bring his lawyer too."

Jesus Christ.

"Can you explain why he isn't with his phone?"

"I can. Because this phone set off that bomb. Now if there isn't anything else, I have a lot of work to do."

"I see. Detective White, is it? I need you to tell me *exactly* where you are. You and I are going to have a long conversation, and maybe at the end of it you should call *your* lawyer."

"I'm at the big white tent. You can't miss me."

It took long enough to get the cruiser to Boston Police headquarters for Corrigan to wonder if walking might have been a better idea. Not that he didn't appreciate the quiet time in the back of the car; it made it possible to lower his head and ignore the madness running rampant outside for a few minutes. On the other hand, if they walked, they probably would have cuffed his wrists in the front, and that would have been nice too.

The car stopped in the station's garage, and then burly cop #2 helped him out of the back. He didn't know their names. He tried asking for them in the future, but didn't get any response, so he never bothered to actually ask.

They escorted him inside, past booking and past the station's desks. The place was half-empty—unsurprising under the circumstances. The officers who were there, all stood where they were to stare at him as he was led through. It was the first time he felt any real concern about his predicament.

His eyes landed on one officer in particular. The cop's name was Wilcox. Corrigan was glad to see the man hadn't retired yet.

Wilcox stared along with everyone else, but upon finding his gaze met, gave the tiniest of nods.

Then it was off to one of the holding cells and—mercifully—the removal of the cuffs.

Completely alone for the first time all day, Corrigan spent a few minutes enjoying the full range of motion of both his arms,. Then he worked through a couple of exercises he designed for himself, to verify that he knew where the present was. It was a cycle of clapping, stomping, and hand-waving repeated several times, with periods of what looked like deep concentration in between. Anyone monitoring him on the security feed would no doubt have a lot of questions about what was going on in the cell, because it looked like an overly complicated rain dance, but he had no better time to do this and it was something that had to be done.

Moderately satisfied that he'd gotten his head in order, he sat down on the holding cell's small cot and tried to work out what had actually happened with the bomb.

It wasn't something that was easy to explain to other people. When asked how far into the future he could see, his usual answer was that it was about five seconds, but that wasn't really true. He could see further, it was just that what he saw didn't make any sense. It was an uncertainty barrier of sorts: beyond a point, the future became a morass of competing outcomes with roughly equal likelihoods. Since he could see all of the possible outcomes, the pile of undifferentiated results was impossible to interpret.

But *within* that barrier, Corrigan knew everything that was going to happen. It was a closed logical circle: the future in that five or so seconds was definitely going to happen because Corrigan could see it about to happen, and he could see it about to happen because it was definitely going to happen.

That was the problem with the bomb not going off. It wasn't simply a matter of the person with the trigger deciding not to blow up the bomb. It didn't work that way.

Only one person could explicitly alter the future in that five-second window, and Corrigan Bain was that person.

I did alter the future, he reminded himself. By taking himself, Maggie, and Duplass away from the center of the blast he made an explicit alteration of the future. The problem, as Maggie had already pointed out, was that he didn't do anything to stop the bomb. The only person who could do that was the one who put it there in the first place.

"They can do what I can do," he said aloud.

It was the only possibility. The bomber must have seen Corrigan alter his own future, and that forced the bomber to alter his as well, and not trigger the explosion.

Briefly, he considered whether he had already seen this bomber: the Kilroy, standing in the middle of the Commons, shrieking just as the bomb went off. It was also capable of altering the future, only because it wasn't the future to a Kilroy; it was the present.

The idea of one of these creatures deciding to go from the occasional murder to acts of terrorism was truly frightening, but incredibly unlikely. It didn't jibe with what Corrigan saw, either. He saw a Kilroy in pain, because large-scale explicit alterations of the nearby future was a special kind of agony for them. The Kilroy could have been blaming Corrigan for the bomb, possibly, but it wasn't the cause.

Plus, if the Kilroy was in the room, Corrigan definitely would have noticed him. And whoever did this *had* to be there, in person, to see Corrigan altering his own future.

This made sense for a few other reasons. For just about anyone else, being in the room when a bomb explodes is a suicidal act. If they were a fixer too (Corrigan never developed a better name for what he did) they could map out the future well enough to know exactly where to stand to survive the blast. And being a miraculous survivor of a terrorist attack was an excellent alibi in this instance.

Sometimes, when Corrigan altered the future substantially, he caused a reset of sorts, where the five-second future-track vanished for a heartbeat or two. (This was exactly what caused the Kilroys pain.) In that heartbeat, he was stuck in the present, as unsure about what was going to happen next as anybody. The same thing could have happened to the bomber. In that half-second, he wouldn't have known where to be. Blowing up the bomb then would have been an *actual* suicidal act.

It wasn't a stretch to imagine someone else out there with his abilities. He'd already met one such person in his life. It was a long time ago, when he was a child, and the man was long-since dead, but if there was one, there almost had to be others.

The door at the far end of the room opened. Corrigan was in one of two decent-sized cells, which were intended to hold a number of people, temporarily, before they were taken elsewhere. Given the mayhem of the day and given it was the middle of the day in the middle of the week, it didn't strike Corrigan as terribly odd that he was the only one being held.

The cop who walked in had sergeant's stripes. Tall and thin, he carried himself like someone who used his height to intimidate. He also looked pretty angry.

"I'm glad you're here," Corrigan said. "I need to contact Maggie Trent. I've figured out something."

The sergeant didn't answer. He stood at the bars and stared down at Corrigan.

"Did you hear me?" Corrigan asked. "Agent Maggie Trent. She works for the FBI. I have information for her."

"Stand up."

"Okay."

Corrigan thought maybe he was being moved, but a quick look at his future said otherwise. Something much less pleasant was happening here.

He stood, and walked to the front of the cell.

"I'm not supposed to question you," the sergeant said. "Orders from the chief. We're supposed to leave you here until he gets back. I guess he's gathering his evidence first."

"All right. I didn't do anything, so I don't know what evidence he expects to find."

"Yeah. Sure thing. I'm sure it's just safer keeping you here. Away from things that go boom."

Corrigan realized the camera was off. It was a low-grade security camera in the top corner of the room, inside a cage. It had a red light on the front that indicated when it was active, and that red light wasn't showing. Corrigan couldn't recall if it had been when he was first brought in.

"Sergeant..."

"Will Pekoe."

"Sergeant Pekoe, I need to make a phone call to FBI Senior Agent Margaret Trent. Do you know her?"

Corrigan was doing his very best to appear normal and calm and reasonable. He was pretty sure it wasn't working.

"My sister's name is Janet. Janet Pekoe, up until she married. Now it's Janet Baskin. Like the ice cream place."

"Sure, okay."

"Baskin, like Jimmy Baskin. Her husband, my brother-in-law. Great guy. Did a tour in Iraq. IED stuff. Really hard-core. Jimmy worked the bomb unit around here."

Corrigan didn't say anything. He didn't need to look into the future to see that there was nothing to say that would sound anything other than confessional.

"I just wanted you to know the man's name, Mr. Bain. That's important to me. Now, you'd like to make a phone call, is that right?"

"Yes, sir."

"Sergeant Pekoe."

"Yes, Sergeant Pekoe, I'd like to make my one phone call."

"Of course you would."

The sergeant pulled out a key ring and unlocked the door with his right hand. His left hand was pulling the nightstick from his belt.

In the future, Sergeant Pekoe would be hitting Corrigan with that stick. The first swing was going to be at the stomach, and the second was going to be over the top of the head. The future got a little blurry after that, which could have meant Corrigan lost consciousness from the second shot.

Corrigan tried out a few other futures to see if there was a way around getting roughed up that didn't include fighting back, but nothing worked. As cliché as that seemed to be, Sergeant Will Pekoe was prepared to beat the crap out of Corrigan. *He was reaching for my gun* was going to be the excuse, surely, assuming he even felt like he needed one.

All Corrigan really wanted was to make that phone call, and then wait for everyone to sort this out and go after the person who was actually responsible for the bomb, but he was in no mood to get the crap beaten out of him in order to get to that point. He'd been looking ahead at his options for defusing this situation since Pekoe walked in, and nothing appeared to work.

The good news, he needed to get out of this cell in order to work on what had actually happened with the bomb, and he was about to get that opportunity. The bad news, he was going to end up a fugitive.

Pekoe's first swing—the one that was supposed to hit Corrigan in the stomach—missed, because his stomach wasn't there anymore. The stick connected with the bars of the cell instead.

"I just want to make the phone call," Corrigan said, his hands up. This would do no good whatsoever, but in the event he was wrong about the camera being off—or if there was an active audio component—he wanted that on the record.

Pekoe turned beet-red, an incoherent grunt slipping from his lips. The second swing would have connected with Corrigan's temple if he had let it, but he ducked and backpedaled into the cell.

Off-balance when he didn't expect to be, the sergeant stumbled forward and nearly went to the ground. It would have been funny under different circumstances, in a *Three Stooges* slapstick sort of way.

But then he went for his gun, and Corrigan knew it was time to do more than just step out of the way. Before Pekoe had the gun all the way out of the holster, Corrigan lunged forward, whacked the sergeant on the wrist and knocked the handgun free. It skittered across the floor and landed on the other side of the cell door.

Spinning under a clumsy swing of the nightstick, Corrigan took the legs out of under Pekoe, who ended up smacking his head against one of the steel bars. It was the least harmful of the possible outcomes. In all the others, he lost consciousness, and in one of those it looked like he broke his neck.

A few seconds later, Corrigan was standing outside the cell with Sergeant Pekoe's cell door keys, gun and nightstick, while the sergeant was on the other side, holding his head and looking confused.

Corrigan locked the door.

"Goddamn you," Pekoe muttered.

"I told you, I just wanted the phone call," Corrigan said. "This wasn't my idea."

CHAPTER FOUR

All units, be on the lookout for Corrigan Bain. Suspect is described as a white male, approximately six foot three, two hundred and forty pounds, brown hair, fifty years of age. Suspect assaulted an officer of the law and is considered dangerous.

—BOLO issued by BPD, two hours and ten minutes after the explosion

By just about any standard, it had been an unusual day in the life of Sal Wilcox.

It began so normally, he couldn't entirely put together the details of the morning—what time he got to the station, who he talked to on the way, what he ate for breakfast, how the traffic was—because it was so standard his memory didn't bother to jot anything down, and what he recalled specifically felt like it happened a week earlier.

He did remember where he parked the cruiser, because that became important later, so it was possible the information was in his head and just waiting to be needed. It was only he would probably never have to wonder whether he got a jelly doughnut or a cruller in the context of aiding and abetting a fugitive's escape from police custody. There were frankly very few situations in which that information would have been relevant.

Corrigan Bain.

Sal didn't think that was a chip he was ever going to have to worry about getting cashed, because he didn't think he'd see the man again. Four or five times in his life he even managed to convince himself that the person who answered to that name wasn't real, that Sal had invented him to explain an otherwise inexplicable event. Or, when he was feeling particularly religious, that Bain was a manifestation of some manner of divine will.

But Corrigan was as real as anyone. And now everybody in the Commonwealth knew his name.

When the news footage of a strange, temporarily-unidentified-man flew across news sites and social media platforms, Officer Sal Wilcox was probably one of the few people in the world who immediately understood what he was watching, because he knew what Bain was capable of. He'd spent a really long time trying to talk himself out of that understanding, which is what one did when facing a reality-shaking premise.

The man who was acting like a maniac on television could see things before they happened. He called himself a fixer, but really, he was some kind of guardian angel, whether he looked the part or not.

When they first brought Corrigan into the station, Sal was pretty confident he was about to have a rough day. That assumption was cemented the second Bain looked across the room and locked eyes with his.

He remembers, Sal thought.

Sal could already imagine how it was going to play out: Wilcox, getting called into an interrogation room where Sergeant Pekoe would be waiting, to ask him about his relationship with the suspect. Corrigan would surely drop the name of the cop whose life he saved, as a way of convincing everyone he was a good guy.

It would have made more sense—from Corrigan's perspective—if Sal Wilcox had become the kind of cop he thought he was on his way to being, back when he was younger and dumber and thinner, and having his ass saved by a big, ugly angel. But he didn't have the kind of influence necessary to make a difference here.

Bain wouldn't know that. He would think it was time to call in a favor. Instead of getting Corrigan out of trouble, though, it would get Wilcox *into* trouble.

Sal would still do it, if asked. He'd walk into a room and say *Corrigan Bain is a standup guy who can see the future*, and it would burn down what was left of his career. It's what you do when a guy saves your life.

Corrigan then lowered his eyes and pretended they didn't know each other, and kept on going to the holding tank without a word. Wilcox went back to what he was doing, while the room murmured.

"Was that the guy?"

"Who is he?"

"The one from the video?"

"That son-of-a-bitch."

Sal kept his mouth shut, then logged onto the Human Resources page and checked the status of his pension.

A frantically busy hour went by. Calls were coming in through *9-1-1* about packages all over the city, and they didn't have nearly enough bodies to handle it. Vacations were getting canceled, days off were getting reversed, uniforms were coming back in from everywhere to help. And Wilcox, who spent about 60% of his days behind a desk, was going to have to get out there too.

He was preparing to do just that, when he found the note on his desk.

It was a piece of scrap paper, folded in half and left on the keyboard. It had to have been put there when he was in the john.

Meet me in the garage—Corrigan.

Wilcox looked around: no bodies, no carnage, nobody doing anything different than they had been before he left for the toilet. The door to the holding cells was still closed. No alarms were going off.

Yet nobody else could have possibly left that note, so Bain was clearly no longer locked in a cell.

Shoving the note into his pocket and not telling anyone about it would be the first time Wilcox broke the law that day.

"Hey, I'm heading out," he said to Lois, who occupied the desk next to his. She was eating a microwaved lunch of what smelled like old broccoli, and working at the same time. She'd clearly just gotten back from the break room and must have been in no position to see Bain walk past.

"I'll probably be right behind you," she said. "Be safe."

"Yep."

He grabbed his keys and his jacket, his heart pounding.

Look normal, look normal, he told himself all the way to the staircase.

There were cameras. Sometime later on this day somebody would be looking at Sal Wilcox as he left his desk to go out on assignment, and they would ask themselves, *does he look nervous?* And that would be the end for him.

It was two flights down to the basement garage, which was nearly empty. Six functional cruisers were parked down there, plus a couple of unmarked, and a half-dozen disabled vehicles waiting on repairs the budget didn't have room for yet. For similar, budget-related reasons, roughly half of the garage lights were out and awaiting replacement.

The newest light to go was right near the door to the stairs. Its absence plunged a whole corner of the garage into darkness. Sal was pretty sure that light had been working fine when he checked in earlier that morning, but that had been ages ago, when the world was still normal.

"I didn't know if you'd come," Corrigan said. He was standing in that dark corner. "Careful, I had to break a bulb."

Sal took a step forward, heard the crunch of glass under his shoe, and stepped back.

"Of course, I came," Sal said. "What can I do for you?"

"I need a way out of here."

Sal looked around.

"There's only one camera," Corrigan said. "I checked already. It's near the door. We're okay."

"You're sure about that?"

"No, but every other camera I've seen in this place is about fifteen years older than it should be. If there's a more modern one in this building, and they decided to put it in the garage, I don't know what to say."

"I'm gonna walk to my car. I back out, I stop, you have about ten seconds to get into the back seat before I start driving."

Wilcox had been a cop for thirty years, but he still remembered what it was like to be a teenager in the city, having just gotten his license, seeing a police car behind him and wondering if he'd done something wrong. That was how he had felt when he left the squad room, and how he felt walking alone through the garage, and how he expected to feel for the rest of the day, and perhaps the foreseeable future.

The slight tremble in his hands caused the keys to fall to the ground. He grunted, leaned over and picked them up, and tried the door again.

Everything's normal over here! he thought.

The cruiser started up. He backed out and turned the wheel to point the hood of the car toward the exit, a maneuver which hid the right side of the vehicle from the stairs and the camera at the gate. That was the side Corrigan jumped in on.

A second later, Bain was lying on the floor in the back.

"Ok, go," he said.

And goodbye to my career.

"I almost didn't recognize you," Corrigan said, later, still on the floor of the car.

"I got older," Sal said. "And bigger. So did you, but you're not the kind of guy people confuse for someone else."

"Sorry about this. I didn't have a lot of options."

"Did you do it?"

"Of course not."

"I had to ask," Sal said.

"I understand."

"You should have stayed in the cell, man. You're just adding to the problems."

"Yes," Corrigan agreed. "That would have been preferable."

The streets were one giant traffic jam. Boston wasn't a large city, so if one main thoroughfare closed down unexpectedly, it tended to have an impact on every other street, sometimes all the way out into the suburbs. Boston Common was hardly the most-traveled part of the city, but it was right between the business district and the theater district on one side, and the edge of Back Bay on the other. A little further in one direction and city hall, the aquarium, and everything up to and including the

Southeast Expressway got clogged up. In the other direction, Mass Ave, Kenmore Square on into Brookline, the Turnpike, and parts of Cambridge. Or, a third direction, past the theaters and into Chinatown, and South Boston.

It wasn't the most efficient getaway ever, basically. They were stop-and-go as soon as they got out of the garage. After fifteen minutes, they'd only traveled two blocks. Sal could have hit the siren and cut through some of it, but the idea was to call less attention, not more.

On the other hand, if the people in the station realized Corrigan was in the back of Sal Wilcox's car, they could probably catch up to them on foot.

So far, that hadn't happened. The radio was full of chatter, but no BOLO had gone out.

He was kind of afraid to ask why that was.

"Where am I taking you?" Sal asked.

"I don't know. Someplace safe, with a phone I can use. Maybe some food."

"Home?"

"I'm pretty sure it's not safe for me to go home."

"Then name a place. I'd like to say I'm happy to help, but to be honest the sooner you get the hell out of the back of my car, the better for me, you understand?"

"Yes."

"I mean, you saved my life, and I'm grateful. But I'd like to stay out of prison if that's okay with you."

"I understand," Corrigan said. "I'm just not clear right now where to go. I need a little quiet. Some sleep, maybe. But I can't think of anywhere that isn't connected to me in some way."

Wilcox sighed.

"I can."

I t was a different city thirty years ago. Not as different as it was in the Seventies, with the bus strike and all that, but different anyway.

The Washington Street L had just come down. That was a raised track for the subway that was just as dilapidated and unsound-looking as the neighborhoods it went over. That was always the problem with raised tracks. They blocked the sunlight from everything underneath, which made everything underneath dirty and cold and unpleasant. The same was true with the raised highway that cut through Boston until the Big Dig buried the Southeast Expressway underground and brought sunlight to sections of the North End that hadn't seen the sun in fifty years.

When the Washington Street tracks came down, they revealed a part of the city that maybe should have remained hidden a little longer, until someone showed up with a little paint or something.

Sal was still a young man: thin, and optimistic, and maybe a little too confident. He'd been on the force for five years and had the rookie beaten out of him already, but still mostly got treated like one by his partner, Moe.

Moe was bigger than Sal would ever be, and would end up dying on the job of congestive heart failure six years later. Since Sal mostly thought of his partner as a racist jackass, it wasn't the sort of loss he ended up lamenting.

It could be called ironic—for how Moe ended up dying—or just cliché, but when the call came in they were actually arguing about doughnuts. Sal could remember the details of that argument because it had started the day they partnered and didn't end until the day Moe died. It was also the only safe thing for them to talk about, since they disagreed stridently about everything else.

They were on a late-night shift in Roxbury, an area of town that—along with Mattapan—was mostly black. Sal never really knew if his partner was a bigot because of the area he policed, or if that was just an unfortunate coincidence. Whatever it was, the disdain pouring from his mouth regarding the people he was there to serve and protect was constant—which, again, was why they argued about doughnuts so often. It was the only thing Sal could stand to listen to.

The call was in response to a burglar alarm going off at one of the downtown liquor stores. It was two in the morning, which was around when those things started to roll in. Almost every time, it ended up being a false alarm for some reason or another. Since the liquor stores downtown all had heavy metal roll-gates and bars on the windows, Sal didn't want to be there on the day the alarm was legit; the guy who could get through those gates was a guy he didn't care to meet.

His memory was a little sketchy on the rest of the details, as they pertained to the liquor store itself. It was a thing they ended up doing almost every night—stopping the car in front of a shop, getting out, looking around, telling dispatch to reach the owner or the alarm company or both—so Sal couldn't quite recall how this particular stop ended with him chasing someone on foot.

But give chase was what he did. As the youngest and most capable of rapid movement, that was his role in the partnership. Moe's part was to get back in the car and try to follow the chase in the vehicle, and call for backup if needed. It wasn't a bad division of labor so long as whoever they were chasing continued along a path a car could follow.

This kid didn't do that. He darted down an alley, and then it looked like he disappeared into a particular building. Sal followed without thinking, which was neither wise nor necessarily protocol. Thirty years later, he still couldn't recall what the suspect was supposed to have done, but whatever it was didn't warrant barging into an abandoned row house at two in the morning, without backup.

Sal cleared the first floor and then the second. The place was completely empty, which was frankly not a good sign. Even the squatters knew better than to be in this place. That was what he'd tell himself later.

By the time he reached the third floor he was pretty winded, and thinking maybe he'd picked the wrong building. Then he noticed there was someone else on the floor with him.

"Hey," Sal said. "Police, get your hands up."

His flashlight beam only hit the guy's pants at first, so he didn't register right off that this wasn't the guy he had been chasing.

"There you are," the man said.

He was a big, rugged-looking dude, not attractive or unattractive so much as facially interesting in a memorable way. He had on a leather jacket and big construction worker boots. He was also white, and therefore definitely not the perp.

"Show me your hands," Sal repeated, putting his own hand on the butt of his unclipped gun.

The man raised his hands.

"I've been wondering if I was in the right place or not," the guy said, amiably.

"What are you talking about?"

"I don't usually have appointments in the middle of the night; I was worried I got confused about the location."

"Pal, I don't know what you're talking about. Pretty positive whoever you're here to meet, it isn't me."

"No, it's you. The time is right."

"The time for what?"

"I don't really know. I haven't been doing this for very long, but...well, something anyway. I'm here for a reason. We'll know soon enough. Can I put my hands down?"

The guy was obviously certifiable. But he was also all the way on the other side of the room.

"Go ahead," Sal said. "You on something?"

"I don't...drugs? Drugs, no I'm not on any drugs."

"Do you own this place?"

"No."

"So, you're trespassing."

"I guess so. Did you want to arrest me for that?"

"Don't know yet."

He used his flashlight to check out the rest of the room. It was what might be called an open floor plan if he were selling the property. More accurately, it looked like a few walls were missing.

"See anybody else come up here?" he asked the man.

"No. Were you looking for someone?"

"I chased I guy, yeah. You sure nobody else came up here?"

"Honest."

"Well, I'm gonna take a look around anyway. You stay put, we'll figure out what to do with you later."

Sal took two steps forward, and there was a loud groan from the floor.

"There we are," the man said.

Sal was halfway through the floorboards before he even realized what was happening. He would have fallen further, but the weirdo from the other end of the room launched himself across the wood surface, belly-first, like he was helping a kid out of a swimming pool. He caught Sal's right arm with both of his.

"I got you," he said calmly.

A second earlier, Sal's right hand had been on his gun. Now he could hear the revolver slap the floor one flight down. He must have started to pull it instinctively when his feet went out. Those feet were still dangling in the air.

"This whole floor's gonna give," he said to the stranger. "Let me go, it's only about ten feet."

The guy didn't answer right away. He just stared at nothing much for a few seconds.

"I can't do that," he said after a time. "The second floor won't take it. You'll end up in the basement. Give me your left."

Sal tossed his flashlight over the guy's shoulder, then reached up, locked wrists with his savior's free arm, and let himself get pulled up. A minute later they were both on the solid part of the third floor.

"Hey, thanks," Sal said.

"Don't thank me yet," he said.

The building groaned.

Until right then, Sal didn't know buildings could groan. Not the gentle settling sound of an old structure passively adjusting to gravity, but a loud, feral noise, the kind of thing people blame on angry ghosts. It was an elephant roaring or a whale dying, something to be both heard and felt.

It was a discomfiting noise for anyone who'd spent their lives in buildings without thinking about how far away from the surface of the Earth they actually were.

"What the hell was that?" he asked.

"The building's coming down," his new best friend said. "It's condemned; didn't you see the sign?"

"I went in the back. Why're you here, if you knew it was condemned?"

"Had to be here. Come on, we don't have a lot of time. I'm Corrigan, by the way."

Sal got to his feet, grabbed his light, and followed Corrigan down the stairs.

"One sec," he said. "I gotta get my service piece."

There was no door to open to get onto the second floor. He could see the gun; it was only a few steps away. But when Corrigan put his hand on Sal's shoulder and told him to stop, he listened to the man.

"I'd argue about this, but you're going to insist the paperwork for a lost revolver is worse than death, and we don't have time to have that conversation," Corrigan said. "Do you trust me?"

"How much do I need to trust you right now?"

"If you go get that gun, you're going to end up going through this floor like you did the last one. But I can get it."

"Yeah?"

"Like I said, you have to trust me."

"All right, sure."

Corrigan looked the room up and down for a second or two.

"Stay in the doorway," he said. "No matter what."

The act of retrieval took only about thirty seconds, but to get to the gun Corrigan approached from a peculiar angle, taking steps the way a guy sneaking through a minefield might. Sal honestly couldn't decide whether this was completely nuts or not.

He reached it, though, and when he made it back to the doorway he handed it right over.

Then the building started coming down, and they had to run.

The stairwell was the sturdiest part of the row house, but that didn't mean their descent was easy. There was plaster-dust, and splinters, and dirt billowing from doorways and windows, and the noise was awful. It sounded like something was eating the building from the top floor down.

Corrigan had his arms around Sal's shoulders, and was actively guiding him out. It was a halting, graceless dance routine with odd stops and pulls and pushes, and sudden shifts in speed. Once, Corrigan stopped them dead, turned around and covered Sal while a beam collapsed nearby.

It was like being escorted by a psychic fireman.

They got out of the building, and kept on going until they'd made it halfway down the alley.

Sal was on his knees coughing up dust for a few seconds before he could speak.

"How'd you do that?" he asked.

Corrigan was leaned up against the brick wall of the alley. He looked pretty spent.

"It's a little complicated. It's what I do. I'm a fixer."

"A fixer?"

"If something bad is about to happen, I go and fix it so it doesn't happen. Like I said, it's complicated."

Sal stood, and offered his hand.

"I'm Sal Wilcox, and I don't understand how you did what you did, but it saved my life and I appreciate that. You ever need anything from a cop, you look me up. Corrigan, right?"

"Corrigan Bain." They shook on it. "And maybe someday I will."

*

They were still six blocks away when the BOLO went out.

"Assaulting a police officer?" Sal said, over his shoulder. Corrigan had remained on the floor for the entire trip, and probably wasn't all too comfortable back there.

"That's not really how it happened," Corrigan said. "Your sergeant is a little excitable."

"But he's okay?"

"He was conscious when I left the room. He's probably more embarrassed than anything."

"The cameras, though, how did…you know what, I don't

think I want to know any more. But, he came after you, huh? Is that what the deal was?"

"That was the deal. You want to turn around? I could tell them I overpowered you too, made you drive me out."

"No, but when you do get caught, make sure it's not anywhere that connects us. And maybe don't tell anyone how you made it out."

"Wasn't planning on it."

Sal turned off the main street and down an alley so narrow there was only room to get out of the cruiser on one side. He came to a stop.

"Where are we?" Corrigan asked.

"Roxbury. C'mon, we should get you indoors. For all I know your face is already all over."

Out of the car, they went halfway down the alley to the side entrance of a building whose front door was on a different street at the other end of the alley. Corrigan stopped, and looked around.

"You're joking."

"Don't worry, this one isn't gonna collapse on our heads."

He brought Corrigan to the third floor, just because that seemed like the most poetically appropriate thing to do.

"I own the building," he said at the door. "About ten years ago my wife—my ex now—thought I should invest some of the overtime into real estate, and I didn't know enough to say no to her about it. I own a few properties in this neighborhood. Gentrification, right? This one, though. I think the ground is cursed or something. I can't get anybody in here."

"This isn't the same building?" Corrigan asked.

"Nah, not really. I kept one wall, that's it. Same basic design, though."

He opened the door to a large common area. It was the open floor plan Wilcox still saw sometimes, in his nightmares, but this one was open without the sacrifice of any of the retaining walls.

"I got it for cheap. Price of the land, basically. Lots of loans available to people interested in investing in this part of town. If you've got some money, might be worth checking out yourself."

"Except this building is vacant."

"Like I said, the land might be cursed. Buy a lot in a different part of the neighborhood, you'll make out, I'm sure."

He stomped on the floor to emphasize his point that the new version was plenty sturdy.

"And the furniture?" Corrigan asked.

"I got this idea maybe it would move if it was fully furnished. But nobody officially lives here. It's got electricity and heat, and the phone even works."

"Well. This is much more than I could have hoped for. Thank you, officer."

"Hey, there was a debt. And now it's cleared."

"Now it's cleared," he agreed. "But I need three more favors from you before you go."

"Ah, c'mon. As it is, if you get caught here I'm dead twice over. My name's on the damn building."

"I won't get caught here. It's not much, I promise. I need the phone number for that phone, and I need you to deliver a message for me. Oh, and some food. Unless the refrigerator's stocked."

Sal really wanted to get out of there and back on the street. The sooner he got the GPS in the squad car away from this location, the better.

"There's Chinese take-out around the corner," Sal said.

"Right, I'll just have them deliver to the vacant building."

"Okay, I see your point. Who's the note for?"

"You aren't going to like the answer to that."

CHAPTER FIVE

*What I want to know is, was he really a guest? Or did he manifest
bodily into the room?*

—anonymous commenter on the *'Corrigan Bain = K'* message
thread, FindTheBostonFixer.com

Maggie looked at her phone. Again.

Over the past six hours, it was fair to say she'd spent more time staring at the face of her phone than she'd done anything else. And as with every other time, there was no new information.

The two things about the phone which held her interest in particular were the time—it was probably dark outside now, but she hadn't been near a window in two hours and couldn't verify this—and the number of messages and/or missed calls, which remained distressingly unchanged.

About ten hours had passed since Corrigan saved the lives of everyone at the ceremony, including about three-quarters of the people who now shared the conference room with her. It had been a wild ten hours.

"All right, we're going to get started," Justin Axelrod said.

Justin was Maggie's boss, the Special-Agent-In-Charge for the state of Massachusetts, and probably the most important person at the table who hadn't been nearly blown up that morning.

Various mini-meetings broke up as people took seats around the long conference table. She knew only half of them: the people from her task force, including David; Detective Joe White, with whom she'd had five loud altercations already; Chief Gregorian of the BPD; and a representative from the mayor's office named Cindy Lane. Everyone else was some version of law enforcement, political animal, media liaison or technical expert.

The conference room was hidden on a top floor of the downtown police headquarters. The choice of venue carried a certain jurisdictional weight, especially considering one of the matters currently under dispute was whose case this should be.

"I'm gonna start with everything we know," Axelrod said. "This'll be review for most of us, but let's make sure we've level-set the facts before we start arguing about what we *don't* know yet. Mikey?"

Mikey was the kid running the projector and the laptop that was attached to it. Maggie thought he looked twelve, but conceded that every new agent looked like that to her nowadays.

The first image was a stock photo of the State House.

"At 10 AM, a ceremony honoring the work of many of the people in this room began...around here."

Justin had a laser pointer, which he used to identify a second-floor window on the western side of the building.

"At 10:42 AM, this happened."

Mikey cut to video footage taken from the foot of the stage, showing a crazed-looking Corrigan bum-rushing Maggie and

Jim Duplass. The shot froze just as he landed atop the deputy mayor.

The ten-second scene had been playing on news channels and all over the Internet for the entire day. She had seen it a few hundred times and hated everything about it, from the way it made Corrigan seem like a madman to how her butt looked when she was thrown to the ground.

The image froze on a shot of the side of Corrigan's face.

"This man is Corrigan Bain," Axelrod said. "We'll be talking about him shortly, but let me just say that a fair number of the people in this room know Mr. Bain personally. I've met him twice myself. I don't know right now the extent of his involvement in anything that happened today, but I want to be clear about one thing: regardless of what that involvement is, we owe it to our dead, and our city, to get to the truth. If the truth is that Corrigan had a hand in things, we will find that out. And if it's true that he saved the lives of some of the people at this table…if it's true that this man is a hero, well, we're going to find that out too."

Justin didn't make eye contact with Maggie once during this speech, and neither did any other person in the room. It was awkward. But, at least she was *in* the room.

"According to reports from the scene—we don't have any footage of this part right now, but you guys have been pretty consistent in your stories—the first person to act *after* this happened was Agent Trent, who upon being informed of a bomb by Mr. Bain, took the necessary steps to get the building evacuated. That was nice work, Maggie."

Joe White glared at her. She wasn't looking at him, but she could feel his eyes nonetheless.

She was told White was a good cop—about five people made a point of saying this already—but so far, she hadn't seen evidence of it. He was jumping to conclusions all over the place.

"The threat got run up the flagpole, State House protocol kicked in, and everybody got outside okay. A couple of scrapes and bruises, nothing serious. First responders to the scene did a nice job keeping a lid on a crazy situation. Good work all around. Now, I'm told that at that time, Mr. Bain was taken into custody. Is that accurate?"

"We hung onto him for questioning," White said. "He wasn't under arrest."

"He could have left if he wanted to?" Justin asked, for clarification.

"If you want to put it like that, sure."

"He was cooperating with your investigation is the point I'm trying to make, Joe."

"Sure. I mean, he wasn't telling me anything, so I don't know if you want to call that cooperation or not."

"Fair enough. Let's fast forward. Bomb squad arrives. Who briefs them?"

"I did that," Chief Gregorian said.

"Okay. They go in. Fifteen minutes later, they send out a runner with the word that they've got a live one. After that? We've got a lot of uncertainty."

The image cut to a still of the State House, immediately after the explosion. Justin pointed to a spot where there used to be a window, and a wall.

"This is early, but so far it looks like the epicenter of the blast was about here. You'll recall that the room where the bomb was found was over *here*. The implication is that they were in the act of removing it, rather than that the bomb became independently ambulatory. I'm gonna table any discussion about why they were doing that for now."

Maggie remembered the last time she worked with the men from the bomb squad. Then, the device in question couldn't be secured to the full satisfaction of the team, so they destroyed it in a reinforced drum. That drum was large and extremely heavy, and was ferried around the city on the back of a flatbed truck. What probably happened at the State House was that they were moving the bomb to get it to the drum, but until someone could confirm that, she understood why the question was an open one. Because the other possibility—that they thought it had been safely disabled, when it wasn't—was scarier.

Justin nodded at Mikey, who went to the next image. It was a photo of the bomb, taken with a camera phone.

"Roughly four seconds before the bomb went off, this image and two others were uploaded to a cloud server shared by the joint domestic terrorism task force. It was sent from Tom Osteen's phone. Tommy didn't make it."

Maggie swallowed hard. She needed to have a good cry about the loss of Tom Osteen and the rest of the team, but now was not the time.

Justin continued.

"Current thinking is, he took these pictures and pointed them to the shared drop box so when he had a signal again they would upload automatically. Here's the problem: Tommy's phone got a signal while he was still next to the bomb, which means the jammer failed, for at least long enough for that to happen. In that same window, the bomb was triggered. Go to the third image?"

Mikey forwarded to the third picture, which was a close-up of one component of the bomb. It was the reason these images had ended up in the joint task force mail drop.

"Maggie, why don't you tell us what we're looking at?"

The image captured a cell phone that was obsolete about ten years earlier, wired to a block of C-4. Drawn in black marker on the explosive was a peculiar symbol: a straight line, or staff bisecting a half-circle, with flat lines drawn off the ends of the circle. It looked almost like an ergonomic crucifixion cross.

"This is a signature," she said. "The type of wires used, the explosive, the phone and especially the symbol are all things we've seen before. It's the same design used by Borowitz and Ledo."

There was a murmur in the room, as this was evidently news to some people.

"I'm sorry," Cindy Lane said, "But aren't both of those people in custody?"

"Yes, they are."

Nick Borowitz and Sharon Ledo had been brought down by Maggie's task force eight weeks ago, at which time—for reasons having less to do with law enforcement and more to do with politics—victory was declared and medals were handed out, and the task force was shut down.

Maggie had never been fully convinced they'd arrested and/or killed all of the parties involved, but Nick and Sharon weren't talking, and the FBI needed a win. And it *was* a big victory. She just thought there was more work to be done.

"So that means...?" Cindy asked. "I guess I don't understand."

Justin answered. "It means an associate of Borowitz and Ledo is still out there somewhere. It could also mean the members of the task force were the target. We'll get back to this as well."

As far as Maggie was concerned, the photograph made this entire thing her case, or rather a case belonging to the joint task force she happened to be running. Even if they were the target, they were also the best equipped to take over the investigation. She had spent most of the day trying to make this point.

But then there was the problem with Corrigan, which made demands for her recusal pretty credible.

Mikey advanced the slide, to a shot of a more modern cellphone.

"This phone belongs to Mr. Bain," Justin said. "According to witnesses, he placed a phone call at the same time the bomb went off. Given he was also considered a suspect in the case... sorry, he was being *held for questioning* in the case...this coincidence is a little peculiar. According to the records *on* the phone, no calls went through. We've reached out to the provider to find out if anything else was transmitted from the phone at around that time. A text message or something."

There were hundreds of people in Boston Common at that time, who were either about to place a call or already on one. Any one of those cellphones could have triggered the device, and the only difference was that Joe White wasn't staring at them when the bomb went off. On top of that, Corrigan didn't even use the phone.

She'd been making this point all afternoon—that what Joe witnessed was just a coincidence—but somehow nobody else could see the logic in it. Corrigan attracted coincidences like blood attracted sharks, but that was also something nobody was ready to hear.

Everything that happened after that sort of hurt her case, too.

"Detective White placed Mr. Bain under arrest at that time," Justin said, "and took the phone as evidence. Mr. Bain was driven here, and held a couple of floors down in one of the tanks...and that's where we have a new problem, don't we?"

"Any leads yet, Justin?" David asked.

"Not at the moment, no."

Justin's response was directed at Maggie. She wasn't sure what to make of it, except maybe to warn her to keep quiet.

"You all know this," he continued, "but let's make sure we're keeping to the same page. Corrigan Bain escaped police custody a little over an hour after he was walked in the front door. According to the sergeant he assaulted—Will Pekoe, if anyone knows him, they're saying he'll be fine—Bain asked for his phone call and surprised Will when the door was opened."

"I'm sorry, can I stop you?" This was from Jeanine Mastrangelo, the task force's ICE liaison. "I've heard this a couple of times now, and…look, I don't know the sergeant, but that story's a little thin. Don't you think?"

"Pekoe's good police," Chief Gregorian said.

"Nobody's saying he isn't, but look: Pekoe goes in alone, right? Is that even…Detective White, is that protocol? Guy's your only suspect in the bombing, and this sounds like drunk tank procedure to me. Have you checked the security footage?"

"I get your point," White said, "and I promise we'll be talking to the sergeant after he's cleared, but we've got a bigger problem here. Our lead suspect is in the wind; I think we should focus on that."

"Did the tape show him attacking Pekoe?" David asked. "I think I'd like to see that, Joe."

"Camera didn't show anything. Looks like there was a malfunction."

Jeanine laughed.

"A what?" she asked. "Say that again."

"The camera that covered the cells wasn't on," Joe said. He at least had the sense to look embarrassed about this.

"All right," Jeanine said. "Look, again, I don't want to step on toes here, but if I could point out the obvious? It looks to *me* like your bigger problem isn't that this Bain guy escaped, it's that you've got someone in your station who helped him get out."

"That's unjustified!" Gregorian said.

Maggie stifled a laugh, and made a note to buy Jeanine a drink if they ever got to a point in this awful day where they had time for one.

"I'm sorry, sir, but I know where those cells are and it's three flights of police and security doors between the bars and the outside," Jeanine said. "He had to have had help. Probably the same guy who turned off the camera." She looked at David. "Tell me I'm wrong."

"I don't think you're wrong," David said.

"Mikey," Justin said, "do you have the security feed loaded?"

"Sure thing," Mike said. He was interfacing the projector with a laptop; going from the prepared presentation to the security footage meant going back out to the desktop and initiating the camera feed stored on the computer.

"We're still looking this over, right Joe?" Justin said, while Mike got to it. "I've only seen it once myself. Didn't plan on sharing it until we understood what was going on, but...well, have a look."

A grainy black-and-white image jumped to life on the projector screen. It was security camera footage, as promised, filmed from a ceiling corner. Maggie recognized it as the open-desk layout on the floor outside the holding cells. It was where Corrigan would have had to go after leaving the cell.

The floor was half-occupied with office personnel—mostly uniformed officers, with a few civilian employees. Out of context it might have been a midnight shift, or a precinct in a tiny suburb.

Corrigan showed up in the top right corner of the screen, walking slowly past two unoccupied desks. Ahead of him, an officer was bent over a desk, examining something being shown to him by a second, seated officer. If either one was to turn around they would see Corrigan standing there, but neither did.

Looking like a man avoiding obstacles only he could see, Corrigan stutter-stepped and dashed from spot to spot, right through the center of the room. One second, he was upright, the next he was crouching. Twice, he walked in a circle. Nobody saw him.

After four minutes of this, he ended up at the other side, where he exited to get to the stairwell.

The footage ended.

"So," Justin said. "We have no idea how he did that. Maggie?"

Maggie was surprised they were even talking to her.

"He was lucky?" she offered.

She knew exactly how Corrigan did what they just watched him do, but didn't think she could explain it.

"Does he have some special training we need to be aware of?" White asked her.

"Like what? He's a ninja?"

"Now look—"

"No, *you* look, detective," she snapped. "You arrested him for making a phone call he didn't make, claim he assaulted a cop while the only camera that could have recorded that mysteriously stopped working, and then your guys let him walk out of the station without anyone saying boo and somehow, *somehow* it's all his fault. Because you've got a gut feeling or some shit."

Justin stepped in. "Maggie, that's enough."

"I don't think it is. Corrigan saved my life this morning. He saved the lives of a lot of the people. And the *police* want him accountable for the lives he didn't save."

"How'd he know the bomb was there?" White asked. "Is he psychic?"

You're pretty close, Maggie thought.

"You don't arrest the hero for being a hero," she said.

"Sure, unless that's the whole idea."

They had been arguing off and on for most of the day, starting when she arrived at his tent about fifteen minutes after Corrigan had been taken away in a cruiser. She'd heard everything White had to say—and vice versa—but this was new.

"You mean a hero complex?" David interjected.

"I've had guys pulling files all afternoon downtown," Joe

said, "and his name pops up all over the place. Accidents, near-accidents, people tripping into the street or down stairs, air conditioners falling outta windows, bikers almost getting creamed by trucks...I got fifteen jackets with his name in 'em so far, and I've only pulled from two precincts. It's always the same thing. He was just in the area, happened to notice, did a thing, everybody's okay. This is not normal."

"All right," Justin said. "Okay, I see what you're saying. Make your case."

"I think this guy gets off on acting the hero. Maybe it was legit a couple of times, early on, and he liked it, and wanted more."

Maggie was pretty sure if Corrigan was in the room he would have laughed out loud at this. Staging two or three things a day so they looked like accidents would have been way beyond his—or anyone's—means, but since White didn't know about all of them, he couldn't appreciate how impossible what he was suggesting actually was. Corrigan also spent half of his career trying to figure out how to retire. Thanks to a lot of therapy, he finally had. That he got off on it somehow was comical. If anything, he hated the attention.

"He graduated in to staging things," White continued, "because the little stuff stopped doing it for him. So, he put a bomb in the podium in a place he was gonna be, when there were gonna be a lot of cameras around to catch him being a big hero. And hey, maybe the bomb was supposed to go off."

"It would have taken out everyone in the room," Jeanine said.

"Then he was expecting a smaller explosion. Wouldn't be the first time some yabbo got the C-4 wrong. Plus, we're all aware of his relationship with Agent Trent. He could have gotten details on the Borowitz and Ledo signature from her."

He looked at Maggie.

"Look, it doesn't make me happy to say this, okay? It doesn't. But it adds up."

"How would he get the bomb into the podium?" Justin asked.

"How would *anybody*? The State House is locked down 24/7 and swept regularly. We don't know. But right now, my money's on the guy who just walked out of a police station completely unnoticed being able to pull something like that off."

The room fell silent while everyone gave that some thought. Some of them were taking him seriously, Maggie realized.

"Justin, come on," she said.

"It's a theory," her boss said with a shrug.

"It's not *close* to one. You *know* we left someone unaccounted for in that case, this should be ours."

"I bet he was counting on that, too," White said.

"I swear to God—"

"Both of you, stop it," Justin said. "All right, here's what I think. Joe, you're already on it, so go find Bain and see if you can make a case. Maggie, you and the task force run the Borowitz/Ledo angle. Whoever closes the case first wins. Does that make everyone equally unhappy?"

There were nods and murmurs and a couple of sighs, but no vocalized dissent, not even from Chief Gregorian, whose toes Justin Axelrod had just stepped all over.

"Good. Daily briefings, keep the chain-of-command, you're all professionals here. Don't forget we lost four guys today. By this time next week, I want the name of the people responsible to be on every headline in the country. Got it?"

The meeting broke up. Maggie rose along with everyone else and started for the elevators. They would have to get back to the FBI offices to reopen a lot of files, and she had no intention of waiting until morning to start doing that.

Justin pulled her aside before she made it very far, into a private room off of the conference room.

"I need to ask you this," he said. "Do you know where he is? No bullshit."

"I haven't talked to him since we got out of the State House together this morning," she said.

"That isn't what I asked."

"No, I don't know. I assume he didn't go home, and that if he had, Joe would have had someone there to arrest him."

"Okay," Justin said. "I'm asking because they're going to do the same thing. The longer he stays in the cold the worse this is going to look, you know that."

"I do. But I don't know where he is or where he would go. He also doesn't have any special combat training, he doesn't know how to build bombs and never would if he did, and he wouldn't have been aware of B and L's signature because I didn't bring my work home with me. This is all a misunderstanding."

Justin nodded gently.

"I believe you. But we have to let them run their investigation, especially because their suspect has a special relationship to you...to us. There can't be any question of us holding out."

"I get that. And thanks for not pulling me from the case."

"You know it best. Just don't cross up with them."

He clapped her on the shoulder and left her alone.

She sat there in the conference room by herself for a few minutes, wondering if she had just lied to her boss or not.

CHAPTER SIX

Call him a hero if you want. What I see is a crazy person running around Boston, and an FBI that is either unable or unwilling to bring him down.

—Anita Hoffman, Good Morning Boston, AM 670

There was a solid three or four seconds of panic and confusion awaiting Corrigan when he woke up. He didn't know where he was, or how he got there. The entire previous day had disappeared, and he was supposed to be awakening next to Maggie, in his own bedroom.

Instead, he woke up alone in a strange place that looked like it belonged on a furniture sales floor.

"Right," he said aloud, listening for the temporal echo and not hearing much of it. He may have woken up in the wrong place, but his head was straight, and he felt like he'd gotten a decent amount of sleep.

A few minutes later, he was in the galley kitchen, eating leftover *lo mein*. The kitchen looked a lot like a show room kitchen, and the living room like a furniture show room living room. The open floor plan just accentuated the effect, since the *living room*, such as it was, had no walls to define it: only a couch, two chairs, and a television on the wall.

Wilcox appeared to have gone to Jordan's Furniture and just started pointing at set pieces in order to furnish the place. Corrigan, a man who had only just recently invested in curtains, could hardly blame the guy.

The TV looked functional—Corrigan could see the red indicator light on the bottom of the console from the kitchen. He found the remote for it on the couch, and flipped on to one of the local channels.

Unsurprisingly, the bombing at the State House was dominant. Maybe also unsurprisingly, Corrigan was a part of every story.

The news channels kept shuttling between *Corrigan Bain: Menace,* and *Corrigan Bain: Hero,* with hardly any nuance between those two poles. Interestingly, both versions also called him the prime suspect in the bombing, a conclusion arrived-at absent any direct input from law enforcement. It was enough for most of the local cognoscenti that he had been taken into custody after the bomb detonated, had since escaped that custody, and was currently wanted by the BPD, albeit for escaping custody and not terrorism.

"Actually, that's plenty," he said aloud. "If it weren't me, I'd think I was guilty too."

He turned the TV off.

I should turn myself in, he thought.

It was probably the most productive thing he could do with his time. As long as the police were out looking for him, instead of looking for whoever was actually responsible, they were putting the city at risk. The way to resolve that was by taking himself off the board.

He walked back into the bedroom—the only room with real

walls in the condo aside from the bathroom—and sat on the bed to figure out how that would work.

He could pick up the phone, call Maggie, tell her he's coming in. She'd make sure nobody tried to shoot him on the way, probably. And when he got there, if this Detective White wanted to know how Corrigan knew about the bomb, he'd just explain it. Again. Only better, and with illustrations or something. It wasn't that Corrigan's talent was a secret; it was more that getting someone to believe it took a lot of patience, and this cop didn't have a ton of patience the last time around.

There were people he could call. Smart people from MIT. Erica Smalls would be happy to help, if they could find her. Maggie had a whole file on him somewhere, in which his skills were documented in an official government record. He had friends too, friends and people he saved, like officer Wilcox.

Maybe it wouldn't play well in the media, but he just had to convince Boston Police enough to get a statement out that he wasn't a suspect any more, and when the real bomber was caught everyone would forget about Corrigan.

So, upside: he'd eventually get his name cleared, provided nobody shot him or tried to beat him up in a prison cell again. Downside...he'd be in jail for a little while, probably.

Or, until the actual bomber set off another bomb.

This bothered him more than he thought it probably should, but if this bomber had Corrigan's skills, Corrigan should be the one to stop him.

Like it was his responsibility.

He didn't know where to begin, though. He couldn't just walk around the city hoping to spot anomalies, not when everyone *in* the city was looking for him. He needed Maggie, and the FBI.

He reached for the phone. That was when he saw the note pad.

It was Sal Wilcox's pad. He handed it over when Corrigan wrote the note for Maggie, and Corrigan hung onto the pad when Sal left. Keeping it next to the bed was an old instinct.

Corrigan didn't remember getting up during the night and writing something down, but obviously he had, because now there was an address and a time written on the pad, and it was in his own handwriting.

"Crap," he said. "I thought I was done with this."

I t was six in the morning, and Maggie was sitting at her desk, reading the note for the fiftieth time and still not really sure what to do about it.

She hadn't bothered to go home. It wasn't worth the hassle, even if it meant getting a little more rest, and maybe a better set of clothes than the gym sweats from the bag under her desk.

Technically, she still had a condo of her own. It was in Brookline, in a spot where she could decide to eat only Korean takeout she'd never tried before, and not starve for a solid six months. The place was small, and hard to get to—there wasn't any off-street parking, which made it awful in the winter—and so she hardly ever went there except to update the clothing she kept at Corrigan's.

His condo was much nicer. It was in a high-rise guarded by an extremely efficient concierge with a view that caught the fireworks on the Fourth, a private parking area underneath, an in-house dry-cleaning service, and a few other amenities she had no idea could exist outside of a five-star hotel. She mostly stayed there, and when she thought of herself *going home*, that was the first place that came to mind.

But she also thought of Corrigan as home. Strange, annoying, occasionally infuriating Corrigan Bain, the guy she never expected to actually end up settling down with. The guy whose most unique quality made him a social nightmare, and sometimes landed him in situations like the one he was in now.

Where the hell are you, Corrigan?

Both condos had been searched, and of course he wasn't in either of them. Detective White asked her for permission to put a trace on their joint bank account, which was granted. These things weren't going to get him his man, but he had to try. Corrigan, she told him many times, was independently wealthy. It was entirely within his means to keep another place in the city, and maybe even a money stash. If it was something he chose to keep from Maggie, he could do that too.

She didn't think he *did*, and she also made that perfectly clear, but it was financially within his power.

It was a difficult balancing act. She didn't want them thinking Corrigan had a bomb shop hidden somewhere, but she also didn't want them to think she was withholding information.

What she couldn't tell them was that if there was anyone in the city capable of evading police custody, it was Corrigan.

So, rather than go to either home, she slept on the couch in her office, for as much sleep as there was to get. It was hardly the first time, but hopefully the last, only because she was looking forward to a bigger office in the near future, with a better couch.

That was provided this whole thing didn't blow up in her face.

She smiled.

Let's not say that one out loud around here.

The couch was comfortable enough for two-hour catnaps. She probably got less than that, because of the note.

There were a lot of problems with the note. First problem: it was from Corrigan. About that there wasn't a question, even though he never signed it. She knew the handwriting, and the message was of the sort that could only have come from him.

It read: *The bomber is a fixer.*

Someone at BPD headquarters slipped this note into her jacket pocket sometime between when she arrived at the station and when she went into the conference room for the big meeting. The only time she could remember being separated from the jacket was when she left it on a chair at a desk on the third floor, while she was thirty feet away, hitting up the candy machine for something bad involving chocolate. The chair sat right in the middle of the precinct floor, and was surrounded by cops. So, either Corrigan had also developed the ability to turn invisible, or a police officer put the note in her jacket.

That was the second problem: its presence indicated Corrigan was getting help from someone in the Boston PD. She didn't know who it was, but by not disclosing either this fact or the fact of the note itself, she was officially withholding information, which she'd promised Justin she would not do.

The third problem was that she could think of nothing more terrifying than a terrorist who saw the world the same way Corrigan did. The fourth was that there was no way to explain to anyone else why this was terrifying.

"Morning," David said, from her doorway. He had two coffees in his hand; one of them was for her, and that was a great thing.

She put Corrigan's note down and dropped a file on top of it.

"C'mon in," she said.

"Sleep here?"

"Yeah, how do I look?"

"Like you slept here."

"That is exactly the look I was aiming for. Is everyone here, or just you?"

"It's only six-thirty," he said, "so it's just me."

"Teacher's pet."

"That I am. Where do you want to start?"

She put her hand on the file hiding the note.

David would know what to do with it, she thought.

He was BPD; he could get something going without causing a mess. She could trust him.

But she also remembered how ready he was to question Corrigan's intentions the day before. Maybe this wasn't the time to show it to him.

"I thought we'd go through whatever we have on the crowd in the room," she said.

"Most of the cameras were covering the stage."

"Yeah, I know, but I bet a few of them continued to record when we all started running. Let's start with the news stations and see what's there."

"What about Nick and Sharon?' he asked. It had become office-normal to refer to Nick Borowitz and Sharon Ledo by their first names, as if they were a part of the team, rather than the targets of that team.

"What about them?"

"If there's someone from their group that's still blowing up things, wouldn't they be the ones to ask?"

"Yeah, but not yet. They refused to tell us where the missing munitions were *before* some of it was used down the street. I can't see either of them giving us more to work with now. I want to go at them with more."

"Okay. News feeds, then."

J oe White hadn't had a splendid couple of days.

Nobody in law enforcement had, so it wasn't really worth complaining about, necessarily—he wasn't dead, for instance, so it definitely could have been worse—but he was starting to get the idea that the bad time he was having was uniquely tailored for him, somehow.

It was like everyone decided to stop making sense all of a sudden.

This was what he was thinking as he stood in front of what appeared to be a shrine dedicated to Corrigan Bain. The center-piece was a blown-up digital photo that was not of tremendous quality. It showed a partial profile of Corrigan's face and his beefy shoulder as he was walking away from the picture-taker; clearly not something for which he posed. It wasn't recent: the subject looked younger, and the clothing worn by the other people sharing the sidewalk with him had a certain pre-2010 vibe.

The image had already been manipulated into something to share online before being made into a poster. It was framed in a thick black border, and written on the bottom of the border, in white letters, was the question, *DO YOU KNOW THIS MAN?*

Below that was a link to a website FindTheBostonFixer.com.

The rest of the wall had what would have been called news-paper clippings about ten years ago: mostly printouts of head-lines from blogs and more official providers of news. It was a collection of stories with happy endings.

"I admit, the wall is a little embarrassing," said the owner of the wall. Her name was Monica Devereaux. She was a short-ish woman somewhere north of her twenties, dressed in sweats and an oversized t-shirt, long hair pulled back but nonetheless pointing in several directions at once, with librarian-petite glasses that didn't match her round face. Joe decided she was probably very cute when she felt like being cute. On this day, greeting Boston PD in her own apartment, she didn't feel like being cute.

It did look like she made an effort to pick up, but only in a regional sense. The edges of the living room spoke of a profound historical clutter only recently reallocated. The shrine to Corrigan was sort of the centerpiece, but not really. The two computer monitors on the desk beneath the shrine were the real anchors. Everything in the apartment seemed to orbit those monitors.

And, presumably, the computer attached to them. Joe wasn't clear which silver rectangle was the actual computer—there were several on and under the desk—but imagined at least one of them was.

"Is this all you do?" he asked. She was standing next to the desk, madly shifting her weight from one foot to the other. He couldn't tell if she was excitable or if she had to pee.

"The website? No, God, of course not. I do a lot of game design, mostly freelance. Mostly from here, but I have a couple of stringer jobs that get me out. I have to meet people sometimes just to, you know, make sure I haven't turned into a troll. Not an Internet troll, like the kind under bridges. Not that I have a bridge. You get what I'm saying."

He didn't know what an Internet troll was, and how one might differ from the kind found under a bridge, but thought it was probably not all that important.

"But the past 24 hours, it's been all this," she added. "I dropped everything. Hey, can I get you anything? Water? I don't drink coffee, but I have some energy drinks if that's what you're looking for. Sorry, I've been up for like thirty-six hours I'm a little...you know, my social skills can suck when I've been awake this long."

"No, no thank you, we're fine," Joe said, speaking for himself and the uniform that came with him. "Tell me how all of this started. You began this website when?"

"Seven years ago, almost to the day. I didn't think we'd ever get this far, either. It's like finding Bigfoot living in a trailer park and working a nine-to-five. Or, you know, discovering your guardian angel lives in a condo down the street. Because that's what we're talking about, right?"

"Guardian angel?"

"Well... yeah. That's what he is. But you guys must know that already."

There were a couple of different ways Detective White could have handled Corrigan's escape from custody. Officially, the man was only wanted *in connection with* the bombing at the State House, and for escaping custody. The latter charge carried real penalties, but Joe wasn't going to be publicizing it, because it was honestly a little embarrassing. He also didn't want to be anywhere near a microphone when explaining *how* that escape had taken place.

To that end, he already knew how Bain had gotten out of his cell and why the security camera didn't record it; Sergeant Pekoe was being reprimanded quietly, very far from the FBI and the press. Nothing after that made any sense, though. Joe appreciated that Corrigan could have been defending himself—they were probably not charging him with assault at this point—when he ended up on the other side of the bars, and given the mood of the sergeant, Joe could even understand the impulse to get out of the precinct before someone else showed up to "question" him. But most people, facing that dilemma, wouldn't have been able to do what Corrigan did.

After the BOLO went out, they couldn't very well pretend that the man in the video warning everyone about the bomb hadn't been taken into custody shortly after. There were political reasons—illogical ones—not to call him a suspect, however. Those reasons where why, when Chief Gregorian delivered the morning statement, he only called Corrigan a *person of interest*.

If it had been White, he would have called Corrigan a suspect. That was what he was, and anyone who thought otherwise was engaging in some kind of weird, magical thinking that baffled the detective.

Until there was an explanation that didn't include fairy tales or psychics, Corrigan *had* to be considered an associate of the bombers. The world just didn't work any other way.

After the chief's press conference, calls began pouring in from all over the city, which was expected. A little surprising, though, was that roughly one in ten of those calls directed the police to Monica Devereaux's website. It turned out that while the Boston Police had been looking for Corrigan for the past twenty hours, Ms. Devereaux had been looking for a whole lot longer. And she wasn't the only one.

———

"You know that huge escalator in the Porter Square station?" Devereaux asked. "That was where I met him."

"And that was seven years ago?"

"Yeah, I remember because it was like a week before my birthday. So I get vertigo sometimes, right? It comes and goes. Sometimes it's bad, most times I'm cool though. This wasn't one of those cool times, but I had a place I had to be, near Porter, and I'd never been there before—to the station, I mean—and I didn't know about the escalator. Like now I know I can get off at Davis and walk a little more, but I didn't back then. Anyway... and I don't even remember what I was late *for*, isn't that weird? Anyway, I got on the escalator. But something like halfway up, I completely lost track of where *up* was, and next thing I know I'm falling and I don't even realize it. I'm just leaning backwards more and more. That was when he caught me."

"He was behind you on the escalator and he caught you?

That hardly seems..." Joe didn't finish the sentence. He pointed to the poster instead.

"Oh, but you don't get it, dude...sir...officer?" Monica said.

"Detective."

"Right. You don't get it, detective." She was getting more animated as the story went on. The enthusiasm that created an entire cult website was beginning to surface. "He *wasn't* behind me. I was alone on the escalator until I started falling, and then I wasn't."

"I don't understand."

"I didn't either! I was like, 'where did you come from?' and he said it was his job, then he apologized for almost being late and rode the rest of the way up to make sure I didn't fall again. Then when we got to the street he totally just *vanished*. Like, I turned to ask him his name and he was gone. Swear to God."

Joe thought she was exaggerating, or her memory wasn't being honest with her. He didn't think Corrigan Bain could literally vanish. If he could, he wouldn't have had to walk out of the police station like that. On the other hand, if Joe didn't have that on camera, he might have been prepared to consider her interpretation.

"And *fixer* was what he said his job was?"

"Right. I asked him why fixer, and he said he fixes accidents before they happen, and I was like, you mean like a guardian angel and he just laughed and said sure thing."

Joe nodded.

"Can we sit?" he asked. He pointed to her futon couch, a modest distance from the altar to Corrigan, which was starting to annoy him.

"Sure, yeah."

She cleared off some books that looked like they carried some import related to computer coding, and they both sat down. He took out his notepad.

"I've been in that station," he said. "That's the one with the bronzed gloves next to the escalator, isn't it?"

"I think maybe. Truth, I didn't go back to that station, but I think I remember seeing something like that."

"When they finished the station, they bronzed some of the work gloves belonging to the guys that built the place, and fixed them to the flat down-slant between the up and down escalators. I'm pretty sure the real reason was to keep somebody from trying to slide down it and kill themselves at the bottom."

"Okay."

"What I'm thinking is, if I'm on the down escalator and I see someone about to fall, and I wanted to get over to the up escalator, I'd grab one of those brass gloves and swing over. It'd be tricky, but it could work."

"Sure, that makes sense."

"Where I'm going with this, Ms. Devereaux, is to say perhaps Mr. Bain didn't appear out of nowhere but from the down stairway."

"Oh yeah, I know exactly what you're saying. He probably did do something like that, and I was pretty disoriented, so maybe."

"So...?" Again, Joe gestured to the altar on the wall.

"Yeah, no, you still don't understand. He might've done that to get behind me, but he had to *know* to do that before I started falling. There's no other way. Plus, he told me he was there to save me. 'Cuz he followed me through the gate to the street. He would've had to pay his fare again, right? I don't think he was there to catch a train; just me. Hey, that's pretty good: *instead of catching a train, he caught me.* I should add that."

"To what?"

"The website. The site's blown up, that's why you're here right? Ooh, can we pretend I didn't just say *blown up?*"

The rat-a-tat of Monica Devereaux's speech pattern was beginning to give him a headache.

"Don't worry about it. But tell me about this website. How did you go from that chance encounter to this whole thing?"

"Yeah, I can be a bit of an obsessive sometimes."

Joe laughed.

"I know," she said. "But, so, I told friends about this guy who saved me and how weird the whole thing was, and next thing, I was on local pages telling people about it and asking if anyone had a similar thing happen to them."

"You didn't take that picture?" He pointed to the blurry shot in the middle of the altar, that he was going to be mentally referring to as the *Bigfoot* picture going forward.

"No, that was taken downtown by a second-hand witness. Someone who wasn't rescued, but saw it happen. That's really rare. So far as I've been able to tell, most times the only one who even realizes something happened is the one he saves, so nobody thinks to pull out their phone and get a picture. Up until yesterday, this was the only shot of him we've been able to get."

"*We* being everyone on your website?"

"Yes."

Joe spent a little time on the site before reaching out to the site owner for this interview. About three-quarters of the first-hand encounters the contributors claimed to have had with the man in the picture were frankly ridiculous: he could fly, and disappear at will, had incredible strength, and so on. The legend on the main page claimed each contribution was vetted beforehand. He failed to see what the minimum standards were for this vetting, because *reality-based* was self-evidently not a factor.

"And none of your contributors know anything else about him, other than what they posted?"

"You'll have to ask them, although...you know, everyone uses a handle, pretty much. I only know like five of them in real life, if that's your next question. But yeah, like I was saying, before yesterday this was all we had. Didn't have a name for him until the news guys gave it out."

"I see."

"Maybe if you told me what you were looking for?"

"We're looking for *him*."

She laughed.

"Awesome, so you came to the one person who has documented proof that she doesn't know where he is? That's really funny."

"I'm open to any insights you may have."

"You and everybody else. I gave a radio interview an hour ago, and I'm pretty sure I just got an email from a producer at channel five. But look, the only thing I have to say is, if you think he's a terrorist or something, you've got it wrong."

"What makes you think he's even a suspect?"

"C'mon, everyone does. You're all wrong, and I'll tell that to anybody who asks. I have no idea how he does what he does. He could just be really lucky, I don't know. But what he isn't is a guy who'd slip a bomb into the State House."

"You know this from one two-minute encounter seven years ago."

"Me, and a hundred other people who had the same kind of encounter, yeah. Oldest story on the site's from nineteen years ago, by the way. He's been doing this for a while."

"We need him to answer questions regarding what happened yesterday. So if you happen to get some information that would be of use, I'd appreciate it if you gave me a call."

"Ha, okay."

"That's funny?"

"If he doesn't want to talk to you he's not going to talk to you. I heard he literally vanished from police custody. Like, into-thin-air stuff."

Joe shook his head. He was too weary to be surprised that this information had, in some form, escaped into the world.

"That isn't the case. He was released prematurely."

"Okay, call it that, then. Point is, if he doesn't feel like *being* in police custody, things like him getting released prematurely are bound to happen. I think you guys are going about this all wrong. You should be asking for his help."

"That's what we're trying to do."

"No, no, no, you're asking him like you think he's to blame. You shouldn't be asking him how he knew about the bomb, you should be getting him to help you find the next one."

If we catch him, there won't be a next one, Joe thought. He would have asked her what made her think there was going to be another bomb, but in assuming there would be, she was only aligning with the media's current assessment of the situation, as well as that of his superiors. Better to plan for the worst and be pleasantly surprised.

"Like I said, if anything comes your way that you think would help, give me a call."

He stood and extended a business card.

"Sure," she said. "I'll be happy to."

He didn't think that was true at all.

"So how do you think he did it, Ms. Devereaux? Really."

"How he knew about the bomb?"

"All of it. But yes, the bomb. You watched the same footage I did."

In the brief amount of time he'd had to check, there appeared to be as many theories online as there were people, but the hero/not-hero split looked about even.

"I'm sticking with guardian angel, detective," she said. "But if I ever see him again I promise I'll ask."

CHAPTER SEVEN

It was apparently not possible for attorneys to dress down.

The young man was seated in the back corner of a particular Brookline sandwich shop at the specified time, sipping a coffee and facing the glass façade. He looked a little nervous, and a lot like a lawyer who was trying not to look like a lawyer.

Corrigan stood on the other side of that glass picture-window, shading his eyes and peering in. Nothing appeared to be out-of-sorts, either in the present or in the near future, so he went in and sat across from the kid, who nodded at him casually, like he was in the middle of a spy caper, but otherwise didn't acknowledge that he'd been joined at the table.

Corrigan silently requested a coffee from the waitress, who was across the room. Then he waited to see if the kid felt like talking first. He didn't, So Corrigan jumped in.

"What's your name?" he asked.

"Bill."

"Bill, I'm Corrigan." He extended his hand for a clumsy, brief handshake. "You look a little nervous."

"Sorry. I am."

The waitress brought the coffee over, and a menu, and disappeared.

"Just relax, nothing's going to happen," Corrigan said. "You're meeting with a client, right?"

"Yes sir."

"I'm just a client."

"Yes sir, only I can't really stop there, if I'm questioned, since you just introduced yourself."

"You'll have to pretend I didn't."

He grimaced.

"I'm kind of hoping nobody asks," he said, "so I don't have to confront that particular moral quandary, sir. It's in the bag under the table, by the way."

Corrigan didn't look, but he kicked the satchel with his foot to confirm the existence of the bag.

"I had to go to two branches to get that much," Bill added.

"It's not a lot."

"Banks don't carry a lot anymore. Everyone's electronic."

"Well thank you. It should be plenty, until I can clear up this mess."

"Yes. About that? I think I'm supposed to tell you to turn yourself in and let us sort things out."

"Us?"

"The...the firm."

Bill's employer was the second-largest law firm on the Eastern seaboard. His reticence to say their name out loud was noted by Corrigan without comment. It was fair to say that most people in the greater Boston area wouldn't recognize the name of the law firm, but it was still a good instinct.

Being the second-largest law firm on the Eastern seaboard didn't necessarily mean much of anything in this context, though, since that law firm only handled estates, property transactions and other legal business settlements. What Bill was talking about seemed to be somewhat outside their area of expertise.

"I didn't do anything wrong," Corrigan said. "And you're just delivering funds to a client. Nothing illegal about that, is there?"

"There might be, sir. Since I'm acting under instructions from my boss, and he's acting on instruction from one of the partners, I think I might be okay. Although if any one of the three of us is going to get arrested, it isn't them, so...I'm not in a good position, Mr. Bain. I feel the only way to improve that is to once again advise you to surrender."

"I'll consider your advice, then. I just can't follow it at this time."

"Thank you."

Bill looked over his shoulder, and around the room, two things that weren't what he should probably have been doing, which was leaving the diner.

"I'm not supposed to ask you this," he said. "But I'm going to anyway."

"You want to know what I need the money for," Corrigan said. He looked into the future for that.

"As I said, it's a good deal of cash. If you need to escape Boston, we can arrange to wire funds."

Corrigan had a good grip on how his head worked these days. He knew he wrote the message on the nightstand to himself, and he knew this meant he'd gone into the future during the night, rather than dreaming like a normal person would. He was pretty sure this was his unconscious mind's way of coping with his sense of helplessness: i.e., give him somebody to save so he could feel useful again. The helplessness came out of being unable to predict the future as it pertained to massive explosive devices.

That didn't mean he could ignore the date, time and location he'd written down. Regardless of his motivation, it still meant someone was going to need help, and he was the only person who could provide it. Not so long ago, he'd have called Dr. Ames to hash all of this out, but Corrigan couldn't do that, because he'd buried Ames eighteen months ago.

"I understand," he told Bill. "I have an appointment in the city that I can't be late for. We'll see what happens after that."

Using the law firm was the only way Corrigan could think of to get cash, without alerting the police as to his whereabouts or compromising Maggie in some way.

He and Maggie were in the midst of the slowest crawl imaginable toward an endpoint that would either be marriage or death from old age, depending on what came first. It was a pace in which living together made sense only if she kept her apartment. They shared a bank account—only for saving up for a vacation—which was the extent to which they were legally entangled.

The same baby steps defined everything from laundry to dinner, and it was this way because they'd spent so much time in an on-again-off-again thing, it was impossible to tell if they were together for good this time, or if they simply forgot to break up. Every new suggestion—should they refurnish the living room? Buy new dishes? Invite the neighbors for a drink?—was floated with the caution of a landmine sweeper.

Despite all of that, most of Corrigan's liquid accounts were either connected with Maggie or were only a step removed from something a clever investigator could attach to her somehow, he was pretty sure.

It was possible he was being unnecessarily cautious, if not actively paranoid. It had only been about twenty-four hours since he'd left the police station, which was probably not nearly enough time for them to figure out where he banked, and set up some kind of alert system on his funds, provided such a thing was even possible. But if this Detective White was smart, he'd go to Maggie first to find out where Corrigan's money was, and if Maggie was smart she'd tell him.

That left the funds Maggie didn't know anything about.

This wasn't actually true. She knew the money existed, but she didn't know how much of it there was or where it came from. If asked, she would *maybe* be able to furnish the name of the law firm acting on Corrigan's behalf, but that was about all.

It was a lot of money, enough that asking for sixty-thousand of it in small bills wasn't a problem for anyone other than the kid who had to draw the funds and slide it to him under a table.

An hour after leaving Bill in the diner, Corrigan turned seven thousand of the cash into a used motorcycle, purchased out of the back of a dealership willing to skip some paperwork for an extra grand. The seller either didn't recognize Corrigan or didn't care.

The next step was to find a place to sleep at night. He figured he was welcome to crash at Sal Wilcox's money pit of an apartment building as long as he needed to, but that seemed like an innately bad idea. As long as Sal knew where he was and also remained employed by the Boston police, it was an obvious risk.

There was a motel on Soldier's Field Road that fit his needs nicely. From that location—and it helped that Corrigan knew his way around the city better than a cab driver—he could get into town five or six different ways, quickly, and get back out of the city just as fast. That was especially true on a motorcycle, as long as he was willing to take the occasional risk.

It was after three by the time he got himself set up in a room. He had no clothes to unpack—clothes shopping would have to come after his appointment—but he did have a bag of other necessities that were perhaps unique to his particular profession.

The first of these was a map of the city and the surrounding suburbs. He took down the motel's understanding of what framed art was supposed to look like and taped the map up in its place. On the bedside, he put a note pad and paper, and a black magic marker.

He took the marker and traced the map carefully with his finger until he found the spot he was looking for.

"Hudson Street, five-twenty PM," he said. He dotted the spot with the black marker.

"Maggie, I'm sorry, but that's the craziest thing I ever heard."

David said this with a tiny smile, as if hoping she would reveal that this was all a joke, and allow him to enjoy claiming that he never *really* believed her, but hey, good try anyway.

They were sitting alone in an unused office off the main bullpen in the FBI headquarters. It was the end of the day, and they'd both seen direct sunlight exactly twice, in the service of a couple of hasty cigarettes.

Maggie was bone-tired. She couldn't remember the last time she felt this exhausted, even on the many, many occasions she worked through the night for a case.

It was the stress, probably. Corrigan had been missing for more than a day, and she couldn't pretend that wasn't bothering her. He might be the most capable person on the planet, but that didn't make it easier to not know what was happening with him.

On top of that, there was the shared stress her team was experiencing. Someone tried to kill them, and that sort of thing was usually worth a month or two of mandatory therapy that nobody had time for. The possibility that the assassin was someone they'd let escape—even though the investigation had been closed under protest—only made it all worse.

Everyone was on edge, on little sleep, and on far too much coffee, paired with not nearly enough food. And they all had the same unspoken question for her: *what are you not telling us, Maggie?*

She *was* keeping things from them, and it had to stop, because if Corrigan was right about the bomber, everyone was going to have to adjust their world view very quickly or a lot of people were going to die.

David was the test subject. It wasn't going well.

"It explains things, though, doesn't it?" she asked.

"Well sure. If you said he was a wizard, that would have done it too. You're not serious, right? *My boyfriend is psychic* really isn't going to get us anywhere."

"I never said he was psychic, I said he could see the future."

"Maybe it's the lack of sleep, but I don't see the difference."

"I've got a couple of MIT physicists on speed dial who can explain exactly what he does, and how. That's the difference. He's not reading tea leaves."

"Okay, fine, if I leave this room thinking this isn't some kind of extended prank, I might need to talk to one of them."

Maggie only had one on speed dial, he was retired, and she hadn't spoken to him for almost three years. The other one graduated and left the city. She therefore hoped David wouldn't ask her to do this.

Instead, she handed him a case file that was more than five years old. It was a copy; the original was archived. Back when she made the copy and stuffed it in her drawer, she asked herself what possible reason she had for doing so. Now, she was thanking the prescience of her past-self, because this was the exact occasion for it.

"The science is bookmarked," she said. "It'll make your head hurt, but it's all there."

He put the file on the table without opening it.

"All right. Let's say I believe you. You told me he can see something like five seconds before it gets blurry. But there's this whole fixer thing. How'd he know where to go every day?"

"Ahh...dreams? Kind of? He travels ahead in his sleep. It's...I know, don't make that face, I know that sounds crazy."

"Yes, that part in particular."

"But it stopped. He started getting clearer information, like people's names and exact addresses. For most of the time he only knew to go to a certain place, but he didn't know what was going to happen until he got there. He started to get better, and remember more, and then a lot of the time he didn't even have to actively rescue anybody in person when a phone call would do it. A couple of years ago it stopped completely, and that's when he started saying he was retired."

"But not the part where he sees the immediate future."

"I don't think that's something that will ever stop."

"All right, but the next contradiction is that the bomb didn't go off, right?"

"Yes, but..."

She was interrupted by a knock on the door. Jeanine poked her head in. "Hey guys, pizza's here. Also, more footage. Wanna watch? Unless there's something more interesting in here."

Jeanine was probably talking about the unopened case file, but since Maggie was almost positive J thought something was going on between her and David, it could have been a more scurrilous suggestion.

"We can take this up later," David said, picking up the file. He looked at Maggie. "Right?"

"Yeah. Jeanine, where'd this reel come in from?"

U ncut footage from the day of the bombing had been rolling in one file at a time since mid-morning. All three of the local news stations had a camera at the scene, plus two local cable news channels and a half-dozen people with camera phones recording things for posterity. The news channels were easy enough to tap. A lot of the time, a subpoena was needed first, but everyone seemed content to trade footage for access, in the event the footage proved useful.

So far, none of it had been. The team now had six different angles covering what happened on the stage, and the best thing that could be said about it was that Maggie liked her outfit that day, and thought she looked pretty good before her boyfriend knocked her over.

What they needed was someone who was pointing their camera the other way.

Maggie and David walked into the video room, which was low-tech by most modern audio-visual standards but a step up from a lot of the regional field offices. They had two HD monitors, five standard ones, several options for video play-back depending on what medium was being used, and stacks upon stacks of outdated equipment that ended up being useful more often than expected. It was actually sort of amazing how much information could be found on outmoded storage formats. This was probably the only room in the city, for instance, that still had use for a machine that could read a five-and-a-half inch floppy disk.

"We're here, we're here," Maggie announced. "Have you seen it yet?"

"Waiting on you," Patel said. He was the team's information forensics expert, which would have made his Indian heritage a tad stereotypical if he weren't a born-and-bred Southern Californian. "This is the last news crew, let's all say a prayer."

He hit play, and the footage popped up on the main HD monitor.

It jumped right into the middle of Duplass's speech.

"This isn't the whole thing," Jeanine noted. "And where's the sound?"

Patel checked the file. "No sound. This is everything we got."

"Wonder what they're hiding."

"I'll call 'em back," Brian said from the back corner of the room. "They've been jerking me around on this all day."

"Hey, maybe they *are* hiding something," Jeanine said.

"Probably caught the bad side of the reporter's face or some shit," Brian said.

"Blah-blah-blah freedom," David said, more or less along with Duplass's recitation on the video footage. The other shots had sound, so they'd heard his speech repeatedly already. It stopped sounding inspirational a long time ago. "C'mon, cameraman, be a pro, give us some audience shots for background."

The camera turned to the left a tiny bit.

"Wait, here it comes!" Patel said.

"C'monnnnnn," Maggie said.

The shot panned left. The exhausted task force cheered as a group, at what was the high point of their day.

"Hold it, hold it, hold it, don't swing back..." Patel said.

The terrible irony was that for this particular media professional, the footage he shot was probably of no use at all to his network, because he happened to be covering the crowd at the same time Corrigan was running across the stage. That made this camera the only one in the room that failed to record the viral event.

By the time the camera swung back, Corrigan, Duplass and

Maggie were off the stage and at the cameraman's feet. Then he was getting bumped into by the deputy's security team. The last piece of the video was of the ceiling of the room, before it cut out.

"I think he fell over," Patel said. "Probably broke the camera, or I would think he'd have tried to capture the evacuation."

"Roll it back," Maggie said.

Patel rewound it to the part where the camera swung left.

"Hey, in back there," Jeanine said. "Another camera, from the back of the room. Did we get their footage yet?"

Patel paused it.

"Who is that?" Brian asked. "Is that channel four?"

"No, four shot from the left side, we have theirs already," David said. "I don't know that we saw anything from that angle."

"Weird camera, too," Patel said.

The image was blurry from the motion of the cameraman, but the guy in the back of the room had what looked like a camera, except it was partly attached to the right side of his face. Instead of looking through a viewfinder, it seemed as if he was wearing one.

"Play it through again," Maggie said.

It was easy to pinpoint the moment Corrigan ran across the stage. If they had audio, it would have been even easier, but as it was everyone in the room jumped, gasped, and expressed surprise in a range of other ways.

All except for the mystery cameraman. He didn't budge at all.

"You know what?" Maggie said. "That isn't a camera."

"What is it, then?" David asked.

"It's something else. We need to get Erica Smalls."

"Who's that?" Jeanine asked.

"She's a physicist. We're gonna have to reach out to MIT. They should be able to track her down."

Hudson Street was in Chinatown, a district that was barely more than three city blocks. There were a lot of Asian restaurants and grocers crammed into those three-odd blocks, though, and by five o'clock it was full of foot traffic, and the roads were packed with cars.

When he was doing appointments regularly, Corrigan learned a few tricks about rush hour, the first being always leave a half an hour earlier than you think you should. If you can't do that, be prepared to stop at a certain point and carry forward on foot. The motorcycle served both concerns, in that it was much easier to maneuver around tight spaces in the city, and it could be parked on a sidewalk in a pinch. Nobody much cared for a motorcycle parked on a sidewalk, but he tended to get away with it because he rarely left it for long.

Corrigan had three spaces rented in the garage under his condo building, which he used to store two bikes and one car. He'd much rather be driving one of those bikes than the one he'd bought off the back of the lot, but to get one of them he'd have to retrieve the keys in the condo, then get into the garage for the bike, then out of the garage. He was pretty confident he could do this even if the police were watching, so long as they weren't actively camped out in his living room, but there was no need to provoke them if he didn't have to. Plus, they'd track down the plates as soon as he parked it.

He managed to find a spot for the bike that was probably legal, located about four blocks from the address, and walked the rest of the way on foot, arriving fifteen minutes before whatever it was that was supposed to happen.

The address was a hot-pot restaurant. He walked around the sidewalk in front for a few minutes looking for anything that might be a likely trigger for an accident: potholes, pavement cracks, unsafe stairs, and so on, like he was an OSHA inspector for the department of public works. He'd gotten good at this sort of inspection because he had to do it a lot. On about half of his appointments, he knew only a little bit about what he was doing at a given location, often not knowing for certain whether it was an indoor event or an outdoor one, so he had to do a lot of advance work.

He once again reminded himself that could have just skipped the appointment. That probably wasn't a big deal now that his head was straight. Used to be, he skipped or somehow failed to save someone, he'd get haunted by whoever he failed to save. He wasn't *really* haunted—they weren't really the spirits of dead souls, if that was even a thing outside of movies—he just had an active unconscious mind that was sometimes interested in driving him literally insane. It took a lot of therapy and a lot of sleeping pills to get past all of that, with the takeaway being, he was pretty sure if he failed *now*, he had the tools to cope.

At the same time, if he had the means to save someone, better to do it than to not, just in case. Plus, saving people was supposed to be a good thing to do.

There wasn't much of concern outside the restaurant, and he had a sense—he called it that but it was probably a memory from the night before—that this was going to take place inside.

The interior of the restaurant was surprisingly spare. Wood counters made up a square bar space with customers facing in on three sides. Every seat had a hot water bath built into the counter in front of it. The dining area was more than half full, and was a somewhat even mix of business-people and tourists.

"For one?" the hostess asked. She was standing at a podium right near the front door.

"It looks like my friend's not here yet," he said. "Is it all right if I wait?"

"We can sit you."

"I'd like to wait. She'll be here in a minute, I'm sure."

"Okay."

She shoved a menu into his hand, gave him a generic hostess smile, and gestured for him to stand aside so she could greet whatever additional customers might drift in.

He stepped past her and into a void between the door and the entrance to the bathrooms. There was still a couple of minutes to go; he spent it pretending to look at the menu while studying the room.

He couldn't quite understand why he was there.

Really, when it came to appointments, that was his normal state, which was to say he almost never knew who was going to require saving, before they actually required saving. But whatever was about to happen in this restaurant had effectively pulled him out of retirement, and there didn't appear to be any kind of opportunity for an event of that scale to take place in this location.

None of this makes sense, does it? he thought.

Fixing something in a restaurant usually involved saving a choking victim. He used to think there was some greater or lesser choking likelihood based on the kind of food served at wherever he happened to be, but he once saved a girl from choking on ice cream, so there was no telling. This place had a lot of large portion vegetables and meats, though, so choking seemed like a good bet.

The conceit of hot-pot dining, was that everyone got their food raw and cooked it in the broth simmering in front of their plates. There were no knives in evidence, just chopsticks and tongs.

He focused on the futures of the diners, looking for the one who was most likely to start laughing at the exact wrong moment, or shove too many things in at the same time. In doing so, he nearly missed the groaning noise.

It came from the ceiling. He heard it before anyone else because he heard it first in the future, but when the room caught up the restaurant quieted down considerably.

It sounded like an animal. More precisely, it sounded like what a made-up animal in a sci-fi movie might sound like: an alien, or a dragon. It was the low baritone of a predatory creature.

Except it wasn't actually any of those things. Some monsters were real, but this wasn't one of them. It was a water pipe.

He dropped the menu and ran to the spot where the ceiling was going to come down. There was a couple dining there, halfway across the room, staring in mild confusion at the growing bulge over their heads. They were about to be crushed by a three foot piece of rusted metal piping, propelled ahead of a large quantity of water.

Neither impact looked deadly, but he wasn't going to watch the whole thing play out to be sure. He didn't have time.

There was also no time for tact. All he could do was pull their chairs backwards, somewhat violently.

The action caught the man—a white male, slightly over-weight, a little balding, in a business suit that had seen a lot of years—off-balance. He ended up toppling over onto his back, which was fine because he landed far enough away from the source of the danger.

The woman was a problem. She was younger and fitter, and dressed more informally. She was either a mistress or his daughter; there didn't seem to be any other options. She had enough of an opportunity to recognize a man seemingly assaulting her, and leapt to her feet as the chair fell backwards beneath her.

"Hey!" she shouted. That was all she got to say, as the ceiling came down right then.

Corrigan wrapped his arms around her and took her to the

floor, away from the falling debris, with one ceiling tile narrowly missing his head.

The rusty pipe landed where she had just been standing, and impacted the floor with a disconcerting degree of force.

Next came a ton of water. It was, thankfully, not so aggressive as to present an immediate threat of death, and it was also not sewage, which was great. Corrigan jumped to his feet—the water already ankle-deep—and helped the woman up.

"Sorry," he said, "I didn't have a lot of time."

She nodded wordlessly, and pushed past him to help her friend and/or father/or whatever they were to one another off the floor.

Water was still coming through the pipe at the kind of rate that would give the restaurant's insurance company a migraine, but it was no longer an active crisis, and getting the restaurant evacuated didn't take any special skill. Corrigan mostly blended in with the rest of the room as they made their way out, hoping as he went that nobody would take the time to look carefully enough at his face to recognize him.

Someone there *did* recognize him, but not in a way he was expecting. It happened once he was outside and drifting away from the crowd, listening as fire truck sirens grew louder and trying to remember which street he came down so he could get back to the bike.

"Aren't you the boy scout?"

He was in the middle of a chattering crowd of thirty or forty people, all making a tremendous amount of present-tense and future-tense noise, but this woman's voice came through clearer than anything else. It took him a second to understand why: she was speaking in the future.

The only other person Corrigan ever knew, who could do what he did, was an asylum patient named Harvey. Harvey used to speak to the twelve-year old version of Corrigan by talking *only* in the future. When Corrigan asked him how he did it, Harvey said, *just decide to speak, but when you get there, don't.*

Whoever this woman was, she had just accomplished the same trick.

Corrigan spun around, trying to pick her out of the crowd, but it was impossible. The people from inside the restaurant had already commingled with gawkers from the street, and now it was much too crowded for him to cope. To pick her out, he needed her to speak again, or to do something *wrong*, something out of place with the future. But everyone followed their own paths and said the things they were about to say.

"Who are you?" he said aloud, in the present and the future.

His question caught the attention of four or five confused people, but none of them had an answer, and the woman didn't respond.

The firetrucks were getting closer, and a second set of sirens —police—were joining them. It was time to get out of there.

Just as he was fleeing the scene—walking rapidly, with purpose, trying not to draw *too* much attention—he saw something else unexpected. There was a Kilroy, across the street, staring at Corrigan.

Corrigan ignored it, and kept going.

CHAPTER EIGHT

Kiki: After what happened in Chinatown, I'm ready to say it.

Bill: Don't.

Kiki: I'm gonna say it.

Bill: I mean, they already, they'll make fun.

Kiki: I don't care. I'm excited. I'm pumped. I'm gonna say it. Boston has its own superhero.

Bill: She said it.

Kiki: And in just a minute, we're going to have a woman who just might agree with us. Her name is Monica.

—Transcript, Boston Morning Nosh with Kiki and Bill

Silly season for the media began on the third day.

The news outlets—local and then national—were given a lot to work through on the second day, when both the BPD and the FBI had morning and evening press conferences, in which they rehashed everything that had already been mentioned in the press conferences that took place on the evening of the bombing. Mostly, there wasn't anything new to say so instead things that *weren't* true were listed.

Did someone claim responsibility? No.

Was a suspect under arrest? No.

What about the rumors that...? No.

Big stories like this—and Maggie had lived through a few —relied as much on controlling the rumors as the facts, and on ignoring the out-and-out lies if belief in them ended up being useful. The people responsible were listening too, after all.

The media couldn't cope with a long investigation, though. The twenty-four-hour cycle needed regular feeding, so it was always a good idea to hold back trivial information to dole out later, just in case. Justin called it kindling. Maggie preferred to think of them as the control rods in a nuclear reactor; without regular application, there would be a meltdown.

But this story was too big and the information the FBI doled out was too small, and so on the morning of the third day, the meltdown began. The subject of the meltdown: Corrigan Bain.

There was a good deal of restraint shown on the subject of Maggie's boyfriend, all things considered. Was he the hero or the suspect? Since law enforcement couldn't decide, neither could the various media outlets, but in their speculation they generally stuck to the available facts, which was nice.

But then the facts started to get weird. A little more than twenty-four hours after the bomb, a local web designer who had built a fan page devoted to Corrigan, years earlier, was given all the air time she wanted on basically every network that wanted her, and every network wanted her because she had one hell of a story.

The media still seemed to be pretty good about this, by not giving much credence to the woman's claims, an omission of tacit support that left the impression she was a crank.

She wasn't. About half of what Monica Devereaux had to say about Corrigan was wrong, but she was right about the important stuff. Maggie just happened to be one of the few people alive who knew it.

But then, just in time for the late news, a new photo emerged, and the story that came with a photo was odd enough to start tipping everything over.

A pipe burst in a restaurant in Chinatown at the start of the dinner rush. It was one of those stories that didn't even make the news unless it was a slow news night or unless someone was killed. Nobody had been killed or even hurt, according to most accounts, but one of the reasons for that might have been that Corrigan Bain was in the restaurant when it happened.

She knew Corrigan well enough to appreciate that this was not the sort of place he would visit for dinner, especially not when he was wanted by the police. This was an appointment, which meant he'd come out of retirement.

She wondered if it was intentional, or if it just started happening again, like in the old days when it seemed out of his control. Either way, the timing was pretty terrible. If nothing else, it lent credence to part of Joe White's argument that argued Corrigan liked being a hero, because here he was acting the hero when he should have been either hiding, or turning himself in to clear his name.

With this new tidbit—and no real news to go with—the media had gone from passively speculating on Corrigan's guilt or innocence to aggressively arguing it one way or another. Suddenly there was no gray area in which to work: he was either a completely innocent man who by coincidence, or some sort of magic, had acted heroically a whole lot; or he was a sinister, attention-seeking monster.

Maggie was watching a nine AM news show when she saw what had to be the bottom of the speculative news barrel. An expert—in something, who knew what—was explaining how it would be possible to deliberately cause a water pipe to burst.

It was ridiculous, but maybe not surprising. According to David, the BPD was checking into the possibility of an explosive in that Chinatown pipe. Crazy, maybe, but that's what you do when you have no leads.

That appeared to be where everyone was, by day three—no leads—which was why the media was starving and people were talking about Corrigan so much, and also why Maggie was sitting in the middle of a roomful of case files with no useful information in any of them.

It was a crime with a ton of evidence, and no suspects. More precisely, it had two suspects, but they couldn't have done it, because Maggie already arrested them.

Sharon Ledo and Nick Borowitz were both in a federal penitentiary after a slam dunk trial. Both were in prison for the rest of their natural lives, although some legal team somewhere was probably thinking up a challenge to that decision, in light of the past three days. It was neither the largest nor most complicated case Maggie had been a part of, and Borowitz and Ledo weren't exactly criminal masterminds, but when it came to domestic terrorism investigations, it was a fine bit of work.

They should have kept it going. Some of the evidence led in other directions, but after the main cell/cult was arrested—thirty-two people were taken into custody, total, and seven more would have been had they not died in a firefight with law enforcement—the investigation was shut down.

"You want me to reassemble the cork board?" Jeanine asked. She was unpacking one of the dozens of file boxes: the one that had the pictures they used to visually illustrate the investigation. It was mostly for show, for when someone with a bigger title walked in and asked for an update.

"I'm thinking no," Maggie said. "Not unless you want to rearrange it so Sharon and Nick aren't at the top of the pyramid anymore."

Brian held up a picture of Corrigan.

"We could put him at the top," he said.

"Not funny," Jeanine said.

"It's a little funny," Maggie said. "But please don't."

Maggie sifted through the box in front of her. There was nothing new to be found in it, as any one of the task force members could attest to, having each done the same thing she was doing, two or three times.

The case originally came together from a bunch of pieces of things that only made sense when lined up correctly. There was chatter, some of which turned out to be benign, some being the sort of noise that causes law enforcement to sit up and start writing down names. It was the *fuck the government* sort of rhetoric that might be ignored if the person saying it was a disgruntled teen with a black-light in his bedroom and too many piercings, but which was taken more seriously when coming from a man in his twenties.

The chatter couldn't be connected to anybody, though, not for a long time, so it sat out there on a file, waiting to be attached to something that gave it meaning.

Elsewhere, an army officer with the Corps of Engineers went missing one day. Sharon Ledo was a lieutenant when she disappeared, a Fall River girl who was working in Concord for the US Army. Sharon was such a clean-cut all-American type, that even though there was ample evidence her departure had been voluntary—she'd packed her bags—she was still treated as a missing-person rather than an AWOL army officer. Not that the available details added up to terrorism, either. Not at first.

A few months after Sharon's disappearance, customs intercepted a package of electronics which included components that could be used to detonate a package of C-4. At the same time, the online chatter started to get a lot more specific. And then, one morning, someone found a device sitting in a cardboard box underneath a pedestrian footbridge in Charlestown.

It was crude, even by the high school science fair standards against which it was initially judged. It consisted of a brick of clay attached to a car battery and some metal rods, a half-dozen entirely unnecessary extra wires, and an old cell phone.

A woman walking her dog came across it, and thought enough of what she was looking at to contact the police.

The respondents included Tommy Osteen, Maggie's friend from the bomb squad. Tom recognized two things: the bomb wouldn't work as designed; if it *had* been designed properly it would have taken down the steel footbridge, because the C-4 was real.

Maggie was looking at a photo of that bomb, taken by Tom nearly two years earlier. It wasn't like the later devices, which had to be destroyed because there was a good deal of uncertainty behind the best approach to dismantling them. This first one was dead on arrival, and that was fortunate, because after it had been made safe, the police reached out to the FBI for help sourcing the explosive, and they wouldn't have been able to do that if it had been detonated.

The device really did look like something a kid could have made. The first time she saw the photo, her instinct was to reach out to the colleges to see if any film students could lay claim to what appeared to be a half-decent cinematic prop.

Nobody called in a threat before the device was discovered, and nobody laid claim to it after it had been found. This ended up being a pattern for the entire investigation, which was somewhat infuriating but also instructive. Whoever was behind the bombs didn't want to voice anything. For the same reason, the media wasn't nearly as engaged as they could have been under the circumstances.

Her team shared the bomb's schematics with every Bureau

office in the country, and soon, three more devices had turned up: in San Diego; in Omaha; and in Miami. All three were destroyed. Based on the on-the-ground assessment, the Miami bomb would have worked perfectly; the only thing keeping it from doing so would have been reluctance on the part of the bombers.

That would mark the last time they discovered an explosive *before* it went off.

Unless we're counting the State House bomb, she thought.

David stuck his head into the room. They had claimed one of the larger conference rooms in the FBI for the unpacking of these files, just as they had taken over the A/V room more or less completely. They also had the full and complete assistance of every single on-duty FBI agent in the building if they wanted it, so basically their bomber case was the only thing anybody was working on.

"Guys," he said, "you don't have the TV on?"

"We didn't like what was on," Brian said, nodding to Maggie. She'd turned it off shortly after hearing about how her boyfriend sabotaged city plumbing in his spare time.

"Turn it on. I'm not promising you'll like it, but it sure sounds like a lead."

It was set to channel four, which a little while earlier had a national news show running. It was showing anchors from the local desk now, a sure sign that something new had broken. The hosts were an older white male with a trustworthy face and a twenty-something woman showing exactly the correct amount of cleavage for this time of day. Maggie couldn't remember their names, because every channel had their own version of these two people, with the only apparent distinction being the ethnicity of the female anchor.

Digitally projected behind them was a symbol Maggie was entirely too familiar with. It was the same symbol found on the

C-4 brick on the first device, and on every other one since, including the one that killed Tommy.

The male anchor—she thought his name might be Chet—was in mid-sentence when the sound kicked in.

"...sent to all the local news stations this morning. Again, the message appears to be from the people responsible for the State House bombing, but that has *not been confirmed*."

"Of course it hasn't, you assholes," Brian said. "You didn't talk to us first."

"What's the message?" Jeanine asked. She was asking the television.

"Once again, here is the message," possibly-Chet said. His face was replaced by a full-screen text box, showing the symbol, followed by two words:

FREE THEM

"How do they know that's from the bombers?" Jeanine asked.

"The symbol," David said.

"Yeah, fine, that's how *I* know, and how *you* know. How do *they* know? We kept it out of the papers."

"Good question," Maggie said. "Brian, get them on the phone. All of them. We need to know when this went out, who got it, where it came from, why none of them called us first. If this was sent from a single location we need to be at that location right now."

"Yeah," Brian said, already pulling out his phone. "I have some people to yell at. They should know better than to run with something like this. Imagine if this was some kid with a fax machine."

"Right, except it's not some kid with a fax machine."

He nodded. "No, it isn't."

Maggie looked at David. "How long ago did this story break?"

"Less than ten minutes."

"We shouldn't have found out like this."

He got where she was going. "They were as surprised as we are. I caught a call from Joe on my way to you, asking why we're keeping secrets."

"Who do you think they're talking about?" Jeanine asked. "In the message."

"*Free them?* I'm pretty sure we all know who," Maggie said. "And in an hour or two, so will the rest of the country, I'm guessing."

Her cell phone rang. She expected it to be Justin, or perhaps someone higher asking for an update, but she didn't recognize the number. The voice was familiar enough, though.

"Something's going to happen," Corrigan said, before she could even get to hello.

***

It was nearly a minute of *hang on guys, I have to take this* and *lemme move to my office, one sec* bits of stalling and hopefully acting normal in front of her trained team of investigators before Maggie could get alone. That moment of quiet was found in the affectionately-termed *junk room*, which was where all the electronic components that weren't being used in the A/V room lived. It was pretty much the only place guaranteed not to have anyone in it, and it was windowless.

"Where are you?" she asked.

"I'm not going to say, Maggs. You know why."

She sighed. "Dammit, you're not making any of this easy."

"I know, I'm sorry. Look, the messages started again. I don't know why, and I'm not remembering the dreams any more. It's like it used to be."

"That's all on you, babe, you know this," she said. "You made it stop before."

"Did I? Or did it just go away?"

"It was you."

"Maybe. But it's back again, and I have appointments, and maybe that's a good thing. I don't know. I just can't surrender right now; you understand that, right?"

"Something big is going to happen, you said."

"Yes. Tomorrow."

"Where?"

"I'm not...I can't tell you, Maggie."

"Of course you can," she said.

"I'm not sure if I can stop it this time. I don't want you there."

"Corrigan..."

"I heard a voice, Maggs."

"You're hearing voices?"

"Not voices, just one voice. Never mind, I can't explain right now. The police are already here."

"Jesus Christ, Corrigan, just let them take you in and we can—"

"I gotta go. If I don't talk to you again...I'm sorry. I'm doing my best."

"Don't hang up, don't..."

He hung up.

"Dammit," she muttered, resisting the urge to throw her phone at one of the walls, where it would surely win against the thin plasterboard.

She opened the door to find David waiting in the hallway.

"That was him, wasn't it?" he asked.

She sighed. "Get in here. I don't know what to do."

C orrigan hung up the hotel phone and snuck another peek at the parking lot. A second cop car had already arrived. He was going to have to get out before any more showed up.

It had been a rough morning. He awoke with a start, the sense memory of what he saw coming next still fresh, which was to say that his chest hurt, because that was where the bullet was going to hit him.

He visited a particular point in the future that had two deeply unpleasant outcomes, and the really bad thing was that the gunshot was the least-bad option.

Aching from the memory of his own death-that-hadn't-happened-yet, he dutifully got up and marked the location on the map, then went to the bathroom to check himself in the mirror. He half-expected to find, if not an actual bullet hole near his heart, some sort of bruise. There was neither.

He felt better after a shower, but then faced a new problem: he was in dire need of some coffee, and food.

There was a pancake house down the road, but he had to think eating there was an unnecessary risk. A drive-through would be better. In the meantime—and this was his only real mistake of the morning—he figured he could tide himself over with a snack from the vending machine in the hotel lobby.

The woman at the counter recognized him. She didn't say so, but he could tell.

The first police cruiser showed up twenty minutes later.

"And now you're out of time, Corrigan," he said.

His voice wasn't echoing, which indicated he had a good grip on the present. That was going to be important shortly.

"If it's ten-thirty, it must be time for the first false alarm," Aaron said with a laugh, when they got the call. He and Janet had barely been in the cruiser twenty minutes before they were directed to the motel down by the river. It was the fourth false identification they'd answered since yesterday, and now that this Corrigan guy was national news—because of whatever the heck went on in Chinatown—it was probably going to be all they did for the entire shift.

"There's a lot of big white guys in this town," Janet said.

"No shit, we're about to meet every single one of 'em."

It was ten minutes to the motel, and they were the second car there.

"Who is that?" she asked. "Did they call for back-up? Are we back-up?"

"Doubt it."

It was Caldwell and Drew. They stepped out of the office just as Aaron was parking.

"Hey, fellas," Janet greeted. "You get this call too?"

Caldwell met her at her door. He was almost exactly the same dimensions as the guy they were there to check out, and probably thankful to be on duty for all of this so he didn't end up having someone calling the cops on him.

"Morning, Tate," he greeted. "The office says our man's staying in seventeen."

Caldwell towered over her, but didn't make her feel like he was doing it on purpose, which she appreciated. She always liked him. His partner was an ass, but he was okay.

"That's great. How come you guys are here on our call?"

"Word from on high, two cars for every positive ID."

She looked over at Aaron, who had apparently just heard the same from Drew. He rolled his eyes.

"Fellas, there aren't enough uniforms in the state to cover that," she said.

"Hey, word from on high, like I said," Caldwell said. "Let's get this done, maybe we can squeeze in a coffee at that IHOP up the road, huh?"

Room seventeen was directly across from the office, which unfortunately meant they were convening in sight of whoever occupied the room. That didn't become an obvious problem until the four of them were halfway to the door, when said occupant stepped out and started walking away from them at a steady but brisk pace.

That sure looks an awful lot like our guy, Janet thought.

"Excuse me, sir?" Caldwell said, from across the lot. "We'd like to ask you a few questions?"

The guy started running.

"Dammit, go!" Caldwell gestured for the three of them to sweep around.

The man from room seventeen—she wasn't ready to say this was Corrigan Bain yet, but it was probably Corrigan Bain—was sprinting along the carpeted runner that ran in front of the doors to the rooms. To his right was the parking lot, and ahead was a corner leading to more rooms and more cars. The whole building was flanked on two sides by busy roadways. Unless he was going to a vehicle, he had nowhere to run. Of course, he *had* to be going to a vehicle, for that same reason. Nobody who was staying at this motel got there on foot.

Caldwell fell in behind the suspect, while Aaron—the fastest of the four—looped around and ahead, but not before the man they were chasing made it past the corner. Janet lost sight of both of them.

It seemed like things went much too quickly after that. When she stepped through it all in her head, later, it seemed as if from this moment until it was all over the morning had gone into fast-forward, only she was stuck at the same speed somehow.

First came the gunshot. Her partner was the only officer not in view, so it was either his gun or the suspect's. When it rang out, the first thing she registered was Drew, a few paces behind, radioing *shots fired, shots fired* into dispatch.

Then Janet had her gun out. She couldn't remember drawing it, but she had, because there it was in her hand.

She rounded the corner on the outside of the parked cars, slowly, gun raised. To her left, Caldwell was coming around with his service revolver in hand. A Cadillac Escalade separated them.

"Mr. Bain?" she shouted. "Come on out. Let's not have this get out of hand."

The cars were only one row deep, but everyone these days drove enormous SUV's, and on this morning, they seemed like an impenetrable phalanx. She remembered—oddly—her grandfather, a World War Two vet, a Normandy survivor, complaining for hours about the gigantic hedgerows of the French countryside, and felt like for the first time, she understood the problem.

She found Aaron behind the fourth car. He was on his side, awake, a cloth shoved in his mouth, his hands cuffed. She holstered her weapon and knelt down to check on him as Caldwell continued past with a silent nod.

"Hey, buddy, you okay?" she asked, un-gagging him.

"It's him," he said. "Be careful."

She heard what happened next, but as with Aaron, didn't see it happen.

"Don't move, police," she heard Caldwell say. Then came a loud THUMP and the unmistakable sound of a gun bouncing on pavement.

"Go," Aaron said. "Hurry."

She hopped up as Drew ran past, then another gunshot and car window glass shattering, more thumps, a thud, and a car alarm was going off. The epicenter was three cars down, between a Honda and a Mazda. There was glass everywhere. Caldwell was on the ground, cuffed, and a stunned Drew was lying across the hood of the Mazda.

"Corrigan Bain, freeze!" She barked. Her gun was drawn, her hold was steady, and she was a solid five paces from him. When she thought about it later she decided the only reason she didn't unload on him on the spot was that he was unarmed.

"Hi," he said. His hands were at his sides, palms down in a *keep calm* gesture. "Everything's okay, I just can't be arrested right now."

"GET ON THE GROUND!"

"You really need to listen to me, officer. Look, I'm not threatening you, okay? But if you try to shoot you're going to miss and hit the room window behind me, and I can't promise there isn't anyone in there. I don't want someone to get hurt, but I can't let you shoot me either, do you see my problem?"

"Get down on your knees, RIGHT NOW, Mr. Bain, or..."

He took a step forward, and she shot him.

Or, she should have. She was aiming at his chest, and it was a large chest. There was no real way to miss him at this distance, despite which she missed him completely. As predicted, the bullet shattered the panoramic window of the hotel room behind him. She had exactly enough time to register this before he hit her in the stomach with his shoulder.

He carried her a couple of feet before she landed hard on her back, gasping for air and no longer in possession of her gun. Expending hardly any effort, he had her cuffed, and then there she was, on the ground in the middle of the lot.

"Sorry," he said. "Let me get you out of the street. Don't want you to get run over."

He picked her up and sat her down next to the front wheel of the Honda.

"That's better."

"Corrigan Bain, you have the right to remain silent," she said. "You have the—"

"Later," he said. "I told you, I don't have a choice here. If you arrest me, a lot of people are probably going to die. It'll make sense later, I promise."

He stared for a second or two at the shattered picture window. She would later dwell on that moment for a while. It was inexplicably creepy.

"Good news," he said, finally, "the bullet didn't hurt anyone. Sorry, I have to go."

He picked up a duffel bag from the ground and ran off. A second later, she heard a motorcycle engine.

CHAPTER NINE

—comment from @fixertramp27, FindTheBostonFixer.com

Calls were coming in from all over the city. Either Corrigan Bain was actually five people or he was some kind of magician, and Joe was starting to think both theories had merit.

It began early, with the incident at the motel on Soldier's Field Road. That was the real Bain, certainly, but it didn't seem possible that he was acting alone, because one unarmed man fleeing the police doesn't just disarm all four of them, leaving three awake but cuffed—with their own handcuffs—and one needing hospitalization for a concussion. According to officer Tate, Bain also managed to dodge a bullet, which was some kind of *Matrix* bullshit Joe really didn't have the patience to listen to.

An hour later, Chief Gregorian was updating the press and

asking again for the public's help in locating Corrigan Bain, only this time it was for assaulting police officers and resisting arrest.

It had been three days since the State House bombing, and suddenly Boston had something to *do*. Unfortunately, what the city as a whole decided to do was pick up the phone and report every sighting of a large white male. It got so bad so quickly, dispatch developed a triage approach: one unit if the suspect had a leather coat and combat boots, two if he could be connected with a motorcycle, and no units if he was described wearing different clothing or if he was no longer in the area at the time of the report.

It was a logistical nightmare. Bain was everywhere, all the time. On four different occasions police had eyes on him, only to have him vanish or something.

On top of that, Bain kept saving people, somehow. About two hours after the chief's press conference, a dozen people confirmed Bain on State Street. Eyewitnesses had him parking his bike at a fire hydrant, running twenty feet to an adjacent corner, and pulling a tourist on a cell phone out of the street before she was run down by a city bus. As soon as she was safe he ran back to his motorcycle and drove off.

The whole thing happened in under a minute. As one witness said, "it was like he was supposed to be there."

Forty-five minutes later, three people identified him at a construction site in Allston. From the sidewalk—he never went past the hard-hat-only sign—he chucked a rock at the head of a guy standing on an open girder, thirty feet above the ground. The rock hit the worker in the helmet and did exactly no harm to him, but *did* make him stop moving to figure out what just happened. Then a brick fell right past his head, dropped by the guy a couple of levels up.

"I would'a been standing under it," the worker told the news crew, an hour after the incident. "I don't know how he knew."

By three in the afternoon, there had been five confirmed sightings, seventeen possible sightings, and two impossible rescues. All of it was buried under a thousand unconfirmed reports, about three hundred of which claimed they witnessed Corrigan Bain flying through the air.

So, it wasn't a great day. Joe and the BPD were being made to look foolish by one easily recognizable guy who had an uncanny ability to evade capture.

Joe was beginning to think none of this was going to get them any closer to catching the bomber, either. As much as he was convinced Bain was connected, he couldn't ignore the creeping sense that maybe this was a trip in the wrong direction. The news media changed its mind hourly about him, and White could see why.

At three-thirty, the FBI called.

"Detective White," Agent Trent greeted. "We need to talk."

"Is it about catching your boyfriend?"

"Yes it is. When can you get here?"

"Full disclosure," Trent said, just as soon as David closed the door. She put a cell phone on the conference room table and slid it into the middle. "He called me."

"When?"

"This morning. You can check the phone for the call time yourself or ask the phone company, but if you're looking to ballpark it, the last thing he said before hanging up was that the police were there."

"He called from the motel."

"Yeah. I didn't know that at the time, and even if I had there was no way I could have gotten word to you before what happened there happened. I wanted to tell you before it came out another way."

She meant, in case Joe ever got around to subpoenaing her phone records or setting up a trace. He hadn't, but that was because he'd been unable to convince a judge to allow either of those things to happen to the phone of an active federal agent who was by all accounts cooperating with the investigation.

"Did he hurt anybody?" she asked.

"One concussion. Mostly just bruised some egos. We think he must have had some help, though. We're looking into it."

David shared a glance with his FBI friend. Joe remembered thinking, the first time he saw these two work together, that they were involved in a way that was more than just business-related. He didn't think so anymore, only because Maggie Trent was in the process of throwing away her career for her boyfriend, and that kind of devotion isn't the sort of thing you cheat on.

"Why do you think he had help?" David asked.

"Four cops? C'mon. Like I said, we're still piecing it together, but there had to be a second perp."

"Maybe not, Joe," he said.

"Yeah? What Kool-Aid you been drinking over here, Davey?"

David placed a large folder in front of Joe.

"We have a lead," he said. "But you're not going to under-stand that lead until you accept a couple of things."

"What kind of things?"

"Corrigan can see the future," Trent said. "A couple of days ago it wasn't necessary for you to believe that, but that's not true anymore. Open up the folder and we'll walk you through it, and when we're done we can talk about how to catch the real bombers."

After an hour, all anybody had accomplished was to give Joe White an enormous headache.

The folder was a case file. He recalled the case, because at the time it impacted his job a little. MIT students were dying at an unreasonably high rate due to a collection of apparent accidents and suicides. One of those kids had been his DB until the feds turned up. He never knew why that happened, but here it was: some science fiction kind of crazy was the reason.

Planted in the middle of the file was a set of notes specifically about Corrigan Bain. It had words in it Joe was pretty positive the author just flat invented—chronoton, for instance—and sentences containing phrases like *contingent temporal events*.

A week ago, he would have called it an elaborate hoax.

"You've read this whole thing?" he asked David.

"I did. I also followed up with the school. I'm waiting on a call back from the professor who authored those notes, but I understand his health is failing so that might not happen."

"Convenient."

"If you say so. Look, Joe, it took me most of the day to come to grips with this, but I think it's legit. I really do. Everything in there fits with what we've been seeing."

"Fine, but none of it tells me why Bain isn't a suspect."

"It should. It explains how he knew the bomb was there," Trent said.

"Actually, it doesn't. It explains everything else, but not that."

"No," she agreed. "You're right. But we have something that does."

She nodded to David, who flipped open a laptop, typed up a couple of things, and then spun it around so Joe could look at the screen.

"Who am I looking at?" he asked.

"This guy was in the back of the room during the speech."

First glance, it looked like the man had a camera, but that wasn't right, because he was wearing it. The lens was too short and covering one eye. There was tech on his arm, too, and he had a microphone next to his mouth.

"What's he wearing?"

"That's the interesting thing," Trent said. "Here's what I think it is. I think it's a mobile version of the device the MIT lab was working on. It's described in the case. The original was destroyed, but it's possible the research wasn't. We've reached out to an expert."

"Save me the reading and tell me what it does."

"If I'm right, it allows the wearer to see the world the same way Corrigan can."

"Or maybe he's wearing some kind of funky camera."

"Sure," David said. "Could be."

"Any chance you ID'ed this guy?" Joe asked.

"No, but he turns up elsewhere," Trent said. "We went back and looked at all the surveillance photos we had of Borowitz and Ledo. He's in three of them."

"How was he not arrested before this?"

"I said he was *in* the photos, but not engaging Nick or Sharon. He was in the background every time. Crowded coffee shops, that sort of thing. We never noticed. Even if we had, there wasn't anything actionable."

"So what's his name?"

"We don't know. We're tapping federal databases to get a facial match, but no luck so far."

"Well somebody out there knows him. We can call a press conference in the morning, plaster his face everywhere, see what shakes out."

"I don't think we have enough time for that," Trent said.

"How do you figure?"

"In the call, Corrigan said something big is going to happen tomorrow. I'm betting this man is going to be involved."

Joe threw his hands in the air. "Of course. Did he say it like a threat?"

"No."

Joe got up and paced the small office for a few seconds, because he was about to start yelling, and that was probably not going to be productive in this situation.

"Look," he said, "no offense intended, Agent Trent, but this is exactly why you shouldn't be anywhere near any part of this."

"I don't understand."

"A suspect in a terrorist attack called the personal phone of an FBI agent eight hours ago and intimated that another attack would be taking place tomorrow. That agent sat on the information for the entire day, because he said it nicely. Imagine for just a second that you're not the agent, and the guy on the other end of the line isn't your boyfriend, and tell me why I'm not arresting everybody for impeding."

"I already told you why," Trent said. She had the good sense to at least look a little shaken.

"Because he can see the future."

"Right."

"He's not abetting a terrorist cell; he's just a weatherman."

"We told you this was going to be tough to get a handle on," David said.

Joe sighed. "Did he say *where* or *when*?"

Trent hesitated.

"I asked him. He wouldn't tell me."

"Great. So now we got him on withholding information regarding the commission of a crime. Add that to assaulting the police and resisting arrest. That's just today."

"I think we can agree Bain handled that situation about as

well as it could be handled," David said, without laughing or anything. Joe couldn't believe it.

"For Chrissake, Davey, the way to handle it was to not resist arrest! I got every blue uniform on triple overtime looking for him right now, and if he had just surrendered this morning you know what I'd have time to do? I'd have time to find this asshole with the funny camera on his face, and then maybe that *something big* you're talking about is something we get to stop like it's our job to do."

"You need his help," Trent said. "If he surrendered, he'd be out of the rotation. From his perspective, he didn't have a choice."

"Tell me, please, why after all these years I suddenly need the help of a freak who thinks he can see the future, just to do my job."

"Because if we're right, the guy in the picture can *also* see the future," David said.

"Right. Your boy beat up four cops so tomorrow he can put himself in harm's way, because according to you that's what he does. And he doesn't want anyone else to know where this is going down for what reason, exactly?"

They shared another of their damn looks.

"He might think we'll just get in the way," David said. "You *have* tried to arrest him twice now."

Joe looked at Maggie Trent. She looked like she just swallowed a bird.

"What did he say on the call?" Joe asked. "When you asked him for the address?"

"He said he didn't want me there because he wasn't sure he could stop it," she said.

"Okay. Well that's really chivalrous and all."

"Joe..."

"David, if the goal here was to get me to call off the manhunt for Bain, it's not going to happen, and the reason it's not going to happen is because wherever this guy is going to be tomorrow is where *I* want to be too. Even if he has nothing to do with the bomb, it sounds, from where I'm sitting, like he's going to be near the next one before it goes off. If he's not gonna tell us where and when that is, we'll have to follow him around until he shows us. You wanna help me get him off the street, I'm all ears. Otherwise I have to go."

Joe got up, and heel-turned for the door.

"Okay," Trent said. "Hang on a sec."

"I'm listening," he said.

"Did you check the hotel room?"

"Personally? No. All the guys at the scene ended up cuffed. We put up some tape. Why? Think he's got a hostage in there?"

"There might be a map of the city in there."

"Well that's great. You've cracked the case; I always wanted one of those."

"No, that's not...If he's working again, he might have a map. It'll have where he's going next, Joe."

CHAPTER TEN

We're getting reports of an incident at the Prudential Center Mall. No details yet, but motorists may want to steer clear of that area for now. We will update you as soon as we know more.

—Local NPR

Corrigan used to plan out little trips in his head, back when he was working as a fixer full-time. They were his vacations, the things he would have been able to do if he had a normal job with regular hours, with someone to cover for him on days off.

It wasn't a regular anything, though. He was the only one who did it, so there was nobody to cover for him. No trips to an exotic island somewhere, or weekend jaunts down the coast in his private boat, or even a chance to spend time in a nice hotel a long way from the Boston area. None of those things were possible because accidents happened every day, and somebody had to be there to help.

One of his dreams had been to own a really nice sports car. For years, he thought about getting one, even though he knew perfectly well he'd never get to really use it. Sure, he could drive it locally, but that wasn't the place to tool around in an expensive car. It also wasn't *just* a sports car; the idea of it was linked to the notion of freedom, of being able to point it in a direction on the highway and start going.

When the messages finally stopped, and he retired, one of the first things he did was go out and get that sports car. It was a Ferrari, it was red, and he had to special order it.

The Ferrari was beautiful. It was also utterly unnecessary.

He'd never driven it. He didn't even tell Maggie about it, because he was embarrassed about the whole thing. Instead, he rented a storage locker in a warehouse facility in Medford, visited a couple of times a year, and waited for the day his life and the car would make sense together.

After what happened at the motel, he was pretty sure he wasn't safe renting a room somewhere else, unless he intended to stay up all night waiting for someone to kick in the door. He was also afraid of reaching out to friends and didn't think he could rely upon any of his former clients more than he already had. The storage facility was one of the few things he had a key to that Maggie didn't know about, and the car was the closest thing around to a bed.

It wasn't a bed, though. The crick in his neck and the pain in his knees told him as much when he woke up entirely too early the next morning. It was a sports car, it was gorgeous, and it was not all that roomy. He made a mental note to covet extra-large SUV's the next time he fantasized about luxury vehicles.

He'd also gone and revisited the site of his imminent demise again overnight. Even had he recalled next-to-nothing on awakening, the fact that his chest hurt again—and now, so did his stomach—would have reminded him of the trip.

He *did* remember, though, and some things had changed about the future between his trips there. Other than the stomach pain, (which he took to mean he was getting shot more than once now) there was a police presence that hadn't been there the night before.

Wonder what changed, he thought.

Then he climbed out of the car, stretched, and automatically sought out the two things he usually went to first, on getting out of bed: the map, and the toilet.

There was no toilet in the storage unit. There was also no map. He left it in the motel room.

"I can't believe I did that," he said aloud.

He wondered if the bomber was willing to reschedule.

A quick drive—on the motorcycle—got him to the nearest public bathroom. It was a surprisingly sanitary men's room attached to a fast food place almost nobody took seriously as a breakfast option. It was therefore nearly empty save for a number of bleary-eyed counter staff who looked unlikely to recognize close relatives, never mind a wanted man like Corrigan.

The bathroom was the first chance he had to examine himself in the mirror. He looked pretty much exactly like someone who hadn't shaved for a few days and who just slept in a car should expect to look.

"Busy day ahead," he told his reflection. "Gotta swing by the condo first."

The police car that had been parked directly in front of the building was replaced after the first day by an unmarked vehicle, but only after Diego complained. It was something he would have never considered doing had he not also been wearing The Jacket at the time.

Such was the power of The Jacket. It was a large, deep blue

blazer, with a coat of arms on the left breast above the heart that matched the sigil on the sign near the private entrance. The sign read: the Kensington. If you owned one of these jackets you were a certified *concierge,* which made you the most important person in a large building occupied by some extremely important people.

That was how Diego liked to think of himself when he was at work: extremely important. It wasn't really true, but pretending it was helped him keep his back straight and his eyes forward and his voice firm and measured.

The Jacket was what gave him the authority to walk across the street, after that first day, and notify the officer that he had to relocate his cruiser to a less visible place, because it was upsetting the residents.

The car was on the street, so by having left the grounds of the Kensington, Diego had technically stepped outside of his kingdom, but since the police were asking Diego—and all the other concierges on staff—for an extremely difficult favor, he felt as if he had a little clout.

It worked, anyway. The cruiser was replaced by the unmarked car, and the residents stopped having to explain to their guests why there was a policeman outside, and everyone was happy. Diego could still see the car out there—it was impossible not to, if one spent enough time looking out onto the street—but it wasn't obvious enough to create a spontaneous conversation piece.

There was still the matter of that favor. On the one hand, it didn't seem like the sort of thing that would have to be executed. This was self-evidently the opinion of the police, who sent only the one police car to monitor the scene. If they were anticipating 702's arrival they would no doubt insert a more overwhelming presence, perhaps even stationing an officer inside the condo itself.

On the other hand, the needs of the residents were supposed to be paramount, and 702 was a resident just like everyone else. Diego could think of a dozen other residents about whom a visit from the police would be no great shock, and he liked to think that their reliance upon him—the man who decided who was, and was not, allowed onto the elevators—was one of the reasons they chose to live at the Kensington in the first place. Calling the police on one didn't seem at all in the spirit of things. That would remain the case whether it was law enforcement or ownership telling him to make that call.

It was likely moot, though, because 702 wasn't going to be showing up, so Diego wouldn't have to even worry about it.

Then—of course—he showed up.

"It's Diego, isn't it?"

Diego looked up from the mail he'd been sorting, and there was Mr. 702, in an otherwise empty lobby, looking as if he'd just spent the night on a bench somewhere.

The owner of condo 702 was not the sort of man to be mistaken for someone else. He looked like the person Diego might hire to unclog a toilet in the building, and not at all like someone who would own one of those toilets.

"Yes. Yes sir, it's Diego. How can I help?"

To his own ears, he sounded nervous. He hoped that didn't telegraph too loudly.

"I need you do to me a favor, Diego," 702 said. "I know there are some officers outside, who I think are expecting a call from you just as soon as I walk away."

"Sir—"

"No, it's okay, I don't want you to get into any trouble. I would just appreciate it if, when you do make that call, it's not for another five minutes. And if you could tell them I took the stairs and not the elevator, that would be great."

"I could just not call them," Diego said, too fast, too loudly.

He was certain this was unconvincing, but equally certain if 702 asked him to not make that call, he would probably agree not to.

"No, if they find out I've been here some other way, the first thing they'll do is check the surveillance footage and see us talking right now. But if you make the call, they might not even think to look at it. Like I said, I don't want you getting into trouble on my behalf."

"It's only, five minutes isn't much time to get in and out, sir."

"Don't worry about that. I just need a couple of minutes in the condo and I'm good. Can you do this for me?"

"Yes, sir, of course."

702 extended his hand, and they shook on it.

"They're right out front," Diego said. He could see the car from where he was standing. "How did you get inside without them seeing?"

"Just lucky, I guess. Now remember, five minutes."

"Five minutes, and the stairs, yes."

As 702 ran for the elevators, Diego marked the time on his watch.

The man in the photograph had a distinctive nose. It was the thing Maggie always ended up focused on. The nose came to an upturned point, as though he was perpetually disgusted.

They had all sorts of facial recognition software at their disposal, and Patel was using it to within an inch of its life. He was convinced if this guy turned up anywhere with a camera, be it an ATM or in the crowd at a political rally from ten years ago, he'd find him. She didn't trust any of the technology half as much as she trusted her own eyes.

Check for that nose, she thought, whenever he brought in an update. *We'll find him because of that nose. Let me look.*

The picture continued to be their only live lead. There was some hope among the task force that the media outreach which resulted in four local stations broadcasting the *Free Them* message at more or less the same time, would result in something the team could use. But no matter how far down that rabbit hole they went, the end result was, they couldn't get anything useful. It was received at the same time in all of the stations, in a tip line mailbox, but sent from four different IP addresses.

Maggie was having someone who knew more about this than she did, check up on those addresses to see if any of them represented a clue, but she wasn't holding out hope.

As for how the stations knew the message was legitimate: they didn't. The stations were in contact with one another, and used the fact that they all got the message as proof that it was valid. Or something. After a few minutes on the phone with one of the more sane producers, Maggie came away with the impression that they all ran it because they all assumed someone else was going to, and they didn't want to not have the story themselves.

Borowitz and Ledo were two possible leads, insofar as they were the people whose freedom everyone figured was being negotiated. Maggie had a couple of local (to their respective prisons) FBI agents drop in on them, to see if they were willing to talk. She didn't expect cooperation, and ended up proven correct. Sharon Ledo had never said more than a couple of words from the moment she was arrested, and continued to be exactly that reticent. Nick Borowitz had a history of being very talkative, only not about things pertinent to his case.

Also, he only acted friendly to certain people. Maggie was one of those people; if she had time, and thought Nick would give her something, she'd give it a try. But not yet. Too much could happen in the three days it would take her to get to Nick and back again, and she wasn't going to risk that, when he wasn't going to give her anything.

Anyway, he didn't talk to the agent the FBI sent. She—and Maggie made sure a woman was the one visiting Nick, as this was the first step in getting him to talk freely—said that all she got from him was "an undefined trepidation". Maggie wasn't sure how to interpret that.

Maggie was outside, working through all of this in her head and smoking a cigarette with David, when her cell phone vibrated with a message.

She expected it to be an update from Patel, but it wasn't from him. It was a picture, of her own bedroom.

"What the hell?"

"News?" David asked.

She scrolled down to the text that followed.

What did he take? it read.

"It's Joe," she said. Rather than play text tag all morning, she called him.

He picked up on one ring.

"Is there still someone in the condo?" she asked.

"Yeah," Joe said.

"Have them send me as many pictures as they can."

Ten minutes later she was back inside and looking at a dozen half-decent photos of the condo. It was disorienting, because it felt like she was looking at a crime scene, rather than the place she called home.

She forwarded the images to her laptop, and dialed Joe and the cop who took the photos—a Cambridge officer named Fisk —in a conference call.

"Tell me what happened," she said as she combed through the images. She hadn't been to the condo since the mess began, and couldn't remember how clean or dirty it was, or where things had been left.

"The man at the desk tipped us," Fisk said. "We called in backup and headed up, but he was already gone by then. Suspect took the stairs, so he can't have had more than a few seconds inside before he had to turn around and run."

"He had more time than that," she said. She was looking at the last outfit she saw Corrigan wearing, now on the floor of the bedroom. "He changed clothes."

"Not much longer, then," Fisk said.

"He went out a fire door, Agent Trent," Joe said. "We know what time the alarm sounded. His window was pretty tight."

Then your math is wrong, she thought. Corrigan was a fast dresser, but not that fast. And he couldn't climb seven flights of stairs any faster than the next guy.

But that wasn't really what was important. This was a huge risk for him; she had to figure out what in the condo made that risk worth it.

"Fisk, can you go back to the bedroom closet?" she said.

"Sure, what are you thinking?"

"There's a foot locker on the floor in there, do you see it?"

She could only see the corner of the locker in the photo Fisk sent, and was pretty sure that was where it was supposed to be. It didn't look disturbed.

"I see it. Should I open?"

"What's in there, Trent?" Joe asked.

"A couple of things," she said. "I keep work gear in there, and he has a strongbox with cash in the bottom."

"Cash," Joe repeated.

"He can't use his cards, right?"

"He probably could. We haven't been able to get a freeze on the funds yet, to be honest."

"Found the strongbox," Fisk said. "It's locked, but it doesn't feel empty."

Maggie was running through a mental list of what she would expect to find in there other than money, and came upon a terrible thought.

"Hey, can you send me a pic of the inside of the footlocker?" she asked.

"Sure," Fisk said. "Hang on."

"What kind of things did you say you kept in there?" Joe asked.

"Gear," she said.

"Yeah, I heard that, but what kind of gear?"

"You know, fun stuff with our letters on the back. Windbreakers, a couple of flak jackets."

"Gift shop shit."

"Sure."

"Here you go," Fisk said. Her phone thrummed and her laptop chimed, and then she had the new image in front of her.

Did I leave it here?

She couldn't honestly remember. It was a terrible thing to lose track of, but she might have done exactly that. The problem was, she hardly ever had to use one in her line of work.

"Is anything missing?" Joe asked.

"Fisk, on the floor of the closet, is there a clear space in front of the locker?"

"What do you mean?"

"I mean, before you opened it, did you have to kick anything out of the way first?"

"No. There's some shoes, but they weren't in the way that I can remember. You guys should get a maid, y'know; I bet this building has a service."

"Yes, thank you."

"Something's missing, isn't it?" Joe repeated.

Come on Maggie, was it here, or did you leave it in your apartment?

"Maggie, talk to me," Joe said.

"Detective White, I'm going to be honest with you. It's possible I kept a handgun in that locker."

The Prudential Tower—the Pru—was the second tallest building in the city after the nearby Hancock, although it was difficult to see any real height difference from most perspectives. The Pru was somewhat more recognizable, and demonstrably more popular, both for the observation deck on the top floor (although it was closed almost all the time) and the shopping mall at its base.

The mall was no more or less spectacular than any other mall in the state—the stores were perhaps a touch more upscale, the products a little more current—but the scale seemed greater. That may have been because the indoor arcade that included the mall also had a convention center, two hotels, and a church. It was also attached to another mall: the even more upscale Copley Place (with a third hotel above it). From end to end, it was possible to walk ten city blocks without setting foot outside, which was particularly useful when shopping in the winter.

It was exactly the sort of place Corrigan avoided under any and all circumstances, outside of the job. He would rather a city street, which may be at times no less busy, but where cars had a boundary condition that prevented them from moving sideways or up. Crowds of people were far less predictable, and their futures were a nightmare because of it.

He stood at the edge of the mess, near one of the doors.

It was hard to breathe and harder to focus. This was a Sunday afternoon, and despite four days of active, public concern regarding bombs in public places, the mall was full: solo shoppers, couples, families, tourists. Everyone had a cell phone, and Corrigan had no cover. He couldn't anticipate somebody recognizing him and calling the police and didn't have a way to prevent it from happening short of wearing a mask, which would have drawn more attention. He had to assume the police were going to be notified, and soon.

No, he thought, as he spotted three police officers in different parts of the promenade. *It's worse than that.*

Uniformed law enforcement's presence in the mall was definitely up. That wasn't so bad, because Corrigan could avoid the ones he could see; it was the ones dressed in plainclothes that were going to be a problem. He didn't know if there were any, but it seemed like a reasonable assumption.

He had, after all, left them a map. If they knew about all the other jobs he'd marked on it already, they had to know this was the only location he hadn't been to yet. Especially if Maggie explained to the cops how this worked.

It was sort of okay. He wondered if an unconscious mechanism in his head decided it would be best if he left the map behind, to give the cops an opportunity to show up at the Pru, without their presence being Corrigan's fault. Because it was definitely the case that something bad was going to happen in this mall; it was probably better that the police were there for it, if only to help with the evacuation.

Or they can take it from here and I'll go home, he thought.

He was kidding. It was going to be a bomb, and he was going to have to stop it himself. He already knew this.

He took a deep breath, adjusted his jacket, and headed in.

———

When it was only Corrigan Bain the Boston Police were looking for, the tip line was reliably busy. It was worse, certainly, after Bain had been connected with the assault of police officers, but not all that much more reliable for it. But when the chief held a press conference Sunday morning asking for help to identify the guy the FBI found—the nameless man in the background, wearing a camera—it tripled the call volume immediately. European-looking white guys with dark hair and pointy noses were apparently the second-largest population of white male humans in the city after big, burly guys who looked like Corrigan.

By Noon, the police had a list of fifty names to follow up on, which was great except they had exactly two detectives free to perform those follow-ups. Joe White was one of the two, and he wasn't really all that free.

"Send them to the feds," he told Doris, when she brought him the first set of names. "Have 'em run it against what they've got, save us the door-to-doors."

The phone banks were in the building, two floors down from Joe's desk. Most of the 911 service was remote, in conjunction with the phone company support, but tip line calls got forwarded directly. Every now and then, he'd head down there to listen to the noise of the city trying to help him stop a bomber. Sometimes it was reassuring.

An hour after Doris's first visit of the day, right past one in the afternoon, she called his desk.

"I think we have something, you want to come down here?"

A few minutes later he was looking at a map of the city. There were red pins stuck all over it. He already knew each pin represented a possible Corrigan Bain sighting. There were a lot of them. There were also blue pins on the map, but only a few.

"Blue's our mystery man," Doris said.

"We just asked for an ID."

"Sure, but we get what we get. We're getting sightings."

"Okay."

"In the past thirty minutes, we've received fifteen calls about Bain. Five of them put him here."

She stuck a new red pin in a spot on the map that had been almost blank.

"That's near the Prudential Center," Joe said. "Isn't it? It's one of the three possibles."

"It's near, yeah."

The Pru was the worst of the possibles, the one he hoped was incorrect, like maybe Corrigan's black magic marker slipped when he put that particular dot on the map.

There were three locations on the map they couldn't account for, meaning they couldn't confirm that Bain had been there in the past, so he might still be going there in the future. Joe pulled some of the resources busy following up on the tip line calls, and stationed officers at each of the three.

Since the other two locations were outside a hospital, and at the mouth of the harbor, he'd been very much hoping to hear that Corrigan had been spotted at one of them instead. Or anywhere else, really; anywhere other than the biggest indoor mall in the city.

"I'll reach out to the uniforms on the scene," Joe said.

"Do that," Doris said, "but that's not why I called. At the same time we were getting those calls about Bain, we got three for our mystery guy, and all three of 'em put him *here*."

She stuck a blue pin a few inches from the red one.

"I'm not seeing what you're seeing, Doris."

"That's because you shop for clothes at Goodwill, Joe. This spot here? Copley. That one there is the Hynes. They connect in the middle."

"You're telling me both of these men have been spotted at the same time, and in the same place."

"I'm saying, they might be meeting in the middle. I mean, I don't have a vector on them or anything, but if I were betting, it would be that they're heading toward each other, not away."

"How good is this information, do you think?" he asked.

"I'm not going to ballpark it for you. That's what you get paid for. For every five calls I have saying Corrigan Bain is around here, I have another five putting him in five other parts of the city."

———

The various sales corridors converged on a central point, appropriately labeled Center Plaza, and it appeared Corrigan's feet were leading him there, but before he even got halfway he noticed that one of the police officers was following him.

He was able to confirm this by stopping, and looking into one of his futures. In that future, immediately after making eye contact with the cop—he was baby-faced, and looked like he graduated high school at the same time as the Academy—the officer would shout at him to stop and raise his hands. Then Corrigan would turn back around and start running.

Corrigan didn't like that future very much, so he picked the one where he didn't turn around.

That the officer hadn't attempted to detain Corrigan reflected a certain prudence on everyone's part, considering he'd disabled a team of four the last time around. Whatever was going to happen next wasn't going to involve only four cops. It was going to be a large response team.

But first, there was going to be a gunshot.

It wasn't the cop. The shot would come from in front of him, from somewhere not yet in view. Even with the tremendous ambient noise in the mall, the gun report would be loud and recognizable. The people around him would be looking around with confusion.

Was that a gun?

Ahead, the shoppers close enough to the noise to feel threatened by it would begin to run towards Corrigan, the people wondering if they heard what they thought they heard would figure out that they *had*, and the stampede would begin.

That was a few seconds away, still; Corrigan began to run toward the noise before it was a noise.

This had a predictable immediate consequence. The cop, assuming the suspect he was tailing was attempting to get away, shouted: "Corrigan Bain, don't move!"

The people between them parted, and the ones in front of Corrigan got out of the way too, and for about two seconds it was just Corrigan and the police officer running through the mall.

When the gun ahead of them went off, Corrigan made sure both his hands were visible, just in case the kid thought his suspect was the one firing something. Corrigan didn't have time to deal with him drawing the wrong conclusion at the wrong time.

It might have worked.

"Shots fired, shots fired," he heard the cop shout into his shoulder microphone just before both of them were overwhelmed by the crowd fleeing the middle of the mall. Corrigan had a little trouble stepping around the stampede—the future was always a mess in the middle of a panic—but surely the policeman was having much more of a problem.

If Corrigan wanted, he probably could have circled around, run with the crowd, and gone right past the cop and out the exit.

Instead, he pressed on, until he reached Center Court.

Under normal circumstances, this area would have been full

of people crisscrossing their way to various sales corridors from other sales corridors. Its centerpiece was an Information desk and a map of the mall.

Most of the people had cleared out already, because of the man with the gun. He was standing next to a terrified-looking woman Corrigan felt like he should recognize. Both of them were next to the information desk, which was either unmanned or occupied by someone who had ducked out of sight.

The man with the gun had on an odd contraption. It was some sort of exoskeleton, with metal rails running down his arms, meeting at circular joints. It looked like his legs had the same thing going on, too. On his head, he was wearing a steel headband with an eyepiece over his right eye.

It looked like something between a rehabilitative support system and a device from a science-fiction movie. Corrigan wasn't sure if he was supposed to take him seriously or not. The gun in his hand said *yes*, but it was really hard to look past the cyborg suit.

The man looked at Corrigan and smiled.

"Is it you?" he asked. He reached up and pulled another lens down, to cover his left eye. "We've been waiting."

In the future, the man fired a shot at Corrigan, which he evaded easily. The bullet shattered a glass display and gut-shot a mannequin.

The future caught up, and the man fired, the mannequin went down, and the guy smiled because Corrigan had stepped aside.

"It *is* you," he said.

Then the man's future disappeared.

Corrigan took a step back, instinctively. An armed man was standing in front of him, and Corrigan couldn't predict what that armed man was going to do next, and that was a bad situation indeed.

"How are you doing that?" Corrigan asked.

"I'm a magician," he said. "OFFICER! STOP RIGHT THERE!"

The cop had reached the scene. Corrigan turned around to see that the kid had already gotten his gun out, but didn't look all that clear on who he should be pointing it at.

"Drop the gun," the cop said.

"I don't think I'm going to, no. Do you see the girl on my right?"

The woman looked utterly terrified. She was short, with spiky black hair and an incongruous overcoat. She was sweating. Corrigan didn't think the overcoat was entirely to blame for that.

"Miss, are you okay?" the officer asked.

She shook her head *no*.

"It's all right, Monica, you can show them now," the man said.

The girl named Monica nodded quickly and took off the coat. Underneath, she had on a T-shirt, a loose pair of jeans, and a large explosive device.

"Help me, please..." the girl said quietly.

Maggie was about to head to her apartment, to hunt down that missing gun, when David burst into her office.

"Something's going on at the Pru," he said.

Ten minutes later they were racing across town in his car, lights flashing, trying to catch up with a convoy of other police cars heading in the same direction.

She got a call through to Joe White on only the tenth try.

"Bad time to talk, agent," he said.

"Gimme the short version."

"Your boyfriend, your mystery man, and a big thing that goes boom. Did you find that gun?"

"Didn't get a chance to look yet," she said.

"We're considering him armed right now, Maggie."

"I know. Tell me about the other guy."

"I don't have details yet. I'll let you know."

The man's future kept blinking in and out. It wasn't clear to Corrigan whether he even knew it was happening, or if he had any control over it. One second he was about to move his arm, and then he did move his arm, and then the next motion vanished and Corrigan saw him the same way everyone else did. It was like watching a television channel whose signal was getting interrupted arrhythmically, except it was in 3-D, and felt much more immersive.

It was having downstream effects all around. The girl with the bomb, for instance, still had a definite future, but that future was in part reacting to the future of the man beside her. Since *his* future was hidden part of the time, it looked as if her future-self was wrestling with a ghost.

Corrigan wondered if this was what vertigo felt like.

"What should I call you?" Corrigan asked. He desperately wanted to look away, before he started throwing up right there, but knew taking his eyes off the armed man with the unpredictable future was a bad idea.

"Bernard," the man said.

"All right, Bernard. What do you want?"

He laughed.

"You got the message already," he said. "Free them. HEY! KID!"

He was shouting past Corrigan. Corrigan turned around to

check on the trailing cop, who had taken cover behind a free-standing kiosk selling microwaveable pillows. He was speaking furiously into his mic, and his gun was still drawn. He didn't know he was being spoken to.

"KID!" Bernard repeated. He turned back to Corrigan. "Well, anyway, that's my demand, and that's why we're here. Free them. He knows. When everyone else gets here I'll tell them the same thing."

Corrigan had no idea who was supposed to be getting freed, but had a strong suspicion that whoever it was, the demand wasn't getting met and the bomb was going to be set off. What he didn't know was what Bernard planned to do with himself when that happened. Corrigan could still remember what it felt like to experience the last bomb, and was pretty positive the only reason he survived was because Bernard didn't end up setting it off.

Was he hoping to survive that last blast? Because standing right next to the girl wasn't the best place to be when this detonation happened. But suicide bombers don't usually need hostages.

"I don't know who *they* are," Corrigan said. "What does she have to do with any of it?"

"Oh, she's for you! Don't you recognize her?"

He did, but he wasn't sure why. He looked her in the eyes.

"Did I save you once?" he asked.

"I run..." she said quietly. "I run a website..."

"She's your biggest fan, Corrigan Bain," Bernard said. "I couldn't think of a better person to bring along."

"So the plan is...I'm sorry, Bernard, I'm trying to get the whole picture here." It was so hard to look at him. "If the police don't free someone for you, you're going to blow all of us up? It doesn't sound like a really great plan."

"Oh, no, no, that demand was yesterday's demand. We

contacted the media with it, and nothing happened. Today is the consequence of not meeting yesterday's demand."

"You're going to set off the bomb?"

"Unless you can stop me."

"That doesn't make any sense."

"The world is a complicated place."

———

From Joe's perspective, the time it took to get from the curb to the center of the mall was somewhere between goddamn forever and a fucking eternity. There were approximately ten million people in the way, too, because other than the gunshot, somebody pulled a fire alarm, so an entire city's worth of people dropped everything and got the hell out.

There was already a news van out front, which was just ridiculous. He had fifteen police cars ignoring all traffic lights to converge on the mall at the Pru, and a damn news truck beat them there.

"Make a hole!" Joe barked on exiting his car. The uniforms who'd gotten there ahead of him were already focusing on crowd control, pushing the shoppers away from the entrance.

Joe found Sergeant Pekoe at the door. Pekoe was supposed to be suspended, but Joe couldn't think of any good reason to bring that up at this moment.

"Will, establish a perimeter," he said.

"How far?"

"The goddamn river, if you have to."

A firetruck siren sounded from a block or two off.

"Have them help. I don't think there's a fire. And someone get me a bullhorn."

———

Police officers were converging on the scene. Since the Center Court could be accessed from multiple directions, each direction got at least two cops. All of them followed the lead of the first responder—the kid hiding behind the kiosk—by seeking cover. Bernard was clearly aware of the crowd they were attracting.

"How does it work?" Corrigan asked.

"The bomb?"

"Yes, the bomb. I see a cell phone hooked up to it. Do you have a trigger or something?"

"Don't worry about that."

"Sort of difficult not to. Is that as big as the last one?"

"Bigger. We have a surplus of C4."

"Great."

"Yes, it will probably destroy a decent amount of the mall. I toyed with putting us out there, to see if we could bring down the building."

The building he was talking about was the Prudential Tower. Bernard was standing in front of an exit that would put him in a small courtyard directly at the base of the Tower. Corrigan wished he *had* decided to stand out there, as the blast would surely be less lethal in an area with no ceiling.

"With a little luck," Bernard added, noting the increased law enforcement presence, "we'll wipe out half the police force in the city."

"You'll also die with them," Corrigan said.

"There's that, yes. But my god is particularly vengeful. Why haven't you tried to stop me yet?"

"You haven't done anything yet."

"That's not an answer, Corrigan Bain. You're the city's guardian angel, according to Ms. Devereaux. Haven't you been reading your own press?"

"I've been busy."

"Well, you are. And I'm a threat, so do something."

"I don't really do this, Bernard," Corrigan said. "I'm not even sure why I'm here, because typically I don't deal with this sort of thing."

"Saving someone?"

"No, I mean murder. I don't get involved in murders, just accidents. To be honest, I'm surprised I was even notified of this little party. It's not my thing."

Bernard didn't respond right away. He acted as though he were listening to something, only there was nothing to listen to aside from the wailing of the fire alarm.

"We find that *very* interesting," he said after a time.

"You keep saying *we*. Who is we?"

"There is myself, and there is the voice inside my head."

"Tell me about this voice," Corrigan said.

"No, I don't think I will. Your *accidents only* rule must have been very convenient over the years."

"How do you mean?"

"You never had to get your hands dirty. Never had to pick sides. An accident has no subjectivity. Not like murder."

"You have a higher opinion of murder than I do."

Behind them, Detective Joe White had just arrived at the scene. He made his presence known immediately, with a bullhorn.

"CORRIGAN BAIN, PUT YOUR HANDS IN THE AIR, TURN AROUND, AND STEP AWAY FROM THEM." White blared.

Corrigan thought it was telling that White decided to address Corrigan first, when he was self-evidently not the biggest threat at the scene.

Bernard smiled.

"Don't do it," he said. "If you walk away I'll set off the bomb."

"Even if he decides to shoot me?"

"Oh, especially then."

Not much about the scene made sense. There was a man in some kind of robot gear standing in the middle of Center Court, holding a gun. Two paces to his right was a girl wearing a bomb. Four paces in front of him was Corrigan Bain.

It didn't make sense because the man didn't appear to have any kind of trigger.

The girl could have one. Nobody seemed to be able to get a clean look at her hands, so a suicide bomber couldn't be ruled out. It was just that this *also* didn't make sense. Suicide bombers didn't typically wait until the building was cleared before setting themselves off, and they weren't known to bring friends along.

Also, the girl was Monica Devereaux. Joe thought she was weird when he interviewed her, but not this kind of weird.

He waved Newton over.

"No demands?" he asked.

Newton was the first on the scene. He'd already been following Bain before the gunshot caused the mass exodus.

"He hasn't communicated to anyone other than Bain," Newton said.

"Did you try?"

"No sir. He shouted, but I didn't engage."

"Good, that's good. Nobody's been blown up or shot since you got here, that's the best you can do."

"Yes sir."

"I'm gonna get Bain the hell out of there and then reach out. Newton, I need you to get on the comm and see if anyone here has a confident shot. Do it quietly."

"Yes sir. Sir? On who?"

"Any one of them, Newton. Nobody *take* a shot. I just want to know what I have."

"Yes sir."

Joe lifted his megaphone.

"CORRIGAN BAIN," he said, "PUT YOUR HANDS IN THE AIR AND TURN AROUND."

<hr>

"How are you going to set off the bomb?" Corrigan asked. The girl whimpered and eyed the cell phone attached to the bomb. Corrigan wanted to say, yes, he saw that, but Bernard doesn't have a phone in his hands. Only then did it occur to him there was someone else involved.

Bernard didn't have the trigger, because someone far removed from the blast site had it.

The voice inside his head, Corrigan thought.

Corrigan started checking the area for a camera, then realized he was being stupid about this as well. Bernard was *wearing* one.

"CORRIGAN, ONE MORE TIME…"

"He told me I can't leave!" Corrigan answered. He snuck a peek over his shoulder in the future and placed Detective White at the far end of the room behind a column in front of the *Game-Stop.* That's where the megaphone was sticking out. It was a long way away. The perimeter established by the police was based on cover, and there was no cover in the middle of Center Court, so they weren't any kind of close.

There was a pause. He could imagine Joe White cursing to himself and probably thinking up a way to blame Corrigan for all of this.

"ALL RIGHT. YOU WITH THE GUN. YOU HAVE A BOMB AND TWO HOSTAGES. TELL US WHAT YOU WANT."

Bernard looked at Corrigan. His future blinked in and out of existence four times.

"I'm not speaking to them," he said. "Tell him we already made our demands."

"You want me to say that?"

"Please."

"Even if it doesn't make any sense?"

Bernard smiled.

"We asked that they be set free, and that hasn't happened. We had this conversation, boy scout."

"Okay, I'm going to stand up and turn around and convey that to Detective White. Will that be okay?"

Corrigan was about ten feet from Bernard and Monica. He could close that distance in four steps if he charged. If he could see Bernard's future with any kind of consistency, he'd try it.

"Yes," Bernard said. "Go ahead. You can see the future; you already know it will be okay."

"But you can also alter the future."

"Oh, very good."

Corrigan sighed.

"You know what," he said, "this is ridiculous. None of this makes sense. According to you, that bomb can level the mall, and now you've got half the police force in your blast radius. You want me to tell the cops that you have no demands, because today is all about the consequences of you not getting your demands met, but that just means you're going to detonate the bomb. As soon as I tell them that, they're going to start to look for options to shoot you without setting it off. If this was really about punishing the city for not meeting your demands, you would have set off the bomb, and you wouldn't even need to be here to die with it."

Bernard laughed.

"You're right; we're being disingenuous. This was all about you, Corrigan Bain."

The guy with in the robot suit wasn't answering. Joe managed to scare up a set of binoculars to get a better look at the situation, but what he was seeing made no sense at all. Suicide bombers don't take hostages, and Monica Devereaux—who looked terrified—was clearly not there voluntarily.

Bain appeared to be trying to resolve this situation, so the good news was that he was probably not a terrorist. That was great, except he was also not a cop, and there continued to be no plausible explanation for how he ended up being the first person on the scene.

According to Officer Newton, Corrigan started running toward Center Plaza before the gunshot. Agent Trent would have Joe believe this was because her boyfriend could see the future.

He still wasn't buying.

Joe didn't know if Corrigan was armed. That seemed like a small thing in light of all the other variables in play, but it was something Joe also had to take into account.

But the focus of the problem was the guy wearing that weird apparatus. It was great that all the people the city was actively looking for, in connection with the State House bombing, had decided to go shopping at the same time like this; better-or-worse, by the end of the day they'd probably be closing that case. Joe just couldn't figure out how to do that without adding to the body count.

They needed more time. The bomb squad was still a half an hour out, the nearest sharpshooter team was another hour, and since nobody knew exactly how big of an explosion to expect, the entire Prudential tower was currently being evacuated, which was probably going to take all afternoon. If they could establish a dialogue with the instigator, they could at least get a clue about how long they had before they had to make hard decisions, like who to shoot in the head first.

"Joe," Maggie Trent said. She'd come up behind him while he was busy holding his breath. "What's the situation?"

"No idea," he said. "Nobody's talking."

She grabbed the binoculars from his hands without asking, and looked at the scene.

"Jesus," she said. "The bomb. Did you look at the bomb?"

"I've got nothing else to do, so yeah."

"It's got a remote trigger, like the one in the State House."

"What's your point?"

"The trigger man might not even be here, is my point. Can we jam the signal?"

"Not before the bomb squad gets here, no. We can shoot the guy in the robot suit now, cross our fingers and hope for the best, but other than that..."

"Do you have a shot?"

"I was joking, Agent."

"I wasn't. I don't think we have a way out of this, other than Corrigan coming up with a solution on his own. We'd be better off if you established a perimeter outside of the blast radius, either way."

"How far?" Joe asked.

She looked at the device again, through the binoculars.

"Um...Jesus. Okay. Maybe outside the mall."

"Can't get a shot if we're not in the building," Joe said.

"You also don't need twenty men to take the shot. I'd get some bodies away from here, if I were you. That's twice the size of the State House bomb. I'm surprised she can stand up straight."

"What do you mean, this is about me?" Corrigan asked.

"I would have thought it was obvious, by now," Bernard said. "This was all to draw you out and see what you could do."

"Super. You could have just asked. I mean, I'm flattered."

"You're a wild card. We had to make sure we eliminated you first. To be honest, we had no idea someone with your capabilities was out there. It's a shame to have to kill you, but here we are."

"Maybe I should have a direct conversation with the voice inside your head," Corrigan said.

Bernard smiled gently. His future blinked out again, and back in, and out. In the micro-second it was available, Bernard pointed the gun at Corrigan.

"I think we've said enough," Bernard said. Then he did as anticipated, and pointed the gun at Corrigan.

"What's going to happen next is that I'm going to shoot you. If you let me do that, I'll surrender, and the bomb doesn't explode."

Corrigan couldn't tell if that was how the future was going to actually play out. All he saw—and felt—was the bullet hitting him in the chest; Bernard's half of the future was missing.

"Okay," Corrigan said.

"Okay? You agree?"

"Yes. Go ahead and shoot me."

Without preamble, Bernard pointed the gun at Corrigan's chest, and fired.

Corrigan altered his future, but not in a way that resulted in him not getting shot, as he felt as if he needed to hold true to the promise to allow this to happen. Instead, rather than stand still, he charged.

The load hit him in the chest, right around the heart, and was not fatal. The flak jacket he'd taken from the condo earlier that day absorbed the worst of it.

It still felt like he'd been struck in the ribcage with a sledge-hammer, but that was why he rushed forward in the first place. His momentum carried him forward despite the impact.

Bernard got off a second shot. This one hit Corrigan in the stomach, under the vest, and was probably fatal.

But not right away. He had enough life in him to connect with Bernard, knock the gun away, and come down hard on top of him on the concrete floor.

The camera lens on Bernard's head shattered. Corrigan got up onto his knees and slammed the man's head on the floor with his left hand, while his right hand sought out the wound. He was unreasonably preoccupied by the notion that his guts were about to pour out of the wound. Black patches began appearing at the edge of his vision, and the pain was kicking in.

He was pretty sure he was dying.

Not yet, he thought.

"Come here," he barked at Monica.

She was terrified to move.

"Quickly!" he said.

She stepped closer.

"Kneel, quick, I can't stand," he said. "Hurry."

She crouched down next to him, tears streaming down her face.

"We're not," he said, in response to the question she hadn't asked yet. He was losing track of the present already; that was bad.

"Are we going to die?" she asked.

He could hear all kinds of shouting. People were running towards them. He had almost no time.

He looked at the bomb, tried five things in the future to

disable it. Four of them set off the bomb. The fifth—yanking the cell phone at the center off of the device—was the only one that didn't.

He ripped the phone off the bomb. The future continued to exist.

Then he collapsed. He could hear Maggie screaming his name, and Joe White barking orders. He wanted to apologize to Maggie for getting himself shot again, but he couldn't seem to move his mouth.

Police officers wrestled Bernard to his feet. Despite the multiple blows to the head, he was conscious, and smiling at Corrigan.

Then the world went black, and Corrigan Bain died.

PART TWO

Shiva Ascendant

CHAPTER ELEVEN

Days later, there are still more questions than answers.

After an incident that left one man dead and another in custody, the country is looking for an explanation. Who is Bernard Jenks? How is he connected to the EJF? And what did Corrigan Bain have to do with any of it?

Police, the FBI, ATF, nobody's talking. Even the local blogger, who was at the center of it all, has dropped out of sight.

Americans want answers. Americans deserve answers.

—Washington Post editorial board

Erica Smalls stole into Boston in the middle of the night, on the red-eye from JFK. By then, it had been a little over two weeks since Agent Maggie Trent turned to an associate in the FBI headquarters and suggested someone get Erica on the phone, and approximately ten days since a terrorist threat in the city of Boston ended with the death of Corrigan Bain.

There were reasons—some of which might, in a different context, make for a funny story about irony and whichever fickle god was responsible for institutional bureaucracy—why it took so long to put Erica and Maggie on the phone together. One of those reasons was that Erica Smalls happened to be working for the speculative technologies division of a large Japanese corporation. This meant (although it didn't have to, as they had offices all over the world) that Erica was *in* Japan when Maggie first thought to reach out.

This wouldn't have been a huge problem if Maggie knew she was trying to reach an American citizen working overseas, but she didn't. The last thing she had on Erica was that she'd graduated from MIT, and then left the city.

The alumni board at MIT appeared to be equally unclear on what happened to Erica after graduation. They last had her working for a think tank in Palo Alto, but she was poached from that job after less than a year, and hadn't updated the school. Likewise, the think tank didn't feel comfortable disclosing Erica's new position to either MIT or the federal government.

Meanwhile—and this was where the god of bureaucracy really stepped up—Erica had been trying to get a hold of Maggie Trent at the same time.

Corrigan was the reason Erica got to see that MIT graduation, when so many of her friends did not. She was also better acquainted with exactly what Corrigan could do—and how—than Corrigan himself was, which Erica thought probably made her valuable in a moment when it looked as if he'd gotten something wrong. So, when Erica saw the viral footage of the man who saved her life acting like a crazy person, she did all she could to get in touch with Maggie Trent of the FBI, if only to ask, *how can I help?*

But she didn't have Maggie's number, or Corrigan's number, and they didn't have hers. This was probably an oversight on someone's part, except that Erica explicitly recalled thinking that if they needed to reach one another again, that would mean something awful was happening. Erica had been hoping they were past all of that.

She kept trying to get through, even after the media reported that the threat was over, and began the debate (still ongoing) over whether Corrigan Bain was a hero or a co-conspirator. It cooled the switchboards enough that one day, finally, Erica gave her name to someone close enough to Maggie to remember that Maggie wanted to talk to Erica. Twenty-two hours and three flights later, Erica was landing at Logan International Airport.

Maggie met her in baggage.

"Hey," Erica greeted, with a hug. "I didn't expect you to show in person. Aren't you kind of important?"

"Depends on who you're talking to.," Maggie said. "I was up anyway."

The wait for Erica's one bag to come down the carousel was interminable, and conducted mostly in silence. They had a thousand things to discuss, but every subject mandated privacy first.

Finally, they got the bag, and made it to Maggie's car.

"He's not really dead, is he?" Erica asked.

Maggie hadn't even started the car yet.

"Not currently," Maggie said. "He also hasn't woken up yet."

"I'm sorry," Erica said. "Are you okay?"

"I'm just tired, thanks. But we have a lot to go over. Let's get you to the hotel so you can start first thing."

"I'm still on Japan time. Why don't we get started now?"

Maggie grinned. "I was sort of hoping you'd say that."

The news media didn't know what to do with what happened in Center Plaza.

What was known was that there was a hostage, a man with a gun, a bomb, and Corrigan Bain, the erstwhile most-wanted-man in the city. When it was all over, Corrigan had been shot twice—once in the bullet-proof vest he was wearing, once in the stomach—and died at the scene...for about sixty seconds. He died again at the hospital, for seventy-three seconds, but had not died successfully since. The public didn't know all of that—that he died, certainly, but not that he had been revived—although nobody scheduled a funeral, which was certainly notable. And the one family member anyone was able to identify—Corrigan's mother—had dropped off the grid entirely.

It was also known that he was shot by the man with the gun, who was now in custody. Identified as Bernard Jenks, his last known address was in Quebec, Canada. Various media personages had written entire biographies of Mr. Jenks that would only end up useful to the people responsible for his high school alumni newsletter. Nothing about his life history could explain how he ended up standing in a mall under the Prudential with a gun and a large bomb.

Perhaps the most notable thing about the biography of Bernard Jenks was that there was more information available about him than anyone had been able to uncover on Corrigan Bain, and the media had an extra week to work on Corrigan.

Then there was the hostage, who should have been an absolute fount of information, given it was a blogger with whom the city was already intimately familiar.

In the four days between the bombing of the State House and the incident at Center Plaza, Monica Devereaux had been interviewed (television and radio) over a dozen times, and profiled twice by local and national print media. For someone who was a self-described introvert who actively sought out a profession that allowed her to work alone almost exclusively, she had pushed the envelope of overexposure to its upper limit. It seemed likely that, had it gone on for another week, everyone would have been sick of hearing from her.

Then she ended up in the middle of the story, instead of a prescient website owner on the fringes. It was known that she was the one wearing the bomb, and it was known that she was not a willing participant in the proceedings. She was a first-hand witness to the shooting of Corrigan Bain by Bernard Jenks, and she was there (of course) when Corrigan deactivated the bomb... somehow, despite having no training anyone could verify, on the deactivation of explosive devices. In fact, most of what the media definitely did know, they knew because of an initial interview with Monica, after she'd been taken from the scene.

It was only reasonable to expect that she would be available to provide additional details. However, after that on-the-scene conversation with a local TV outlet, Monica Devereaux stopped talking. Her website, while still active, was being held aloft by commenters. She posted no updates, and hadn't even returned home, according to the multiple print reporters camped in front of her apartment building.

Beyond what was known, was everything that could only be guessed at. Nobody was really sure why Jenks shot Bain, while the twenty-odd police officers and FBI persons at the scene neither shot anyone, nor prevented anyone from getting shot. Devereaux did not—in her one interview—explain how she ended up kidnapped (presumably) and taken to the mall with a bomb on her chest. Speculation abounded, as speculation tended to do: were Jenks and Bain working together? Was the shooting due to an argument? How could Corrigan Bain deactivate a bomb that was supposedly the same kind of bomb that had flummoxed professional bomb deactivation people four days earlier? Did this mean he was involved all along?

Some of the questions being asked were the same ones being asked by law enforcement, albeit privately. The biggest such question was: what exactly was the point of all of that? The bomb never went off. The BPD and the FBI knew perfectly well that Bernard Jenks had no demands, and never interacted—aside from a couple of orders shouted at the first-responder—with anyone aside from Bain, and Devereaux. So why was he there?

This was the kernel of missing information that drove the media mad over the course of the week, following Bain's public death. The official statement from the Boston Police was that the case was closed, the bomber responsible for what happened at the State House had been captured, and everyone was safe now. But Bernard Jenks was a black hole in terms of information, which meant there was no storyline to follow that could button up the story. The public needed a manifesto, or a statement of intent, or...something. Just a note on a napkin that read, "I don't like Bostonians", in Bernard's hand, would have done the trick.

It wasn't that law enforcement had made it impossible for anyone from the press to get this information; they didn't have it either. Since his arrest, Jenks had only spoken a dozen words. Two of those words were, "not guilty". They were spoken at his arraignment, and it looked to the assembled press as though the words came as a surprise to the court-appointed attorney standing next to him.

He was being held at the Suffolk County Jail until his trial date. Which just meant that BPD, the Suffolk County Sheriff's department, the District Attorney, and the FBI had until then to figure out what in the hell was actually going on.

Hopefully, Corrigan Bain would be able to answer some of that, but the odds were pretty good that—while he was not actually dead—he would never regain consciousness.

———

There were several different ways to get from Logan Airport to the FBI offices at Government Center. The way Maggie decided on, without really thinking about it, took them past the Nashua Street location of the Suffolk County Jail.

She'd spoken to Jenks personally, on three occasions. It was very much the case that *she* spoke, rather than that they spoke with one another, because he continued to be unhelpful. He didn't behave like a man who was concerned about spending the rest of his life in prison, certainly. If anything, his demeanor leaned hard in the direction of religious fanaticism. Specifically, the, *my reward will come in the next life* component.

"So that's it?" Erica asked, regarding their conversation up to that point. "You guys really don't know anything more than the papers do?"

"Depends on which papers you've been reading," Maggie said.

There were a bunch of conspiracy theories out there. The one that was most interesting had Corrigan as part of a secret government program whose goal was...well, it varied. This theory had it that he didn't die, but was simply reassigned, after being outed by the press. The flashpoint for that theory appeared to be a blurry photograph that surfaced after the incident at the Pru. Someone got a shot of him being loaded into the ambulance. He was rocked to the side as he was loaded, which revealed a portion of the back of the bulletproof vest. It was hard to tell, but it looked like the words FBI were emblazoned on it.

Maggie happened to know that those letters really were on the back of the vest, because that was what he'd taken from the condo that day. (And not her gun, which she found in her own apartment a day later, still in its case.) It didn't mean Corrigan Bain was a CIA agent with superpowers; it meant he was dating an FBI agent who was in the habit of leaving unusual articles of clothing in his house.

But at least that theory was rooted in some sort of reality.

"Well, okay," Erica said, "but none of that explains why I'm here."

"No, it doesn't," Maggie said. "I've only told you what we *know*. There's a big pile of stuff we don't understand. That's what you're here for."

"Ooh, mysterious. I'm flattered. I guess I'm pretty good with things that are difficult to understand. What are we talking about?"

"You're also the only expert on the subject who's still alive," Maggie said. "Someone built one of your devices."

"One of my...devices?"

Erica looked confused.

"A more advanced version of the thing you guys were working on at MIT. I thought you would have figured that out by now, just from the reports."

"To see the future? Like Corrigan does?"

"Yes, exactly. You know, because that was what we were so hung up on, the day of the bombing. How could Corrigan have thought a bomb was going to go off, when it didn't? Didn't you wonder that?"

"I did, yes, but...tell me more about this device."

"I'm taking you to see it right now. It's portable; Jenks was wearing the thing when Corrigan took him down, and it's still mostly intact."

"Oh, is that where the android story came from?"

Several conspiracy theories posited that Bernard Jenks wasn't fully human. That Erica was citing this particular bit of weirdness implied that she had indeed been reading *all* the available news.

"Yeah. It's a suit, kind of."

Erica stopped talking. They'd just gotten off of Storrow Drive and were making their way down Charles Street—past the old location of the Suffolk County Jail, which was now (of all things) an upscale hotel. She appeared to be looking at the scenery. On the other side of the river was the tail end of the MIT campus, briefly visible as they made the turn. Maggie thought at first that this was what had brought on the sudden solemnity in her car's co-occupant. Then she realized Erica's lips were moving. She was doing calculations or something.

Erica Smalls was probably the smartest person Maggie would ever expect to know personally, and she'd met a lot of smart people. That she also looked like a fashion model was something Maggie was trying not to take personally.

"It's impossible," Erica said, some three blocks later. "That's why."

"That's why what?"

"You said you thought I would have figured that part out already from what was available to the public, and you're right; I would have if was possible. It's not."

"Well that happens a lot, doesn't it? Around Corrigan?"

"That's true."

"I mean, we had to deal with invisible creatures murdering people last time around, right? It's impossible, until it isn't."

Erica looked like she was going to say more on the subject, but pulled it back.

"Maybe I should look at the device first," she said. "Then we can have this conversation again."

J oe White was surprised to discover David Spence waiting for him in front of the jail, rather than Margaret Trent. It had been Maggie the last three times. This either meant she had something more important to do, or she'd decided this was a waste of her time. Joe was leaning toward the latter, only because he was pretty sure it was a waste of *his* time.

"Where's your girlfriend, Davey?" he asked, while Dave extinguished the cigarette he'd been enjoying from less than fifty feet from the front door, contrary to federal regulations.

Joe always thought Dave was a good cop, but he was also someone who liked to break little rules, because he wanted to be the kind of guy people thought of as a rule-breaker. It was the same reason he enjoyed letting people—people who knew his wife personally—think he was having a thing with Maggie Trent. It was mostly an idiosyncrasy with him: Joe didn't think he was someone willing to break the important rules. Dave wouldn't pocket cash from a drug bust, or beat down a suspect, or plant a drop piece on a perp. But he wanted to be thought of as someone who *could* do those things.

It was probably the kids. Or the premature balding. Whatever the reason, it was why Joe tended to prefer not to work closely with him, good cop or not.

Plus, Maggie was easier on the eyes. She continued to annoy the hell out of Joe, but he couldn't deny that.

"She's not my girlfriend," David said. "Do you have a new set of questions for our friend today?"

"Nah, same ones. Figure I'll just keep asking until he gets bored of 'em. You?"

"I don't have a list. This is my first time, I thought I'd just wing it."

"Oh, and you didn't answer my question: where's Agent Trent? She get tired of this guy already?"

"Maggie's consulting with an expert right now."

"An expert? In what?"

David shrugged.

"That's all she told us."

"Does this expert have a name?" Joe asked.

"I'm sure he does. Most people do. You ready?"

The Suffolk County Jail was a maximum-security facility full of short-term residents who were either on their way to prison or exoneration, depending on how expensive their lawyer was, and perhaps also on whether or not they were guilty.

In order to get in to see Bernard Jenks, White and Spence had to sign in at the first desk, show some paperwork with the D.A.'s signature on it at a second desk, surrender their firearms at a third desk, and then wait at a fourth desk for a half an hour, while the prisoner was moved from his extra-secure private cell and his attorney—who was waiting at a fifth desk somewhere— was brought in to represent his client's interests. They would all meet in an interrogation room, where the two police officers were allowed to talk to Jenks for as long as an hour.

They were also allowed to record the conversation. If the perp felt like confessing—he'd already pled not guilty, but stranger things had happened—they were allowed to hand him a pen and paper so as to formally document that confession. They were allowed to tell his attorney to let the man write, in the event the attorney felt obligated in some way to advise his client not to confess under these circumstances, as surely the correct way involved a plea deal with a representative of the District Attorney's office.

They were not allowed to beat the shit out of the guy. Joe checked the paperwork, and that was definitely not allowed.

After all those desks—plus a dozen doors that had be

unlocked for them—they were escorted into the room. Jenks was cuffed to a steel table, next to a P.D. named Landon. Joe had never met Landon outside of this room, and didn't know what kind of person he was when he wasn't going full-on attorney, but he seemed like an okay enough guy. Probably not a cross-the-room-to-shake-his-hand kind of guy; more of a nod-hello type. It was hard to say, because the kid was a little green.

"Landon," Joe greeted, shaking the attorney's hand across the table. "This is Detective David Spence."

David and Landon shook, and then everyone joined Jenks at the table.

"We have a few questions," Joe said. "And we're hoping your client can answer them this time."

The questions were indeed the same ones they'd asked every other time they spent an hour with Bernard Jenks. They were interesting questions, if only because they illuminated precisely how little the FBI knew. Landon, for instance, probably found them extremely interesting.

About half, if answered, would be a tacit admission of guilt for a crime Jenks had already pled not guilty to. Whenever those kinds of questions came up, Landon advised his client not to answer. His client didn't, but he wasn't answering anything either way. On the second try, Joe snuck in, "what did you have for lunch today?" and Jenks still didn't answer. He smiled, though, so he wasn't deaf.

They went through all of them anyway.

- *Why did you blow up the State House?*
- *What were you hoping to accomplish at the Prudential?*
- *Did you act alone?*
- *What is your connection to Nick Borowitz and Sharon Ledo?*
- *What does the device we found you wearing do?*

- *How do you know Corrigan Bain?*

There were more. It went on like that for almost the whole hour, and included multiple visuals. They would slide a picture to him: the symbol on the bombs, which they asked him to explain the significance of, or a picture of the apparatus he was wearing, perp shots of Ledo and Borowitz, and so on. He'd look at each picture, consider whether or not to respond, and then lean back and look away. Every single time.

Joe was ready to renegotiate the no-beating-the-shit-out-of-him rules. Instead, he closed up his folder, thanked Landon for his time, and told David it was time to go.

"I have one more question," David said. He'd been silent the entire time, so this was a treat. "Mr. Jenks: is it over?"

Landon quietly advised Jenks not to answer. Jenks nodded. Then he answered.

"No," he said quietly.

Joe nearly fell over.

"Again," his attorney said, louder now, "I'm advising my client not to answer."

"Oh, shut the hell up, Landon," Joe said. "We know. It's on tape. What did you say, Bernard?"

Bernard had a certain expression he stuck to when declining to answer questions. It was kind of a middle-distance meditation look, like he was finishing up an especially relaxing yoga class or a really good bong hit. He looked different now. It was like David had unlocked him or something.

"I said no, it isn't over," Bernard repeated. "And it's Shiva."

"What is?" David asked.

"Have you ever witnessed a miracle, detectives?"

"What, like ever?" Joe asked. "What kind of miracle?"

"Any kind. Have you seen the impossible and known what you were looking at was a miracle?"

For some reason, the first thing Joe thought of was watching that surveillance tape of Corrigan Bain eluding an entire floor of cops to sneak out of the precinct. That seemed ages ago, so it was surprising to find it so readily available in his recall.

"Have you?" David asked.

"Yes, I have," Bernard said. "I saw an act of God."

Joe and David shared an uncomfortable look.

Joe wasn't all that familiar with the terrorist cell David worked on with the FBI, but he didn't think religious fanaticism was a component.

"God, huh?" Joe said. "Which one?"

"The only one that matters. I look forward to the day you witness your first miracle, Detective White."

"Okay, forget all that," David said. "What do you mean when you say it isn't over? Do you know about another attack?"

But then Bernard had that unhelpful expression again, and Joe knew they'd gotten all they were getting out of him for that session. Their hour was up anyway, a point Landon emphasized by getting to his feet, and tapping his wristwatch.

"Detectives, I'm afraid it's time."

Joe thought the attorney probably wouldn't have stood in the way of them getting more questions answered, had his client not returned to his prior reticence already. He was probably as curious as they were.

"We'll talk again soon," Joe said, to Bernard, who ignored him. Then David tapped on the door, and they were being escorted all the way back out again.

They didn't speak about what had just happened until after they'd reclaimed their service weapons and made it all the way outside.

"What the hell did that mean?" Joe asked.

"I don't know," David said. He was lighting up another

smoke. "But I'm going to be listening to that tape for the rest of the month until I figure it out."

"I'll make you a copy. But this smells wrong. I never saw a religious angle before. Weren't your guys anarchists?"

David puffed and nodded. "Their politics were surprisingly scattered, to tell the truth. They were radicalized, but their philosophy wasn't...I mean, maybe I'm not the one to say, because I don't study these kinds of groups for a living, but I never heard anything from Borowitz or Ledo that sounded coherent enough to build a revolution on."

"Yeah, I get you," Joe said. "You expect something interesting enough to worry about it getting onto the Internet. Something to keep the kids away from."

"Right. They had the words and all, but it never seemed like they believed them. I thought they mostly just wanted to blow shit up and needed help doing that. Borowitz has some charisma to him, so I thought of it as more of a Manson thing. What do you think Shiva was?"

"Yeah, that was weird. I think he was talking about the symbol we showed him."

"You think?"

"'It's Shiva', he said. Doesn't fit any other context that I can see."

"The Hindu destroyer-god," David said. "A cool thing to put on your bombs, I guess. I mean, if you just got out of high school."

Joe was about to suggest they contact their various superiors and let them know that Bernard had begun talking, and what he had to say was kind of terrifying, when an alarm sounded.

"What's that?" Joe asked.

It was coming from the jail.

"I dunno," David said. "Let's go see."

Erica's biggest fear was that Maggie was correct, and someone had duplicated the work of the MIT team with which she was most closely associated during her time there.

They'd built something extraordinary. It should have been the most important discovery of the past fifty years, both for the technology they invented and the physics that made that technology possible.

What happened instead was that they discovered a new life form, something that lived at the edge of time. Kilroys were what they called themselves.

They didn't appreciate being discovered, and so one of them took it upon itself to murder everybody connected with the project. All except Erica, although if the knife it plunged into her back landed an inch to the left, that wouldn't have been the case. She ended up in a coma, not altogether unlike the state the man who ultimately saved her life was in now.

Corrigan was the only one who could stop the rogue Kilroy, because he was the only one capable of seeing it without the aid of a machine.

Considering all the damage done to her as a consequence of that project, nobody would have blamed her had she simply moved on, and never discussed it again. She actually did try this. The problem was that she'd spent two of her four years in graduate school solving a very specific, extremely complex problem, and now that it was solved, she couldn't very well unsolve it, or somehow find a way to make it so it didn't actually work out. The tools were all there; someone else would get to it one day. So, she decided she may as well get the credit for it.

She used the work as the basis of her doctoral thesis, and then after graduation formally published it, in a series of three papers. The papers were a combination of her pure math, and theory, co-authored by her and a retired professor named Archibald Calvin. Calvin didn't actually do any of the writing, but he did vet them, and received co-credit for the fact that it was sort of his theory in the first place.

Carefully omitted from any of her papers, was a practical application of the theory. It didn't lend itself to *any* practical application, in its native form, because the technological component sprang from the combined genius of Archie Calvin, and the long-departed professor Michael Offey. They were inspired by the existence (known only to Calvin at first) of Corrigan Bain. In other words, the two of them started by knowing a practical application existed in the form of a human being who could view the world in a particular way, and then worked out—in broad strokes—the physics that made such a thing possible.

When Erica published, she started with the math and worked in the other direction, which was *far* more complicated. This accomplished two things: it erased the line between the theory and Corrigan Bain; it made it so anyone looking for a practical application would have to first understand the math at least as well as Erica did. This was probably arrogance on her part, but she was pretty sure there were only about a dozen people in the world who could make that claim.

Erica had no illusions that she'd managed to prevent anyone from reinventing their machine, ever, but hoped it would be at a time in the future when other advances would make it less likely for anyone to anger the aggressive lifeforms at the edge of the chronoton. And if she was wrong, maybe she would be in a position, at that future date, to offer advice to whoever was close.

Don't let them know you can see them, she thought.

She was wrong, of course. About just about all of that.

Erica received a number of offers from the private sector after graduation, all significantly more lucrative than the offers she was getting from the academic side. Money was something that had always been an issue for her—she attended MIT on scholarship, but that didn't mean there weren't bills facing her at graduation—so it wasn't a trivial consideration. Still, she could survive just fine on the academic income, and that was where she was leaning.

Then she met with a Japanese company called Takani-Ko. Their presentation included proprietary blueprints for a device so similar to the functional one she'd seen at MIT, she wondered if they'd happened upon the design somewhere.

"How close are you?" she asked them.

But they weren't close at all. What she was looking at was an artistic rendering of an idea from a not-yet-funded project. Hiring Erica would get them a lot closer to that funding.

"I'm going to tell you a story," she said. "If you believe me, and still want to offer me a job, I'll take it."

She told them about the Kilroys, and what they did to her classmates. She expected one of two outcomes. Either: they believed her, and decided to never build this machine because of the consequences, or; they didn't believe her, wouldn't hire her, and would still never build the machine because they lacked funding.

But Erica was always better at equations not involving human beings, who often behaved irrationally. They made her an offer.

For the first year, she was installed in a stateside think-tank the company co-financed, where she worked on aspects of their design and a few other things, like the theoretical existence of a species that lived in the future. (The think-tank was multi-discipline, so it was ideal.) Then the project got funding, and she was off to Japan.

One of the goals of the project was to solve for the Kilroys, which the Japanese were taking very seriously. The short-term solution—

the part of the pitch dealing with them that was approved—was to build in a filter. The reasoning was, if the Kilroys became murderous when observed, they could build a filter into the device to ignore them. Users wouldn't have to pretend they didn't see the Kilroys; they literally wouldn't see them. It was risky, because in order to design a filter like that, the team would have to first use it to observe the species, so that the machine could learn to ignore them. If that wasn't handled well, they'd be right where they were at MIT.

But that was a concern for the future. The new device hadn't been built yet. It wasn't even in a prototype stage yet.

That obviated Erica's second-biggest concern, which was that if somebody was copying the MIT project, they were doing it using tech stolen from her Japanese company. But once she was left alone in the room with Bernard's device, it became clear that this was a different design altogether.

None of this was why she'd told Maggie that the portable device Erica had been told to expect was impossible. She knew before she even laid hands on it that it didn't do what Maggie thought it did. But it took her most of the morning to work out what it *did* do.

It was well past Noon by the time she called Maggie in to discuss what she'd found. Erica knew this more by the fact that she'd been brought both breakfast and lunch during her time in the conference room.

Maggie arrived to discover Erica had claimed almost every corner of the room, with two open laptops, a marker-board, and pieces of the device scattered across the table.

"Okay," Maggie said, rubbing her eyes. Erica thought Maggie had probably just finished a nap in her office across the hall. "What do you have?"

"Let's start with this," Erica said.

On one of the laptops, she hit play, and they both watched—

for the thousandth time—Corrigan tackling Maggie and Deputy Duplass off the stage.

"You said before, that you were surprised I hadn't worked out that there was a mobile ATSV out there—"

"ATSV?" Maggie interrupted.

"Advanced Temporal Segment Viewing. It's what we called our machine."

"Right. Go on."

"I didn't assume that, because nobody using an ATSV could have done this to Corrigan. This was an explicit alteration of the near-future. We couldn't do that."

"Why not? You see something that hasn't happened yet, you can just make sure something else happens. What's the big deal? Corrigan does it."

"Corrigan is different," Erica said. "He exists across the time-line. As a person who is *also* in his own future, he can act to change it. We were just viewing. This is complicated, and a little hard to get your mind around, but the very fact that the future happened the way we saw it happen was what made it possible to for us to view it in the first place. The last word in ATSV is *viewing* for exactly that reason."

"So this isn't a portable ATSV."

"It isn't. But that doesn't mean it's not pretty advanced tech. At first, I thought it was just a kind of broadcast camera or something. The optical part's shattered, so it's hard to tell. But the parts of it that go down the arms and legs...here, do you see this? This is hydraulics. Starts at the base here, where there's a transmitter/receiver device, and it's powered by a battery, down there. This is the kind of thing you'd give to someone who had limited use of their limbs. I assume Jenks isn't a cripple?"

"No, he's not."

"I didn't think so. Look, I'm not an expert in this kind of tech, but I think what we're looking at is a rejiggered virtual reality rig, only there's no video game involved."

"Yeah, nope, I don't get it."

"Okay. Bernard puts on this headset, right? He sees through the goggles, or whatever. Someone somewhere else has a matching rig, and they put on theirs, and now they can see what he sees. Go a little further, line up the arm attachments and the leg attachments. Now, the other person, who can see what Bernard sees, can also move Bernard's arms and legs for him."

"What you're saying is, the person on the other end of this suit can see the future, and manipulate Bernard into changing it."

"Basically. I mean, this is still incredibly advanced. And I haven't figured out how they resolved the video feed problem yet. Corrigan can't look at a live video feed and see the future on it—I asked him, once, because we were never sure—so whoever designed this bridged that gap. I think it was with this right-eye optical thing. It's the part that's broken, of course. But if you want I can reach out to a couple of people and try to get the tech sourced."

Maggie was lost in thought.

"Maggie," Erica said.

"Sorry, what?"

"I said I can try to get the tech sourced, if you think that will help."

"Yes. Yes, sure, whatever you need. Keep it on the down-low but...sorry, so, the person on the other end of this rig, they couldn't be using one of your ATSV's there either, right? Because they still wouldn't be able to alter the future."

"Yeah, that's right."

"*The bomber is a fixer*," Maggie said.

"What?"

"Corrigan sent me a note before everything went down at the

Pru. *The bomber is a fixer.* I assumed it meant this device here gave Bernard Jenks the ability to do what Corrigan does, but I was wrong. Whoever was manipulating Bernard is also a fixer, and they're still out there somewhere, which means we're in a whole lot of trouble."

CHAPTER TWELVE

*I think he IS dead, and I think nobody's talking about all he did to
save the city because of that. Because of the next time, when he could
have saved us but didn't, because the police killed him, because they
didn't know better. They're saving face ahead of time, you know?*

—anonymous comment to
"Rumors Continue to Swirl Around Reported Death"
The Boston Globe

There should have been someone at the front desk. Joe
and David were at the desk not ten minutes earlier,
when they were checked out by a uniformed corrections officer named Janice Chapman. Janice smelled like winter-
green and looked like someone's grandmother, and would
probably be the last person Joe might consider deputizing in the
event a fugitive needed hunting down, but such was the nature
of public service. She looked fine for manning an open-area
desk, as the first of many bulwarks against proceeding into the
county jail.

In that, Janice was not alone. The desk area was a small

bullpen space, on a raised platform, such that all entrants had to look up, as if beseeching the mighty Oz for a favor.

Janice was no longer there. Neither was anybody else.

The alarms they heard going off from the outside were much louder in the lobby. Joe could scarcely imagine a scenario in which Janice might, on hearing the alarm (which perhaps meant a prisoner was attempting to escape?) grab her service revolver, and race inside to cut off the breakout.

"What do you think?" he asked.

"Prison break?" Dave suggested.

Joe took the three steps leading up to the platform, and looked around the desk.

"Shit," he said. "Yeah, but from the outside in. Call an ambulance."

Janice was lying in a heap on the floor under the desk. Someone had cold-cocked her, but it looked like she was breathing.

Dave got a look for himself.

"Jesus," he muttered, pulling out his phone. "Who does this?"

Dave had only just connected with the emergency dispatch when they both heard gunshots from deeper inside. They looked at one another.

"Tell 'em we're going to need backup, while you have them on the phone," Joe said.

Janice's keys were missing, but that didn't end up being as much of an issue as it could have, once they discovered the first door was unlocked.

They both drew their guns, and proceeded down the hall, to the second desk.

It was also now unmanned, but without anyone unconscious behind it.

"Maybe we should stop here," David said. "You figure they

have some robust processes in place to prevent this kind of thing from escalating, don't you?"

"A lockdown procedure."

"Yeah, exactly. Nobody's making it back out to the street that isn't supposed to, and even if they did, I mean, we're in the middle of the city. How far can they get? Plus, this place is full of armed men dressed in uniforms, and neither of us are wearing a uniform today."

"You don't want to get shot."

"Do you?" Dave asked.

"Not really."

Another gunshot sounded.

"That was just ahead of us," Joe said. "I agree with everything you just said, but at the same time, I'm worried people need our help right on the other side of that door there. If we're looking at an active shooter situation, maybe we should be the ones who tried to offer assistance, instead of the ones who waited outside for the cavalry."

Dave nodded.

"Yeah, okay. Get your badge out."

He stepped behind the desk and looked around until he found the buzzer for the next door.

"C'mon, I'll buzz you through," Dave said. "You hold the door open and don't get shot."

It was an equitable division of labor only because Joe did not get shot, as requested. He held his badge out in his left hand and his gun in his right, and shouldered open the door.

The next room was an anteroom to the gun locker, where they had been expected to check their weapons before proceeding. From this point, there were five additional doors, leading to different sections of the jail. The one they'd taken before ultimately led to the room where they spoke to Jenks. Joe didn't know for certain where the other four went, but assumed the cells were at the end of at least one.

Nobody was in the anteroom. Dave followed him through the open door, and confirmed this.

"We were just here," Dave said. "Where the hell is everyone?"

There was a caged window at the other end of the room with a door next to it, so whoever got stuck pulling cage duty had a way to get in and out. Their last time through, they retrieved their service revolvers from the window. There were lockboxes on the other side, and a ledger to record who checked in what, so everyone got the right guns when they came back this way.

A few minutes earlier, there were at least two people on the other side of the window.

Joe peeked through the bars.

"Hello?" he shouted. "BPD, is anyone back there?"

He couldn't see anyone, but the angles were terrible. That was made obvious almost immediately, when the door to the cage flew open, springing an officer with her gun out.

"Whoa, whoa, whoa," Dave said, his badge up high. "We're the good guys."

"Jesus Christ," the officer said.

Unlike the last corrections officer they'd seen—Janice—this one looked like she would be good to have around when assembling a posse. She was about five-nine, her brown hair in a ponytail. She looked athletically fit, which wasn't something that could be said about a lot of people who worked full-time in a jail. It also didn't describe Joe or Dave, really, but Joe tried not to think about that.

On the other hand, she nearly shot them, so there was some room for improvement.

"What's going on?" she asked. "The alarms, why are the alarms going off? Who are you guys?"

"Boston Police," Joe said. "And I think we know as much as you do. Are you okay?"

"I'm fine. I was out back when the alarm started. Mike was supposed to be at the window, and I don't know where he's gotten to."

"Out back?" Dave asked.

"Yeah, the...the john. Did you guys hear the gunshots? I thought they came from that way."

"No, we just came from there," Joe said. "They came from here."

"Not this room. I'd know. Guessing wherever Mike went is wherever those gunshots came from, because it's not like he's lying on the floor back here. He's a little too big to miss."

"What's your name, officer?" Joe asked.

"Sheila."

"Sheila, the place has procedures, doesn't it? Nobody's breaking out, right?"

"Yeah, that's right. Honestly, detective, this is only my second day. I'm up to speed on the drills, but I haven't been in one yet. I don't think we drill for breakouts so much."

"Why is that?"

"People in here are facing trial, sometimes for things where they aren't the most important person. Informants, like."

"*Possible* informants," David said. "Someone who might cop a plea to get a lighter sentence. I understand."

"Right, the worry is someone breaking in here to shut someone up."

"They still wouldn't get out again," Joe said.

"Yeah well, we've gamed suicide runs," Sheila said. "Who are you guys here to see, anyway?"

"Dammit," Dave said. "What cell is Bernard Jenks in? Joe? Do you know?"

"Right now, I don't even know which door leads to the cells. Sheila?"

Sheila took a second to look at each door.

"You don't remember?" Dave asked.

"I told you, it's my first day."

"He buzzed us through, last time," Joe said, pointing to the door he and Dave went through to get to the interrogation room.

"Right, the buzzers are labeled," Sheila said. "Hang on."

She disappeared to the other side of the cage, and after a short delay, one of the doors started buzzing.

"Got it?" she asked.

Dave found the correct door, and pulled it open, partway. He looked at Joe.

"Maybe she should go first," he said. "She's the only one in uniform, and I'm growing increasingly uncomfortable with the likelihood of going down by friendly fire."

"Let's just find Bernard and sit on him," Joe said. "It'll be all right."

"You think he's a target."

"I can't think of anyone else in here who could be, can you?"

"It's a big jail," Dave said. "There's no telling."

"Who's this Bernard?" Sheila asked, stepping out of the back room. Dave was holding the buzzed-open door.

"From the scene at the Pru," Joe elaborated.

"Ohh, him! Oh hey, you're the guy. I knew I recognized you. I saw you on television. You arrested him, huh?"

"Maybe we can hold a confab on this later," Dave said. "After we figure out who's shooting guns and all. Officer...Sheila?"

"Binney" she said, tapping the nametag on her ill-fitting shirt. Day one uniforms never did fit well, Joe thought.

"Officer Binney," Dave said, "you want to take point?"

"Sure, detective."

She stepped past him and into the hallway on the other side of the door. Dave went through next, with Joe in back.

The hallway was long, with barred windows on one side, just high enough to make it hard to see anything other than the sky. The sunlight offered almost more illumination than the flashing emergency lights that were busy visually affirming the existence of an alarm in the building.

There was a steel door at the far end, with a Plexiglass window that had bars on either side of it. It was a security door somewhat similar to the sort one saw on the back of armored cars, including a round opening big enough to insert a gun barrel.

Sheila looked through the glass on one side of the door.

"Hey," she said, waving. There was a camera in the corner above the door.

Dave took up a spot at the window, pressing his badge up against the bars. This left almost no room for Joe to get a good look at what was on the other side. He could see a desk back there, and a uniform behind that desk. It looked like he was holding a rifle.

"We're in lockdown," the man behind the desk—Joe assumed—said, through an intercom. "What's going on out there?"

Dave stepped up to the camera, beside Sheila Binney.

"We're responding to gunshots," Dave said, showing his badge to the camera. "BPD. We're looking to secure our prisoner."

"Your prisoner is secure," the man on the other side said.

"You don't even know who we're here for."

"Doesn't matter, all the prisoners are secure."

"What about the gunshots?" Sheila asked. "Pretty sure they came from down here."

"Hang on."

There was a delay, as the fellow with what Joe thought was a rifle got up from behind the desk to stand by the door. He heard a metal-on-metal sound that took him a few seconds to process.

It was the security plate on the gun port in the door. The man on the other side was readying it in case he needed to fire his weapon through the hole.

It's probably a shotgun, Joe thought.

Joe remained a few paces from the door, with an eye on the other end of the corridor. This all felt wrong. The guard on the other side of the door was acting appropriately to armed persons who declined to leave, during a lockdown; Joe couldn't really begrudge him that.

If they were wrong about the source of the gunshots, though...if they'd come from a different direction, it was possible they had managed to put themselves on the bad side of a dead-end, especially if that door stayed closed.

They were in a position to be taken from behind.

"There were no gunshots over here," he said. He was still using the intercom, through a speaker in his hand. His other option would have been to shout through the gun port.

"But you heard them?" Dave asked.

"Just the alarms, sir," he said. "You people need to return to your stations or evacuate the premises until this gets sorted out."

He looked at Sheila.

"You should know this, it's procedure," he said.

"I think you'd better open up," Dave said. "We heard gunfire from this direction, and so did Officer Binney."

"Until that alarm is resolved, sir, this door stays closed."

Dave looked at Joe.

"What do you think?" he said.

"Something doesn't feel right," Joe said.

"Yeah, I agree."

He looked at Sheila.

"Do you know this guy?" he asked.

"First day," she said. "So no."

"What's your name, officer?" Dave asked.

"Sir, I'm going to say this again," the guard on the other side of the door said. "There are procedures in place for this situation. Head back the way you came, because if I follow those procedures to the letter, I'm supposed to treat all three of you as hostiles, and I don't think you want me to do that."

To illustrate this point, he held up the gun.

Dave looked at Joe.

"I don't think he knows his own name," Dave said.

Dave appeared to be thinking the same thing Joe was: that the guy with the rifle might not belong in that uniform.

"Tell you what," the man said. "You head back down the hallway, and ask Binney what my name is, since he's so sure the gunshot came from down here."

This got everyone's attention. Dave pointed his gun at the guard's head, which was at best a symbolic gesture given he'd never be able to shoot through the glass.

"Who are you really?" Dave asked. "Who are you working for? Why are you here?"

"I said—"

"Ask Binney, we heard you. But Officer Binney is standing right in front of you."

He looked down as Sheila, who was a full head shorter.

"Binney is a guy," he said. "I don't know who you are."

Sheila sighed, and turned around.

"He's right," she said. Then she shot David Spence in the head.

Joe reacted badly, which was to say that he had no reaction other than shock, and this was the wrong moment for that. She disarmed Joe with her second shot, which struck him in the shoulder and knocked him to the floor, his gun down the hall and well out of reach. Then she spun around and fired twice through the gun port, paused, and then fired again.

She re-holstered the gun, and then turned back to Joe.

"Tell me something, Detective White," she said. Sheila's demeanor had changed considerably in the past three seconds. It was as if something predatory had crawled into her skin.

She knelt down next to him, and smiled, while he did his best to get off the floor.

"When you had guns trained on the back of Corrigan Bain's head, were you really going to take the shot? Do you think he would have let you? I've always wondered."

His mouth was moving, but no words were coming out. If she could lip-read, she'd realize he was attempting to Mirandize her.

"You're going to pass out now," she said. She stood and pulled out a key ring that was covered in someone else's blood. "Goodbye."

***

Joe was out for about fifteen minutes. He couldn't be sure exactly how long, because he neglected to look at his watch before blacking out, but that seemed about right.

He came to, in the hallway, right where he'd been shot, with the alarms still going off and the lights still flashing. The headless body of David Spence was still where he'd last seen it too, only now it looked as if part of Dave's shirt had been torn off.

Joe sat up. The room spun counter-clockwise when he did this, but tolerably slow.

His shoulder was bandaged. That was where the parts of Dave's shirt had ended up: somebody performed a quick battle-field dress on his shoulder wound. It was pretty expertly done, if only temporarily helpful. He thought he was probably not at risk for bleeding to death in the next hour, but should seek out medical attention after that.

Sheila must have done it. He couldn't imagine why, given she was also the person who shot him, but there weren't a lot of other options, unless headless Dave managed it somehow.

Joe's gun was where he dropped it, and Dave's gun was next to his body. This was another thing that made very little sense, but Joe decided he was in the middle of an afternoon where a whole host of things were going to stop making sense, so he may as well roll with it and move on. He got to his feet, wobbily, and fetched his gun. Dave's he left where it was.

His right arm was useless, so he stuck the gun in his pocket —the holster was in the wrong place, if he wanted to draw it lefty—and picked up his badge, thinking that it was more likely to save his life going forward.

That it was possible to go forward at all was obvious as soon as he took a look at the steel door. It was ajar. Given this was the kind of security door that was built to self-close, the fact that it had not done so meant someone (Sheila, again, surely) had propped something in the jamb to keep it that way.

"She wants you to follow her, idiot," he said to himself. "Don't fucking do it."

He immediately ignored his own advice, and went through the door.

The guard's body was just on the other side. Joe counted three bullet wounds: in the knee, the stomach and the head.

She fired three times, he remembered, *through the hole in the door.*

Only three shots. And they all landed.

"Just lucky," he said. "That's all."

He stepped over the guard. The room on the other side consisted of the desk he saw from the window, a second desk, and a cabinet containing multiple rifles, riot guns, and gear. Joe didn't know enough about what was supposed to be in the cabinet to be able to tell if something was missing, but there certainly did seem to be room for more guns than there were actual guns. Already, the one that could have been on the floor next to the guard's body was missing, so that meant Sheila probably had it now.

There was another door at the other end of the room, and two more dead bodies: more of the sheriff's men. Joe checked one to confirm he was dead. The other one was self-evidently so; it looked like a bomb had gone off on his chest, which is what happens when you're shotgunned at close range.

On the other side of the far door—it was propped open as well—were two more doors, and another body. This one had her throat cut.

Joe was having a lot of trouble processing all of this, in the context of it having been performed by the petite, young Sheila, who simply didn't look physically capable of all of this, never mind mentally. It was clear by now that he was dealing with one of the accomplices they were certain Bernard was working with, but he just couldn't jibe that fact with what he thought he understood about her, in the few minutes in which they interacted...before she blew Dave's head off his shoulders. It was a good argument against profiling, he decided, because she would have been the last person he'd have associated with the word *terrorist*.

There were more gunshots. He had three doors to choose from, but there was someone firing a gun behind only one of the three, so that was the one he decided to go through.

It led, finally, to the cells. Joe was kicking himself for not already knowing more about the Suffolk Jail than he did— although he couldn't have anticipated this particular need—but he knew not to expect a prison-like scene. It looked a little like slightly upscale single-occupancy public housing, with one wall replaced by bars on each of the rooms.

None of the first cells he saw were occupied.

He walked to the end of the long corridor and turned...and nearly had his head blown off. He fell back behind the corner of the wall again.

Someone at the other end was in a shoot-first-ask-later mood.

Joe stuck his badge around the corner.

"BPD," he said, as loudly as he could. "I'm here to help."

A tremendous amount of gunfire followed, but none of it appeared to be aimed in his direction. He poked his head around.

It was another long corridor, ending at what looked like a balcony. Another guard's body was lying still at the edge of the railing. There was a firefight going on, on the other side of that railing.

Nobody was actually shooting at Joe on purpose. There was a pitched battle in the room with the balcony, though. He headed towards it, wondering as he went how many people Sheila had with her, and if they were all dressed like guards, as she was. In short, although he had yet to come across another living employee of the jail, if he did, he wasn't positive he could trust them.

That realization, coupled with the active fire in the upcoming room and the fact that he was still losing blood, should have resulted in him making the rational decision to turn heel and head out while he still could.

He kept going.

The railing was the end of a raised walkway that overlooked what appeared to be the jail's cafeteria. The walkway was designed to provide elevated fire positions to guards in the event there was a need to shoot at someone in the middle of the floor.

When Joe got there—picking up the dead guard's rifle on the way—this was exactly what was happening.

There were a dozen round tables staged in strategic positions around the cafeteria, and nobody at or under those tables; it was mid-afternoon, and between meal times. But Sheila was there, right in the middle of the cafeteria floor. She was taking on constant fire from three directions on the elevated walkway, and was still standing.

"Jesus Christ," Joe muttered. "Is she bulletproof?"

He confirmed that the rifle in his hands had a few rounds left, and took aim himself.

That was when he realized what he was actually seeing.

Sheila was doing something like dancing. It was an awkward dance, and might less charitably be termed a series of brief seizures, but its goal was not aesthetic; she was dodging the bullets, somehow.

Joe took aim at her head, and fired. Just as he did this, the head moved away from where it had been, seemingly after he pulled the trigger but before the bullet had a chance to get there.

That wasn't what happened; it couldn't have been. She was moving before he fired the shot, but after he decided where he was aiming. She'd anticipated the need to move her head—without knowing he was even there, because he was behind her.

After moving her head, she turned to look at Joe. She flashed a devilish smile, and a wink.

Someone gave a signal Joe didn't see, and the hail of gunfire ceased. A quarter of the way around the circular balcony, one of the guards stood.

"You on the floor," he barked. "There's no way you're getting out of here. Surrender if you want to live."

She laughed.

"Darling, if you could shoot me, you would have already."

To punctuate this point, she drew a handgun and fired it, but not at the guard who'd issued the command. He stood at her twelve; she fired at her three. The bullet hit the guard who was positioned there, in the forehead.

Everyone left—this was just two guards now, and Joe—opened fire again. This time, it seemed as if Sheila had run out of patience with the entire exercise. She continued to pirouette around the room, as bullets struck the tables, the floor, everything but her. Her impatience was expressed facially; she looked the same way someone might look if they'd just missed the bus, or dropped an egg. Aggravated, somehow, that this was what it had come to.

Given she was reacting this way to a constant hail of gunfire left Joe with the impression—although this was surely the blood loss talking—that he was dealing with an especially annoyed god.

Joe could barely see straight, and the room was spinning, such that he would have had trouble hitting a stationary target in his current condition.

He kept shooting, though, as useless as the effort was. Then two things happened: Sheila decided to finish off the rest of the room, with two staggeringly difficult shots; and Joe ran out of bullets.

Sheila realized this before he did. Her gun was pointed at him, and for a few heartbeats he thought this was the moment when they both fired, like the last scene of a western. But then she smiled, and he heard the tell-tale click of an empty chamber.

"I let you live as thanks for all the help," she said. "Take the charity, and stop being so stupid. Don't follow me again."

She knelt down and picked up a new gun, then sauntered out of the cafeteria.

Joe heard shouts, and more gunshots, and then nothing. He tried to get up again, but this time it looked like he was staying where he was, either until someone found him and administered first aid, or he bled out and died.

Have you ever witnessed a miracle, detective?

That was what Bernard asked him.

"Shiva," Joe said. "The name is Shiva."

CHAPTER THIRTEEN

Police aren't talking, but as we all know, this is happening in the same place the notorious terrorist Bernard Jenks is being held. Coincidence? We'll have to wait and see.

—on-the-scene Eyewitness News, Channel 7 Local

The Suffolk County Jail took up what was a mental dead spot on the area maps most locals carried around in their heads. It wasn't far from the Museum of Science, the Garden (where the Celtics and Bruins both played) and the Charlestown dock where Old Ironsides lived. One could exit an Italian restaurant in Boston's North End and reach the front door of the jail in a walk that was scarcely a mile, if one were so inclined.

The fact that a large portion of the citizenry was unaware of this had to do with the fact that nothing of note ever happened at the jail—which is an absolute minimum expectation when it came to places housing criminals.

The problem with all of this was that there were a large number of roads which went around the jail, and a profound number of cars used those roads daily; they connected Route 93 to Storrow Drive along one direction, and one part of Cambridge to one part of Boston along another direction.

So, when the Suffolk County Jail, and everything within a half-mile radius, went into total lockdown, all of these roads were closed. This had a drastic effect on traffic for the entire metropolitan area that was far worse than what transpired a few weeks earlier, at the State House.

Maggie had to talk her way to the scene, because between the Boston Police, the Cambridge Police, the state police, the Suffolk County sheriff's department, and the FBI, basically everyone in the state with a badge had an interest in what was going on at the jail. It was officially Sheriff McCarthy's scene, though, and he was there in person to make sure the place wasn't overrun by uniforms.

She could barely pick Lou McCarthy out of a lineup, but he knew enough about her and the investigation she was heading to recognize that granting her passage was a good idea, especially since she had two men inside already.

Dave and Joe were actually BPD, and only Dave was even attached to Maggie's task force, but she wasn't going to let McCarthy's failure to see the distinction get in the way of things.

"Have you heard from either of your guys?" he asked her, as soon as she reached his command center. There was hardly any room available to establish a perimeter beyond the walls of the jail itself. They were standing at the back of a police van in the parking lot of a credit union.

"No," she said. "I've been trying."

"They were here for Jenks?" he asked.

"Yeah."

She'd only gotten a cursory look at the scene on the drive-up. They gave her an escort down Storrow and onto Nashua Street, which encircled the jail, but that told her about as much as a rubbernecker checking out a crash on the highway might get, which wasn't much.

"Can I get a sit-rep?" she asked. "What do we know?"

"Not a fucking thing," McCarthy said. "Step into my office."

The back of the van was taken up by an overhead map of the area, on a card table.

"We got the place surrounded," he said. "Not that it was hard to do, it was built surrounded."

"Maybe you should pretend I don't know anything at all," she said, "and start at the top."

"It's an active shooter situation, agent," he said. "That's all we know for sure. I've got two-hundred and twelve employees in the building, most of 'em unarmed and hunkered down in their offices, waiting for an all-clear I can't give."

"No eyes inside?"

"Working on it. Cameras are a closed system, which makes sense for not wanting anyone outside the place to jack into the feed, except for now when we're the ones trying."

A radio at the front of the van squawked.

"Excuse me," he said. He stepped away, to engage in a long exchange with whoever was on the other end of that radio.

Maggie stood at the back of the open van, and tried to take in the entire scene. She could see the steps leading to the front of the jail from there, as well as the ring of law enforcement vehicles. It didn't look like anybody was in charge, which was partly true only because when something like this happens—and nothing like this had ever happened before—it causes a lot of jurisdictional issues. McCarthy was the county sheriff, and the county sheriff ran the jail, so he was officially in charge. Except he didn't really have the manpower to run what amounted to a siege attack on a fixed battlement, especially since some of his people were inside, and thus not free to mount an attack from the field.

After that, it was the Boston Police, who did have the manpower. Depending on whether there was anybody inside, communicating with the outside, this would either be treated like a terrorist attack or a hostage situation, which meant it fell in the same nether space as the events at the Pru.

Then she thought of Corrigan, and how great it would be if he were there to help out. Having him in a hospital bed instead of free to save the day made all of this just that much more terrifying. That she had been unconsciously relying upon his seemingly mystical abilities as a backstop to the unknown, for all this time, was a jarring realization, but no more so than the fact that Maggie had to fight off tears two or three times a day whenever she thought he might die in that bed.

"What do you kind-of know," she shouted to McCarthy, as soon as she heard his call end.

"We kind-of know that an unclear number of individuals shot their way into the jail portion of the building."

"As opposed to?"

"Transpo, booking, property. The kitchen. It's a big place."

"Not a disgruntled employee, then."

"We can't rule it out, but I don't think so."

"Anyone made it clear?"

"Nobody's tried. Procedure's to sit where you are and wait for us to go in and get you."

Maggie took another look at the door.

"Looks like a clean go," she said.

"Yeah I agree. But look, we've got reports coming in from all over the building, from everyone with a cell phone, meaning everyone except the people in cells, and a few of them have a phone too. Nothing we're getting back makes sense. What we know is there are bodies, and there continue to be reports of gunshots, but nobody's straight about from where and by whom. Could be the good guys, or the bad guys. Thing is, there are a few dozen armed good guys in there, so this thing should be over, and it's not. That either means a small army of bad guys breached the place, or something I don't understand right now is going on. We think it's isolated to the cells, so in a few minutes we're sending in a team to evac the admin section, and then maybe we can get a few witnesses in front of us who are making sense."

"Got it. So why am I here?"

"You've got men inside."

"Sounds like everyone with a badge and a local address has someone inside."

"Yeah."

He looked off into the middle distance for a second, seemingly able to shut out the tremendous amount of noise and activity swirling around them: sirens, dome lights, a helicopter overhead, horns in the distance, people shouting, people running, orders being barked. It looked like everyone was in the middle of shooting a movie, but half were on the wrong scene and hadn't figured that out yet.

"I'm leaning on the theory that Jenks is involved in this," McCarthy said.

"I don't disagree," Maggie said, "but what makes you say that?"

"He's the only terrorist on the premises today. But that's not the only reason. White and Spence were the last two people to enter the building."

"I thought you didn't have any eyes inside."

"I don't, but the cameras out here belong to BPD. Alarms sounded, and then White and Spence ran back inside. It was only after that we got word this was a hostage-slash-takeover scenario, which by procedure meant nobody followed them in until we got an idea of who, and why, and so on. You understand that because this is a jail, containment is one of the things we worry about a lot more than if this was just an office building. Most times, we just focus on getting everyone out. Here, we worry about getting *almost* everybody out."

"I understand."

"So let's pretend whoever stormed this supposedly impossible-to-storm facility was doing so in order to get to Jenks. You worked the case. The other one, Ledo and Borowitz. My understanding is, Bernard Jenks is connected to them. I think we all thought that whole case was put to bed on account of everyone got a medal, but obviously not. Do you have any idea who could be behind this?"

Maggie remembered what Erica Smalls said, just a few minutes before word came down that the jail was under attack: there was someone on the other end of the device Bernard used, and that someone could see things the same way Corrigan could.

"Let's just say we left some leads on the table," Maggie said. "But I don't know who they pointed to. Aside from Bernard Jenks."

"Right. Well, we know it's not him."

His radio squawked again. He stepped away to deal with it, while Maggie pulled out her phone and tried David for the hundredth time and Joe for the fiftieth. She was trying to ignore the creeping fear that the reason neither of them were answering was that they were dead, a fear that only intensified as soon as McCarthy confirmed they were seen re-entering the building after the alarms sounded.

As before, nobody picked up.

The plaza in front of the jail was filling up with officers in riot gear. It was BPD's spec ops, and they looked like they were about to charge up the steps and breach the door. She wondered if McCarthy was aware of this, and decided probably not. The chaos she'd witnessed to this point was self-evidently due, in part, to the fact that nobody was sure who was in charge, so everyone decided it was them.

Then her phone rang.

It was Joe.

"Are you okay?" she asked. "Joe? Are you okay? Is David with you?"

The line was open, but if someone on the other end of the call was speaking, she couldn't hear them.

"I've been trying to reach you," Maggie said, in case this helped. "Are you there?"

The plaza was turning into a case study on the importance of clean jurisdictional claims. McCarthy's people were trying to tell the Boston Police that they couldn't breach, and BPD was telling the sheriff's deputies that it wasn't their call to make. McCarthy was on the radio in the back of the van, holding two separate conversations and shouting in both of them. Everyone had a stake in this.

"They're about to breach, Joe," she said. "Can you tell me where you are?"

"Don't..." Joe creaked.

He was barely audible. Maggie stuck a finger in her other ear to try and drown out the ambient noise of the plaza, and ducked around the side of the van.

"Don't? Don't breach? I'm not calling the shots, I can't stop them."

She could pick up background noise now, around Joe. Someone in the distance was shouting in pain. She wondered if that was David.

"Don't let her escape," he said. Joe's breathing was ragged, and his words were forceful, as though just this amount of work was taking all he had.

"Who is *her*?" Maggie asked.

"Don't...let her escape," he repeated.

"Give me more, Joe. Tell me what happened."

Joe didn't answer. She could hear him breathing, which was probably ultimately a good sign, but in context was mostly just alarming.

Meanwhile, cooler heads appeared to be winning the scene on the stairs in front of the prison. McCarthy had stepped out of the van and was in conversation with the head of the spec ops team, and nobody was running at the doors. Maggie thought someone probably realized they were all on camera—local media was covering the scene from a great distance, but the camera on the news chopper was all-seeing—and decided to at least try looking more professional.

"Joe, tell me how many there are," Maggie said.

She got a grunt, and a sharp inhale.

"We're all dead," he whispered.

"What? What does that mean?"

Joe didn't answer, and she couldn't hear his breathing any longer.

Doesn't mean he stopped breathing, she thought. *He just dropped the phone.*

From halfway across the open plaza, McCarthy caught her eye and waved her over.

They were going in.

Erica thought it probably wasn't okay for her to just wander around the FBI, but at the same time there was hardly anybody around to stop her, which was how she eventually ended up looking at a visual breakdown of the State House bombing. It was pinned to a corkboard wall, with connecting bits of yarn, just like they did it on television. She couldn't decide if this low-tech method of breaking down the case was fantastic or not. She'd seen more interactive displays on weather forecasts, but at the same time, it was just like TV, and that was a little cool.

Maggie left Erica in the care of someone named Francie, about two hours earlier. Then Francie handed her off to George, a half hour after that. George disappeared a short time later, although Erica wasn't sure when, since he didn't announce he was stepping out. He just sort of drifted off or something.

There was a lot going on, so it wasn't like babysitting the civilian was necessarily a priority. The offices had televisions all over the place, and all of the sets were tuned to the local cable news feed, as the events at the jail unfolded. This would surely take up every available agent's time, as it should. Erica was pretty sure Maggie was already at the scene, and maybe so were Francie and George. Plus, Erica had a visitor's pass around her neck, and had already been vetted for some top-secret info (or, whatever it was called here) in the form of the device she'd spent most of the morning examining.

She decided, shortly after George disappeared, that she'd run out of things to learn from the apparatus. It was possible there was more there, and perhaps, had she been involved in ATSV design rather than theory, she'd be in a position to glean that information. But her technical knowledge had an upper limit.

The problem of bridging the video gap remained unresolved. She could say with some certainty that with the virtual reality device attached to the exoskeleton, it was possible for the person wearing it to be physically manipulated by the person on the other end of the device, but even if that person was like Corrigan, the information coming through the feed shouldn't have been any more special than it would be if it was Erica on the other end instead.

She managed to isolate the solution to that mystery to one

component: a rectangular device strapped to the back of the exoskeleton. She at first thought it was a battery, until she found the actual battery, and then she didn't know what she was looking at anymore. It was clear that all sorts of wires led into and out of the rectangle, but she couldn't figure out why, or what it did.

She needed to open the box up, which meant getting her hands on whatever kind of screwdriver handled the screws in question. (Neither the flathead nor the Phillips' head she'd been provided fit.) This necessitated poking her head out of the conference room that had been the entirety of her experience in the FBI to this point, to ask for help.

That was when she realized how empty the place was, and how she ended up wandering into the room with the yarn on the wall.

Maybe the first interesting thing to come out of this discovery was that the State House bombing was evidently connected with the Borowitz and Ledo terrorist case. This connection had been made by linking up a symbol on the bomb to a symbol on an earlier device. Erica found that particularly interesting, because the mystery component—which she was walking around with, although she probably wasn't supposed to be—had the same symbol on it. It was barely visible, because it had been applied to the same part of the rectangle that rested on Bernard Jenks's back, and so had been partly rubbed off. But it was definitely the same thing.

"Hey, can I help you?"

The voice made her jump. It belonged to a guy who looked like he had some Indian heritage. The accent was pure Southern Cali, though.

"Oh, hi!" she stammered. "Sorry, I didn't...I shouldn't be here, right?"

She held up the visitor badge.

"You're the consultant, huh?" he said, with a thin smile.

"How'd you guess?"

"George described...um, yeah, sorry, he asked me to look in on you, and I straight-up forgot. I'm Patel."

He extended his hand, which she took.

"Is that your first name or your last name?" she asked.

"It's Agent Patel. Mike. Mike's my first name, but everyone calls me Patel."

"Okay, should I call you..."

"Patel is fine. It's not actually Mike, it's Madhavaditya but really, literally, nobody calls me that, not even my parents."

"Okay, Patel. Nice to meet you. I'm Erica."

He was doing that thing guys did around her sometimes, which was to babble awkwardly. She could only guess at what, exactly, George said to Patel when describing her, but Erica could turn heads, whether she wanted to or not, so it was probably some combination of crude and flattering, as was just about typical. Patel's current struggle appeared to be with the fact that he found her attractive, which was overriding the problem of finding her where she wasn't supposed to be.

She pointed to the television, currently airing what looked like the beginning of a battle incursion of some sort.

"This is crazy, huh?" she said, nodding to the screen.

"Yeah, they're going in," Patel said. "We've got people...hey, you probably aren't supposed to be in here. I don't want to be rude or anything, but..."

"No, it's cool, sorry."

She held up the component.

"I'm looking for something that can help me open this. Take a look?"

He squinted at the screw heads, and then smiled.

"Yeah, that's a T15," he said. "I got one. Is that from the thing?"

"It is. I'm trying to figure out what this piece does."

"Awesome. C'mon, let's pop it and find out."

It was almost another hour before they finally breached. It took that long for McCarthy and BPD Chief Gregorian—who arrived at the scene about twenty minutes after Maggie—decided they knew enough to at least secure the front lobby. They were still getting conflicting information from inside the jail, but the consensus was that the gunfire had stopped.

The lack of communication with the perpetrators of the attack remained troubling. Nobody was even sure what to call them: terrorists, anarchists, bombers, hostage-takers...none of that seemed appropriate until they had a good idea what their intent was. They also continued to not know how many hostiles to expect.

Getting inside would enable them to patch into the internal security loop, which was a start.

Maggie geared up in a spec ops vest and helmet, and was one of the last through the door. She glad to go, even without being sure why she was invited; her entire reason for being there was to establish contact with Joe and Dave, and she'd done that, even if that didn't result in useful information.

Unless we're all dead *is useful information*, she thought. *Maybe we should expect zombies?*

The large, glassed-in front lobby took ten officers only about thirty seconds to secure, at which point Maggie and McCarthy and a half dozen of his deputies went in.

The BPD spec ops team was being run by an officer named Huang, whom Maggie met for the first time two minutes prior to the breach. He seemed to possess the degree of hyper-competence you really want to see in a police officer whose job involved handling military-grade firepower.

"Lobby's secure," Huang said, when she and McCarthy made it inside. "Two behind the desk."

"We'll hold here," McCarthy said. "Start with the cells."

Huang took five and went through the door that led to the jail cells.

Maggie had been in this building a couple of dozen times, and all but one time had gone through that same door. It was where Dave and Joe would have headed.

She pulled her phone out and listened again. The line remained open. Since Joe wasn't talking, the call served a new purpose: a beacon. When the team got close to finding him, she'd know it.

So far, nothing. That just meant he made it past the first room.

The front desk was on a raised platform. She stepped up and went around. The *two behind the desk* Huang mentioned were a pair of deputies, either unconscious or dead. Both were women, one old and heavy-set, the other looking like she was too young to die like this.

A corrections officer with some basic medical training was kneeling over them.

"How are they?" Maggie asked.

"This one's out," he said, meaning the heavy-set one.

"Out, dead?"

"No, no. Unresponsive, but not dead. She took a hard blow to the back of the head. That one's awake, but groggy."

At the door, another ten officers entered. Half went toward the jail door, the other half to the administrative side. Someone must have decided it was safe enough to start getting people out.

Maggie knelt down next to the younger one. Her eyes were

blinking open. There was blood on the back of her head. Her nametag read *Binney*.

"Hey," Maggie said. "Officer Binney, is it? How are you doing?"

The girl looked at Maggie for a long second.

"Hi," she said. "You're FBI, huh? I've seen you."

"Yes."

She helped Binney sit up.

"What happened?" Maggie asked.

"I was hit. I was hit from behind. I can't remember...Oh my God, is she dead?"

Meaning, the heavyset one across the floor.

"No, she's not dead," Maggie said. "Look, we're a little behind the eight-ball here. Can you tell us anything that can help? Like how many there are?"

"Don't know. Five? I think five. Felt like more, but I only saw five."

"That's very helpful, officer. Were they armed?"

"Not when I was looking at them, but it...it was a surprise. I'm sorry, I can't remember how I ended up on the floor."

"What's your first name?" Maggie asked.

"Sheila."

"Sheila, I'm Maggie. Do you have any idea why they might be doing this?"

"No, sorry."

Sheila touched the back of her head and winced. Her hand came back bloody.

"Oh geez," she muttered.

"Paramedics are right over there," Maggie said, nodding to the front door. "They'll have you out in a second."

"Okay."

"Did they say anything? Anything at all."

"Who? Oh. I'm sorry, Maggie. It was blitz attack, I think. I think it had to have been. God, my head really hurts. I wish I had more for you."

"It's okay."

The medics got to work on the older one first. Maggie really wanted to get over to McCarthy, who was working with a tech to get the internal video monitors to do what he wanted, but now that she'd traded first names with Sheila Binney, she didn't feel like it would have been right to walk away until a paramedic arrived to claim her.

"Hey," Binney said. "I remember."

"Great, what is it?"

"No, I'm sorry. Not that."

She blushed a little, perhaps a good sign she hadn't lost a lot of blood.

"You were dating that Corrigan guy, weren't you?" Binney said. "That was you, right? How is he doing?"

"He's…he died." Maggie said.

"Well, sure. That's what the story is."

McCarthy got a picture. Maggie could see some of the scene from over his shoulder.

"Maggie?" Sheila said.

"Yeah?"

The images were black-and-white, and not in focus, and Maggie was several feet further than she should be for optimal viewing clarity, but already, she'd spotted three bodies.

"How is he, really?" Sheila asked. "Is he gonna pull through?"

"They think he'll be fine. Look, I have to go. The paramedics will be with you in a few seconds. You okay?"

"Yes, of course. You go. I'll let you know if I remember anything."

"Good," Maggie said. "Thank you for the help."

All concern regarding whether or not Erica was where she should be, was discarded as soon as she handed Patel a problem to solve. He took her to a room at the far end of the floor, well outside the realm of the central bullpen space, which he called the junk room. It was where old electronic equipment went to die.

In a way, it reminded her of the lab at MIT, where they first cracked the advanced temporal viewing problem, and in so doing, ensured most of them would end up being murdered.

Kilroy.

Hardly a day went by when she didn't think about him, even though Corrigan assured her that the creature was dead. Once you've been introduced to the idea of an invisible, unstoppable killer, you don't really forget about it.

"Have a seat," Patel said, pointing to one of only two chairs not currently holding up a piece of equipment. He left the device in her hands and dove into the workshop, looking for the peculiar screwdriver they needed.

The biggest difference between this room and the one at MIT—aside from the part where nobody was inventing a new technology at the FBI—was that in their old lab it was basically impossible to tell if you were looking at a discarded scrap of electronics, or at a piece of something important. Erica remembered three different occasions in which she picked up a discarded bit of nothing, only to have it light up because it was plugged into something else. On one of those occasions, she got a light shock, which should have discouraged her curiosity a lot more than it actually did.

She was examining a radio that looked like it was state-of-the-art the same year she was born, when Patel found the right tool.

"Here," he said, clearing a space on the work bench, by unceremoniously shoving everything that was on it aside. Evidently, nothing there was going to be shocking them. She put the rectangle down, and he extended a light over it.

"You don't know what this is?" he asked.

"It's the only part of the thing I can't figure out," she said. Then she explained her theory that there was someone on the other end who was actually manipulating the wearer. It went a little easier than she expected, as evidently Patel had been briefed already on what Corrigan Bain was capable of.

"That's nuts," he said. "If I'm being honest, I'm not sure I believe any of this, and my boss is dating the guy."

"It's real. I should know. I probably have a file here somewhere; look me up sometime."

"I'll do that," he said. "All right, here we go."

He got off the fourth screw, and lifted up the rear casing.

Erica leaned in for a better look, which didn't help much because she still didn't know what she was looking at.

There appeared to be a relay of some sort in there, and something that may have been a second battery, but everything else was just a bunch of wires leading to a central device: an oblong black cylinder.

"Fractals," she muttered.

"What's that?"

"It's just...every time I dig deeper, I find a smaller version of the same unknown. I don't recognize that thing there, do you?"

"Nope."

She picked up the rectangle, carefully, so the contents didn't spill out if they were so inclined to do, and rotated it. She was afraid to touch anything inside without knowing its function.

"Do you think I can take a picture of this?" she asked.

"Depends on what you want to do with it."

"I might know someone who can help us figure out what we're looking at."

"Um...Agent Trent will have to clear that."

"Yeah, I understand. Let me..." She held up her cellphone. "I won't send it anywhere, but before we start pulling this apart, let's...you understand."

She'd already taken two pictures before he had a chance to consider the point. She didn't send it—the folks in the lab in Japan who might know what it is were asleep right then, anyway.

"Just, clear it with Maggie," Patel said. "I like my job, okay?"

"I will, I promise."

He took the device from her and started poking around inside of it.

"I'm thinking maybe we don't need to know what this does," he said. "What we need is to find someone who does know what it does."

"You mean like Bernard Jenks?"

"No. Yes, he would know, but he isn't speaking to anyone. And also..."

Patel drifted off. He was looking at a TV monitor in the corner of the room. The television wasn't on, but she got the point. Jenks was in the jail that was currently under siege. He could be dead, or no longer in custody, so for a lot of reasons, he wasn't going to be available for questioning any time soon.

"I mean, this was manufactured," he said. "So who manufactured it?"

"That's a really good question."

"Thank you. You already thought of it, which is why you wanted that photo."

She laughed.

"Maybe," she said.

"Did this come from the company you work for? Is that your concern?"

"I don't think it did, no."

"that's good."

He picked up a pair of needle-nose pliers, pinched the sides of the black cylinder, and pulled it from the casing. The thin wires going through both sides of it came up with it, so without wire-cutters it wasn't going far, but it did give them a better look at the thing.

"If we can get this under magnification," Patel said, "there could be a trademark stamp on a component."

"Or a serial number."

"Yes. Here, hold the pliers. I think I have a magnifying glass somewhere."

He handed off the thing awkwardly. The room they were sharing wasn't all that large even without the electronic detritus; with it, they had only a few feet of common space, so there was a lot of incidental contact going on already.

To get the pliers and the device from him meant, effectively, holding hands and then spooning for a few seconds until he got past her and to the shelf on the left wall. She didn't mind, because he wasn't being gross about it. If anything, she wanted to tell him to stop looking so embarrassed.

Something inside of the device caught her eye. It was a flash of illumination, coming from underneath the cylinder. She pulled it further away, to get a better look, and was nearly convinced this was a trick of the light—or her eyes, telling her she should have taken a nap by now—until it happened again.

"Hey," she said. "Out of curiosity, did the bomb squad look at everything before it was sent over here?"

"Yeah. Of course. You worried that's gonna blow us up? It's really too small. Plus, you disconnected it from its power source when you took it off the exoskeleton."

"It's got a battery." She pointed to it. "That's what that is. Also, it's blinking."

"Really?"

He took it from her to check for himself.

"Next question," Erica said. "I know when you guys brought this into the building, you thought it was a curious piece of tech from a closed case, where you had the guy in custody. Did anyone check to make sure this thing wasn't sending out a signal?"

"Sure, of course."

"Maybe you should check again."

He put the device down.

"Yes," he agreed. "We should check again. I think this could be trying to send out a signal now. Let's find out."

"Only now?"

"It would have been scanned. But maybe it's self-activated or...we'll check. Good catch."

He looked at her, and must have seen concern in her expression.

"Not to worry," he said. "We're perfectly safe here."

***

Maggie sat down next to McCarthy, to get a better look at the security monitors. There were ten of them, covering different parts of the facility through rotating camera angles.

It took only a few seconds to spot Joe. He was lying on his side next to a railing.

"There," she said, pointing. "Where is that?"

That's the balcony of the cafeteria," McCarthy said. "Is that your man?"

"It's one of them."

The sheriff's radio—which he had on the counter next to the monitors—chirped to life.

"We got a body here," Huang said.

McCarthy opened the line.

"Can you ID him?"

"Negative. Plainclothes. Possible civilian."

"Send a picture though," McCarthy said. "We'll try and get a name."

"He's got no face, command."

McCarthy shared a look with Maggie.

"Roger that, Captain," McCarthy said. "Keep going."

"Where are they now?" Maggie asked.

"In the airlock."

"Come again?"

"That's what we call it. Between this world and that one. It's two doors down, between the check-in counter and the first riot door."

"Can I go down there?"

"You want to see if it's your man?" he asked.

"I'm missing one, yeah."

"He's not gonna be any less dead if you go down there in an hour. Stay put."

"Command," someone said on the radio. "I have two more bodies here."

"Who's this?" McCarthy asked. Whoever was broadcasting, it wasn't Huang.

"It's Mark, sheriff. I'm at the gun locker."

"One of mine," McCarthy said to Maggie, before answering.

"What do you got, Mark?" he asked. "I thought that room was cleared."

Maggie really wished there was a map she could look at to figure out where everyone was. What she knew was that if Mark was an officer under McCarthy's command, he wasn't at point like Huang's team was. Sheriff's department people were trailing the vanguard.

"BPD cleared it of threats, but they didn't look past the window. Looks like...yeah. It's Billy Drake for sure. They've both been shot but...look, I think the other one's Pete, but his uniform's missing."

"Pete Binney?" McCarthy said, for clarification.

"That's what I'm saying. Lou, one of the perps might be in uniform."

"I'm sorry," Maggie said. "Did he say Binney?"

"Yeah," McCarthy said. "Do you know him?"

"Is there more than one corrections officer named Binney here?"

"I'm not sure. Why?"

"A woman. Was there a female officer assigned here named Sheila Binney?"

"No, but..."

She was running before he finished the sentence, and out the front door so fast, the men covering the entrance from the plaza probably would have been justified in shooting her.

"The ambulance!" she shouted, at nobody in particular.

Two Boston Police ran up and dragged her by the elbows from the middle of the plaza. One of them was Sergeant Pekoe, who she recognized as the one that unintentionally released Corrigan from custody.

"Where's the ambulance?" she barked.

"Are you all right?" he asked.

"I'm fine, goddammit, where is the ambulance?"

"It left a minute ago. Another's on its way. Are you hurt?"

He thought she needed medical attention.

"I need to reach that ambulance. I think one of the people we loaded onto it isn't who she says she is."

"I don't understand."

"Sergeant Pekoe, a terrorist is escaping in that ambulance. Find me a way to get through to the driver."

He grabbed his radio and called downtown. This would require him reaching the 911 desk and then someone from there calling out to the ambulance, and if she was right the next step would be to figure out where the ambulance was and how in the world they'd be able to mobilize a police response that was appropriate to the situation when all the traffic was paralyzed and half the cops in town were standing next to her. But first things first.

It took only two minutes to get the driver. Pekoe handed over his radio.

"Hi, who am I talking to?" Maggie asked. She could hear the siren over the open line, which reminded her the cellphone in her pocket was still connected to Joe.

"This is Valparaiso, who's this?"

"Valparaiso?"

"Iggy."

"All right, Iggy. This is Agent Margaret Trent of the FBI. Can the rear of the ambulance hear us talking right now?"

"Shutter's closed, ma'am. What's this about?"

"I have reason to believe one of the two wounded deputies you're taking in isn't who she says she is."

"Okay."

"The younger one. Her uniform says Binney, but it belongs to someone else. The injury may be fake, and she may be a threat. Do you understand what I'm saying?"

"No, ma'am, I don't."

"All right, either way I'm going to need you to tell us exactly where you are."

"Agent Trent, I think you may have called the wrong ambulance."

"Are you coming from the jail?"

"Yes, ma'am, but we only have one patient in back, not two."

"We sent out two, Iggy."

"I don't know what to tell you, ma'am."

Maggie lowered the radio and looked around. If anything, the number of uniformed officers—Boston Police, State Police, Sheriff's Deputies—had tripled since she was last outside. The woman who identified herself as Sheila Binney could still be there, but she had no reason to be; getting away just meant walking off.

"*Don't let her escape,*" Maggie said. "You tried to warn me, Joe."

And I just told her Corrigan was still alive.

CHAPTER FOURTEEN

*I don't know if this means anything, but I saw some woman in a
uniform running away from the jail at the same time everyone else
was running toward it...*

*...yes I can describe her. Brown hair, ponytail. She was cute. Didn't
look like she was, you know, frantic or anything. Like she was jogging,
like. Holding a pace, you know.*

...it just seemed weird, that's why I called...

—anonymous tip line call

I t wasn't until Erica heard what sounded a lot like a
gunshot that she wished she'd paid better attention to the
layout of the Boston FBI's downtown office.

It could have been something other than a gunshot; she'd
only ever been exposed to the sound of a gun one time in her
life, and that was up-close, at a firing range. This was on a first
date with someone who thought his accuracy with a lethal
weapon was something she would find appealing. It wasn't.

She could recall in vivid detail the volume of the noise, even through the noise-canceling headphones, and the steps involved in loading and firing a handgun. (He wanted her to try. She didn't.) But, interestingly, she couldn't remember the name of her date.

The noise she heard in the FBI offices was similar, but significantly more distant: a muffled *whump*—rather than the *bang* one might anticipate from the cartoons—that she was having difficulty explaining away.

Patel would have known what it was, as surely he had more experience with firearms. But he'd been called away nearly an hour ago, only a few seconds after saying that it would be a good idea to determine if the device still in Erica's possession was actively emitting a signal. What ought to have followed was that he manifested something capable of determining exactly that. But then his phone rang.

What Patel said after the phone call didn't make a lot of sense, but Erica figured she'd get a more thorough explanation eventually, since Maggie was the one who ordered him away. He said Maggie thought Corrigan Bain—who was secretly still alive, hidden in a private bed somewhere—was at that moment in great danger. Patel, and the long-absent George, and everyone else connected to Maggie's team who was currently in-the-know regarding the non-deceased state of Mr. Bain, was heading there to protect him.

Erica was incredibly curious as to how an attack on the jail translated into Corrigan being in danger, but the answer to that could wait.

Patel left, and didn't hand her off to anyone else, because it didn't look like there was anyone left to hand her off to. So, she was back to having free rein over a large portion of what was probably a secure area, surrounded by a host of top-secret things. Likewise, she was left without any answers to her questions, specifically regarding the weird rectangular box with the cylindrical thing-a-ma-bob inside of it.

She *was* able to determine, after about a half an hour of fiddling, that the black rectangle probably wasn't giving off a signal. One of the discarded devices in the junk room was an old oscilloscope that seemed to be functional, and it seemed to think there was nothing to worry about. Probably, Patel had access to a more modern (and possibly more accurate) device that could do the same thing, but this was enough to calm her concerns for the moment.

She examined the contents of the rectangle in every way she could, without cutting any wires or disabling the flashing light. Patel said there wasn't anything that could explode inside of it, but just the same, while it was flashing, it wasn't also exploding; there was no guarantee that if it stopped flashing it wouldn't then explode. Or, something less drastic but also bad.

This wasn't what she was good at, anyway, which was why she wished Patel had given her permission to send the pictures to Saito, before leaving. Saito was the engineer building the machine for Takani-Ko.

There wasn't actually anything stopping her from sharing the pic, just like there wasn't anything stopping her from waking up one of the many computers that were currently in sleep-mode, and poking around, or picking up a file and reading it. She wasn't going to do any of those things, though.

Erica was still sitting in the junk room, lost in thought, when the gun went off. It was jarring—for reasons other than the obvious ones—because she'd been caught up in one of her little reveries, which happened to her a lot while working on a complicated question. Because while she was not good at looking at a piece of technology and working out what it did, she was *very* good at complicated, albeit abstract, problems.

The fundamental issue remained the same: there shouldn't

be any way a live video feed offered some kind of future-sight, without that video feed being connected to an ATSV at the source. Since the exoskeleton Bernard Jenks was wearing had no ATSV technology attached to it—she was dismissing out-of-hand the possibility that she was holding a portable one—he shouldn't have been able to do what he did. And what he did was, connect via feed to a "fixer" (Corrigan's word) who could see the future remotely, through Bernard's optical headset.

This should have been impossible, but it was only the first half of the problem. The second half of the problem was that this fixer then manipulated Bernard to alter the future.

It remained the case that every attempt to mirror what Corrigan could do through technology ran into a circular-logic dead-end: the future was viewable because it was probabilistically certain; any effort to alter it would mean it was no longer probabilistically certain, which meant it wasn't possible to view; it was impossible to alter a future that could no longer be viewed, which returned the probabilistic certainty.

In sum, the future could be viewed but not changed, or changed but not viewed.

There was no way around this, unless you were a fixer, like Corrigan Bain, or whoever was on the other end of Bernard's apparatus. Corrigan could do it because his very existence in the timeline was fluid: he existed, perpetually, in the present and the future. He was, in effect, a time traveler capable of zig-zagging between points in a rolling five seconds, in either direction. He was neither fully aware, nor fully in control of this zig-zagging, but that was what he was doing anyway.

To Erica's understanding, it wasn't possible to mimic this. And yet, someone solved the problem, using the device on the counter in front of her.

The gunshot snapped her out of this train of thought, a kind of violence all its own.

She scooped up the rectangular device, and stepped out of the room.

"Hello?" she called out.

The layout of the area she was in was taken up, largely, by an office bullpen: four desks to a row, low cubicle walls, the whole space boxed in on four sides by a walkway. There were private offices on the other side of the walkway, plus some conference rooms, and other kinds of rooms, such as the festival of electronics in the one she was in.

The conference room holding the rest of Bernard's device was down a hall on the other side of the bullpen, as was the TV room she'd wandered into when Patel discovered her roaming freely, but Erica wasn't sure she could retrace the steps necessary to get to that part of the floor, because she hadn't been paying attention.

A little further down that hall was the bank of elevators that got her to the floor in the first place. This part of the floor plan was a little clearer, because Erica remembered taking note of the security procedures. Maggie had taken her to a lower floor first, where she signed in and got a visitor badge. Then they stepped back into the elevator and went up.

Erica suspected that if one attempted to reach the floor she was currently on, without first stopping at the lower floor and checking in, the elevator wouldn't go high enough.

"Anybody here?" she asked.

The silence that followed, served as a tacit *no*.

There was another muffled gunshot, and then two more in rapid succession. She decided two things were definitely true: there was an actual gunfight going on somewhere in the building, and it was happening on a different floor.

She remembered there being doors on either side of the receptionist desk downstairs, because she could recall being surprised to not be led through either of them. If the layout was similar, a lot of space was available. Maybe that was why no one was bothered all that much that a visitor was wandering freely on this floor—there were more offices elsewhere.

A fifth gunshot sounded. Only then did Erica think maybe she should devote less time to wondering about the interior design choices of the FBI and more time to getting the hell out of the building.

She ran in the direction she thought the elevators were, and quickly discovered she had the layout wrong, because she ended up in a cul-de-sac with doors to the rest rooms. She was about to turn around, but there was a third door at the end, and it was slightly ajar. The implication of its position was that there was a janitor's closet on the other side, but she could see a glow from a monitor.

She poked her head in. It was a security guard's station. Evidence of a half-eaten sandwich indicated it had been vacated recently.

The television screen showed the downstairs bullpen on five screens and the elevators on one. It didn't look like anyone was down there, except that there was definitely someone firing a gun, so maybe it was more accurate to argue that there wasn't anyone *moving* down there.

That wasn't right either. There *was* someone down there. She saw a woman walking casually down the middle of the main strip of the bullpen. She had dark hair up in a ponytail, and was in uniform. In one hand, she was holding a small box, and in the other, a gun.

The woman's attention was fixed on the box, at first. But halfway out of the room, she performed this weird...shimmy sideways. There was no audio associated with the security feed, but it was happening right beneath her feet, so Erica heard the gunfire just fine anyway. Someone shot at the woman with the ponytail.

But, they missed. After her odd sidestep maneuver, she fired twice at an unseen target at her ten-o'clock. Then she stood still for a few seconds, and continued walking.

The woman dodged two bullets, and fired an apparently lethal shot, without raising her eyes from the box in her right hand. She didn't even look particularly inconvenienced by the incident.

It was the other fixer. It had to be.

"Hey, maybe you should get out of here, Erica," she said, at around the same time the woman with the ponytail disappeared from the office feed and appeared on the elevator lobby feed. Then Erica saw the elevator door open on the feed, and the woman get in.

The door closed, and the arrow over the door became the most important thing in Erica's life.

"Down arrow, down arrow, down arrow," she muttered.

It was the up-arrow.

The list of things Erica thought she should be doing at that very moment was filling up fast. It included: call Maggie; find a gun; find the fire exit; get the hell out of this cul-de-sac.

She deemed the last one on the list the highest priority, until she saw the open gun locker under the security guard's desk. The guard must have opened it to arm himself and run out in a hurry. With any luck, he radioed someone to let them know the office was under attack first, but there was no way to be sure. Already, Erica had some concerns regarding the professional-ness of a guard who left both the door to the room and the locker to the firearms open.

She took the remaining handgun, shoved some bullets (hopefully they'd fit?) in her pocket, and ran out and back down the hall. She got to the bullpen at the same time the elevator let out a distant *ding* on arrival.

At least now I know which direction the elevator is in, she thought.

Not knowing where else to go, Erica sprinted back to the electronics junk room, closed and locked the door. It was, on the one hand, a good decision given this was one of the few rooms she knew of that didn't have glass walls. On the other hand, she was cornered. But the woman in the ponytail didn't know she was there, so…

Erica turned out the light, just to complete the illusion that this was an unoccupied service closet of some sort. All she managed to accomplish was to prove to herself that she wasn't really thinking straight about all of this.

Bernard's device was still blinking. She'd forgotten all about that, until the lights were out and the flashing lit up her hand.

She's here for this, Erica thought. *Of course she is.*

But why? What made it important enough to storm the FBI to retrieve it?

Erica started loading the gun by the light of the cellphone she should have used to call Maggie with. She still could do that, but now she risked being overheard from the hallway, and so considered it a last-resort thing instead of the first thing on the list. Calling Maggie wouldn't do a whole lot if the armed fixer was already there anyway, and besides, someone should be on the way. Erica liked to think one couldn't shoot up a federal office and not have anyone notice pretty close to immediately.

Loading the gun kept her hands busy and her mind free to work the problem, which should have been getting away from the armed assassin alive, but ended up being the same one she was working on before the gunshot.

There was something about this little rectangular device that was making it possible to remote-view the future, and more importantly, to remote-alter the future. Those were two things, not one, and it did both.

No, it's just one problem, she realized. *It's the* same *problem.*

Then it all fell into place in her head, and she knew what she had to do.

Erica turned the lights back on, put the gun down, and started flipping the device around, looking for a spot for a plug. It had been jacked into the exoskeleton by a plug on one end and a clamp on the other, to keep it still. She took that to mean, when the apparatus was powered up, this thing drew from that power source. The tiny battery inside powered the blinking light (whatever that was for) but wasn't powering the device itself.

What she needed, really, was Bernard's apparatus. But there was a super-powered killer between her and the conference room.

Fortunately, she was standing in the middle of a truckload of discarded electronics.

She'd only just started searching when someone tried the handle to the door. That was followed by a light knock.

"Hello in there."

Erica didn't answer; she kept looking instead.

"Come on, I can hear you moving around," the fixer said. "Look, I just want my doodad and I'll be on my way."

"I don't believe you," Erica said.

"I swear. I pinky-swear. If you could see me, you'd see my hand over my heart."

"I don't think so."

The fixer tried the door again, more violently.

"Not that you've got a lot of options, honey, but what makes you think I care if you live or die? Just crack the door and throw it out and I'll go home."

"You went through too much to recover it," Erica said.

"Nah, the office is practically empty. Low body count. What's your name?"

"Erica."

That's it, keep talking, Erica thought. So far, she'd found five adapters; none fit in the plug.

"Erica, I'm Sheila. You know this door is wood, right? I can just shoot it open."

"Did you empty the offices on purpose?"

"What's that?" Sheila asked.

"I said, did you empty the offices on purpose? They're all out because of the thing at the jail, which I assume was also you."

"No, that was for something else. I'm tying up all loose ends today. One of those loose ends used to be in that jail; another other one's in that room. Are you in the FBI, Erica?"

"I'm the cleaning lady."

Sheila laughed.

"You sound too smart for that."

"You're underestimating the native intelligence of cleaning ladies, Sheila."

Erica had nearly exhausted all of the possible options when she saw the calculator. It was an ancient thing, the kind that used to be on banker desks before computers were in wide use. It had a roll of ticker-tape paper in it and a printer to record every mathematical calculation. She remembered seeing the exact model on Professor Offey's desk at MIT. He treated it like a prized artifact.

This one wasn't prized by anybody; it was stuck at the edge of a counter in the Bureau's room-sized junk drawer, but that wasn't what was important. What was important was that the plug end that went into the back of the calculator also fit into the rectangular device. The other end of the cord was taken up by a big square plug that fit into the wall.

She connected everything together.

"Look," Sheila said, "I'm being nice. I don't have to be. But you know, the longer I stand out here, the more people I have to kill on my way out of the building. You're putting a lot of badges at risk, Erica, and there's no point. You must realize by now that nobody can stop me. Your only chance to live is to open the door."

"You're right."

The device appeared to be powering up. There was no sound to it, or lights, or bells, but it vibrated gently in her hand. Quietly, she reached across the room and unlocked the door. Then she picked up the gun, stepped back behind a stack of retired computer monitors, and said a quiet prayer to all the available gods that she'd figured this out correctly.

"So are you gonna open the door?" Sheila asked.

"It's open," Erica said. "Come on in."

Sheila turned the knob, and pushed the door open.

"Thanks," she said. "I'm actually out of bullets or I would have shot my way through. I appreciate your help."

"Good to know."

Erica had the gun—which she really hoped she'd correctly loaded and enabled—pointed right at Sheila. Despite this, Sheila didn't seem particularly concerned.

"I'm a trained killer, Erica," she said. "Don't be ridiculous. Put the gun down and hand that over. I mean it; I won't hurt you."

Erica shifted slightly, and Sheila blinked and shook her head. It was incredibly subtle, but not to someone looking for it.

"Let me ask you something first," Erica said. "Can you see my future?"

She fired twice.

Of all the things to come out of this day, Erica never expected to wish she'd spent more time on the firing range, with the guy whose name she couldn't recall. If she'd taken the opportunity that date provided, to fire a handgun for the first time in her life, she might have learned to expect that shooting it would pull her aim up and to the left. Also, the recoil was far worse than what she expected.

The first round hit Sheila around the collarbone near the right shoulder, even though Erica had been aiming for her heart from only fifteen feet away. The second shot missed everything but the ceiling.

Sheila fell backwards and out of the doorway, staggering in the direction of the bullpen.

Erica ran to the hallway, meaning—foolishly—to pursue. Her nerve lasted exactly as long as it took to determine that the cord powering the device wouldn't let her get past the doorway.

A blood trail led across the bullpen, to parts unknown. The fire exit, probably, but Erica wasn't going to follow the trail to find that out. Wounded or no, Sheila was a trained killer, and Erica Smalls was still just a physicist.

She nearly stepped on the black box on the floor; it was the thing she saw Sheila using on the security camera. Erica picked it up, put it in her pocket, and stepped back inside the junk room. Then she locked the door, and called Maggie Trent.

CHAPTER FIFTEEN

We have unconfirmed reports of a second attack at the Government Center offices of the FBI. Chet, I think it's clear right now that the city of Boston is under attack.

—on-the-scene news report, Channel 4 Local

There were bodies all over the first floor.

It probably only seemed that way; Maggie was clearing an office space she was intimately familiar with, a place that wasn't by any stretch expected to be a risky location; just the opposite, considering the security involved in making it that far.

The people who worked in the FBI offices had no reason to expect that they would be caught in a shootout *here*. In the field, sure, although that was highly unusual as well.

She counted three dead before she found someone alive, but unconscious and wounded. She was pretty sure his name was Ken. There was nothing she could do for Ken, but ambulances were on the way. Hopefully, they would arrive after Maggie cleared the building of threats, and before Ken bled out.

This doesn't happen, she thought.

One woman, with Corrigan's gift but apparently missing his moral compass, had done all this. It seemed impossible, and that was without even taking everything that happened at the jail into consideration.

Maggie cleared the floor quickly, and made it to the fire stairs. She was about to head up, when the elevator doors dinged.

She wasn't expecting Sheila to return to the crime scene by way of the elevator—or, at all—so Maggie didn't have her gun up when the doors opened. The same could not be said of Justin Axelrod.

"It's me! It's me!" Maggie said, when Justin stepped off the lift, gun at the ready.

"Trent!" he exclaimed. "What happened here!"

"It's been a busy day," she said.

"No shit. I was with the mayor across the street when I got word something went down here. I thought it was a misreport, after the jail."

"It wasn't."

Right after Maggie got off the phone with Erica, she called in the breach. Since nobody had ever done that before, as regards FBI headquarters, she really didn't know what the procedure was supposed to be. She didn't expect *no* response, though, which was essentially what she was seeing, to this point. Then again, a breach at the jail fell under the same rubric; a lot of people were dealing with impossible things at the same time.

Probably, everyone was just a little too busy.

"I've swept this floor," Maggie said. "People are down, ambulances are coming. I'm heading up. I think we missed all the fun, though. Come on, I think I saw a blood trail on the stairs."

She did indeed. There were drops of blood in both directions. From what Erica told her, this was probably Sheila, exiting the building.

"If we have any manpower left," she said, "we need someone to figure out where these stairs exit, and throw up a cordon of the neighborhood."

"Right now? That would take an act of God. Who did this, Maggie?"

"Same person who shot up the jail earlier today."

"Person?" Justin asked. "One person? This was a team, right?"

Maggie briefly considered heading down, because Erica didn't need to be rescued, according to Erica. There was time to enter into a pursuit. But it had been at least a half an hour since Maggie got the call; unless Sheila was lying unconscious in a pool of blood somewhere beneath them, she was long gone.

"There's a couple of things you're going to have to understand, Justin," Maggie said, as they both headed up. "And I don't think I have time to explain it to you yet."

There was more blood on the landing to the top floor. Maggie swiped her badge and pulled the door open, being careful not to touch any of the blood, which would be useful if they ever wanted to ID Sheila.

"I'm not really satisfied with that response, agent," her boss said.

"I appreciate that, sir. Do you remember the video of Corrigan sneaking out of the precinct?"

"I do, yes. Clear over here."

They'd made it onto the floor. He was sweeping one side of the bullpen.

"Imagine someone with the same skills, but now put a gun in their hands."

"Skills? All I saw was a lucky guy sneaking out of an almost-empty building," Justin said.

"Yeah, I figured you'd say that. She's connected to Borowitz and Ledo, anyway. We know this much. I'm expecting to get confirmation shortly that Bernard Jenks is dead. I'm pretty positive that was why she hit the jail."

Maggie followed the trail of blood to the junk room door. She knocked.

"Erica, it's Maggie. It's clear, you want to open up?"

"Okay, hang on," Erica said through the door.

"Who's that?" Justin asked.

"Someone who can explain how only one person did all this," Maggie said.

Erica opened the door. She looked like she was on the wrong side of an adrenaline rush.

"Hi," she said. Then she hugged Maggie for a few seconds. "Sorry I...I borrowed someone's gun, I probably wasn't supposed to do that."

"It's fine. This is Justin Axelrod, he's the Special Agent in... he's my boss. Justin, this is Dr. Erica Smalls."

"Oh hi," she said.

"Hello, sorry, excuse me for a minute," Justin said, holding up his cell phone.

Erica turned to Maggie, while Justin stepped away to take the call.

"I heard what you were saying. You're right; she hit the jail to kill that Bernard person, she told me so. Then she came here for this."

Erica held up a black rectangle.

"Is that part of his suit?" Maggie asked.

"Yep. I know why she wanted it, too."

"What's it do?"

"That's complicated. But if we can figure out how to mimic it, we can stop her."

"Okay, the paramedics are downstairs," Justin said, hanging up. "And Jenks is dead. I just got confirmation. You said this person is connected to Borowitz, are you a hundred percent on that?"

"I am," Maggie said.

"Okay. You're leaving town, now. Go interview him."

"We've already tried that," Maggie said, "and I have too much to do here."

"*You* didn't try it. He'll talk to you, we know this. We can cover things until you get back."

"Justin, the whole city's gone to hell. My place has to be here at least until the smoke clears."

"I understand," he said. "But believe it or not, we have other competent people working here. It's two days, and it's an order."

She sighed.

"There's a lot you don't understand. The file. I'll get you the file, ask..."

She caught herself, because the next thing out of her mouth was going to be *ask Dave*, and he was still missing.

"If you're going to stop the person who did this," Maggie said, "you are going to need an education on some things that you'll have trouble believing, okay?"

"I'm sure," he said. "But Dr. Smalls here can explain everything, right?"

"I'll need a few hours," Erica said.

"I'll make time. It'll be fine Maggie. We can run this without you for a couple of days, but I can't get anything out of Nick Borowitz. You know it makes sense. And...I promise, as soon as Corrigan is awake, you'll be the first to know."

Maggie turned away for a second, because she didn't want it to be about that. It *was*, but she didn't want it to be. She probably could have left to talk to Nick before, but she didn't like the idea of being out of town when Corrigan's condition changed, in either direction.

"I'll get my go-bag," she said. All the clothes in her go-bag had been worn at least twice, because she never seemed to find time to go home and get a change of clothes, but she was pretty sure nobody at the prison was going to mull over the cleanliness of her appearance.

"Sorry," Justin said, before she was out of earshot. "I forgot. There was more news from the jail. Joe and David...you probably knew this already, but they didn't make it."

That felt like getting punched in the chest. In the past ninety minutes, Maggie had gone from being afraid that she'd accidentally put Corrigan's life in danger, to nearly getting her civilian consultant killed. She had almost completely forgotten about Dave and Joe.

"That thing in your hand," Maggie said, to Erica. "What's it do?"

"I'll need some time to explain," she said.

"But we can kill her with it?"

"Yeah. Yeah, I think so."

"Good. I'm looking forward to that."

The entire world was fuzzy.

At first, it was something that really bothered Corrigan, but after a few...hours? Days? Weeks? He'd gotten used to it. Now, he hardly even questioned it anymore. It was just a fact: the world was fuzzy, and that was all.

What he questioned instead was the word *now*. To say that *now*, the world was fuzzy was to tacitly accept that the *now* he was currently experiencing aligned with the commonly held understanding of the term.

He ruminated on the word *now* a distressingly long time. Well over a decade, at least, back before the world became manifestly fuzzy, when time adhered to some basic commonly agreed-upon standard. Corrigan had a sliding *now*. Usually, his *now* hovered near the edge of everyone else's, such that he could see the popular present from where he was.

He thought about *that* present—when he thought of it at all—as where he left his body, because stuff that happened to his body in that present was more or less irreversible, whereas all of his other *nows* could be altered. They weren't chiseled in stone. They were imprecise. They were fuzzy.

Corrigan couldn't figure out where he left his body, and that was a problem. He kept wandering around the fuzzy world, expecting a clue to be forthcoming, but nothing came.

He was beginning to wonder if something had happened to his body that he either didn't know about, or used to know but could no longer remember.

It's not fuzzy, he thought. *It's imprecise.*

It was something he had to keep reminding himself. For some reason (there was a reason, he didn't know the reason but there was a reason) he was walking around in his own future. That was what this fuzzy world was.

He used to visit the near-future all the time, in his sleep, when he was working as a fixer full-time. The problem had been that he didn't know he was doing it, so when he woke up with a specific location in his head, and then visited that location, he ended up in a position to save someone. He interpreted the appointments as messages from "the universe", which was what one said when not wishing to invoke a particular deity.

It was all him, though, looking at where he was going to be the following day and reporting back to himself.

The fact that this was circular logic never bothered him all that much, because it was a complicated problem, and he hated complicated problems. It was why when he first met Archie Calvin—an MIT professor who happened to be extremely good at working out complicated problems—he was happy to share what he knew and let the professor work out what it all meant.

It became a less pleasant relationship later, but he and Archibald did eventually break bread and settle things.

He was thinking of Calvin at this moment, the fuzzy world of the current *now* he was stuck in, because it would have been a good idea to have someone around who liked complicated things, if only to tell Corrigan why he was there and how to get back.

He'd already arrived at the conclusion that he was not asleep. He never spent this much time in the fuzzy future before, and that was definitely not a good sign. Granted, a comprehensive understanding of the passage of time was essentially impossible, in this place, but it *felt* like this was much longer than it should have been, and that was good enough.

If not asleep, he didn't know what his other options were. Probably not dead. If he were dead, he'd have to re-examine his interpretation of what the fuzzy future actually was, since he couldn't very well be wandering around in his own future if he had no future.

That left *coma* as the best guess. He decided that was probably it, but then balked at fully accepting this explanation, because he couldn't recall entering into a circumstance where a coma was a feasible consequence. An accident, surely, except that he was maybe better than anyone on the planet at avoiding accidents.

Leave it alone, he thought.

He was walking along a street, somewhere in downtown Boston. He couldn't tell where, because according to his own future, it was not at all certain he would end up standing there at all. This was something he'd worked out only recently: sometimes, he could see buildings and street signs perfectly well, and it was everything else—people, cars, etc.—that was fuzzy. Other times, everything was. Corrigan figured since it was unlikely for the physical architecture of the city to have, as a whole, such an uncertain future, the only way it made sense for it to be fuzzy was that the likelihood of him standing there was low.

But that wasn't the most interesting thing he'd worked out, in his mini-vacation in the fuzzy future. He might have also come up with an explanation to the circular logic that didn't bother him in the first place.

He noticed, while standing on a far more distinct street in another part of town, that certain things were *slightly* less fuzzy, meaning they were more likely to happen. Every now and then, these slightly-less-fuzzy, slightly-more-certain events involved someone getting hurt. And when *that* happened, Corrigan heard it very clearly.

The fuzzy future wasn't just a visual murk: there were sounds, and smells too. Auditory fuzziness sounded like white noise that rose and fell somewhat like the tide, if the tide had no pattern to it. The more certain something was, the easier it was to pick out real words (fuzzy words were an alphabet soup of nonsense), and those real words were typically very loud.

Future-walking Corrigan didn't need to walk all over the city looking for accidents before they happened; he just had to listen for them.

Corrigan was pretty proud of himself for having figured this complicated thing out, even though all he was really doing was finding words to explain something he'd clearly been instinctively aware of for years. He thought maybe the next time he spoke to Calvin, he'd tell him about it. This was an exceedingly optimistic thought, because Archie Calvin's fading health had, of late, kept all visitors away, and also because Corrigan didn't think he'd ever find his way out of the fuzzy world to have that conversation.

That answer didn't really explain why he hardly ever managed to stop deliberate acts of violence, unless it was true that most deliberate acts of violence had hardly any screaming.

"Kora-gan-see."

The voice floated above the white noise, as crisp and clear as a slap in the face. Corrigan spun around, because it seemed as if it had come from behind him.

There wasn't anyone there. Well, that wasn't fully accurate; there were two-dozen semi-people there, but all of them were so indistinct that it seemed unlikely any were capable of speaking with such clarity. Even if what they said was weird, and almost gibberish.

I've been called that before, he thought. But he couldn't remember when, or by whom.

"I need to focus," he said, aloud. He heard his own voice clearly, and didn't know if that meant something or not. Two of the blurry humanoids looked at him when he spoke, and then continued on their way down the sidewalk.

I am in the future, he reminded himself. He wasn't a ghost, and he wasn't spirit-walking, or whatever. He hadn't left his body; he'd jumped ahead to where his body *might* be, in however many hours, days or weeks from the present he happened to be standing. He had to get a hold of this, and find his way back again, because he didn't know what would happen if his consciousness was in one of his possible futures while the present-tense version of his body died, and he wasn't nearly curious enough to find out.

I'm in the future and I've wandered into a place I'm not likely to be, he thought. *I have to find out where I'm more likely to be. That's where I'll find myself.*

He reached the corner of a busy street. He couldn't tell which one, but when he looked left and right he could see some distance, so it was probably a major tributary, since hardly any Boston street went straight for more than a block or two.

Everything to the right was louder. When he stood still and stared in that direction for a while, it seemed as if the buildings along there were...crisper, somehow. He headed in that direction.

"Kora-gan-see waken."

It was the voice again. The people around Corrigan were becoming more distinct as he walked, and the white noise of the neighborhood was clarifying into clearly identifiable noises with directionality. Which was why this time, Corrigan was pretty sure whoever said that wasn't around him. It was coming from somewhere else.

"Who are you?" he said out loud.

A blurry man stopped in front of him.

"I-buh-you-hablyee-suhsuh-buddy-la," the man said, which didn't mean anything. Or rather, he said seven or eight things—all of which, on their own, meant something—but at the same time. Then he brushed past Corrigan and headed down the street.

The gibberish was a good sign that he was heading in the right direction, Corrigan decided.

It was evident that even if he could hear the phantom speaker that kept calling him *Kora-gan-see*, the communication wasn't two-way; he should stop trying to talk back. Maybe if he could remember who called him that, it would help explain who belonged to this voice, but that was one of several things he should have remembered by now, and couldn't.

Another block down the street and the buildings started to come into focus. He was heading in the direction of greater likelihood. One of the things now in focus was a street sign: he was on Massachusetts Avenue.

Ordinarily, this would be useful information, but Mass Ave went from South Boston to Lexington; it was possibly the longest uninterrupted non-highway in the entire commonwealth. Knowing he was on it was about as helpful as knowing he was still in the city.

What he really needed to know was what part of Mass Ave he was on, and after another two blocks he did. Up ahead, the largest building he could see was also the one that was the most in-focus.

It was the hospital.

There was a dull pain in his stomach that either wasn't there before, or was there but he had simply been ignoring.

No, that wasn't it. He was getting closer to his present, and in the present, his stomach hurt. It hurt less, or not at all, in the future. He wasn't just walking through the geographic space occupied by the future-state version of Boston; he was traveling backwards in his own timeline.

Probably. He decided he didn't want to understand it any better than that, so he balled up the whole idea and shoved it back in the box in his head, where he kept annoyingly complicated things.

"I was shot," he said. The memory rushed back suddenly, and brought with it a sharper pain in his abdomen. Two of the people on the sidewalk stopped to address his revelation, delivered a couple of gibberish sentences, and then gave him wide berth.

He crossed two more intersections, getting closer to the hospital with each step. The pain was becoming more difficult to ignore, because he was heading toward it. This perhaps explained how he ended up lost in the fuzzy future in the first place; he was escaping the pain.

He came to a stop when he reached the front entrance of the hospital, because the entrance was in nearly perfect clarity, and that was jarring after all the fuzzy-walking he'd been doing. He blinked a couple of times, and then, arrestingly, was no longer on the outside looking in. He was in the lobby, and coming out.

The pain in his abdomen had crested into a constant ache, dulled by medication that also made him feel sluggish. He was in a wheelchair, and being met outside by four police officers, at the curb, next to an armored van.

"Are you sure/up/this/okay/for/you?"

A woman asked him this. She was pushing the wheelchair. It wasn't Maggie; he thought he recognized her, but couldn't recall from where.

Future-him thought the answer to this question was, yes, he was sure.

They pushed out through the front doors. It was nighttime, suddenly. Corrigan wasn't sure how that happened, but at this point he was a passenger, so he put it in the box with everything else.

The cops—he didn't recognize any of them—looked extremely concerned about the best way to get Corrigan into the van waiting at the curb. They were sweeping the courtyard, guns out, which was the sort of thing one saw on television all the time and hardly ever in real life.

When Corrigan and the woman pushing the wheelchair got through the doors, he stood, and started walking to the van under his own power. His legs had that familiar ache of disuse, as if he'd been in the chair for a month. It also felt like someone had sewn his belly-button to his ribcage.

Stitches, he thought. *Gunshot. Surgery. Hospital.*

He only got three steps before there was a loud BANG, and one of the officers went down. Someone was shooting at them. The remaining officers split between trying to get him back inside and responding to the threat, and at first it seemed to

Corrigan as if there were suddenly twice as many cops in the courtyard as before. That wasn't it: their futures split.

The whole area in front of the hospital erupted into a blur of possible actions, Corrigan included. In one, he shoved the girl with him back inside. In another, they both went in. In a third, they made for the van, whose doors had opened.

Amidst all of this, a figure emerged. She was a brown-haired woman, shorter than Corrigan, dressed in a cop uniform but clearly not a cop. She had a bandage on her right shoulder and a smile on her face. She wasn't moving like anyone else, although it took him a minute to see the difference: she was moving contrary to her own future. This was causing what she should have been doing in the next five seconds to collapse and disappear.

When he saw someone with no future, it usually meant they were either not moving, or they had just died. (The third option was that they were not there, and he was seeing a ghost. He'd never seen a ghost when sleepwalking into his own future, as he was clearly doing at this moment, so he discounted the possibility out-of-hand.) Since the woman with the bandage on her shoulder was neither dead nor not moving, this was something new.

Not new, he thought. *Harvey moved like this too. So do I.*

She dodged two blurry police officers' attempts to subdue her, by shooting one and throat-punching the other. Both were done without the use of her right arm, and yet almost effortlessly.

Then she looked Corrigan in the eye, leveled the gun at his face, and smiled.

"Time to go, boy-scout," she said.

"Kora-gan-see."

Corrigan woke with a start.

He was in a hospital bed, and it was daytime. Sunlight

streamed in through one of the two windows, the other blocked by a shade.

A woman—the same woman who in the future would be pushing him outside in the middle of the night—was sitting in a chair next to the bed, doing something on a computer in her lap. Now he recognized her. She was the hostage. At the Pru. Where he'd gotten himself shot.

Monica something.

She wasn't alone, although it was pretty likely she didn't know it. Sitting in the second chair was a bald man in orange coveralls. He had terrifyingly long fingers, that gave the impression his arms were actually what was too long, and his mouth was larger than it should have been. Corrigan knew—but couldn't at this moment see—that the mouth was full of shark-like teeth.

It was a Kilroy. And it already knew Corrigan was awake.

"Oh, hello there!" Monica said.

Corrigan didn't answer. He was too busy trying to confirm that he actually *was* awake—a reasonable concern under the circumstances—and whether he was seeing what he thought he was seeing.

The Kilroy in the room was messing with his head. Monica whatever-her-last-name-was, made for an excellent lighthouse, notifying Corrigan of where the present was. He'd heard her greeting quite clearly, twice, with the second one signifying where the present was. That was good. Also, he *only* heard it twice, which indicated his perception wasn't muddled. When things got bad, her three words, spoken only once, would have been jumbled from repetition, across her five-second timeline.

The Kilroy, meanwhile, lived on the other end, in the near

future. Seeing it in the chair sent Corrigan's heart rate soaring, which, thanks to the device he was hooked up to, was something Monica—and probably a nurse somewhere—now knew. The last time he saw a Kilroy, the creature was actively interested in murdering not just Corrigan, but everyone else too; Corrigan's pulse jumped because he thought he was going to have to defend himself.

It didn't appear to be a threat to Monica, which made some measure of sense. The last Kilroy wanted to kill anyone with a proven capacity to see it. The only ones who did this were the MIT team of scientists, of whom Erica Smalls was the last remaining member, and Corrigan himself. Whereas Monica had no idea she was sharing the room with a monster.

Corrigan didn't know why the Kilroy was there, but he also didn't know why Monica was there. He'd never really speculated on what he might expect upon waking up in a hospital room, because that's not the kind of thing one game-plans for, but now that he'd done it, he realized he was expecting, at minimum, Maggie Trent by his bedside. Or his mother. A face, anyway, more familiar than that of Monica...*Devereaux*, he remembered.

According to Ms. Deveraux's website and her many appearances on television, Corrigan saved her life once, and she'd been kind-of-stalking him ever since. He was faintly amused to discover that he was some kind of Boston cryptid all these years, although he couldn't actually recall saving Monica's life. He figured she'd changed her hair since, or something.

"Yes, hello," he said. Then he said it again, to make sure he addressed her in the correct time-frame.

"I'm so everybody glad Monica hi I'll tell them."

She couldn't decide what to say first, so her future was all over the place. To Corrigan, she said half of three different things at once. He decided maybe his head wasn't as clear as he'd thought at first.

"You're Monica," he said. "And you want to tell them I'm awake."

"Monica so long Dev I've been you saved Devereaux right I'll."

"I'm awake," he repeated. "And you should tell them I'm awake."

He wanted to go back to sleep, frankly. This was exhausting enough.

The Kilroy got to its feet, which just made matters worse. In Monica's uncertain future, she would be leaving the room, and the Kilroy would be occupying the space by the bed at which she was currently (possibly currently) standing, but from Corrigan's perspective they were there at the same time, turning the two of them into a foggy hybrid that was a little terrifying. He wondered if he was healthy enough to get out of the bed and defend himself if it came to that, and decided probably not.

Then Monica left the room, and things got much easier, because the Kilroy had no uncertain future making everything blurry, and he was easy to concentrate on. The downside was that it meant Corrigan was on the wrong side of Professor Calvin's chronoton.

"Kora-gan-see," he said.

It was hard to tell, because the face of the Kilroy was so alien, but he seemed almost placid. Corrigan stopped worrying so much about his inability to defend himself. Besides, he was unconscious until a few minutes ago. If this thing wanted him dead, there was no power on the planet capable of stopping him.

"Yes," Corrigan said.

Corrigan's understanding was that the word 'see' in the title the Kilroys gave him was literal: he could see them, and therefore he was a 'see'. In the linguistic soup of bastard English that they used, it made as much sense as anything.

It wasn't really the seeing that caused them distress, as existentially interesting as that idea happened to be. Corrigan could both see and alter the future, and manifest alterations caused them pain. The one time he was on their end of the timeline when such a manifest change transpired, it caused *him* pain too, so he could almost understand.

"Kora-gan-see," it repeated, this time while pointing at Corrigan with one of those alarmingly long fingers. Then it tapped its own chest. "Kilroy-prime."

"It's nice to meet you, Kilroy Prime."

He tried raising his arm to shake hands with the Kilroy, which was a tremendously bad idea all around. His arm was tethered to the bed because of the IV attached to it, and the Kilroy's fingers ended in sharp claws. Shaking his hand would probably result in a severed artery or something.

They didn't shake. Kilroy Prime nodded its head to acknowledge the greeting.

"What are you doing here?" Corrigan asked.

"Kora-gan-see-fix."

"Fix?"

"Fixer-fix."

"Corrigan is a...I called myself a fixer, yes. I fixed the future. It was my job, sort of."

"Kora-gan-see-fix. Fix."

This is going nowhere, he thought.

"Look, you can keep saying that word if you want, but you have to say other words too, or I'm not going to understand."

"Fix-see."

"Yeah, I don't..."

Monica's re-entry was telegraphed by the Kilroy, who could see into the hallway. She was about to come in with a woman Corrigan recognized as an FBI agent, from Maggie's team.

"Help-fix-see," the Kilroy said. Then he stepped back and let the two women enter. Corrigan flat-out didn't understand anything they said to him, because he was firmly focused in the future and they were talking over each other all the way down the timeline. He waited until the Kilroy left the room, and then tried to recalibrate.

"Stop talking," he said, to both of them. "Just for a minute. Then you can tell me everything."

CHAPTER SIXTEEN

The FBI has, so far, released photos of exactly one person. Call me crazy, but unless this woman conducted two high-profile attacks on these facilities all by herself, there's something they're not telling us...

...no, I don't imagine what it could be.

—Counterterrorism expert Jacob Clark,
CNN live coverage

Maggie got the news that Corrigan was awake, just as she climbed aboard the helicopter that took her to Hanscom. That was where the military plane, which then took her to Lee County, Virginia, was taking off from. It was the only way out of town; all commercial air travel to and from Boston had been shut down.

She wasn't in a position to turn around. As it was, her travel arrangements—including making certain she got in to see Nick immediately, rather than in the 'several days' the prison initially insisted on—practically required an act of Congress to secure.

Tearing all of that up so she could visit Corrigan, who wasn't going anywhere, wouldn't be well-received.

Justin promised to put Corrigan on the phone when he could, and since he had the good sense to sound apologetic about demanding Maggie leave town in the first place, she thought she could hold him to that.

She kept getting updates of the situation on the ground, while en route. In addition to Joe, Dave, and Bernard Jenks, the assault on the Suffolk County Jail killed thirteen deputies and wounded seventeen more. There were also three dead and two wounded at Boston FBI headquarters. That body count would no doubt have been higher had the place not been nearly empty at the time. It would also have been higher by at least one civilian life, had Erica Smalls not proven to be extremely resourceful in a time of crisis.

If Maggie hadn't moved members of her team to the hospital to guard Corrigan against an attack that never came, they might have been among dead. It was ultimately a happy accident: by ordering them into what she thought was the line of fire, she was actually taking them out of it. This didn't mean Justin wasn't slightly uncomfortable with the process resulting in that decision. He hadn't said so, but he probably thought had there been more people in the office, Sheila would have been stopped, and they wouldn't be closing down the Eastern Seaboard to get her into custody now.

But there would be video of what happened at the jail. He would reconsider, once he saw.

There was a loud buzzing, as the gate she was standing in front of slid open, and allowed her and her FBP escort to step into the next room. Getting into the penitentiary was like

clearing dull trials in the most boring version of Dungeons &
Dragons imaginable. Every section had a desk behind bars, with
a person at the desk who wanted to see your papers, and your
ID, and for you to answer some questions. She'd checked her
weapons already at one desk, and gotten patted down at
another, and thought maybe this next one would have a blood
test or a current events quiz.

She'd been through all of it before, because this was not the
first time she'd been to the prison for an interview with Nick
Borowitz. It was, however, the first time she'd arrived with something that might get him talking.

The process was a little like what it took to get in to see
Bernard Jenks, she thought. This was probably her mind trying
to find a way back to David and Joe's final hours, because for
some reason Maggie couldn't stop thinking about that. It wasn't
just that she should have been there instead of Dave, although
that didn't help. Theirs were the personal faces she could put on
a tragedy that was otherwise too monstrous to grasp.

It wasn't true, anyway. Lee Penitentiary was a super-max, and
Suffolk County jail wasn't. What Sheila did at the jail was impossible for anyone who wasn't like her; pulling off the same thing
at the prison was impossible, period.

Probably, she thought.

The guy at the third desk asked for her name, ID, and paperwork, so she slid them across. Then he asked who she was there
to see.

"Oh," he said. "You're from Boston, huh? We got word to
expect you."

She just nodded, and waited for him to clear her to move on.
He looked like he was ready to have a much longer conversation,
before deciding this wasn't the time.

Maggie had checked in twice with the office already since
landing. Maybe the only good news, at the end of this long day

—it was nearly 10 PM—was that Sheila hadn't turned up anywhere else with murder on her mind.

The first press conference happened while Maggie was in the air; a photo was shared, and the tip lines were opened, to see if anyone knew of Sheila's whereabouts. It was the same as one of the photos Maggie had with her—a still shot pulled from the security cameras at the jail. They were showing the same photo to a lot of paramedics and emergency room employees at the same time, in the hope that Sheila sought medical aid after the gunshot.

The hospitals were a dead-end so far, and the police tip line had exploded, but with no good leads.

It's early, she reminded herself.

Besides, she wasn't positive she wanted Sheila found, not yet, not unless it was dead somewhere in an alley after having succumbing to blood loss. Otherwise, if they wanted to stop her, they were going to need a fixer, and Corrigan wasn't ready yet.

The next door buzzed.

"You can go on," the guy in the cage said. "Room twelve."

He handed back her papers and ID, and waved toward the door helpfully.

Her FBP escort—his name was Clint, and that was all she knew about him—led the way to room twelve. He cleared the room first for her, then brought her in, to sit at a steel table that was bolted to the floor. There was only one other door in the room, on the opposite end, which opened as soon as she took her seat, and the door she came in through was closed by Clint from the outside.

Two guards entered, with Borowitz between them. He was leg irons and handcuffs, and all of it was chained together, so he couldn't walk; he could only shuffle.

Nick Borowitz was a handsome man with blue eyes and a

disarming smile. So handsome was he, the first time his picture appeared in the papers, he started getting fan mail.

From what Maggie had been told, the fan mail deluge never stopped, even after the trial. There was a man at the penitentiary whose job it was to screen all of the mail before Nick got to see it, but there was far more mail than could be screened adequately by one man, so most of what he received was sitting in boxes, somewhere in the building. On the list of things Maggie expected to accomplish: collect all the unopened mail and send it to Quantico, where recruits with free time could go through everything, to check for communications from Sheila.

She'd probably have to get the opened mail too, but that might take more doing, unless Nick felt like handing it over.

Nick smiled when he saw her at the table. He had a natural charisma. It was easy to see how he could convince a certain kind of person to commit acts of terrorism in the name of *A Cause*. Which was why he became the target of Maggie's investigation fairly early on, and also why once he was caught, there was a strong push to close the investigation.

Maggie had misgivings then, but she couldn't express them in a way anyone above her found compelling. Now, of course, everyone wanted to know why she closed the investigation when there was clearly more to it.

There were too many things about the case that just never made sense. Nick was a California guy, who looked like he was born to have his picture taken next to a surfboard on a beach somewhere. He, and a small gathering of friends, assembled what could charitably be called an environmental activism group, whose initial foray into the public consciousness consisted of petitions and loud appearances at town councils in various parts of the state. There was a distressingly long list of things they were against, and none of it was a secret because they also had a website.

They were also incredibly harmless; doing the kinds of things bored upper-middle class white kids did with their time when they hit their twenties. Really, the only threatening aspect of the group was the name they went by: The Environmental Justice Fighters, or EJF. Like a lot of these groups, it was a hyperbolic title, adopting the language of violence while supporting non-violent protestation. Of course, once the EJF became associated with actual acts of terror, the media *loved* the name.

The violence was confounding. At some point in the evolution of the EJF, the group transformed from a collection of like-minded kids worried about beach erosion, to a cult of personality orbiting Nick Borowitz, and later just a cult, period. That tipping point—when they went from passing out pamphlets to doling out explosives—was the subject of an entire psych department in the FBI, because nobody quite understood it. There were thousands of small groups that looked just like the EJF, but none of them took the same turn, and everyone wanted to know what happened differently this time.

But, the facts were clear enough, even if the motives—and the development of those motives—were not. Pretty, charismatic Nick recruited a lonely, disgruntled army officer named Sharon Ledo. Sharon had access to military-grade weapons and explosives.

There was another grey area here, because nobody had figured out yet how Sharon was able to use that access to get as much C-4 off the base as she had. Her access could put her in the room with a tremendous quantity of it, but that wasn't the same thing as being able to walk off the base with a supply, and yet that was what she did, despite the ample security measured in place to prevent any such thing.

After that, and after Ledo went AWOL but before anyone noticed the missing C-4, bombs started turning up, first in random spots—like the one under the bridge that first got Maggie's attention—and later at some government buildings, which changed the dynamic of the threat significantly.

This was another element of the story that never made a lot of sense. After he was arrested, Nick went to great lengths to justify their actions in the context of their stated interest in the environment, but even if one allowed for the possibility that he was deeply unstable, it didn't make a lot of sense. He argued that the only way to save the environment was to topple the United States government, and sure, that was an argument to be made in the abstract, but the execution of that plan was rather dubious. Even arguing that it might be possible to topple the entire government with some well-placed bombs, their list of targets was strikingly random.

In the early days of Nick and Sharon's terror campaign, the randomness of the targets was their biggest ally. The EJF-connected bomb that caused Maggie's local case to turn into a nationwide investigation was the one received by a federal judge in Tallahassee. It didn't go off until it had already been placed safely in the bomb squad's iron drum, and the judge was fine. The second was at the home of a postal inspector in rural Ohio. That one did go off, destroying the house and killing him, his wife, and the family dog. It was initially attributed to a gas leak, and not connected to EJF until much later. Even if it had been recognized as a bomb right off, associating it with the event in Tallahassee would have taken a remarkable leap.

The EJF also had a habit of not taking credit for their bombs, even after another three turned up (in Dearborn, Providence, and Albany.) By then nine deaths could be attributed to the group, and Maggie finally managed to convince her superiors that there was a terrorist group operating inside the United

States, and that group was annoyingly declining to take credit for their actions.

This was another reason the EJF evaded capture for longer than they probably should have. Bombs and an at least semi-coherent message are recruitment tools for terrorists. Their behavior fit the pattern of a serial bomber, not a team of environmentally conscious anarchists.

It was thus the case that Maggie Trent knew just about all there was to know about the apparent charismatic leader of this little group, Nick Borowitz, long before anyone else. She remembered running through all of the likely reactions she would get from Nick after she apprehended him—assuming they were able to take him alive—and hoped that one of those reactions would include a nominal explanation of what he thought he was doing with all of this. When the day did arrive, and Nick and Sharon were taken into custody, his response was oddly underwhelming.

He didn't react like a fanatic. He didn't react much at all, actually. Maggie couldn't even put words to his emotional response until later, after he'd been put in the back of the police van.

It was relief. That was his reaction.

The guards sat Nick down, looped his chains through a bolt on the floor and a second on the table, and then left the room.

"Hi, Nick," Maggie said. "You're looking good."

"No, I'm not," he said, "but thanks for saying so."

His right eye was a little swollen, and his lip was cut. His hair was trimmed short in the way a barber with clippers and no professional training might do it. It looked like he hadn't been eating much, and had seen very little sunlight. But, his blue eyes were just as blue and his smile no less brilliant.

She pulled her phone out, set it to record, and put it between them. Then she read off the time and date and identified the two people in the room, for whoever transcribed it later.

"So, what can I do for you?" he asked.

"Have you been watching the news?"

"Not really. Why, did something happen?"

He was grinning as he said it.

"Right," she said.

Maggie opened the Manila folder that had been inspected by three different sets of guards, and slid one of the photos across the table..

"Who is she, Nick?" she asked.

He picked up the picture with his shackled hands and looked at it for a few seconds.

"Not a great angle, huh?" he said.

"She didn't pose for us, no."

"Is that a guard uniform?"

"Nick."

"I mean, it looks like there's a name tag there."

Maggie pushed across the other two photos, which weren't a whole lot better.

"I don't know who she is," Nick said.

"C'mon."

"No, no, you don't understand. I'm not going to do that thing where we go back and forth and I play coy about not knowing her, and you dangling some kind of concession. I know I'm not getting out of here. I mean, I don't know who she *really* is. She killed Bernard, didn't she?"

The fact that the siege on the jail was conducted with the ultimate aim of killing one of its occupants had not been disclosed to the media. It would be eventually—sometime before Bernard's trial date, it was going to have to come out that he was no longer alive—but there was still a lid on that information.

"Yes," Maggie said. "And we think you might be next."

Nick laughed.

"No, you don't," he said.

"No, we really don't. We don't know anything right now, because nothing she's done has made sense. Look, you obviously *do* know who she is. Why don't you give me something?"

"Like I said, I don't know who she is, or where she came from. I'm not saying that to be unhelpful; she just never provided a background story any of us was prepared to believe. But that was normal, you know? We were all using nicknames at the start. Back in Cali, I mean."

"She was with you back then?"

It had been eight years since the Environmental Justice Fighters was founded. They only turned to violence in the final three years.

"Not *that* far," Nick said. "But yeah, when we were still, you know. Granola."

"Sure."

"First time she and Bernard started coming 'round, she said to call her Shiva, and we were all, cool, that's how you identify. He was calling himself...Sundance, I think. I forget. But eventually, we got his real name. We never got hers. Not that it matters, right? You need an origin story, I think, and Shiva doesn't have one of those."

"You don't think that's her real name?"

"I mean, maybe. It's a little on-the-nose, though, right? Destroyer-god and all that."

"How about Sheila?" Maggie asked. "That's the name she gave us."

"Sure. It's pretty close to the same thing. Yeah. Yeah. That seems like something she'd do."

He tapped the image from the video feed.

"You watched this, right?" he asked.

"I haven't had a chance to see the video, no."

"Then you don't really know what she can do."

"I don't need to watch," she said. "I already know."

"No you don't. It's not...nobody who doesn't see her in action can understand what she's capable of. Not really. This is next-level."

Maggie leaned back and took in the entirety of the man before her.

Even when he was beaten and bruised, as he was now, Nick had a certain master-of-the-universe confidence that was impossible to ignore. When he went to trial, and talked about all the crimes of the EJF, it was with pride. He gave the impression that these things were done in his name, by worshippers who loved him. It was a neat trick that she didn't entirely buy into, even if everyone else appeared to. His silver tongue and good looks supposedly talked a dozen trust-fund kids to live a criminal life on the run in the name of a barely coherent philosophy. He convinced Sharon to abandon everything in the name of the same cause. They committed murder for him, a blue-eyed blond-haired Charlie Manson.

And up until this moment, at the table, Maggie assumed whatever Sheila/Shiva was doing, it was done in Nick's name, whether he actually told her to do it or not.

But that wasn't right at all. She had it exactly backwards.

"You're afraid of her," Maggie said.

"Oh, absolutely."

"Is that why you're being so forthright now? Because it would have been great if you mentioned her earlier."

"I can only talk about her because she's already been outed, and not by me."

He held the photo up in his shackled hands.

"This was her coming-out party," he said. "She could've left Bernard to take the rap. *We* already knew what she was capable of, right? Now, Shiva wants *you* to know, and it's not gonna matter what I give up; she'll do what she wants and then disappear. If you haven't already figured that out, now I'm telling you. She can't be stopped, Maggie, and truth is, I'm glad I'm in here and not out there."

Maggie nodded.

"Shiva, then," she said. "Don't suppose she gave you a last name?"

"Yeah, actually."

"Really?"

"I didn't take it seriously. Seemed like it was just some kind of weird joke with her that I wasn't in on, because it didn't match the first name she was giving us, at all. Kinda matches Sheila, though, so now I'm wondering if she was being honest with me that one time. I mean, it's possible."

"What was it?"

"It was, um, something Irish...and Sheila is Scottish, right? I used to know this kinda thing. That's why I'm wondering now... because Shiva, that's Indian, doesn't go right with an Irish surname, you know?"

"Nick..."

"Sorry, I'm trying to remember...Yeah. Corrigan. Pretty sure that's what she said."

Maggie had been interrogating suspects off and on for nearly her entire adult life. She was highly skilled at not reacting to the information she was being provided. In this moment, she was pretty positive she failed.

"Shiva Corrigan," Maggie said. "That's what she said her name was."

"Yeah, or Sheila Corrigan. That sounds like a real name. Do you recognize it?"

"I've heard the name before."

She reminded herself that Nick probably had enough access to the news to have come across the name Corrigan Bain at least a few times by now, and he could therefore be screwing with her.

The problem was that it made sense. Corrigan's first name was his father's surname. Someone turning up with the same surname and the same skillset was too impossible to be a coincidence. But for Nick to have made that up, he'd have to know Corrigan's family history first.

"So," she said, trying to get back to the questions, "Bernard joined at the same time as Sheila?"

"That's right."

"And this was when?"

Nick smirked.

"Sorry, Maggie, I'm thinking about how this is going to sound."

"It sounds however it sounds. Just talk."

"Thing is, you're gonna lose the audience if I keep going. I won't even be in the room, and I can hear them. They'll say I'm doing this to get out of here or...well, shit, I don't know. If I was talking to anyone other than you, I wouldn't keep going."

"Nick, if you *don't* keep talking, I'm going to strangle you."

"Fine. Patsy."

"What?"

"That's what I'm gonna say next. I'm a fall-guy, a patsy, the guy set up to take the blame."

Maggie sat back, stared at the ceiling for several seconds, considered turning off the audio recording and going back to Boston with "Shiva Corrigan" as a starting point, and then reminded herself he was at least giving some real answers for a change.

"Who set you up?" she asked. "Sheila and Bernard?"

"Shiva turned up when we were just going around handing out leaflets and all that other crap. Nothing criminal. Well, no, I take that back, one time we heard about a big meeting between oil company execs at this hotel, so we set up a picket line and called in a bomb threat, so the oil guys would have to go outside and hear us. Wrong hotel but, anyway, we did do that. But that was all. She hooked up with us not long after."

"I remember that. That was before Sharon went AWOL."

"I know. This is what I'm saying. The idea to use real bombs, that was all Shiva and Bernard. I didn't want to do any of that, and I told her as much, but...you know what she can do. I didn't think anyone else would go along with it though. I was wrong there. She knew exactly what I should say to get everyone to sign up. And for the record, I didn't even recruit Sharon myself."

"Was Sheila the one to get the explosives off the base?"

"That was Sharon and Bernard. He had this gizmo he would wear when he went out. I think it connected the two of them together. It was some weird high-tech shit. Don't know where that came from."

"All right," Maggie said. She stood up to pace and run through everything she already knew about Nick, to update all of it with this new information. Then she thought about the cigarette she'd be having as soon as she was back outside. "For the record, what you're telling me is that you were an unwilling participant in all of this, and that the real orchestrator of your terrorist cell is this woman you called Shiva."

He laughed.

"I told you this would happen. The skepticism, right? I hear it. But look, I wouldn't say entirely unwilling. I mean, don't knock being a cult leader until you've tried it, right? The sex was pretty good, too."

"You had a sexual relationship with the woman you're so afraid of, you'd rather stay in here than have your sentence commuted? Because she can't get to you?"

"I was getting sex from all over. Shiva was great, though. Really...really great, and the threat of death kind of worked for me."

"Who picked the targets?"

He looked perplexed for a half-second because this was a strong redirect from the sex conversation.

"She did," he said. "Her or Bernard. He was the one conveying the information a lot of the time, but I assumed the orders came from her."

"Did they explain their reasoning?"

"No."

"Did you ever try to work it out yourself?"

"You asked me these questions before," he said. "After the arrest."

She and other members of her team had taken full advantage of the lax regulations regarding the interrogation of a terror suspect, to question him for over twenty-four hours before his lawyer got anywhere near the room. That he never mentioned Shiva or Bernard said a lot about how afraid he was of her.

"I did," Maggie said, "but that was when we'd been led to understand that you picked the targets."

"Well, same answer. If there's an explanation for who she wanted us to kill, I never worked it out. He built all the bombs, by the way."

"I thought Sharon did that."

"She took the fall for it, but it was him. And another thing...I can't prove this, okay? But the ones that didn't go off, I think they didn't go off on purpose."

"The unexploded bombs provided us with the evidence we needed to catch the entire cell," Maggie said. "Are you telling me Sheila wanted that to happen?"

"Draw your own conclusions, agent. To me, it means she really wanted to kill the ones who actually got killed, and only wanted you to think she wanted to kill the other ones, to keep you from figuring out the connection."

She smiled, and nodded, and paced some more.

"That's a very shrewd observation, Nick," she said.

They had, of course, run the biographical information of every victim and near-victim against every other victim and near-victim already. If there was some kind of consonance between sub-groups on those lists, she'd have known about it a long time ago.

That didn't mean it wasn't a good observation, just that he might be drawing the wrong conclusion.

"Sheila took your little group and turned it into a terrorist cell, and you don't know why. She killed or almost killed a hand-selected group of individuals, and you don't know why. She—or Bernard, now—arranged so that the cell would eventually get arrested, and you don't know why."

"That's about right."

"What about the message she sent to the media?"

"I'm not following. What message?"

"After the State House, she issued a statement to the media: *Free them*. We assume she meant you and Sharon."

"Oh, that. I think that was for us. I mean, hold the theme, right, that it's all some big plan I orchestrated, but I'm pretty sure she did that so you guys would send someone to talk to us. I assume Sharon got a visit too."

"She did, yes. You didn't offer anything, then."

"Nah. The agent they sent wasn't half as charming as you."

"Right."

"Plus, that was the point. As soon as I got those details I got the message just fine. See, that wasn't a demand directed at you, it was a threat directed at us."

"You really are safe in here," Maggie said.

He shrugged.

"Sure, as safe as I can be. I mean, if she wants me dead, I'm dead. Just the way it is."

Maggie nodded, and sat back down.

"Look, Nick, I can't get you out of here. You don't want to get out of here anyway, but you know I couldn't make that promise in good faith. But I can get you other things, for being cooperative. How's the food here?"

Nick had been on a Paleo diet when they arrested him. Needless to say, that was no longer the case.

"It's terrible."

"I can help you with that," she said.

"Can you really?"

"It's just a few phone calls. But you have to give me something I can really work with."

"What, I haven't already?"

"Where did she come from, Nick? I know you said you don't know, but you've got to have *something*. You met her for the first time in California, right? Is she from there originally?"

"No, definitely not. Too pale. All right, yeah. I don't think either of them are from this country originally."

"Bernard's last known address was in Quebec," Maggie said. "We knew that."

"Yeah, but no, not Canada. That hardly even counts. Do they have television in Canada?"

"I think probably, yes."

"American TV, and movies. Someone who grew up in Quebec would have a grip on most of your basic pop culture references, right?"

"Nick, I'm not an expert on Canadian cultural norms. What's your point?"

"Shiva didn't. I don't know Bernard too well, but she sounded like she was raised in a cave or something, when it came to that stuff."

"That's pretty thin."

"Oh, and she talked in her sleep one time."

"What did she say?"

"No idea. It wasn't in English. But it also wasn't in French; I know what that sounds like."

"Russian, German, what?"

"I don't know. Honestly, I didn't think about it at all until just now, so I'm a little worried any guess I have will be based on me misremembering it."

"Or she was just babbling in gibberish."

"Yeah, maybe. I don't know."

"All right. Foreign. Not Canada."

"If I think of more, I'll let you know."

"Okay, Nick. Thanks."

She turned off the record button on the phone and slid it off the table.

"I don't think I can get you any Paleo diet food," she said. "But I can try."

"Actually, I'd kill for a burger right now," he said. "I mean, not literally. You understand."

PART THREE

Family Feud

······························

CHAPTER SEVENTEEN

······························

Nobody's heard from @MDevereaux for nearly the same span of time nobody's heard from K. I think we can all agree he's not really dead, so, I mean, it's obvious isn't it?

They ran off together. Right?

—comment from @LooperSuper7, FindTheBostonFixer.com

Erica's impression of what it must be like to be in law enforcement was permanently colored by television shows, which was sort of amazing given how little TV she actually watched. Not just recently—it almost went without saying that she didn't absorb a ton of network programming in her flat in Japan—but for most of her life.

Yet she still had that sense about how things were supposed to go, especially as regards to the *expository meeting*. That was the part in the program where people who knew what was going on would sit down with people who did not yet know what was going on, and exchange information, when the whole point of it was actually to give information to the audience.

Five days after Erica, for the first and hopefully only time in her life, picked up a gun and shot another human being in self-defense, she was in one of those meetings. It was also five days since Corrigan Bain woke up, which was considerably more important, as far as Erica was concerned, because that had to mean this was all nearly over, and she could go back to Japan, where nobody was (probably) trying to kill her. This was in stark contrast to the Boston area, which seemed strangely bent on having her killed.

The people at the table were a lot more interested in what Erica did five days ago than what Corrigan did five days ago, which just seemed weird.

Justin Axelrod put the small rectangular box—the focus of so much of Erica's time for the past five days—in the middle of the table. Justin was the SAIC, which Erica learned (she had to ask) stood for Special Agent in Charge.

"Dr. Smalls," Justin said, "just to level-set everyone here; can you tell us everything you have on this device?"

"Sure," she said, standing. The unnamed agent, manning the laptop/projector combo at the other end of the room, pulled up a Powerpoint presentation Erica slapped together that morning—under protest, because she hated Powerpoint presentations. She'd been forced to present extremely complicated things in this format many times over, during her collegiate career, and found the limitations in text—and over-reliance on visualized points—so constrictive, it was impossible to use Powerpoint without getting something wrong. Some things couldn't be simplified without ending up incorrect.

She would rather have drafted a long text document and told everyone to read it before the meeting. She was pretty sure that would never happen.

The first slide in the Powerpoint began with *a brief summary of the theory of quantized time: the chronoton, and the malleability of the future.*

Erica was really proud of the introductory section, especially for how she managed to use non-technical terms to explain everything. So when Justin stopped her on the third slide, only two minutes in, she was sort of annoyed.

"Everyone, you have access to this deck, which is an excellent deep-dive into the concepts. I think we need to skip ahead, though, if that's all right, Dr. Smalls."

"Of course," she said. It wasn't all right, and she didn't work for him, so she could certainly say as much, but she didn't.

"I think we'd all like to understand how *you* employed this little box, and how we can use it to our advantage."

Erica flashed back on the moment, not so long ago and not so far from where she was now standing, when she came face-to-face with the woman Karen identified as Sheila (or Shiva, depending on who was talking) Corrigan. It was an unwelcome memory that Erica would probably have to deal with at some point, maybe professionally. For now, it was helpful that the memory was fresh, because the details mattered.

"I don't know how we can use it to our advantage," she said. "I can only tell you how I used it."

"And how was that?" he asked.

"I plugged it in."

Justin was an older man, fit, with white hair that was starting to creep back from his forehead. Erica kind of liked him, especially when he smiled in a semi-flirty way, as he was now doing.

"Maybe *more* detail this time," he said. "I appreciate this is all complicated, and you're trying to meet us halfway. Give us a little more."

Maggie rolled her eyes in the tiniest of unintentional micro-expressions, then looked at Erica again.

Boys, she seemed to be saying.

"I plugged it in using an adapter I found in the junk room." Erica said. "Once it was powered up, as long as I held the device Sheila couldn't see what I was *going* to do. She couldn't dodge bullets, basically."

If anyone in the room didn't believe Sheila Corrigan was capable of dodging bullets, it was because they refused to accept the evidence, which included extensive footage from the security cameras in the jail. Patel—sitting next to Maggie and thus far unable to bring himself to make eye contact with Erica since the start of the meeting—had presented all of that already. Erica thought he probably felt guilty for having left Erica alone, even though if he'd been there he would likely be among the dead.

"Why did that work, and how did you know it would?" someone from Justin's end of the long conference room table asked. He'd been introduced, but she couldn't recall his name. He was the only one there in police blue, though, so the commissioner, perhaps.

"That's where it becomes difficult to explain without going through the deck," Erica said, looking at Justin, "but I can try. Can you bring up the apparatus?"

After a few tries, the agent running the projector found the right picture. It was of the exoskeleton, taken after Bernard Jenks had been arrested, but before Erica had begun taking it apart.

"I was brought here to figure out how someone wearing this could...um...do what Corrigan Bain does naturally."

"See the future," Maggie said. "It's okay, Erica, I think we're all past that now."

"Okay. What I told Maggie was that it should have been impossible, without a lot of complicated optical equipment, and what's in this picture isn't that. I was both right and wrong. It's not the same thing, but the device on the table is actually extremely complicated.

"Here's how it was done. There are actually two exoskeletons. There's this one, and there's the one Sheila must have been wearing. They're paired, so if she needs to get Bernard to move, she can move her own arm wherever she is, and get him to move his arm. So far so good, right? But none of that would work if she couldn't see the future *through* the device. Switch to...should be the next picture."

The next image was a close-up of the rectangular device in the middle of the table, from when it was still installed in the suit.

"This part of the apparatus enabled her to do that, but I couldn't figure out how, at first. Um. Okay, let's talk about it like this. I was part of a project, a few years back, where we built something to see into the near future, and it only worked because the near future had a probabilistically high likelihood. Changing the future collapses the probability, which means the future *can't* be seen, which means I can't change it because I can't see what I'm changing. A paradox.

"That's how I've always explained it, but it's not entirely accurate. I can only see what's happening on the other end of the...I'm sorry, I can't do this without using certain words. We called it a chronoton. It's a single particle of time, in the same way a photon is a single particle of light. It's not *really* a particle, but it worked as an explanation because, well, because the same thing is true for energy quanta. Single, indivisible units..."

Justin was holding up his hand.

"Sorry," Erica said.

"It's okay. Just a little slower."

"Right. The paradox is only a paradox for us. Corrigan Bain can change the future, and so can Sheila Corrigan, which means..."

"Can I interrupt, for a second?" a woman named Cindy

asked. Erica recalled her name, but not what she did. "Can anyone explain why her last name is his first name?"

"We think they're probably related," Maggie said. When Cindy's expression indicated this failed to explain things adequately, Maggie added, "Corrigan is the last name of the man who fathered him. He was a soldier, and that was the name on his uniform."

"You're thinking this gift," Cindy said, "or whatever it is, you're thinking it's something inheritable."

"Yeah, until we come up with a better explanation. Go ahead, Erica."

"What I was saying was, we're stuck at one end of the chronoton. We're part of the future, or, or we're stuck inside of it."

There had been math running through Erica's head ever since she worked this out, and she still hadn't had a chance to write it down, which was unfortunate because it was going to end up being important.

"Basically," she continued, "if Sheila was going to have a chance to see the future through Bernard's eyes, she first had to unmoor him from his end of the chronoton."

This was met with several seconds of silence. She was pretty positive she lost everyone.

"But how did that help you?" Justin asked. "When you powered it up?"

"I understand," Patel said. "If Bernard was a part of the future, he couldn't change it."

"Yes," Erica said. "Although he couldn't *see* that future. The apparatus didn't work that way. Only she could see it."

"You worked all of that out while locked in the closet?" Justin asked.

"Not really. I'd been trying to figure it out all day; I'm just better under a deadline."

Patel appeared to be warming up to the entire concept, even

though he still wasn't ready to make eye contact. He leaned forward, excitedly.

"It took Jenks out of the, um, the timeline," he said.

"The chronoton," Erica said.

"Sure. It took him out of that to enable this woman to manipulate the future remotely. When *you* turned it on, it did the same, and that masked your future from her. That's brilliant."

"Thanks, I'm…thanks."

I'm actually very smart, Erica nearly said.

"That seems pretty useful," Justin said. "Maybe we can expand the technology and cover the whole city."

It was a joke, but Erica took it seriously.

"Well, hang on. We know what it does, but I couldn't begin to tell you *how* it does it. I can't even tell you who built it for her."

This was a not-inconsequential point that had already been made at the meeting. One of the things the FBI did, once they understood that there was advanced tech in Bernard's apparatus, was try and determine if any official branch of the United States government had had a hand in building it.

The answer to that inquiry appeared to be no, although Erica didn't entirely trust this conclusion. It seemed to her, there were enough top secret military/CIA/"deep state" whatevers out there for it to be part of a US program that the FBI simply didn't have clearance for. This belief was largely informed by spy thrillers, however.

Erica herself had made a concerted effort to locate any serial numbers or production stamps on the components. She'd also been given permission to share the photos she took with Saito, her engineer at Takani-Ko. He didn't recognize it, and neither did anyone he shared it with. Saito was extremely interested in getting his hands on it, though, which was likely not going to be happening.

The fact that they couldn't properly source the device was a problem all by itself. Bernard's apparatus was only useful as long as Sheila Corrigan was on the other end of the thing, and since Sheila happened to have committed multiple acts of terrorism on U.S. soil, there was a real possibility that the country was under attack from a foreign actor supported by a sovereign nation.

Although a private company could have done it, almost as easily. That didn't make the answer a whole lot easier to take; it just muddied the possible motives somewhat.

The only thing Erica thought was pretty definitively true, was that the rectangular device on the table wasn't something that had been cobbled together in a back room somewhere. It represented a great deal of funding, and a lot of high-end science It wasn't the kind of thing your average terrorist could build from scratch, basically.

All of that meant it made perfect sense for Sheila to want it back.

"What was its function?" the guy who was probably the commissioner asked. "I mean, why was it even necessary? We're missing two people at this table today, my people, because this woman can apparently walk into and out of any building in this city, with impunity, and kill anyone she feels like killing. It's self-evident that she doesn't need advanced technology to accomplish this. I have no idea how that's so, without invoking *magic* as a part of the explanation, but leaving that aside, why did she need it?"

"We think this was a way to weaponize her abilities without putting her in direct danger," Maggie said. "Bernard Jenks was disposable. She proved that herself when she marched into the jail and executed him. Sheila isn't."

"Dr. Smalls, thank you, you can have a seat," Justin said, recognizing that they'd drifted beyond questions she could directly answer. "Maggie, how far have we gotten in terms of motive?"

"We don't have one," she said, "outside of whatever platitudes to anarchy Nick and his people came up with. As far as we've been able to tell, Sheila attached herself to a group she could manipulate, to give her cover for her actions."

"She picked the targets?" Justin asked.

"Yes. But she never explained her reasoning. Understand that the first thing any of us did here, when we realized these bombs were part of the same case, was to try to establish a connection between the targets. We were never able to. I now think that was the point. It's also why we're still facing the same problem. Because we don't know why she did any of this, we don't know what she's going to do next."

"We're back where we started," George said. George was one of the three FBI agents Erica had been handed off to on the day of the attack. He'd barely stuck around for long enough to leave an impression with her. "We're under attack and we don't know why."

"Yes and no," Maggie said. "The string of bombings across the country, perpetrated by the EJF, served one specific purpose: it put all of us in a room for a big, televised event. We interpreted the State House bomb as retribution for having taken down the cell, and that was reinforced when we got the *free them* message, but I think that was just a smokescreen. That bomb was supposed to be the endgame, and Bernard would have been the dead suicide bomber who took the blame for the whole thing."

"What does that say about the Prudential bomb?" Justin asked.

"I think that was specifically to take out Corrigan," Maggie said. "He was the one to foil the State House attack."

"Vengeance, then?"

"Maybe."

"I'm sorry, this isn't making sense to me," Cindy said. Erica decided Cindy definitely didn't work for either the BPD or the FBI, so that had to mean she was a politician or something, since those were the only kinds of people in the room aside from Erica. "Are you suggesting this woman conducted a campaign over three years, that was orchestrated specifically to get high-ranking members of law enforcement into the same room as the deputy mayor of the city? And then to blow them all up? How could she possibly know who was going to be there?"

"We don't know that," Maggie said, "and yes, it's a stretch. It fits the available evidence."

"That isn't good enough," Cindy said. "The entire state government is on house arrest right now because you've got an assassin who can walk through walls. Do you even know if she's still alive?"

"She can't walk through walls," Maggie said. "She didn't turn up in any hospitals, and she's on every watch list there is. It's always possible she fainted from the blood loss and fell in the Charles or something, but right now we can't assume that."

"When can we start assuming that?"

"Cindy," Justin said, "I think we all feel the same way. That's why we're having this meeting, to see if we can come to an understanding. I would love to tell everyone the threat is over, but while she can't walk through walls—like Maggie said—she can do things we're unprepared to deal with. She could be standing on the other side of the conference room door right now, and we wouldn't know it until we opened the door, and that's the real problem. There's only one person we know of who may be capable of facing her on her terms, and he's recovering from a gunshot wound."

Erica wondered if everyone in the room knew all along that Corrigan had survived the gunshot, or if this had been news to one or two of them going in.

"I need something, Justin," Cindy said. "I need something I can bring back to the mayor, or this is going to get complicated. You have no leads at all?"

"We don't know where she is and we don't know what she plans to do next, no," Maggie said. "If we did, we'd have led with that."

"I'm sorry," Erica said. "That isn't entirely true."

She picked the rectangular device up from the middle of the table.

"We know she wants this."

"Given what happens when you turn that on," Justin said, "I would think she'd want to be as far away from it as possible."

"Yes, except she came for it knowing that already. If this was disposable, she wouldn't have risked storming the FBI to get it back."

"Are you suggesting we use it as bait?" Justin asked.

"That's actually a complicated suggestion," Patel said. "She tracked it here, but we don't know how she did it. We can't use it as bait if we don't know how to disable the tracker inside of it, because according to every piece of equipment we have, there is no tracker. It isn't giving off a signal."

Erica was looking at Cindy when Patel said this; her expression was sort of amusing.

"She really *could* be standing outside the door, then," Cindy said. "She could know where that is right now."

"Probably not," Erica said.

She put the box she'd found in the hallway onto the table. The thing had been fingerprinted—it matched the ones Sheila left at the jail, which didn't help since there was no match for them elsewhere—and tested in every way imaginable. Now it was just something Erica carried around with her.

"She used this to track that," Erica said.

"Even though that isn't giving off a signal?" Justin asked. "Just so we're clear."

"That's right," Patel said. "One of these things gives off a signal that doesn't exist, and the other detects the nonexistent signal. We can't get the one to detect the other, which at the moment doesn't mean it isn't giving off a signal. Only that we don't understand how it is, and how it's getting picked up."

"But, she needs this to track that, and she doesn't have this," Erica said.

"We don't know that at all," Cindy said. "She could have another one of those. I get that she's probably not on the other side of the door right now, but if you don't mind, I'd rather I was in a different place than that thing until we've eliminated the threat."

"The point being," the police chief at the other end of the table began, "we know nothing of this woman's agenda, other than that she wants this box, so we should anticipate that need accordingly."

"That isn't all we know," Erica said. It was something at the forefront of an idea that had just occurred to her. She looked at Maggie.

"Corrigan," Erica said. "She also wants Corrigan. You realized this the day of the attacks, when you sent a team to the hospital."

Maggie...blushed. This was an unexpected reaction.

"I don't know about this," Cindy said.

"I had a face-to-face with Sheila," Maggie said. "At the jail. That's in the report. In that conversation, I inadvertently revealed that Corrigan was still alive. When I realized who she was, I sent members of the task force to the hospital, thinking I'd just made him a target. It was...a heat-of-the-moment thing. She came here instead."

"But you had it right," Erica said. "She told me she was

taking care of all the loose ends. Bernard was the first, and she said the box was *another*. Not *the other*. There was more on her list."

"You're jumping to the same conclusion Maggie did," Justin said. "Right or wrong."

"I don't think I am. I think killing Corrigan was supposed to be the next thing. Look at the order of events. Maggie says the plan all along was to blow up everyone at the awards ceremony, on live television. Maybe it was. But the plan changed as soon as Corrigan foiled it. What did she do next?"

"She tried to kill Corrigan," Maggie said. "At the the Pru. Put Corrigan in a position where he has no choice but to take a bullet."

"Exactly. Guys, I think she's marketing a service."

There was a moment of silence, because Erica had just skipped too far ahead.

"Well that's an interesting theory..." Justin began.

"I'll explain."

"I think we can table that for now."

"Let her explain," Maggie said. "Catch us up, Erica."

"It's proof-of-principle," Erica said. "Or, an audition. Imagine you're Sheila, and you're working with this company, and the company is claiming they can provide, I don't know, political assassination on demand. Something like that; it doesn't matter exactly what. But it has to be one-of-a-kind. If we think about this as a service instead of a politically motivated attack...Justin, what do you think it would be worth to the military or, or, the CIA, I guess. I guess this would be them, right? What would it be worth to know they could kill *anyone* in a way that was completely impossible to trace back?"

"That's really...Dr. Smalls, that's well outside the scope of this conversation."

"But we agree that it would be worth a lot, right? What

happens to the value of that service if it can be proven to *not* be one-of-a-kind?"

Everyone was quiet again. Erica couldn't tell if that was a good sign or a bad sign.

"After Corrigan foiled the bombing the first time," she said, "Sheila arranged to put him and Bernard in the same place. If that bomb had gone off, it would have eliminated Corrigan, the evidence trail *still* would have ended with Bernard, and the proprietary technology on the table would have been destroyed along with it. But then Corrigan foiled *that* bombing too, so she started cleaning house. Bernard had to die, she had to recover this box, and..."

"And she has to kill Corrigan," Maggie said.

There was a pause as everyone worked through that.

"Well, it's a theory," Justin said.

"Does this mean the mayor's office isn't a target any longer?" Cindy asked.

Justin sighed loudly.

"It's *just* a theory," he said. "Pulling the protective details seems like a poor idea right now. But it does give me an idea. Maggie, how is Corrigan doing?"

"He's well enough to want to get out of the hospital," she said. "Which we're taking as a good sign. He stood and walked on his own yesterday. Just to the bathroom, but it was a start."

"His being alive isn't a secret any longer. Not if the one person we were trying to keep that information from already knows otherwise. If she's going to go after him, maybe we can take steps to make sure we're there when it happens."

CHAPTER EIGHTEEN

Dr. Warren: I'm saying if you look at everything that's happened in this city over the past month...if you look at it, and don't even consider aliens, you're fooling yourself.

Dick Jackson: And when you say aliens, you're not talking about illegal immigration, correct?

Dr. Warren: That's correct, that is not what I'm talking about.

—Transcript, from the 'Late night with Dick Jackson' radio show

"You want me to accept a what?"

The room they'd put Corrigan in was on a floor that was officially under renovation, in a wing of the hospital that wasn't typically used for people recovering from gunshot wounds. Not that Mass General had a section specifically intended for the use of gunshot victims, but if they did, it wouldn't be anywhere near the maternity ward that was one floor down.

The reason they had him there, he was told, was to hide his

continued existence from the woman responsible for that gunshot. Since she was supposed to think he was dead, it followed that the rest of the world did as well.

For all these reasons, Corrigan assumed he'd misheard his girlfriend.

"A medal," she said. "For bravery or something. I'm pretty sure the mayor has a few commendations lying around. One of those."

Maggie was sitting in a chair that had been exclusively occupied—up until this point—by Monica Devereaux, despite Corrigan's many attempts to get her to go away.

It had been nice having someone to talk to, at first, especially once it became clear that Maggie's appearances in the ward would be extremely occasional, as long as there was a killer out there. Monica had a lot of questions, and he didn't have anything better to do. Her probing helped him recall the details that had landed him in the hospital in the first place, and that made her pretty useful.

But she wouldn't go away. Even when Corrigan lapsed into silence on a regular basis, and stopped answering questions with enthusiasm, she continued to sit in the chair and tap away on her laptop.

It turned out the fan site she created in his honor had exploded...or gone viral, or something like that...at a time when she couldn't do much more than basic maintenance to keep it running. She desperately wanted to tell everyone what it was like to be rescued a second time by the same guy, but Boston Police asked her nicely (in a way that sounded like an order, even though they couldn't make it an actual order) not to do that. To her credit, she kept quiet, although he got the sense that she was compensating for silence in that part of her life, by filling up all the silence in Corrigan's life.

Her silence wasn't having the expected effect. Basically,

everyone contributing to her website now assumed that since Monica had dropped out of sight, both she and Corrigan were alive, and further, had run off together.

Or something. One afternoon, she went through seven entirely different ridiculous theories, and read ten thousand words of a piece of fan fiction about their entirely imaginary life on the run. Then she laughed at how wrong they all were, and said, "I should write a book or something!" in an offhand way that strongly suggested she was doing exactly that.

It all made him about ten times happier to see Maggie than he would have been otherwise.

"I don't want to tell the FBI how to do things," he said, to Maggie, "but it seems to me this is the sort of thing this Sheila woman is going to hear about."

"Yeah, that's the plan."

"You're using me as bait?"

"Yep. What do you think?"

"I think I liked being in a coma."

"You don't have to do it," she said.

"It was nice and quiet there."

"Corrigan, I mean it. You don't have to do it."

He adjusted himself in the bed. It wasn't the worst thing in the world, having a bed he could turn into a chair with a couple of buttons. His butt was numb, more or less all the time, and he felt a profound need to stretch his legs every half hour or so, but it was still nice. Also, a week ago, he couldn't sit up or move much at all without some pretty intense pain. Even a slight shift like the one he'd just accomplished would have been accompanied by the sensation that his midsection was being torn open.

He could stand now, and walk. He just had to ignore the feeling of his skin tugging at the stitches, and convince himself his insides were not about to spill out, despite how it felt.

He was not in any shape to defend himself properly, but he

could walk across a stage okay. But if everything Maggie had just told him about the woman they were after was true, if they did this he wouldn't be walking off that stage again.

"Give me the details, so I can tell you how many ways it's a terrible idea," he said.

"We haven't worked out all of the details yet. But, we'll stage it someplace where we can control the situation. She isn't bullet-proof, right?"

"She may as well be, if she knows where the bullets are going to hit her."

"You did. Bernard still shot you."

"That was different," he said. "I could have gotten out of the way, but in all the versions where I did, the bomb went off. This is why my weakness isn't her weakness; to me, getting shot to be the lesser of two outcomes. We don't have anything or anyone she cares enough about to protect in the same way. On top of that, she'll know about the trap ahead of time, just like I knew I was going to take a round in the chest."

"Okay. But this is the way it works, Corrigan. Step one is figuring out where she's going to be, step two is apprehending her when she shows up. We don't have any other strategies in our toolkit. Nobody's ever gamed for a scenario where we have to take down a terrorist who can see the future."

"You'll have to work on one," he said. "Is her name really Sheila Corrigan? Because I don't know what to think about that."

"It's too much of a coincidence, isn't it? We can't get anything useful out of the name, because it's too common, so I don't know. But it seems legitimate."

The twelve-year old version of Corrigan would have thought this was the best news ever, because it meant that there was a family of people who shared not just his name, but his abilities. It was a pretty good superhero origin story. Not as good, maybe, as the lab-experiment one, or the father-from-another-planet one (although that was still on the table) but it was pretty good.

"It's too bad she's a violent killer," he said. "I mean if she's a relative. I'd love to know more about dad's side of the family. You know what you're asking of me, don't you? If she can do what I can, I may not be able to see her attack coming."

"You saw the bomb."

"That was different."

"How?"

"The bomb was supposed to go off, and then it didn't. It was the part where it didn't go off that was an alteration of the future. If she reverses that, and the bomb that wasn't supposed to go off in the future, *does* go off, I won't see it about to happen. And she knows it."

"Ah," Maggie said. "Well, I can't do anything about her ability to do that, but I do have something that will keep our intentions hidden from her."

Maggie held up a little rectangular block of metal. It looked like a surge protector. She put it on the floor, and then ran a cord from the back of it to the outlet, and plugged it in.

"What's that?" he asked.

"A magic trick. Do you notice anything weird about it?"

"Not really, no."

Maggie picked it up, and then disappeared.

No, that's not right, he thought. *Her future's gone.*

"Whoa," he said.

"What do you see?"

"You turned into a ghost."

"What do you mean?"

"Please put that down, it's giving me a headache."

She put it down, and her future popped back in.

"Neat trick," he said.

"Why did you say I turned into a ghost?" she asked.

"Remember in the bad old days, when I used to hallucinate entire people? I knew they weren't real because they had no futures. It was like that. That comes from what Bernard was wearing, doesn't it? I recognize the effect."

"Yeah."

"I hated it then, too. Can we make a whole bunch of them?"

"We just have this one."

He laughed.

"You'll definitely get me killed."

"We can take precautions. I know it sounds like a crummy idea, but we don't have any good ones. The only things we're pretty sure about right now are that she wants this device back, and she wants to kill you. At least if we announce where you're going to be, we'll know one place where *she'll* be."

"Except she'll also know it's a trap."

Maggie shrugged.

"It's what we have," she said.

"Hang on."

Something was rattling around in the back of his head: a memory of something.

"I'm supposed to check out of here soon," he said.

"I know. Tonight. We've already worked out the details."

"Middle of the night, out the front door and into a police van?"

"Yeah. Quick and clean. You'll be exposed for only a few seconds. BPD is going to close the entrance and half the block. Wait, did someone already brief you?"

"She was wounded, wasn't she? Right shoulder?"

"I really hate it when you do this, dear."

"She'll be there. Tonight. I saw it happen."

E xcept for two details, the plan to move Corrigan out of the hospital at one in the morning—through a pre-cleared front plaza to a police van parked on a street that had been cordoned off an hour earlier—continued exactly as planned.

The first change: the person pushing Corrigan to the door in a wheelchair was no longer Monica Devereaux. Instead, it was an FBI agent named Vera, who was dressed to look like Monica.

The second: Corrigan wasn't the one who got wheeled out. This was another FBI agent, named Carl.

Carl was about the same height as Corrigan, but not as bulky, so they had to put a bomb vest on under his shirt, along with the flak jacket he'd already planned to wear. But he was still in Corrigan's clothes, his hair was the right color and approximate degree of incipient baldness, and most importantly, he was showing up at the right time and place to be Corrigan. The general opinion was that he looked close enough to fool someone for a few seconds.

They figured that was all they needed.

Corrigan actually left the hospital two hours earlier, through one of a series of underground maintenance tunnels connecting the many buildings that made up Mass General. He—and Monica, whom he decided he was doomed to spend eternity with at this point—were taken down one such tunnel, to an indoor loading dock for the laundry service, and into an unmarked van. At that point, Monica could probably have gone home, but nobody wanted to risk her being seen on the street, by Sheila or anyone else. It seemed like a silly concern, except Sheila and Bernard had already kidnapped Monica once.

They were both still in the unmarked van, with Maggie, at twenty minutes before one AM, across the street from the front entrance. The van was Maggie's command center, where all the video feeds from the area were sent, and from which all of the team communications passed. The FBI managed to rig the courtyard with cameras, which Corrigan thought was pretty remarkable given they only had a lead time of half a day to put all of this together. There were also multiple rings of police and FBI at various points around the entrance, for when Sheila showed up on one of those cameras.

"It's nearly time," Maggie said.

"This is exciting, isn't it?" Monica said.

This was her way of saying she was nervous. She was on a stool near the back doors, her knee bouncing up and down. Even the rhythm was annoying Corrigan.

"You'll be safe here, Ms. Devereaux," Maggie said. "It'll be over soon."

"Oh, I know," she said, winking at Corrigan. Corrigan in turn glared at his girlfriend, who smiled. He was pretty sure she was enjoying this.

Maggie looked at her watch.

"Ten minutes, everyone," she said into the walkie-talkie. "Anyone have eyes?"

She got silence in response, which just meant no, nobody had seen Sheila.

Maggie had everyone check in, then gave the all-clear to the police van. A minute later, it drove up and parked at the edge of the sidewalk.

Two officers climbed out and began to do a slow circle around the courtyard.

The front of the hospital was shaped like a semi-circle, with the courtyard in front of it a cement rotunda. There were tall granite columns between the curb and the middle of the plaza, to prevent anyone from driving their car directly into the front lobby. The police van was at the curb next to those columns.

Corrigan was looking at a monitor, so he couldn't tell if one of the two men had the device. He thought probably not, because that would tip off Sheila too early. There were at least two more officers inside the police van; one of them probably had it.

"Does it look about right?" Maggie asked Corrigan.

"I guess," he said. "I saw it from inside the hospital, not from here. But it's about right."

Maggie nodded, then opened the channel on her radio again.

"It's time. Carl, Vera, you're up. Everyone be careful."

The front door to the hospital slid open.

"I've got someone," somebody on the radio said.

"What do you have?" Maggie asked.

"Someone running. From the north side. Bee-line. One block away."

"It's not a jogger, right?" Maggie asked.

"No ma'am, I think it's her. Should I take a shot?"

"Negative, let her get closer."

Corrigan decided it was strange, watching things on a video monitor that were unfolding just outside. When Sheila Corrigan made it within a few hundred feet of the courtyard, for example, if he'd been looking out the back of the van instead of at the screen, he would have seen her slide between two parked cars. He could have interacted with her directly, which is not something one expects to be able to do when watching something happen on television.

But that wasn't half as weird as what it was like to feel an explosion, an instant before seeing it transpire on the monitor.

Sheila didn't shoot her way into the courtyard, which was what the officers were told to expect. One of them even had on extra armor and a helmet, because he was the one who was supposed to take the bullet.

She also didn't get into hand-to-hand with anyone, or come up to the substitute Corrigan, speak to him, and then shoot him.

(Carl didn't have anything protecting his face, which was where Corrigan remembered her aiming, but it was believed that this would not matter, because by then they would have had her nullified.)

But basically none of what happened in Corrigan's future-view of this evening ended up happening. Instead, Sheila got within fifty feet of the police van, threw a bomb that landed under the rear fender, and ducked behind a parked car.

Corrigan couldn't attest to what happened to the police van, or to Carl and Vera, or to anyone else in the courtyard, because the explosion knocked him over.

They were lucky the whole van didn't end up on its side. It got rocked hard enough that all of them were knocked to the floor, and some of the electronics went airborne, including a monitor. If he didn't know any better, Corrigan would have said they'd just been wishboned by an elephant.

They also lost power. Without the monitors, they were going to have to step outside to find out what was happening twenty feet away.

"Corrigan, are you okay?" Maggie asked.

His side was screaming at him. He hadn't done anything more than jump up and down a couple of times, during therapy. It was enough to convince him he never wanted to jump up and down again. Getting dropped to the floor was a lot worse.

"I'm super," he said. "What happened?"

"Nothing good."

He heard a shuffle of equipment from the part of the van where Maggie was sitting comfortably a few seconds ago.

"Monica," he called out, in the other direction. "Are you okay?"

"Ow," she said. "I think my arm's broken, guys."

"Stay where you are," Maggie said.

"Yeah, no problem. Good thing we're near a hospital, huh?"

Corrigan heard static; Maggie had found her radio.

"This is base," she said. "We took a hit. Check in."

Silence. All they could hear outside was the wailing of car alarms.

Then: "Hey, girl. Is the boy scout there?"

"Who is this?" Maggie asked.

"You know who it is. Come on, I wanna talk to him."

Maggie closed the channel.

"It's her," she said.

"I got that" Corrigan said. He staggered to his feet, got his bearings, and turned to face the back doors.

"Corrigan, don't you dare go out there," Maggie said.

"Give me a gun," he said.

"Absolutely not."

"Then I'll go out unarmed."

"Fine."

She crawled to her feet and stuck a handgun into his open palm.

"I have another piece," she said, "at least let me get out through the front and provide some cover."

"You won't be able to touch her, you know that."

"I know. All the girls down at the club will give me grief if I don't offer covering fire to my boyfriend, okay?"

"Just don't give her a target," he said.

"Same to you."

"I might not have a choice."

He had to step over Monica on the way out.

"Be careful," she whispered.

"It'll be fine. Stay here."

"Thanks, I didn't have any plans not to."

In his immediate future, Corrigan reached the back door, waited three seconds, and then opened it. When he did so, he was not shot, which should have meant he was fine to do exactly that. Instead, he just pushed it open immediately, without the three seconds, pointing the gun Maggie gave him in the approximate direction of the hospital's front door.

He was not shot.

The devastation was pretty impressive. Sheila's bomb took off the back of the police van, which probably meant bad things happened to the officers inside. The two other officers were lying on the floor of the cement courtyard, either dead or unconscious. Likewise, Vera and Carl, who were in a heap near the door and not moving.

There was a crack in the glass of the hospital's façade. A red light was flashing on the inside of the building, creating interesting shadows.

Corrigan had the sense that there was all this motion happening around him, just at the edge of his vision. He was in the middle of the silence—well, all except for the car alarms—immediately following an explosive detonation. What would follow would be a rush of people toward the scene.

Sheila Corrigan, sitting on the messed-up remnants of the police van's rear fender, didn't look concerned about any of that.

Sheila was shorter than Corrigan, and he thought shorter than Maggie too. She had her brown hair up in a ponytail and, unlike the version of the future he saw, she was in black clothing, not a police uniform.

Her right shoulder was twice as large as her left. He thought this must have been the bandage, under her jacket.

"There you are," she said, standing. She had the interesting little rectangular device Maggie showed off earlier, in her right hand. "Thanks for setting all this up for me, I really needed this back."

"I didn't set up anything."

"You kinda did. It messes with your head, doesn't it? You peek into our future and see me gunning for you, and then I do the same and I see...this. How do you think it works? Last one to the future wins?"

"Maybe. Never thought about it. Who are you?"

"Distant cousin, I'm thinking. Never saw you at the reunions."

In his future, Corrigan fired the gun.

"Whoop," she said. In her future, she moved, and pulled her own gun. Then the future caught up and she actually did pull the gun, even if Corrigan didn't end up shooting his.

"Neat, right?" she said. Then she shot in her future. He stepped aside. She caught up, and didn't fire the gun.

"How's the gut shot?" she asked. "You seem to be moving okay."

"I'm fine. How's the shoulder?"

"It's healing, thanks."

"Tell me what you want."

"Man, you are a terrible conversationalist," she said. "You know what I want to know? How come you don't do anything *fun* with your skills?"

"I don't know what you mean."

In her future, she sighed grandly, and walked in a circle, gesticulating. She didn't end up doing that, and the sighing version of the future disappeared. It was the kind of surreal that made Corrigan's head hurt. He was witnessing reactions that were only for his benefit.

The secret future, he thought. That was what he called it when he met Harvey. The old man almost never moved—up until that last day in the hospital—so Corrigan had few chances to process how odd it was.

Regular people had possible futures, but they always ended up on the path of one of those possible futures. Sheila was completely freelancing. She could follow one of those futures, or she could do something entirely different. If it was adequately different, all the other possible futures vanished, so when she did that, for a micro-second, it looked as if she had no future at all. That was when she was most dangerous, but the counterpoint was that Corrigan could do the same thing and was therefore equally dangerous.

"I mean, something fun!" she said, but only in the future. When it came time to actually say it out loud, in the present, she just stood there.

"Tell me why you're trying to kill me," he said, in the same manner. To Maggie, it must have looked like they were just holding a staring contest.

"Fine, fine, Mr. all-business. It's purely economic, okay? I offer a unique service. I can't have you around, proving I'm not unique."

"You've never met anyone like us before?"

"I assumed there *were* people like us, but no. Even if I did, I might leave them alone, as long as they're not on national television acting like a crazy man superhero."

"I wasn't trying to go public," he said. "That was your fault."

"Oh, I know. Man, that was *so* weird, right? I couldn't figure out what happened at first. The future popped out of existence when you jumped up; I thought Bern's equipment malfunctioned. Whoop."

In the future, someone shot her in the head. She moved aside, and fired two shots in the direction of the shooter. It came from up the street, and not from Maggie, who knew better.

"Looks like it's time to go, Mr. Corrigan Bain," she said. "This has been fun."

"Don't suppose you're leaving town."

"I could promise to, but you wouldn't believe me."

"No, probably not."

"Later, then. Keep sharp, heal up, this'll be a blast."

She raised the gun, aimed it at him at first, then turned and fired in the direction of Maggie. The bullets hit the side of the van, but served the purpose of preventing Maggie from doing what she was about to do, which was to shoot at Sheila's back as she ran from the scene.

Corrigan took two steps to follow, until the stitches in his side reminded him he had only just barely graduated to walking.

To reinforce the point the stabbing pain in his stomach was already making, he touched the spot where the stitches were, and his hand came up wet.

Bleeding through the stitches, and I haven't even made it home yet, he thought. *That seems about right.*

To his left, Maggie emerged from behind the van's engine block, shouting commands into a radio. The agents who'd been positioned around the front of the hospital were all running, either toward the immobile bodies in the courtyard or in the direction Sheila Corrigan had fled. It was only ten or eleven people, but suddenly Corrigan realized how unprepared he was, to go back out into the world again. Those ten or eleven people looked and sounded like five times that. His grip on the present wasn't nearly what it should be.

But, he was tired, and stressed, and apparently bleeding.

"Are you okay?" Maggie asked him, in between commands on her radio. Then she asked the same thing a second time. He waited until he was sure she wasn't going to ask a third time, and then responded. To her, it must have seemed like he was *not* okay.

"Don't worry about me right now," he said.

"Are you hurt?" she asked. She also almost asked if he was okay, and if he was wounded, but the one that stuck was *are you hurt?*

"Go," he said. He then added, "I'll stay here" before she could tell him to stay put.

Maggie was intimately familiar with Corrigan's tendency to respond to things that had not yet been said, and so after a quick head-shake, she joined the carnage in the courtyard.

Corrigan leaned up against the side of the van, and wondered if he had an obligation to check up on Monica, who was probably still hiding inside, worried that it wasn't safe yet. Then he wondered if maybe he should call someone's attention to his bleeding. He didn't know how much blood was *too* much, before it was officially a medical problem requiring some manner of triage, but surely someone there did.

Focus, he thought.

The spaghetti-string parade of future-movement had to be put back in the box, or he was of no use to anybody. He picked out one person at random—a paramedic, who had just rushed out of the front of the hospital on his way to the carcass of a police van—and concentrated on the far end of the man's path. If Corrigan were feeling better, that would be the spot where the paramedic appeared the most solid.

Then he saw the one person at the scene, next to the paramedic, who had no visible future.

It was a Kilroy. Possibly, the same one who'd been waiting for Corrigan to wake up. Aside from their sartorial choices, it was essentially impossible to tell them apart. All Corrigan knew for sure was that this was not the same Kilroy who was killing people a few years back, but he only knew that because that particular Kilroy was dead.

It walked through the scene, calmly, weaponless aside from those long fingers and sharp teeth.

"What do you want?" Corrigan asked it, using the same future-only-speak he'd just been trying out with Sheila a minute earlier. Just doing this meant he was going to be fighting a lot longer to relocate the present, but, one thing at a time.

"Kora-gan-see, fix," the Kilroy said.

"You said that before."

Corrigan was very, very glad that so far, this particular Kilroy hadn't expressed any interest in committing murders, because Corrigan just didn't have it in him to deal with both Sheila and a resumption of Kilroy hostilities.

The Kilroy stopped about five feet from Corrigan. It was making an effort to appear non-threatening, which was greatly appreciated. Then Corrigan realized it was probably because he was still holding a gun. He shoved the gun in his pocket.

"Fix," the Kilroy repeated. "She-see, fixer fix."

"She. You mean, Sheila?"

"She-see."

It turned, and gestured at the scene.

"Yes, Sheila did this," Corrigan said.

"Fix," it said.

"I'm trying."

It put its hand on its chest and tapped.

"Kilroy-prime," it said, confirming that this was the same one as before.

"I know." Corrigan said. "Nice to meet you."

"Kilroy-prime," it repeated.

"I know."

"Fix-help."

"Look, I…it's been a long day, and I'm not a linguist. Thanks for not trying to kill me, but I have to…"

He was going to say he had to go help, but he was pretty sure he'd just be in the way. What he really needed to go was get his head right, which wasn't going to happen as long as a creature who was firmly stuck in the future was standing in front of him.

"We can talk later," Corrigan said. "When I'm better."

To emphasize the point, Corrigan showed the Kilroy the blood on his hand.

"Kora-gan-see fix Kora-gan-see," it said.

"Yes. Sure."

It nodded, and walked away.

"Hey," Monica said, from over Corrigan's shoulder. She was looking at the scene in the plaza, which was indeed eye-catching. She couldn't also see the Kilroy, walking along the row of cars. Corrigan had no idea how long she'd been standing there.

"Were you talking to someone?" she asked.

"You heard that?" he asked.

"Just grunts, but, you were making noises. Is this some special fixer thing?"

"Kind of. It's a long story."

CHAPTER NINETEEN

In what police are calling a gas main explosion...I'm sorry, do they expect us to believe this shit?

—former action news reporter Kim Dill, Channel 4 (live mike error)

If there was any good news to be had, it was that this bombing took place in front of a hospital. Everyone who was still breathing by the time Sheila Corrigan vacated the courtyard, remained that way a few hours later. It meant the death toll was confined to two—the men in the back of the police van—rather than six or seven.

This was not a particularly rosy outcome, but by sunrise, it was just about all anyone had to cling to.

The explosion ripped the back of the van open. It began underneath the vehicle, near the rear fender, which happened to be exactly the place to put a bomb if you wanted to target the softest spot in the vehicle's armor. The force of the blast was largely absorbed by the van and the street, which was the only reason the four people in the courtyard survived. The driver was also alive, thanks to the thick steel wall separating the cabin from the rear.

Sheila eluded the dragnet. There had been coordinated efforts to seal off the area, in anticipation of her possible escape from the scene, set up before anybody knew she was going to be lobbing a packet of C-4. It worked fine, in the sense that everyone did what they were supposed to do; the cordon was locked down as soon as Sheila was spotted near the scene.

It didn't matter. Nothing short of encasing the entire region in an airtight force field would do it, and to the best of everyone's knowledge that sort of thing was only available in science fiction books. Sheila Corrigan had the same abilities as Corrigan Bain, so in the same way Corrigan was able to evade police capture for several days, back when he was a suspect, so too could Sheila.

As for Corrigan, as the sun shone over the still-smoking husk of the police van wreckage, he was sitting on the fender of an ambulance, drinking a cup of bad coffee and getting his head in order. He had not torn his stitches, but he did need to be re-bandaged. It came with a lecture from the paramedic who did it for him, about not doing anything strenuous for the next few weeks, which was cute.

"Maybe you should show me how to rewrap it myself," Corrigan suggested, "because this is going to happen again."

Maggie, who now sported a bandage on her head—she'd evidently whacked it in the blast—spent the whole evening on her radio. She wasn't even in the courtyard when Erica arrived.

"Corrigan Bain," Erica said. "How many times do you plan to almost die before I get to say hello?"

"You could have swung by the hospital," he said, standing to give her a hug. "I wasn't almost dying then."

She arrived with a retinue. There was an Indian man by her elbow, sporting a badge on his hip. Corrigan recognized him as a member of Maggie's team. He didn't recognize the other three men in her orbit; it looked a little like she was being escorted by the secret service.

"Sorry," she said. "I should have, but I try to avoid hospitals. I've had my fill."

"I understand."

The last time Corrigan saw Erica Smalls was when she graduated from MIT. He was a reluctant attendee to the ceremony—Maggie dragged him there—and only agreed to go because Erica insisted.

That had been a few years ago. She didn't look any different. But, she was in her twenties—time was kind to people in their twenties. In contrast, he was pretty sure he looked a hundred years older. He certainly felt that way.

"What's all this?" he asked, referring to her escorts.

"They didn't want me to come," she said. "I said I was going anyway, and it turns out since I'm not under arrest and don't work for the government, they couldn't stop me."

"It's a police scene," the agent fused to her hip said. Patel was his name, Corrigan remembered. "You couldn't have come here alone even if you wanted to."

"She tried to kill me before," Erica said, evidently ignoring Patel. "And I shot her, so they're thinking I might be a target. I keep telling them none of it was personal, but they worry. It's cute."

"*You* shot her?" Corrigan asked.

"I had a lucky guess about something."

"Hey," Maggie shouted, from a few yards away. "You shouldn't be here, Erica."

She said it while looking at Patel, who she undoubtedly blamed for this particular sin.

"Well, here I am," Erica said. "Does someone want to tell me how all this went down, or do I need to take a double-secret oath or something first?"

"Handshake," Corrigan said. "It's usually a secret handshake."

"She knew it was a trap," Maggie said. "Corrigan can't seem to explain how she knew, but she knew."

"How'd you even know to set the trap?" Erica asked. It was obvious from the question that she didn't know about any of this until it had—literally—blown up in everyone's faces.

"I saw it," he said.

"In the future? When was that?"

Corrigan hesitated, because *when in the past did you see the future that just happened?* was a distressingly complicated question.

"Patel," Maggie said, "get these two out of here." She looked at Corrigan. "I'll catch up later. If you can figure out how we just got our asses kicked, let me know."

S heila Corrigan reached the door of the shipping container just as the sunrise took away the last of her cover. Her shoulder ached, she felt like she was ready to sleep for the next five days, and the phone inside the container was already ringing, which meant she was going to have to delay the sleep.

She could also not answer the phone, but that would hardly help matters. It would go to voicemail, and then tell the caller that there *was* no voicemail in which to save a message, and then it would disconnect the call. (The automated voice said *goodbye* so officiously, a part of her wanted to find the woman who recorded it and thank her personally.) But then the caller would just call back again.

Turning the phone off was also a perfectly good option. It wouldn't stop the calls, but she could get a little sleep before dealing with the caller, which would be nice. She didn't do that either, because he would know—it would go right to voicemail after one ring instead of eight—and he'd be even more pissed off.

There were perhaps two or three people in the world who Sheila Corrigan was unwilling to piss off any more than absolutely necessary. The guy calling her was one of them.

At the same time, he could wait a little longer.

She stepped inside the container, pulled the door closed behind her, and then slid aside a partition next to the external latch. She reached through the opening and reconnected the counterfeit customs seal that was more or less the only thing keeping her entire operation a secret at this point.

The container was one of about a thousand boxes in the Boston Harbor shipyard. Officially, it was just waiting for a company that didn't know it existed, to lay claim to it and drive it away. Until that time, the seal—which would prove the contents had been inspected and cleared by customs, if it were real—had to remain on the outside of the container.

If customs had actually examined the contents of the shipping container, they probably would have had a few words to say about the C-4.

The phone stopped ringing. Sheila closed the partition, which turned the interior from near-total darkness to complete darkness. Undeterred by this detail, she took three steps to her right, picked up the battery-powered lantern, and lit it up. Then she got the generator going, and the portable heater, which she kept as far as possible from the crates in the back of the container.

Sheila imagined a time in the distant future—farther than she was capable of seeing, and thus the speculation—well after she'd completed the Boston gig and abandoned the rest of the C-4, the shipping container it was in, and the entire country. They'd stolen a *lot* more explosives than they needed to fulfill the needs of the assignment, which wasn't really anyone's fault. Sheila had told Sharon and Nick they didn't need so much, but since Sheila was the only one privy to the actual goals of their little team, she couldn't very well complain when Sharon and Bernard walked as much as they did off the base. And then it was too late, because one couldn't very well flush plastic explosives down the toilet, and sending what they didn't need back to the army—while practical—was a bad idea.

In that imagined distant future, the C-4 would deteriorate, and then one hot summer day it would explode and take out the entire shipyard.

It was a pleasant thought. Sheila knew a lot about making bombs, but less about storing explosives long-term, so she couldn't know for sure when that day might come, but she was looking forward to it. Because, to hell with this town.

The phone started ringing again.

"Not yet, dammit," she muttered.

She sat down on the cot, slipped the left arm out of her jacket, and then went about the painful task of sliding the right arm free.

She still couldn't believe the pretty one shot her. She couldn't believe she was shot, period, but that it was the pretty one to do it was that much more galling. Sheila had been, by her estimation, on her best behavior given the circumstances. She'd planned on letting the girl live, even.

This was why there was no point in being nice.

The battlefield dressing she'd applied wasn't doing the job. Neither was the antibiotic, or the pain pills, both of which she'd stolen from a pharmacy when it became clear the wound wasn't going to heal itself with nice little bandage and some harsh language. What she needed was a hospital.

Maybe a different hospital than the one she'd just blown up.

She changed the bandage, tried to ignore the smell—

unquestionably a bad sign—and dug up the bottle of eighty proof painkiller she had under the cot. After a couple of quick swigs, she recapped the bottle and answered the phone.

"Yeah," she said.

"It isn't done," he said, without preamble. When you're one of the richest people in the world, you don't bother with introductions.

"Half of it's done," she said. "I got the doodad back."

"He's still alive."

"Are you asking me, or telling me?"

"When are you taking care of him?"

"It'll happen. It's just not going to be easy, I've told you this. He's hard to kill, for the same reason I'm hard to kill. I'll do it, I just might have to blow up half the city to get the job done."

"Shiva...get it done and get out of there. We're already writing off this entire affair. The last thing we need is another one of you out there, making news. He's devaluing our patent."

"You're sweet," she said. "I love it when people talk about me like I'm proprietary software. Maybe you should sue him."

"If you think I haven't investigated that option, you're mistaken."

"Right. Well, look. Like I said, I have your doodad, so they won't be tracing it back to your project."

"It's incredibly valuable, so I'm glad, but I'm told it's effectively untraceable."

"Sure."

Sheila thought whoever told him that was lying to him, but that wasn't her problem.

"I know you don't appreciate it when I question your methods, Shiva, but why didn't you end it today?"

"An opportunity didn't present," she said. "And you're right, I don't appreciate it. Is there anything else?"

"No," he said. "But. I do want to correct you on one detail.

You aren't as hard to kill as you think. I will call again tomorrow. Try to answer more promptly."

He hung up. She resisted the impulse to smash the phone into tiny pieces.

Instead, she opened up the map of Boston that had been so handy over the past month. Somewhere on that map was the ideal location for a bomb.

"I'll sleep on it," she said, after a minute. "That's faster."

Then she lay down on the cot and closed her eyes. It was time to visit the future.

"Let me see if I have this right," Erica said. "You were in a coma, and then…"

"It wasn't a coma," Corrigan said. "They told me it wasn't a coma. I just wasn't waking up."

"All right, well, neither of us are doctors, but that sounds like a coma, doesn't it?"

"Sure."

"I mean, I was in one."

"You were, yes," he said.

"Doesn't make me an expert in comas, but I don't remember being all that lucid."

"Go on with what you were saying."

They were in a corner of one of the Mass General Hospital's cafeterias, which meant if they did need an expert on comas, they could probably get their hands on one by standing on the table and loudly asking if there was a doctor in the house. This would likely distress their FBI guards, who had already gone through a lot of trouble to recon the room and secure the corner table. Erica was nearly positive that Sheila wasn't anywhere near the hospital any longer, but given she had already proven capable of getting in and out of just about any building, their need to make sure was only sensible.

"While you were in this not-coma," she said, "you were visiting the future, and in that future, you saw the scene out front. Except it wasn't exactly the scene out front."

"Right. I was supposed to go out the front, under escort. She was supposed to show up and attack us, in order to kill me."

"Did she?"

"Did she show up?" he asked.

"Did she kill you, in this future."

"Yeah, I think so. I woke up before it got that far."

"That's what woke you out of your not-coma?" she asked.

"It was pretty shocking, yes."

"She killed you with a gun?"

"Again, yes."

"Even though you're kind of hard to get a straight shot on."

She remembered the story about Corrigan, from when he was a kid. He'd encountered another person with the same abilities: an asylum patient, who was armed. Corrigan, at twelve, was capable enough to prevent this guy from getting a clean shot off.

"I'm not saying it made a lot of sense," Corrigan said. "But that was how the future played out. So we changed the future."

"Then she changed it even more."

"Yes, she did."

"Which means, she can go ahead, the same as you. You guys are just diving in to a certain point in the near-future, and taking turns altering it."

Corrigan shrugged.

"I've never even done that before. Not like this. I used to... this was how I saw accidents coming, before, when I was still working as a fixer. Accidents are louder. I'd go into the future in my sleep, find an accident, and remember the time and location."

"Then you *have* done it before."

"Yes, but this wasn't an accident I witnessed. It was a murder."

"Maybe there's an exception when you're witnessing your own murder," she said. "I wouldn't invest too much into this being something new for you; pretty sure those rules about only stopping accidents came from your head. There's certainly no scientific explanation."

"Right."

He took a sip from his coffee and looked as if he was focusing on something going on at the other end of the room. This was about normal for him, she decided.

"Your turn," he said. "You shot her. Tell me about that."

Erica walked him through what happened. He looked suitably impressed.

"Maggie showed you the device?" she asked, once the story was told.

"Yeah. It messed with my head. I can see why she thought it would be useful, and why Sheila wanted it back."

"Yes, but...hang on. It was blown up in the truck, right? She didn't get it."

"She did get it," Corrigan said. "I saw it in her hand."

Erica grabbed her bag from the floor and started rummaging around in it.

"Patel," she said, "Can you call Maggie?"

"Sure," he said. "What for?"

Erica pulled out the small plastic box she'd been carrying around since the day Sheila dropped it.

"Tell her I think we have a way to track Sheila Corrigan's location."

The news got Maggie to the cafeteria pretty fast.

"You can track her?" she asked, while still halfway across the room. "Great, where is she?"

"I don't know yet," Erica said. "And it's just a theory."

Maggie sighed, in the way people tended to around Erica, whenever she said the word *theory*.

"What's the theory, then?"

"We use this," Erica said. She put the black plastic box on the table.

"That's the thing that doesn't work," Maggie said. "The thing that doesn't track the signal the device doesn't give off."

"I'm sorry," Corrigan said. "What did you just say?"

"It's complicated," Erica said. "So I've been thinking about it for a while, because I like complicated things."

"Great," Maggie said. "Did you figure something out?"

"Maybe."

Erica pushed the box across the table, until it was in front of Corrigan.

He shrugged, and picked it up. After about thirty seconds, he said, "wow, this is neat."

"Is there something on the display?" Erica asked.

All she'd been able to figure out so far was that the box had a front and a back. The front was clear plastic, but nothing ever came up on it.

"Yeah," Corrigan said. He held it up to show them.

"It looks the same," Maggie said.

"Yes, there's nothing there," Patel agreed.

"It's only lighting up in the future," Erica explained. "That's why we can't see anything. But he can."

"In the...how?" Maggie asked. "How is that even possible?"

"I'm not sure," Erica said. "Objects have a certain permanence, but something happening in the present can stop happening in the future. Assuming the future has some positional indifference, there's no reason to think something can happen in the future and not in the present. I've never seen considered in any work before, but..."

"Okay," Maggie said, "okay, never mind, forget I asked. Corrigan, what does it say?"

He looked at the display again.

"I'm thinking when it gets closer it has some kind of hot-cold component to it," he said, "because there are two parts of the screen. One part has a faintly blinking dot that changes position when I move it. But we're not close."

"And the other part of the screen?" Maggie asked.

"N 42.36, W 71.15. That's all it says."

"Those are GPS coordinates," Patel said.

"Yes, they are," Maggie agreed. "If we find out where it is, maybe we can get ahead of her for once."

"Can we?" Erica asked. "What I mean is, isn't that what happened earlier?"

"She's right," Corrigan said. "That's exactly what happened earlier. I think we can agree, it didn't work the way we wanted it to."

Maggie looked like she was on the verge of a nervous breakdown. Erica couldn't blame her for that; it had been a long night, and this stuff was headache-inducing.

"I can't go to Justin with news that we've located the suspect, again, and we can't do anything," she said. "That's not how any of this works."

"It's near Boston Harbor," Patel said.

"What?" Maggie asked.

"The GPS location."

"Do you think she's on a boat?"

"Could be," he said. "But she doesn't have to be."

"Do you think she's swimming?"

"No, that isn't what I mean," Patel said. "She could be on the shore. These coordinates aren't precise enough."

"I wouldn't be on a boat, if I were her," Corrigan said.

"Why's that?" Maggie asked.

"It would nullify my abilities. If I was out on a boat, and you wanted to kill me..."

"Right, we could just torpedo the boat. I don't think the FBI has torpedoes, but maybe we can borrow one."

"If she was on a boat," Patel said, "it would fit the available information. We've had this woman's photo posted throughout the city; if she was sitting in a room at one of the harbor hotels, I feel as if we'd already know this."

"We'll have to do an aerial survey. Corrigan, how do you feel about a tour of the city in a helicopter?"

He was grimacing before she even finished the sentence. Erica forgot sometimes how different long conversations were for him.

It must be like watching a play you've already read, she thought.

"I'm not fond of the idea," he said.

"If she's on land, we need to know what part," Maggie said.

"If she's on a boat, she'll see the helicopter and know she'd been identified," Patel said.

"She's not on a boat," Corrigan insisted.

"Then we don't have anything to worry about," Maggie said. "Except for how it's apparently impossible to come up with a plan to capture her."

"We can go in with overwhelming force," Patel said. "She's still only one person."

"One person with a large supply of C-4, in the middle of a city."

"That will only do her any good if she knows where to put the bombs, right?"

Maggie glared at him.

"Are you suggesting someone who we already know can see the future won't know where to put her bombs?" Maggie asked.

"I'll go alone," Corrigan said.

"No."

"Maggie, it's the only way. I'm the only one whose movements she can't entirely anticipate."

"You can barely walk, Corrigan. It's not an option."

"Wait, wait, wait," Erica said. "We're not dealing with someone who knows *the* future. She's dealing with likely outcomes, right? Once you've narrowed down her location, the most likely outcome is to go in with a team. So, plan to do that. Walk it right up to the last minute, and then don't. Do something else instead."

"As soon as you say that, the *something else* becomes more likely," Patel said. "Doesn't it?"

"Bourbon," Maggie said, "and a cigarette. Who's with me?"

"I can alter my actions in a way she can't see," Corrigan said. "Plan the assault, I'll order the team's movements myself, and I'll go in."

"Still no," Maggie said. "We need an army of Corrigans before my answer changes."

Corrigan had a *Eureka* expression before Maggie finished talking. Erica wondered if Maggie saw it too, and had just practiced ignoring it, because sometimes it was kind of eerie.

"What is it?" Erica asked.

"I have an idea," he said. "You two are going to hate it."

Sheila awoke with a start, shaking, and covered in sweat. She sat up, slowly, and tried to get her bearings.

I'm in Boston. In a crate. Nothing's happened yet. Remember your training.

She closed her eyes again and took a few cleansing breaths, concentrating on bringing down her heart rate.

Relax.

She could hear the words of the man who taught her how to tap into her own dreams.

The future is what you make of it, he was fond of saying. He had no idea how much more literal that was for her than for anybody else, because she never told him what was really going on when she slept.

She was exploring her own future. It was something she'd done since she was a kid, which—along with the everyday weirdness of seeing things happen a few seconds before they actually happened—made for a pretty messed up childhood. It was years before she worked out how she knew about big events like plane crashes and earthquakes a day or two beforehand.

To her knowledge, she'd never in her life actually had a dream. Everything going on in her head when she closed her eyes was a future-walk, whether she wanted it to be or not. *Prophetic dreaming* is what the first, second, and third person she told about it called this, but they were all wrong. She wished she *could* dream, or at least have a night where nothing went on in her head, and everything shut down, and she could wake up feeling rested. But no. The best that could be said about sleep, for her, was that her body got a chance to rest. Her mind did not.

An apparently inevitable consequence of her weird existence was that she could sleep twelve to fifteen hours a day. There'd been weeks where it seemed as if she was spending more time in the future than in the present.

But this time, she only had her eyes closed for about six hours. Something in the future startled her so much it woke her up. That was why she was trying to relax now: it was so jarring, she couldn't at first remember what it was she'd experienced.

"Benjamin would understand," she muttered. Then she

pushed him from her mind, because he had been dead for five years, and she'd promised to stop letting him haunt her. It would never happen, but she kept trying to banish him anyway; the future was difficult enough without the past poking its head into the room.

He was essentially the closest thing she had to a father, after her real father...well, she never knew what happened to him. The nuns wouldn't tell her. The only reasons Sheila knew a father was at one time in her life was that she wasn't immaculately conceived—surely, had she been, the nuns would have been glad to tell her *that*—and he gave her a last name. Mother, about whom she knew slightly more, had died giving birth.

It was unfortunately also true that every little girl in that orphanage had some variation of a hard-luck story about the-parent-who-loved-her-but-couldn't-keep-her, or the-parent-who-died-tragically, so it was sometimes hard to tell how much of Sheila's recollection was patched together from other girls' stories, and/or wishful thinking, and how much was real.

Benjamin was real. He took her away, helped her hone her skills, worked out surprisingly creative ways to sell them, and only got fresh a few times.

She pushed him out of her head, and tried to remember what she'd seen.

It was important. It was supposed to be a future in which she figured out where to find and kill Corrigan Bain. Obviously, it was going to be more complicated than that.

It shouldn't have even gotten this far. He'd already screwed up her plans twice, the first time at the State House (although this was partly her fault, for not setting off the bomb anyway, even when the future popped out of view for a few seconds) and the second time at the Prudential Center, when he refused to die. It was honestly just bad luck that their paths crossed at all, but that bad luck ruined three years of planning and cost a very powerful man a lot of money.

Basically, even if she didn't *have* to kill him on her way out of town, she would have done it just out of spite.

She tried focusing on Bain, to see if he was in the dream. It didn't work, but there was...

Police, she thought. *And shipping crates.*

"They found me."

CHAPTER TWENTY

"Absolutely not."

Special Agent in Charge Justin Axelrod had a reputation as a reasonable person; the kind of firm-but-understanding guy who was easy to work for. He'd also been known to entertain some unusual solutions to problems, indicating the kind of flexibility of thought that one just didn't see all that often in the ranks of law enforcement's senior management.

But he had limits.

"Can you tell us why?" Maggie asked.

She was thinking about tackling his biggest objection first and working her way down, but the problem was, there was no telling which part of the plan he disliked the most. The whole thing was bonkers.

"I shouldn't have to," he said. "You work for the same FBI I do, and it's located in the real world, and in the real world we don't entertain solutions that apparently involve stopping someone with superpowers."

"I mean, that's a given by now, isn't it?" Erica said.

Maggie brought her along in case they got deep enough into

the weeds for Justin to want a complicated explanation. Plus—and Maggie hated herself for thinking like this—his low-grade flirting with Erica made him easier to manipulate.

"Not officially, no," he said. "If you think anybody in this office is going to be putting *suspect can see the future* on an official report, you're mistaken."

"Okay, but that doesn't make sense," Erica said. "You know she can. You know Corrigan Bain can, too, and I can give you an actual scientific explanation for all of it. Why wouldn't you put it in the report?"

"Erica," Maggie said. "It's okay."

"No, it's important. You can't just pick the version of the truth you're comfortable with."

Justin laughed.

"Never go into politics, Dr. Smalls. Yes, I understand your point. Maggie, why don't we start with this: Corrigan Bain is a civilian. I think we've all learned a lot recently about what he's done for this city, but that doesn't mean we just point him toward the bad guy and step away. That's not how it's done. If you've located her...no, that's not even right, is it? You didn't find her. You found the device she went through all that trouble to retrieve. And you found it using some kind of magical ding-dong only Bain is capable of operating, for reasons I swear to God my forehead will crack open if you try to explain to me again"

"It isn't magic," Maggie said.

Justin shook his head. He looked ready to challenge Maggie on the finer points of how one defines magic, before deciding against it.

"You sent Corrigan up in a chopper with the doohickey, and narrowed it down to a harbor dock, and somehow that didn't immediately trigger a box-to-box search. Did you at least drop a net over the place?"

"We have the gates under surveillance, but we're not going in until everything's in place."

"You don't even know if she's there. Again, you've tracked the device, not her."

"She'll be there," Erica said.

"How do you know?"

"Because she wants Corrigan, and in the future, Corrigan will be on the docks. She already knows this, so she'll be there."

"But I haven't said yes to any of this."

"Not yet. As soon as you say okay to the plan, she'll be there. If you don't, we don't know where she'll end up being."

"Because she saw it happen in the future. That's what you're saying?" Justin asked.

"Yes."

"Did she see *when* it was going to happen?"

"I don't think that matters."

"If she saw it happen Wednesday and we went on Tuesday..."

"Oh, I see," Erica said. "No, it doesn't work that way."

"Dr. Smalls, as far as I can tell, you're all making this up as you go along, to push me in the direction of heavy drug use."

"I know the feeling," Maggie said.

"I mean that whatever day you decide to go is the day she sees it happen," Erica said. "You can change it all you want, but that won't impact her; she'll still get it right."

"You know, she's already considered a terrorist," Justin said. "I can probably get the National Guard involved. Just have them march in and take the docks."

"A lot of them will die if you do that," Maggie said. "Look, I'm not going into this happy either. Corrigan wants to take on a psychopath, and his plan hinges on...let's just say I don't like the plan either. But he says it will work, and I'm out of better ideas. If you want to get past your problem with Sheila Corrigan seeing the future, consider that the alternative is to send people—FBI, BPD, the Guard, anybody—into a fight with someone sitting on a large supply of C-4, who knows they're coming. Sure, they may get her, but how many are you willing to lose to make that happen?"

Justin sighed.

"Except, I do have to send someone in," he said. "This is like that brain teaser. If a man tells you that everything he says is a lie, then his admission is itself a lie. If we make like we're sending in a force, but we don't *really* send in a force, then in the future we don't actually send in that force, and she'll know it."

"Yes," Maggie said. "Unless Corrigan is the one who tells them not to go in."

"I see. What you're really asking is for permission to send in an overwhelming force, with orders to take down the target, and then keep to myself that those aren't really their orders. Instead, their real orders will be coming from Corrigan Bain, a civilian who shouldn't be there in the first place, and isn't even on the chart as far as chain-of-command is concerned. And that magically, if he tells them to do something, the other Corrigan won't be able to anticipate that. Or, or, what? Divine it? This is nuts, Maggie."

"Did you read the report?" Erica asked. "From when I was attacked. Corrigan did this before."

"Dr. Smalls..." Justin began. He caught himself short of saying something that was probably going to be a lot blunter. "Let's just say it's been in the best interest of everyone connected with that case that it is *not* well-read. I mean that for the sake of Maggie's career, and for mine."

"Once again, I can provide ample scientific—"

"Yes, I know. But understand that at least twenty percent of the people reporting to me, think wireless internet access is witchcraft."

He looked at Maggie.

"You're going to be there," he said. It was a question, but he delivered it like it was an order.

"In a chopper," she said, "coordinating from above."

"All right. If anyone asks, your boyfriend's appearance at the scene was a surprise for everyone involved. Set it in motion. Just know that I'm regretting this already."

<hr>

The container terminal sat along a stretch of water called the Reserved Channel, which forked off from the Boston Main Channel that fed Boston Harbor. Beyond the Harbor was the mouth of the Charles River on one side and the Mystic River on the other.

These were parts of the city about which—up until about ten hours prior—Corrigan knew nothing. Then he toured the shoreline in a helicopter, holding a device whose functionality was an ongoing revelation to Erica Smalls, the resident expert in these sorts of things. The tour also included Castle Island, a place Corrigan *had* been to, having visited on foot one time while working as a fixer.

That he could travel to a thing called an island on foot, was just one of the many reasons the collection of land masses and water estuaries in the area remained a mystery. This, despite having spent over two decades staring at a map of the region every morning.

The best explanation for this, he thought, was that he'd never been called upon to save someone on the water.

Once they got the helicopter within a couple of miles, the device switched from GPS coordinates to a kind of throbbing arrow on a compass dial. It pointed them in the correct direction and pulsed more rapidly the closer they came. The consensus: Sheila Corrigan was hiding in the container stacks.

Corrigan and Maggie had to argue a few of the finer points of this for long enough that his head hurt after it was over, and she looked like she needed a smoke. She rightly pointed out that all they'd managed to do was track the object Sheila took from the police van, and they had no reason to believe Sheila was there herself.

Maggie was right, but there were plenty of reasons this was a moot point. For starters, they had no other leads. Also, the thing was clearly something she valued greatly enough to go through law enforcement to retrieve—twice—so she would probably stay close to it. But most importantly, even if they were about to raid a mostly-empty container on a dock, they had to go in assuming otherwise.

None of those were the reason Corrigan went with, though. He argued that all he had to do was make a personal appearance on the dock. Sheila would know he was going to be there, and he would know that she would know he was going to be there, and so on. He could change his future so that he was *not* there, but if he did, it would have to be right before he was supposed to be there, because anything other than that and they risked her seeing the switch-out, like she had at the hospital.

This was the portion of the conversation that spun everyone around. Erica tried to explain it using terms like *contingent probability*, but that only made it worse.

The short answer to all of this was that they had to go in heavy, and Corrigan had to be there.

It took the Bureau the better part of the afternoon to get the terminal closed down. This had to be done quietly, in shifts. They were fortunate that no ship was in, as this would mean a small army of stevedores moving up and down the dock. Then they had to set up a perimeter, which was also not terribly difficult, as every part of the property not up against the water was behind a fence, so they had a starting point.

They ringed the fence-line with a joint combination of members of the FBI, ICE, ATF, and the Boston Police. Corrigan didn't pretend to understand how any of that worked, jurisdictionally, and didn't much care as long as they all listened to him when he needed them to.

It was dark now. That hardly mattered in the container yard, because the place was bathed in the kind of electrical lighting that would fit right in at Fenway Park. Those lights weren't coming at the yard from the same angle of the sun (obviously) so they did have a tendency to create heavy shadows when up against the tall stacks of containers, but it wasn't much worse than being in the city on a moonless night. Corrigan thought Sheila would use the shadows to her advantage, but he planned on doing the same thing, so it was fair.

"Corrigan, can you hear me okay?" Maggie asked. She was talking over the wireless from her position in a helicopter somewhere above.

"I hear you," he said. "Is everyone in position?"

The terminal was broken up into three square sections, each with five rows of containers. Each row was between one and three containers tall. The containers could be moved with a lift, to be loaded on a truck and driven away when it was time to do such a thing. Everything was set up on a grid, with clearly marked sections and lots of straight lines. Corrigan had narrowed the signal down to the 1/3 of the yard closest to the Boston Main Channel, at the mouth of the Reserved Channel, which also happened to be the section with the most containers in it. (In contrast, the middle section was nearly empty.)

If everything had gone according to plan, this section of the yard would now be devoid of all human beings that weren't Corrigan, Sheila, or heavily armored members of law enforcement. Helpfully, the whole area was supposed to be kept sealed by customs, so security was heightened to begin with. That this meant Sheila had been hanging out in the middle of a secure area for an undetermined length of time, without being noticed, just underlined how difficult this was going to be. She couldn't walk through walls—as some had suggested she must be capable of—but it sure seemed that way sometimes.

Corrigan was standing on the inside of the gate. There were three ICE agents with him, including Jeanine, who had been with Maggie's task force almost from the beginning. Corrigan nearly didn't recognize her in all the gear.

Something like twenty other officers had taken up positions along the perimeter fence. The target container was somewhere in the middle of the second row, which was the best Corrigan had been able to pinpoint it. Sheila was surrounded. It was undoubtedly the case that she knew it.

"Everyone's in position," Maggie said.

Corrigan peeked into the future.

"All clear," he said. "Let's go."

Maggie's dislike of helicopters was strong enough that she would have greatly preferred being part of the ground operation for this particular campaign. Everybody down there was looking at an artificially foreshortened life expectancy —and for the most part was unaware of this—but she didn't care. Sitting in a helicopter made her feel exposed, and not in control of her own fate.

We have to force her to change the future, Corrigan said. *A lot. It has to be noisy.*

This was part of the plan-within-a-plan-within-a-plan. The only people who knew about it were Corrigan, Erica, and

Maggie. They didn't tell Justin, or any of the people on the ground. An unavoidable consequence was that people were probably going to die. Maggie didn't care for that part.

She opened up the channel.

"All teams, go," she said.

T here was an opening to a walkway between the containers, directly in front of Corrigan. He headed that way, with the tracking box in one hand and a handgun in the other. Jeanine and the other two ICE agents flanked him. They were helmeted, in heavy battle armor that was about one layer of padding short of bomb-tech gear. Corrigan, meanwhile, was in a bulletproof vest and no helmet. If anyone thought this was stupid, they weren't saying so out loud.

Walking quickly was difficult. The stitches in his side pulled on every other step. He'd been told that no matter how it felt, everything should hold together down there provided he didn't try running. He had no intention to run.

Twenty steps in, and his head exploded. He felt the bullet enter his forehead and the world black out as he died. Death tasted like copper.

He shifted his head out of the path of the bullet. Sheila—it was definitely her—adjusted as well, and the man to his left took a round in the chest. It didn't look fatal, so Corrigan allowed it to happen.

"Sniper!" he shouted. "She's on top of the boxes."

Corrigan's declaration—mainly intended for Maggie—must have been alarming to the ICE agents, because it came before the first round hit the man on the left. Then it did. The guy who took the round fell onto his back, while his partner dropped to a knee, raised his M4 in the direction of fire, and tried to a target.

Jeanine's instinctive response to the gunshot was to jump in front of Corrigan. It was a take-a-bullet move that wouldn't work, long-term, but wasn't a bad temporary solution to his lack of battle armor.

Corrigan pulled Jeanine closer to him, like a shield.

"You," he said to the guy on his right, "drag him out of range. We're going forward."

"Do you see her?" she asked, over her shoulder.

"No, but I know where her shots are landing," Corrigan said. "If you let me guide you, we'll make it to the crates."

In the future, the night sky to Corrigan's left lit up suddenly, and Jeanine took a shot in the right shoulder.

"Explosion to my left, Maggie," he said, while at the same time tugging Jeanine out of the way of the bullet.

***

"Team one, fall back," Maggie ordered. She held her breath and waited for the explosion Corrigan just predicted. It happened, but then so did a second explosion on the right. That was where team three was, and they hadn't been issued a fall-back order.

There were men screaming over the open channel. Maggie switched it off.

"Pilot, we have a sniper on the roof," she said. "Can you see her?"

"No, ma'am," he said, calmly. The surface had turned into a war zone a few seconds earlier; the fact that he sounded unfazed was surprisingly reassuring.

"Get in closer," she said, "if you can."

She switched the open channel back on.

"Team one, report," she said.

Static.

"Team one, report," she repeated.

"This is Phipps, we took a hit."

Bill Phipps was FBI. Most of the rest of team one was ATF. Maggie hated this piecemeal approach to domestic terrorism solutions, but they had to put this together in an afternoon. It made her wonder if Justin's let's-bring-in-the-National Guard idea wasn't so bad.

"Bill, how bad?"

"The blast was directional. We're down two. Wounded, not dead, we're getting 'em out now."

"What do you mean, directional?"

"I mean she aimed it at us. How's three?"

"I don't know. Team three, can you respond?"

More static.

"This is Carson." Janet Carson was on team two. She was BPD. "I can spare some guys for a sweep left."

"Maggie, what's going on?" Corrigan asked.

The set-up was, Maggie could hear Corrigan and all the teams, but they couldn't hear him and he couldn't hear them. She had to toggle between the channels to address them.

"Corrigan, we may have lost your right flank. Team two's gonna send someone around."

He didn't respond immediately, which could indicate he was looking ahead. It could also mean he was out of breath or getting shot at, or just about anything else.

"Corrigan?" she asked.

"Your call," he said. "If we lost everyone…If we lost everyone, the side's clear. Might not be any more explosives from that direction."

"Yeah, I didn't want to say that either," she said.

They were still twenty feet from the relative safety of the containers. Sheila had taken five shots at them, in the future, which was enough for Corrigan to be able to narrow down which crate she was on top of. Nobody else could, because she hadn't actually fired any of the shots.

He needed her on the ground, and was mad at himself for not considering that she might take to the roof.

"I need your gun," Corrigan said. He had his handgun, which wasn't as good for range as the semi-automatic rifle his ICE escort carried.

"We're nearly there," Jeanine said.

"I'm nearly there. You're stopping here. When I say go, hand me your weapon and retreat. I'll cover you."

"Corrigan, I'm here to keep you upright, not the other way around."

"I know that's what you were told."

Corrigan dropped his handgun, jerked her backwards, yanked the weapon away, and opened fire on his best guess for Sheila's location. It might have been the wrong roof, but as long as Corrigan was shooting, she didn't dare take a shot at Jeanine, for fear of exposing herself.

"Get out of range, agent," Corrigan shouted.

The gun was an M4, and Corrigan had never used one before. It hurt. He braced it against his shoulder, like a person is supposed to, and he was wearing a thick vest that covered that shoulder. Despite that, the shock from the kickback traveled all the way down his body. He couldn't shoot and move at the same time—he could barely walk and he could barely shoot, so doing both at once was really out of the question—and he was a terrible shot with a rifle.

Sheila was clearly a very good shot with whatever she was using, but, critically, she didn't come into this already knowing

Corrigan had never practiced with a semi-automatic. She'd figure it out as long as he continued to fail to hit her, but not before his ICE escort made it out of range.

Instead of taking a shot, Sheila responded by setting off another explosion. He didn't see it happening in the future; it was a temporally unscheduled occurrence, just like the one that had taken out team three a minute earlier. It caused the future to blink out of existence for a heartbeat.

Keep that up, Sheila, he thought. *You'll get everyone's attention.*

In time with the new explosion, she got to her feet and jumped from the roof he (correctly) guessed she was on, to the next one over. He took a couple of shots at her in the future, and missed so wildly, she actually stopped where she was to take aim and fire once at him. She hit the ground to his right, but in her case, he was pretty sure she missed on purpose.

Then she pointed the rifle in the air.

***

"Maggie, pull up!" Corrigan shouted.

"Ma'am, I see her," the pilot said.

Maggie was sitting behind the pilot. Next to her, in the jump seat, was a sharpshooter attached to the BPD. As soon as the pilot said he'd identified a target, the officer was readying his rifle.

"Say again, Corrigan."

"I said pull up!"

There was a loud TINK. It sounded like the noise a window makes when a rock hits it, just before the window cracks and shatters.

"We're under fire," the pilot said, still quite calm.

"Pull up," Maggie said. "Get us out."

"The dome's bulletproof, ma'am."

"Swing around, let me get a shot," the sharpshooter said.

"Not everything on this chopper is bulletproof," Maggie said. "I said pull…"

She was interrupted by a series of flashing lights and bleeps and bloops coming from the pilot's dashboard. It looked as if, very suddenly, the helicopter became something difficult to fly.

"Hold tight," he said. "We're losing…"

Maggie lost track of what he said next, because he pushed the helicopter forward, as if he had someplace more important to be. They were no longer hovering over the scene; they were racing above it at high speed.

"I need a runway," he said.

"What happened?" Maggie asked. She had to shout to be heard, between all the noise coming from the dashboard, and the fact that the interior of the helicopter had become a wind tunnel.

"She hit the tail rotor," he said. "Million-to-one shot."

"We have to stay up. The whole team is blind if we don't stay up."

"Our best chance at survival is putting this down right now, ma'am, and that's what I'm doing."

Corrigan saw the whole thing happen, but in a way somewhat different than any of the other witnesses. He got to see Sheila try the shot seven times before getting it right. During that, he tried three times to hit her, and missed all three. She didn't even need to move out of his way.

Then the chopper was wobbling, and turning in a way the healthy ones aren't supposed to, and jetting off. It didn't explode (which was good) and the distraction it provided gave him a window in which to reach the container row (which was also good), but he was pretty sure Maggie was about to crash-land in the harbor...which was bad.

"Hey, Corrigan! Corrigan Bain!"

It was Sheila. She was shouting from whatever container roof she'd ended up on. He lost sight of her when he disappeared into the shadows of the container row.

"What?" he shouted back.

"Why don't you just let me shoot you? Then I can go home, and everyone else can have a nice long life. What do you say?"

"Come on down here, and I'll tell you why."

"Nah, I like the view. By the way, the container you're looking for is right in the middle. Just head to the center and look left."

Keep talking, he thought. As long as she was talking, he had a chance to figure out where she was. He also needed a way to get up onto the containers, but one thing at a time. He started walking in the direction she recommended, but only because that was getting him closer to her voice.

"Is there something more interesting in the container than you?" he asked. "Because you're really what I'm here for."

"That's so sweet. Whoops."

A gunshot rang out, and then two more.

"What was that?" he asked.

"One of your boys got fresh is all. I think he's dead? This is one hell of a plan you put together, I gotta say."

Maggie was supposed to be telling everyone to fall back once Corrigan reached the crates. That was when the plan made more sense, before they discovered Sheila could shoot a helicopter out of the sky.

"Maggie, what's going on up there?" he asked.

"Little busy," she said.

The helicopter didn't travel far. The pilot appeared to have a location in mind for his crash-landing, and fortunately —probably—that location wasn't the middle of the water.

The middle section of the container terminal included a long, straight strip that was uninterrupted by any boxes. It wasn't nearly long enough to land a plane on, but plenty long if one was trying to steer a helicopter that could no longer travel anywhere but forward at a brisk pace.

Maggie only understood a little about the physics behind helicopter travel: not enough to fly one, but enough to know that the tail rotor was there to keep the whole vehicle from spinning in a circle along with the rotors. It appeared to also be true that, when one lost one's tail rotor, the way to keep from turning with the rotors was to floor it.

That was working out great, except that the pilot was accelerating toward the ground. He cleared the tall fence between the two container lots, and then brought the chopper down to just a few feet above the tarmac. Right when Maggie started to worry that the next thing to happen would be him telling them to jump clear, he pulled back on the stick and killed the engine. The helicopter dropped straight down.

They weren't on wheels. Maggie didn't know what to call them—runners, pads, something like that—but they weren't round and they didn't roll and they weren't made of rubber. The whole craft skidded, then, down the makeshift runway. It was tremendously loud, and kicked up enough sparks to blind a person, but there was no ball of fire to speak of, and they didn't flip over.

"Is everyone okay?" the pilot asked, as soon as they were fully stopped.

Maggie looked at the BPD sharpshooter, who gave her a thumbs-up.

"We're good," she said. "Nice landing."

"Thanks."

"Maggie," Corrigan said.

Comms were still up, even if the chopper wasn't.

"I'm here."

"Order everyone back. You have to...Oh no."

"What? What is it, Corrigan?"

"Too late."

Corrigan had been splitting his attention between pinpointing the sound of Sheila's voice, and the downing of the helicopter. He wasn't paying as much attention to the future as he should have been, which was why he didn't realize Sheila's voice was leading him somewhere in particular. Not until it was just about too late.

In that future, he turned the corner. The first thing he saw was two officers at the other end of the corridor, running towards him, guns out, shouting something he couldn't hear.

The second thing he saw, was the stack of C-4.

He never turned that corner. Instead, he spun around and did the thing the doctor told him he should absolutely not do: he ran, as hard as he could.

The explosion sounded like the collision of two freight trains. The fiery blast had only a few places to go before it met with resistance in the form of heavy metal containers, so the impact force took up all the gaps in-between. Corrigan could feel heat on his neck from the fire behind him, while ahead, hot air puffed out of every crack. It was the kind of situation where, if he saw his own death coming up in the next five seconds, there was nothing he could do to change that. Either he outran the blast, or he didn't.

He did not entirely outrun the blast, but he got far enough from it that when it caught up, the experience wasn't fatal. He was pushed, like a BB from an air-gun, down the path, at least fifteen feet before skidding to a stop. He ended up on his back, a few paces from the open space that marked the edge of the containers.

His pants leg was on fire. He took a few seconds to put that out, then lay back down again.

He wondered if his side had resumed bleeding, and if so, if it was the only place. He could also be on fire, in a less obvious part of his anatomy, but he was surprisingly unmotivated when it came to checking for that.

Sheila dropped to the ground nearby. He saw her coming.

"Jesus," she said. She was holding her right shoulder, and looked to have developed a limp. "You are hard to kill, my friend."

He sat up. It sucked. He didn't like it at all.

"Get caught in your own explosion?" he asked.

"It was the only way to get you close enough. You were supposed to die in it, though, so imagine my disappointment. Lost my rifle, too. You?"

He looked around. The M4 he'd just been using was nowhere in sight, and the handgun he had before that was lying on the ground thirty yards away. The headset he'd been using to talk to Maggie was a few feet away. It wouldn't make for a very good weapon, but it was good to know he could get his hands on it if he needed to.

"Looks like we're down to fists and insults," he said.

"Not really."

Sheila pulled a machete from a sheath on her thigh.

"It's not a gun, but I'm pretty good with it," she said.

The fear in Corrigan's voice got Maggie right out of the crippled helicopter. She turned just in time to witness the full glory of a large stack of C-4 erupting in the middle of a jungle of steel. The fireball shot out in all directions. Metal cried. Maggie was blinded, temporarily.

She climbed back into the helicopter and got on the radio.

"Team...anybody. Anybody, who's still out there?"

All she got was a lot of static. Maggie had no idea if there was such a thing as good static and bad static, but if there was, this was definitely the bad kind.

She looked at the officer who'd ridden down the chopper next to her.

"Hey," she said, "that explosion's gonna draw people."

"You want me to call in?" he asked.

The assault team had a staging area a half a mile away, with emergency units on standby.

"Please. Tell them we're not done yet. Tell them it's not as bad as it looks."

"Isn't it?"

"Just tell them."

"Hello?" someone said over the comms. "Maggie it's Jeanine."

"Jeanine, where are you?"

"Front gate. I see the target."

"Where?"

"Facing up on Corrigan. They look like they're gonna fight. We have a shot."

"Negative, don't engage, Jeanine. Hold the perimeter. That goes for everyone else on this channel."

Let's hope this plan works, Corrigan, she thought. *Or we're all going to look pretty bad here.*

"I'm going to make you an offer," Corrigan said, as he got to his feet with tremendous reluctance. "Surrender, and we won't have to go through with this next part."

"Aw, come on," Sheila said, laughing. "You don't think you can take me straight-up, do you? I've been combat training since I was twelve."

He shrugged.

"Okay."

She swung the giant knife at his head, a pretty straightforward attack he stepped away from. She saw his evasion in the future, and altered the attack, which he adjusted to as well. She let that one happen.

Sheila stepped back and reassessed.

"You're moving okay. How's the stomach?"

"It hurts. I see you're mostly using your left arm."

"Yep."

She attacked again. This time, instead of just stepping aside, he moved up and punched her in the face. She adjusted to that, but he still managed to make contact. It wasn't the fully impactful blow he planned for it to be, but it didn't miss entirely.

"Whoa," she said, staggering backwards. "How'd you move that fast?"

"I'm not telling."

He charged right at her. She saw it happening and stepped aside, but again he got there faster than she expected him to. He knocked the knife from her hand and rammed her against the steel wall of one of the containers, his hand around her throat.

He had one chance, right then, to press his advantage and end things. He missed the moment.

Corrigan knew this would happen. The problem was that he'd never killed someone with his bare hands, and while he recognized that this was definitely the time to change that, he couldn't do it.

She rabbit-punched him in the stitches, and he lost his grip. He ended up on his knees a few feet away, while she stayed where she was, against the wall, gasping for breath.

"How the *hell* are you doing that, Corrigan?" she asked.

"Would you believe I'm just faster than you thought I was?"

"No, I would not."

She struck a pose he'd last seen in a martial arts film, which was to say if they weren't in the middle of a life-or-death struggle, he'd find it funny. As it was, he did find it somewhat amusing. Then she launched herself at him, in some wild combination of kicking and punching that would have been impressive if he didn't have the means to evade it. He stepped to the right and threw a punch at her throat...and missed her. She got out of the way.

"You caught up," he said.

"What are you talking about?"

"We're in the future. Have you ever been?"

She looked around, which was cute. The future didn't look any different; that was why it was so hard to tell when you'd arrived there. If they were near anybody, it would have been obvious much sooner, because regular humans tended to be off-focus when viewed from the other end of things.

"You weren't moving faster," she said. "You were moving sooner. That is a trip. And now?"

"Now we're on the other side of time. You can't see what I'm going to do, and I can't see what you're going to do."

She laughed.

"Dude, that was a *huge* mistake. You literally just took away your only advantage."

He had more to say, but unlike when Corrigan had a chance

to finish the job and punted it, she saw the opportunity for what it was, and went right at him.

He was a head taller, and had at least sixty pounds on her, and she was fighting with a bad shoulder, but that didn't matter at all. When she said she'd been combat training since she was a child, clearly, she wasn't exaggerating.

Inside of three seconds, she'd punched him twice in the nose, cut his knees from under him, and done something to his elbow that made it feel like his entire arm had been ripped off. He ended up on his back, blood gushing from his nose, his head spinning, and thinking it would have been awesome if he'd just stayed in bed on the day of the State House bombing.

She had the heel of her palm pointed at his nose, as if it was a loaded gun.

"I'm going to kill you with this next shot," she said. "I just wanted you to know that, before I did it. Oh, and it was nice meeting you. Family should stay in touch, right?"

A hand—an extra-long hand, with an extra set of knuckles and what looked like claws at the end of it—grabbed her by the wrist, and pulled.

The Kilroy threw her a good ten feet.

She rolled into a crouch, and got a look at the thing that had just attacked her.

For the first time, Corrigan saw fear in her eyes.

"What the fuck, what the fuck, Corrigan, what the fuck is that?"

"It's a Kilroy. Ever seen one before?"

Corrigan got up. He was really woozy, but it seemed important at this moment to not show weakness. He didn't know exactly how far this little arrangement with the Kilroy Prime really extended.

"I...I've seen them, but I didn't think they were *real*."

"They are. And they don't like people like us."

"They?"

The Kilroy Prime opened its huge mouth and shouted.

It was a horrific sound. Sheila dropped to one knee. Corrigan nearly ended up on his back again, and he knew it was coming.

"Kora-gan-see-stop-she-see," the Kilroy hissed.

"It talks?" Sheila whispered. "What the fuck."

"I brought you into the future," Corrigan said, "so they could meet you."

She crouched into a battle stance.

"Why don't they like people like us?" she asked.

"Because when we change the future, it causes them pain. I've experienced it from this end myself, and it's awful. You know how the future blinks out of existence for a half second? Imagine living in that future."

"That's stupid, dude." She looked at the Kilroy. "It's stupid... Kilroy, I guess. I do that all the time. He does that all the time."

"It's worse the bigger it is," Corrigan said. "Stepping out of the way of a bullet is bad when you're nearby, but otherwise, it's not a huge deal. Setting off a bomb when it wasn't supposed to off is another thing entirely."

"Aw, come on, really?"

"Really," he said. "They knew you were out there some-where, but they couldn't find you, so they asked for my help. It took me a while to figure that out, because they're not great conversationalists. Also, my last encounter with them wasn't all that fun. As you can imagine."

"All right, well, I guess I'll have to fight this...nightmare first, to get to you. No problem."

"I still don't think you understand," Corrigan said. "This isn't the only one of them. It's an entire species. And you're surrounded."

"Maggie?" Jeanine said.

"What is it?" Maggie asked. "Is something happening?"

She'd managed to salvage a headset from the downed chopper, so she could keep in communication while also running back to the scene. There were sirens in the distance, and two more helicopters were already circling the dock. She was pretty sure they were from the news stations and not law enforcement. There was supposed to be a no-fly over the area, but big explosions draw crowds and that was that.

"Yeah," Jeanine said, "but I couldn't begin to tell you what."

"Just describe what you see."

"All right. Corrigan is just standing there. The target is fighting, but she's not fighting him. She's not fighting anybody. Is he, like, doing this with his mind or something?"

"Not exactly."

"Because he can dodge bullets, so, this looks... I mean, it looks like he's using telekinesis on her."

"Hang on, I'm here."

Maggie got through the gate. The ICE agent who took a round in the chest was sitting up against the fence, and gave a thumbs-up as she went past. Jeanine and the third ICE agent were twenty yards closer, looking deeply perplexed at what was transpiring before them.

In the open space in front of the containers, Sheila Corrigan was in the middle of a life-or-death battle with empty space. And, she was losing that battle.

"Tell me that's not exactly what I said," Jeanine said.

"It's not. What you're looking at, is someone getting beaten to death by a gang of invisible killers."

"No shit."

"I do not shit you, agent."

"Well. That's something for the grandkids."

Sheila looked nearly done, and a few seconds later, she was. She took a brutal hit, one that rocked her head sideways and sent a spray of blood across the pavement, and then she fell over in a heap.

Corrigan stepped forward and stood over her, protectively, and began to talk.

They couldn't hear what he was saying, but it looked like he was in negotiations with the wind. He put his hand on his chest, nodded, and then made a gesture that looked as if he was shaking hands with someone who, again, was invisible.

Then he bent down, picked Sheila up, threw her over his shoulder, and walked her away from the crates.

"Hey Maggie," he said, a little sooner than he should have, addressing a spot Maggie wasn't occupying.

"Corrigan, what are you..."

"Handcuffs. Get handcuffs."

"Is she..."

"Get handcuffs."

He was addressing a space to her left.

"Good, thank you," he said, to nobody.

Jeanine looked at Maggie, confused, then stepped into the space Corrigan was addressing, and held up a pair of handcuffs.

"Yes, I'll put her down for you," Corrigan said. "I'm sorry, Maggie, my head is in the future, I'll be all right in a minute."

CHAPTER TWENTY-ONE

Sheila Corrigan was chained to a wheelchair, awake, and still looking as if she'd been run over by a herd of trucks. Both of her legs were broken, as was her left arm. Her right arm was okay, but the shoulder above it was not. The spot where Erica Smalls shot her had become badly infected, and it remained touch-and-go on whether Sheila was going to lose a limb over the matter. That was before considering the somewhat high likelihood of sepsis.

One of her eyes remained swollen shut, a week after the beating, but other than a lost tooth, she was expected to come out of the recuperation with more or less the same face, without any reconstructive surgery needed.

Sheila and her wheelchair were in an interrogation room in the Boston Police headquarters. She'd been driven there from Mass General in an armored vehicle, guarded by twenty officers in riot gear, down a street that was closed for this reason. All that, despite the fact that she couldn't walk—there was a real possibility she never would again—and was cuffed to the chair.

For the past half hour, Justin Axelrod had been in the interrogation room with her, asking all the obvious questions: who did she work for, what was her goal, and so on. She had, thus far, declined to answer.

"Is she doing anything?" Maggie asked Corrigan. They were in the observation room on the other side of the one-way glass, along with Erica. Erica was supposed to have returned to her job by now, but expressed interest in being present for this interrogation. There were probably a host of legal reasons why she wasn't supposed to be there, but nobody bothered to cite them, and so she was allowed in.

"Anything like what?" he asked.

"In the future. You know what I mean."

"She's nearly answered a few times, but no."

"Maybe she doesn't want to incriminate herself," Erica said. "She doesn't have a lawyer in the room or anything."

Maggie laughed.

"Oh, there won't be a trial," she said. "I think she knows it too. She's going to a black site."

"I didn't think those were real," Erica said. "What about due process?"

"There are loopholes. To begin with, the site isn't on U.S. soil. You would be surprised how much that very fact changes how we interpret our own laws. Besides, do you want to try to explain, in court, who did that to her face? I don't."

"I guess not."

"Anyway, legally, she's dead. Died a week ago in the fight on the dock."

In the future, Sheila kept shooting glances at the window. Justin was in the middle of asking her about the tech she was using, and how expensive it was, and did she want protection from these people? Because he could offer her protection.

"He's here, isn't he?" Sheila asked.

"You're referring to..."

"You know exactly who I'm referring to. I'll talk to him."

Justin turned to the window, and shrugged.

Maggie looked at Corrigan.

"Go ahead, if you want to," Maggie said.

He didn't really want to. He wanted to go back home and be done with all of this. But Justin Axelrod had made all of Corrigan's legal problems go away, so he figured he owed him a little.

"Sure," Corrigan said.

He walked around and got buzzed into the room. Justin met him on his way out.

"Anything you can get out of her will be helpful," Justin said, quietly. "Just keep her talking."

"I'll try."

Corrigan waited until Justin was out, then took a seat. Sheila looked up at him with her one good eye, and tried a smile her face wasn't entirely capable of.

"Hey there, cousin," Sheila said.

"Hi," he said. "How's the...um, how's the everything? How are you?"

"They're thinking I may get to stand again someday, and they're holding out hope I stop pissing blood soon. Those friends of yours went to town, huh?"

"They aren't my friends."

"Right. Enemy-of-my-enemy huh? You're a bigger bag of tricks than I gave you credit for."

"Do you think we are?" he asked. "Cousins, I mean."

"Hell if I know."

"We share a name."

"True. Maybe we're brother and sister, huh? Dad just got around a lot."

"Did you know your father?"

She tried another smile. This one looked like a grimace of pain.

"Yeah, we're not doing that," she said. "I'm not giving up any more information to you than I did to agent asshole. I wanted to thank you for stopping them before they killed me, is all."

"Oh. You're welcome."

"Also, you shouldn't have done that."

"Why not?" he asked.

"Don't get me wrong, I'm really glad to still be alive. Thing is, I'm a *lot* more valuable than you realize. I know they're gonna stick me in a hole where nobody can find me, but I'll help myself out of that hole someday, and even if I don't...they'll come looking."

"They who?"

"Nah. I mean, I wouldn't answer that even if I really knew the answer. I don't. But someone. As far as they're concerned, I'm their intellectual property. They'll want me back. You and me, we'll meet again."

Corrigan smiled.

"You know what your big mistake was?" he asked.

"Not blowing you up the first time, when I had a chance?"

"No. The big mistake was pulling this in my city."

She laughed, and then started coughing. Some bloody saliva came out of her mouth, which she couldn't tend to. As threatening as Sheila Corrigan sounded, she was effectively incapable of moving.

"Luck of the draw," she said. "Unless every city has someone like us, and I don't think it does."

"Could be. Could be there's hundreds of us."

"Daddy really did get around, then."

"He did, at that," he said, standing. His side complained, gently, about this.

Corrigan was a whole lot healthier than he had been a week ago, when he faced off with Sheila on the docks, but the doctors were saying to expect it to be a while before he could move around without some discomfort. Since he'd run out of reasons to put his life in danger, he was anticipating a smooth recuperation period.

"Now if you don't have any information for me," he said, "I'm going to go home and get back to my retirement. Best of luck with the rehab. I'll keep an eye out for you."

"Hey," she said, in the future, just as he was about to put his hand on the doorknob. "If there are hundreds of us, who do you think they're more like? You? Or me?"

He didn't answer. He just shook his head and let himself out of the room.

Maggie, Justin and Erica met him in the hallway a few seconds later.

"I think you can get more from her," Justin said. "You should go back in."

"She has nothing else to tell us," Corrigan said. "It's over. If you're going to lock her up somewhere, you should probably do that. Get her out of the city, at least."

Justin nodded.

"Maybe the CIA will have better luck," he said.

"I don't want to know," Corrigan said. He looked at Maggie. "Can we go home now? My retirement's behind schedule."

Maggie laughed, as Justin excused himself.

"Sure," she said. "We gotta swing by the airport on our way."

"I have a few hours," Erica said. "I wouldn't mind a drink first. Maybe we can talk about what she said to you just now that none of us could hear."

Corrigan smiled.

"Don't know what you're talking about," he said, "but a drink sounds good."

Gene Doucette is a hybrid author, albeit in a somewhat round-about way. From 2010 through 2014, Gene published four full-length novels (*Immortal, Hellenic Immortal, Fixer*, and *Immortal at the Edge of the World*) with a small indie publisher. Then, in 2014, Gene started self-publishing novellas that were set in the same universe as the *Immortal* series, at which point he was a hybrid.

When the novellas proved more lucrative than the novels, Gene tried self-publishing a full novel, *The Spaceship Next Door*, in 2015. This went well. So well, that in 2016, Gene reacquired the rights to the earlier four novels from the publisher, and re-released them, at which point he wasn't a hybrid any longer.

Additional self-published novels followed: *Immortal and the Island of Impossible Things* (2016); *Unfiction* (2017); and *The Frequency of Aliens* (2017).

In 2018, John Joseph Adams Books (an imprint of Houghton Mifflin Harcourt) acquired the rights to *The Spaceship Next Door*. The reprint was published in September of that year, at which point Gene was once again a hybrid author.

Since then, a number of things have happened. Gene published three more novels—*Immortal From Hell* (2018), *Fixer Redux* (2019), and *Immortal: Last Call* (2020)—and wrote a new novel called *The Apocalypse Seven* that he did not self-publish; it was acquired by JJA/HMH in September of 2019. Publication date is May 25, 2021.

Gene lives in Cambridge, MA.

For the latest on Gene Doucette, follow him online
genedoucette.me
genedoucette@me.com

apocalyptically wrong in Sorrow Falls—she's a pretty good person to have around.

As a matter of fact, Annie Collins might be the most important person on the planet. She just doesn't know it.

———

The Frequency of Aliens

Annie Collins is back!

Becoming an overnight celebrity at age sixteen should have been a lot more fun. Yes, there were times when it was extremely cool, but when the newness of it all wore off, Annie Collins was left with a permanent security detail and the kind of constant scrutiny that makes the college experience especially awkward.

Not helping matters: she's the only kid in school with her own pet spaceship.

She would love it if things found some kind of normal, but as long as she has control of the most lethal—and only—interstellar vehicle in existence, that isn't going to happen. Worse, things appear to be going in the other direction. Instead of everyone getting used to the idea of the ship, the complaints are getting louder. Public opinion is turning, and the demands that Annie turn over the ship are becoming more frequent. It doesn't help that everyone seems to think Annie is giving them nightmares.

Nightmares aren't the only weird things going on lately. A government telescope in California has been abandoned, and nobody seems to know why.

The man called on to investigate—Edgar Somerville—has become the go-to guy whenever there's something odd going on, which has been pretty common lately. So far, nothing has panned out: no aliens or zombies or anything else that might be deemed legitimately peculiar... but now may be different, and not just because Ed can't find an easy explanation. This isn't the only telescope where people have gone missing, and the clues left behind lead back to Annie.

It all adds up to a new threat that the world may just need saving from, requiring the help of all the Sorrow Falls survivors. The question is: are they saving the world with Annie Collins, or are they saving it from her?

The Frequency of Aliens is the exciting sequel to *The Spaceship Next Door*.

⁂

Unfiction

When Oliver Naughton joins the Tenth Avenue Writers Underground, headed by literary wunderkind Wilson Knight, Oliver figures he'll finally get some of the wild imaginings out of his head and onto paper.

But when Wilson takes an intense interest in Oliver's writing and his genre stories of dragons, aliens, and spies, things get weird. Oliver's stories don't just need to be finished: they insist on it.

With the help of Minerva, Wilson's girlfriend, Oliver has to find the connection between reality, fiction, the mythical Cydonian Kingdom, and the non-mythical nightclub called M Pallas. That is, if he can survive the alien invasion, the ghosts, and the fact that he thinks he might be in love with Minerva.

Unfiction is a wild ride through the collision of science fiction, fantasy, thriller, horror and romance. It's what happens when one writer's fiction interferes with everyone's reality.

⁂

Fixer

What would you do if you could see into the future?

As a child, he dreamed of being a superhero. Most people never get to realize their childhood dreams, but Corrigan Bain has come close. He is a fixer. His job is to prevent accidents—to see the future and "fix" things before people get hurt. But the ability to see into the future, however limited, isn't always so simple. Sometimes not everyone can be saved.

"Don't let them know you can see them."

Graduate students from a local university are dying, and former lover and FBI agent Maggie Trent is the only person who believes their deaths aren't as accidental as they appear. But the truth can only be found in something from Corrigan Bain's past, and he's not interested in sharing that past, not even with Maggie.

To stop the deaths, Corrigan will have to face up to some old horrors, confront the possibility that he may be going mad, and find a way to stop a killer no one can see.

Corrigan Bain is going insane ... or is he?

Because there's something in the future that doesn't want to be seen. It isn't human. It's got a taste for mayhem. And it is very, very angry.

Fixer Redux

Someone's altering the future, and it isn't Corrigan Bain

Corrigan Bain was retired.

It wasn't something he ever thought he'd be able to do. The problem was that the *job* he wanted to retire from wasn't actually a job at all: nobody paid him to do it, and nobody else did it. With very few exceptions, nobody even knew he was doing it.

Corrigan called himself a fixer, because he fixed accidents that were about to happen. It was complicated and unrewarding, and even though doing it right meant saving someone, he didn't enjoy it. He couldn't stop—he thought—because there would always be accidents, and he would never find someone to take over as fixer. Anyone trying would have to be capable of seeing the future, like he did, and that kind of person was hard to find.

Still, he did it. He's never been happier.

His girlfriend, Maggie Trent of the FBI, has not retired. Her task force just shut down the most dangerous domestic terrorist cell in the country, and she's up for an award, and a big promotion.

Everything's going their way now, and the future looks even brighter.

Unfortunately, that future is about to blow up in their faces…literally. And somehow, Corrigan Bain, fixer, the man who can see the future, is taken completely by surprise.

Fixer Redux is the long-awaited sequel to *Fixer*. Catch up with Corrigan, as he tries to understand a future that no longer makes sense.

———

FANTASY

The Immortal Novel Series

———

Immortal

"I don't know how old I am. My earliest memory is something along the lines of fire good, ice bad, so I think I predate written history, but I don't know by how much. I like to brag that I've been there from the beginning, and while this may very well be true, I generally just say it to pick up girls."

Surviving sixty thousand years takes cunning and more than a little luck. But in the twenty-first century, Adam confronts new dangers— someone has found out what he is, a demon is after him, and he has run out of places to hide. Worst of all, he has had entirely too much to drink.

Immortal is a first person confessional penned by a man who is immortal, but not invincible. In an artful blending of sci-fi, adventure, fantasy, and humor, IMMORTAL introduces us to a world with vampires, demons and other "magical" creatures, yet a world without actual magic.

At the center of the book is Adam.

Adam is a sixty thousand year old man. (Approximately.) He doesn't age or get sick, but is otherwise entirely capable of being killed. His survival has hinged on an innate ability to adapt, his wits, and a fairly large dollop of luck. He makes for an excellent guide through history ... when he's sober.

Immortal is a contemporary fantasy for non-fantasy readers and fantasy enthusiasts alike.

Hellenic Immortal

"Very occasionally, I will pop up in the historical record. Most of the time I'm not at all easy to spot, because most of the time I'm just a guy who does a thing and then disappears again into the background behind someone-or-other who's busy doing something much more important. But there are a couple of rare occasions when I get a starring role."

An oracle has predicted the sojourner's end, which is a problem for Adam insofar as he has never encountered an oracular prediction that didn't come true ... and he is the sojourner. To survive, he's going to have to figure out what a beautiful ex-government analyst, an eco-terrorist, a rogue FBI agent, and the world's oldest religious cult all want with him, and fast.

And all he wanted when he came to Vegas was to forget about a girl. And maybe have a drink or two.

The second book in the Immortal series, Hellenic Immortal follows the continuing adventures of Adam, a sixty-thousand-year-old man with a wry sense of humor, a flair for storytelling, and a knack for staying alive. Hellenic Immortal is a clever blend of history, mythology, sci-fi, fantasy, adventure, mystery and romance. A little something, in other words, for every reader.

Immortal at the Edge of the World

"What I was currently doing with my time and money ... didn't really deserve anyone else's attention. If I was feeling romantic about it, I'd call it a quest, but all I was really doing was trying to answer a question I'd been ignoring for a thousand years."

In his very long life, Adam had encountered only one person who appeared to share his longevity: the mysterious red-haired woman. She appeared throughout history, usually from a distance, nearly always vanishing before he could speak to her.

In his last encounter, she actually did vanish—into thin air, right in front of him. The question was how did she do it? To answer, Adam will have to complete a quest he gave up on a thousand years earlier, for an object that may no longer exist.

If he can find it, he might be able to do what the red-haired woman did, and if he can do that, maybe he can find her again and ask her who she is ... and why she seems to hate him.

But Adam isn't the only one who wants the red-haired woman. There are other forces at work, and after a warning from one of the few men he trusts, Adam realizes how much danger everyone is in. To save his friends and finish his quest he may be forced to bankrupt himself, call in every favor he can, and ultimately trade the one thing he'd never been able to give up before: his life.

Immortal and the island of Impossible Things

"I thought I'd miss the world."

Adam is on vacation in an island paradise, with nothing to do and plenty of time to do nothing.

It's exactly what he needed: beautiful weather, beautiful girlfriend, plenty of books to read, and alcohol to drink. Most importantly, either nobody on the island knows who he is, or, nobody cares.

"This probably sounds boring, and maybe it is. It's possible I have no compass to help determine boring, or maybe I have a different threshold than most people. From my perspective, though, the vast majority of human history has been boring, by which I mean nothing happened, and sure, that can be dull. On the other hand, nothing happening includes nobody trying to kill anybody, and specifically, nobody trying to kill me. That's the kind of boring a guy can get behind."

Nothing last forever, though, and that includes the opportunity to *do* nothing. One day, unwelcome visitors arrive in secret, with impossible knowledge of impossible events, and then the impossible things arrive: a new species.

It's *all* impossible, especially to the immortal man who thought he'd seen all there was to see in the world. Now, Adam is going to have to figure out what's happening and make things right before he and everyone he loves ends up dead in the hot sun of this island paradise.

Immortal From Hell

Not all of Adam's stories have happy endings

"Paris is romantic and quests are cool. But the threat of a global pandemic kind of sours the whole thing. The good news was, if all life on Earth were felled by a plague, it looked like this one could take me out too. It'd be pretty lonely otherwise."

--Adam the immortal

When Adam decides to leave the safety of the island, it's for a good reason: Eve, the only other immortal on the planet, appears to be dying, and nobody seems to understand why. But when Adam—with his extremely capable girlfriend Mirella—tries to retrace Eve's steps, he discovers a world that's a whole lot deadlier than he remembered.

Adam is supposed to be dead. He went through a lot of trouble to fake that death, but now that he's back it's clear someone remains unconvinced. That wouldn't be so terrible, except that whoever it is, they have a great deal of influence, and an abiding interest in ensuring that his death sticks this time around.

Adam and Mirella will have to figure out how to travel halfway across the world in secret, with almost no resources or friends. The good news is, Adam solved the travel problem a thousand years earlier. The bad news is, one of his oldest assumptions will turn out to be untrue.

Immortal From Hell is the darkest entry in the Immortal series.

Immortal: Last Call

"I'm something like sixty-thousand years old, and I've probably thought more about my own death than any living being has thought about any subject, ever. I used to be unduly preoccupied with what might constitute a "good death", although interestingly, this has always been an after-the-fact analysis. What I mean is, following a near-death experience, I'll generally perform a quiet review of the circumstances and judge whether that death would have been objectively good, by whatever metric one uses for that kind of thing. I'm not nearly that self-reflective while in the midst of said near-death experience. Facing death, the predominant thought is always not like this."

A disease threatening the lives of everyone—human and non-human—has been loosed upon the world, by an arch-enemy Adam didn't even know he had.

That's just the first of his problems. Adam's also in jail, facing multiple counts of murder, at least a few of which are accurate. He may never see the inside of a courtroom, because there remains a bounty on his head—put there by the aforementioned arch-enemy—that someone is bound to try to collect while he's stuck behind bars.

Meanwhile, Adam's sitting on some tantalizing evidence that there might be a cure, but to find it, he's going to have to get out of jail, get out of the country, and track down the man responsible. He can't do any of that alone, but he also can't rely on any of his non-human friends for help, not when they're all getting sick.

What he needs is a particularly gifted human, who can do things no other human is capable of. He knows one such person. He calls himself a fixer, and he's Adam's—and possibly the world's—last hope. That's provided he believes any of it.

Immortal: Last Call is the sixth book in the *Immortal Novel Series*, and also the end of a long journey for one immortal man.

Immortal Stories

Eve

"...if your next question is, what could that possibly make me, if I'm not an angel or a god? The answer is the same as what I said before: many have considered me a god, and probably a few have thought of me as an angel. I'm neither, if those positions are defined by any kind of supernormal magical power. True magic of that kind doesn't exist, but I can do things that may appear magic to someone slightly more tethered to their mortality. I'm a woman, and that's all. What may make me different from the next woman is that it's possible I'm the very first one..."

For most of humankind, the woman calling herself Eve has been nothing more than a shock of red hair glimpsed out of the corner of the eye, in a crowd, or from a great distance. She's been worshipped, feared, and hunted, but perhaps never understood. Now, she's trying to reconnect with the world, and finding that more challenging than anticipated.

Can the oldest human on Earth rediscover her own humanity? Or will she decide the world isn't worth it?

The Immortal Chronicles

Immortal at Sea (volume 1)

Adam's adventures on the high seas have taken him from the Mediterranean to the Barbary Coast, and if there's one thing he learned, it's that maybe the sea is trying to tell him to stay on dry land.

Hard-Boiled Immortal (volume 2)

The year was 1942, there was a war on, and Adam was having a lot of trouble avoiding the attention of some important people. The kind of people with guns, and ways to make a fella disappear. He was caught somewhere between the mob and the government, and the only way out involved a red-haired dame he was pretty sure he couldn't trust.

Immortal and the Madman (volume 3)

On a nice quiet trip to the English countryside to cope with the likelihood that he has gone a little insane, Adam meets a man who definitely has. The madman's name is John Corrigan, and he is convinced he's going to die soon.

He could be right. Because there's trouble coming, and unless Adam can get his own head together in time, they may die together.

***

Yuletide Immortal (volume 4)

When he's in a funk, Adam the immortal man mostly just wants a place to drink and the occasional drinking buddy. When that buddy turns out to be Santa Claus, Adam is forced to face one of the biggest challenges of extremely long life: Christmas cheer. Will Santa break him out of his bad mood? Or will he be responsible for depressing the most positive man on the planet?

***

Regency Immortal (volume 5)

Adam has accidentally stumbled upon an important period in history: Vienna in 1814. Mostly, he'd just like to continue to enjoy the local pubs, but that becomes impossible when he meets Anna, an intriguing woman with an unreasonable number of secrets and sharp objects.

Anna is hunting down a man who isn't exactly a man, and if Adam doesn't help her, all of Europe will suffer. If Adam *does* help, the cost may be his own life. It's not a fantastic set of options. Also, he's probably fallen in love with her, which just complicates everything.